ORION
THE VAULTS OF WINTER

'By the gods.' Sephian shook his head as he saw the horses' riders – towering giants with spirals of horn snaking from their ivy-bound hair. Their faces were as pale and beautiful as the moonlight, but their eyes burned with a dark spectral fire.

'The horned riders.' Sephian recognised them immediately and his voice trembled with awe. 'Priests of Kurnous.'

He watched in stunned silence as they thundered past, but then his sense of awe began to be replaced by the same dread that had driven him from the Silvam Dale. This time, however, it was no vague, nameless fear: he knew exactly what made his breath come in short, sharp gasps.

The riders were coming for him.

Suddenly, everything that had happened that evening made sense. As the drumming of hooves filled his mind, drowning out even his thudding pulse, Sephian realised that *he* was the riders' prey.

The hunt was for *him*.

A WARHAMMER NOVEL

ORION
THE VAULTS OF WINTER

DARIUS HINKS

BLACK LIBRARY

For Arthur Charles Hinks. Be happy, my perfect little son.

A BLACK LIBRARY PUBLICATION

First published in Great Britain in 2012 by
Black Library,
Games Workshop Ltd.,
Willow Road, Nottingham,
NG7 2WS, UK.

10 9 8 7 6 5 4 3 2 1

Cover illustration by Slawomir Maniak.
Internal illustrations by Nuala Kinrade.

A CIP record for this book is available from the British Library.

UK ISBN: 978 1 84970 199 0
US ISBN: 978 1 84970 200 3

See Black Library on the internet at
www.blacklibrary.com

Find out more about Games Workshop
and the world of Warhammer at
www.games-workshop.com

Printed and bound by CPI Group (UK) Ltd, Croydon, CR0 4YY

This is a dark age, a bloody age, an age of daemons
and of sorcery. It is an age of battle and death, and of the
world's ending. Amidst all of the fire, flame and fury
it is a time, too, of mighty heroes, of bold deeds
and great courage.

At the heart of the Old World sprawls the Empire, the
largest and most powerful of the human realms. Known for
its engineers, sorcerers, traders and soldiers, it is
a land of great mountains, mighty rivers, dark forests
and vast cities. And from his throne in Altdorf reigns
the Emperor Karl Franz, sacred descendant of the
founder of these lands, Sigmar, and wielder
of his magical warhammer.

But these are far from civilised times. Across the length
and breadth of the Old World, from the knightly palaces
of Bretonnia to ice-bound Kislev in the far north, come
rumblings of war. In the towering Worlds Edge Mountains,
the orc tribes are gathering for another assault. Bandits and
renegades harry the wild southern lands of
the Border Princes. There are rumours of rat-things, the
skaven, emerging from the sewers and swamps across the
land. And from the northern wildernesses there is the
ever-present threat of Chaos, of daemons and beastmen
corrupted by the foul powers of the Dark Gods.
As the time of battle draws ever near,
the Empire needs heroes
like never before.

CHARACTERS AND PLACES

LOCRIMERE
Finavar *the Darkling Prince*
Jokleel *younger brother of Finavar*
Mormo and Mauro *Finavar's scouts*
Gole *tiny forest spirit that stalks Finavar*
Thuralin *old, crippled follower of Finavar*
Alhena *Thuralin's daughter*
Caorann *Finavar's oldest friend*
Lord Beldeas *highborn; Warden of Locrimere*
Lady Ordaana *highborn; wife of Beldeas*
Death's-head *forest spirit that accompanies Ordaana*
Hauran Quillwort *Lord Beldeas's advisor*
Eremon *captain of the Locrimere kinbands*
Ilbrec *guardsman*
Elaeus *elderly healer*

THE SILVAM DALE
Sephian *revered waywatcher*
Princess Asphalia *highborn, ageing spellweaver*
Prince Elatior *the Enchanter; highborn, ruler of the Silvam Dale*
Isére *Sephian's former lover*
Arthron *guardian of the Wilding Tree*
Tethea *guard; deceased*

ARIEL'S COURT
Ariel *the Queen in the Wood*
Laelia *handmaiden; powerful mage*
Khoron Belidae *Ariel's poet and counsellor*
Naieth *revered prophetess*
Othu *Naieth's owl*

Lord Alioth *young noble, brother of Salicis*
Lord Salicis *young noble, brother of Alioth*

THE KING'S GLADE
Orion *Ariel's Consort-King*
Atolmis the Hunter *High Priest of Kurnous*
Olachas *priest of Kurnous*
Karioth *priest of Kurnous*
Ilaruss *priest of Kurnous*
Sélva *priest of Kurnous*

THE BRÚIDD (THE COUNCIL OF BEASTS)
Sativus *forest spirit; resembles a great, noble stag*
Adanhu *forest spirit; resembles an enormous tree*
Amphion *forest spirit; resembles a great eagle*
Drys *forest spirit; resembles an enormous tree*
The Wrach *Keeper of the Dark Paths; the Blind Guide*
Zephyr *forest spirit; resembles a playful child*
Merula *forest spirit; resembles an enormous toad*
Usnarr *forest spirit; resembles a white wolf*
Nembus *forest spirit; resembles a horned serpent*

BLOOD-KIN
Ghorgus Four-legs *lord of the Blood-kin*
Belakhor the Unseen *bray-shaman*
Arghob *Blood-kin warrior*
Morgharon *Blood-kin warrior*

THE VALE OF FINCARA (TURAS-ALVA)
Lord Cyanos *'King' of the alvair*
Elpenor *alvair warrior*
Síngas *alvair warrior*

THE KINDRED OF ARUM TOR
Prince Haldus *Warhawk Rider; Lord of Arum Tor*
Clorana *Haldus's daughter*

BRANCHWRAITHS
Drycha
Liris
Melusine

THE DAEMON
Alkhor

DRAGONS
Tanos
Tamarix

HIGH ELVES
Aestar Eltanin *high elf mage*
Derasa *Aestar's eagle mount*

OTHERS
Gavra and Aefa *figures of asrai mythology*
Nuin *great eagle, ridden by Prince Haldus*
Skólann *great eagle, ridden by Orion*

LOCATIONS
The Sínann-Torr *prehistoric dolmens and sacred stones*
Torr-Goholoth *one of the Sínann-Torr*
Torr-Marloch *one of the Sínann-Torr*
Torr-Cirrus *one of the Sínann-Torr*
Torr-Ildána *one of the Sínann-Torr*
Torr-Dobár *one of the Sínann-Torr*

The Tenderfoot Way *entry to the Wrach's 'Dark Paths'*
The Council Glade *halls of the Everqueen*
Cerura Carn *mound of petrified branches near the Council Glade; a place of contemplation*
Drúne Fell *large hill, south of the Council Glade; the Lost Mountain*
The Iuliss Vale *kingdom in the south of the forest*
The Idolan *sacred lake at the heart of Locrimere, surrounded by a broad meadow*
The Eomain Tarn *mythical mountain pool, supposedly in the foothills of the Grey Mountains*
The Wilding Tree *enormous old hawthorn tree in the Silvam Dale, warped by asrai magic*
Arum Tor *lofty kingdom located in the Pine Crags*
Cáder Donann *highest peak of the Arum Tor; home of Prince Haldus*
The Ìobrass *Lord Cyanos's 'Great Work'*
Líath-Mael *river, of no fixed location*
Coeth-Mara *kingdom in the south of the forest*
Dhioll Hollow *location of the Torr-Ildána*
The Gyre *the Wrach's 'Dark Paths'*

PROLOGUE

A daemon dropped from the sky. Its misshapen flesh was swaddled in a cloud of flies, smoke and carrion crows and as it fell it attempted to right itself, thrashing great, ragged wings and belching out a garbled laugh. The laughter grew, the rolling mass of flies blocked the sun and, for a moment, it seemed as though the daemon's mirth alone would be enough to arrest its fall. Then the whole tangled mess was wrenched onto its back, revealing a second shape, clinging to its tattered gut: an enormous eagle, carrying a silver-clad rider. The bird was as torn and broken as the daemon. As they fell they painted the clouds with their blood, laughing and screeching as they plunged towards the forest below.

The silver-clad rider had the bird's reins in one hand and a lance in the other. His armour was as ragged as the eagle's flesh and his face was pale with agony, but as they plummeted the rider yanked desperately at the eagle's reins and the bird managed another beat of its broken wings.

The struggling creatures lurched back up into the sky,

narrowly missing the trees and looping back into the clouds. As they rose, the rider jammed his lance into the daemon's sagging head. Glistening limbs exploded from the wound, edged with talons that rattled down against the rider's armour. He calmly shook his head and began hacking at them with a longsword. The blade flashed and fell, sparkling in the morning light, and the eagle pounded its wings even harder, sensing that victory was finally within reach.

As they spiralled back up into the clouds, the daemon's laughter grew hysterical.

The rider hesitated, lowering his blade and looking around; straining to find the source of the creature's mirth.

From where he sat there was no way he could have seen the daemon's sword: a slab of rusted iron, nestling in the bird's chest feathers. His first warning was the explosion of blood that washed over him as the sword erupted from between the eagle's shoulder blades.

They dropped again, faster this time, with the rider still hacking at the daemon's rippling flesh.

A few seconds later they smashed through the canopy of trees and the daemon's laughter was silenced. The force of the impact rippled through the ancient boughs, toppling trunks, scattering deer and filling the valley with dust.

Then there was nothing but echoes and the screaming of crows.

Aestar Eltanin drooled blood across his breastplate as he tried to rise. His legs trembled but managed to hold him as he clutched his stomach and moaned in pain. He looked down at his ruined armour and shook his head, then his eyes widened as he recalled his mount.

'Derasa,' he gasped, squinting through the forest gloom. He

was in a small clearing, bordered by an impenetrable wall of bracken and brushwood. The air was thick with the stench of rotting flesh and Aestar grimaced as he looked for the source of the smell. There was a brackish, ominous-looking pool at the centre of the clearing but his gaze moved straight past it to a column of smoke and flies, rising lazily in the south. He tried to move but the thicket resisted. The tendrils wrapped around his shins and sent him crashing to the ground.

'Derasa,' he called, louder. His face was as long and elegant as the rest of him, but as he scoured the trees for his mount, his features grew ugly with fear. He realised it was not just the stink making the air so heavy, there was something else: malice, pouring down on him from all sides.

Aestar peered beneath the ancient yews, noticing how odd they were. The branches were twisted and claw-like, bristling with thorns as long as his fingers. There was no breeze, but the claws were creaking and moving; straining towards him.

He climbed to his feet, taking a metal sceptre from his belt and using it to free his legs. The knotted tendrils resisted, tightening their grip until he snapped them. As the broken thicket fell away it withdrew, worm-like, into the ground.

The sense of anger grew.

'What kind of forest is this?' His voice was muffled and flat and there was no reply. Aestar muttered a long, sinuous word and raised his sceptre. The rod was entwined with coils of silver filigree and at its end was a gleaming eagle's head, holding in its metal beak a sapphire the size of a fist. Aestar blinked as the stone pulsed into life, throwing back the shadows and bathing the trees in cool, blue light.

There was a huge, tawny shape lying crumpled on the far side of the clearing. Aestar groaned as he saw his mount, broken and lifeless, her chest punctured by the shattered remains of a yew. He hurried towards the eagle but pain exploded in his left leg and he fell to his knees, sinking into the stagnant pond. He looked down and saw blood pouring from a deep wound in his thigh. For a moment, the pain of it confused him. As he watched the water turning red he imagined dozens of tiny shapes peering up at him: a bizarre collection of human, avian and insect faces, each no bigger than his thumb and carrying tiny, barbed weapons. They vanished as soon as he tried to focus on them and when he thrust his hand into the water he caught nothing but pallid weeds. He cursed and hobbled on, reaching the bird's side and placing a hand on her blackened feathers.

'Derasa,' he said, his voice cracking with emotion. 'Live.' He allowed his head to fall gently against her noble brow. *'Live.'* She was already growing cold, but he kept repeating his plea all the same, unable to accept the truth. He knew he should move on, continue the fight, but he could not. As branches and leaves continued to land around him, Aestar remained motionless at the eagle's side, paralysed by grief.

The snap of breaking wood dragged him from his reverie. He looked up to see movement in the trees: a flash of pallid green. Aestar's expression hardened as an enormous, sagging face grinned at him through the trees.

'Alkhor!' he bellowed, wrenching himself from the eagle's side and limping off through the bracken.

There was a crash as the daemon turned and fled, dragging its tattered wings through the forest and letting out a gurgling laugh as it vanished from view.

Aestar channelled his outrage through the head of his sceptre. A column of blue flame tore through the trees. 'You're mine!' he cried, lurching through the mass of branches and roots.

The giggling daemon replied by pointing its huge, rusted

sword at him. Disease poured from the pitted iron, twisting branches to create a corridor of blackened decay. Roots shrivelled, leaves withered and thousands of flaccid grubs erupted from the earth. The whole rotting mess hurtled towards Aestar with the force of a landslide.

Maggots and rotting vegetation smashed into Aestar. He tried to leap aside, but his wounded leg gave way and he fell again, rolling awkwardly into a steep defile and landing face down in a reeking brook. The ground shifted and bubbled as the corruption spread. Flies poured into his mouth, crows pecked at his face and filthy water flooded his wounds. He rolled onto his back, moaning and stabbing his sceptre into the mud, filling the gulley with fire.

Flies became dust and crows became smoke as Aestar's fire met the daemon's rot head-on. He rose to his feet, shrouded in light, numinous with fury and howling. 'You are ended!' He wiped the muck from his face and lifted his chin. 'You are *dead*! I will crush your rotten heart.'

More laughter greeted his words, but as the daemon turned and ploughed on through the trees Aestar saw its torn wings pounding uselessly and realised how close he was to the truth. The daemon's movements were erratic and pained. The combined assault of Aestar and his brothers had left it horribly wounded. He allowed himself a grim smile as he staggered off in pursuit, splashing awkwardly through the knee-deep water. His brothers had died. Hundreds of his kin had lain down their lives so that he might reach this point and none of their deeds would go forgotten. As he hobbled after the daemon Aestar swore an oath: he would survive. He would return home. After all these long years he would finally set sail for Ulthuan. He would tell the keepers of the White Tower how fiercely their students had fought; how bravely they had died. He would tell the Lords of Hoeth how he had tracked down this evil and cut it from the world.

Using roots as a ladder, he climbed from the gulley and raised his sceptre higher, throwing blue light deeper into the forest. 'I have you,' he muttered, catching another glimpse of the hulking shape. He scrambled on through the trees, but the daemon's sickness was spreading. Clouds of spores were pooling beneath the eaves, blight was washing over the bracken and a wall of emerald smoke was rolling towards him.

Aestar placed a hand over his mouth and plunged on. As he ran, he called out another spell, pulling back the fumes with his sceptre. The air only cleared momentarily, but it was long enough for the mage to see another vast shape hurtling towards him from the daemon's sword: dozens of crows, slicing through the smoke, filling the air with their scornful din. He raised his hands as they slammed into him. Most died, hitting him with such force their necks broke, but others remained alive, pecking at his face, clawing at his arms and beating their wings furiously against his armour.

'What is the use?' he roared, swinging at the birds and trying to stagger on. 'Why prolong this when I have already…?' Aestar's words faltered as he saw movement to his right. 'Who's there?' he gasped, struggling to free himself from the thrashing wings. There was no reply, but as he fought Aestar saw more shapes to his left: darting, sinuous shadows, moving at incredible speed.

'What is this place?' he cried, slamming his staff into the soil. More blinding light erupted from the sceptre and for a second the birds hung motionless in the air, their feathers rippling with flames. Then the light ceased and the birds dropped to the ground. The smell of cooking meat filled the air.

Aestar forgot his prey and stared into the darkness. 'Who

is that? Are you mortal?' He stepped from the path, straining to make out the vague shapes. It was hard to be sure in the shifting smoke, but it seemed that the trees themselves were leaning towards him. No, not trees. These were giants of some kind, with tall, knotted coronets and lichened claws. The mage shook his head in confusion and redirected his light, trying to make out the towering figures in more detail. As his blue flame pierced the gloom the spectres evaporated, leaving nothing but vague shadows, and even they disappeared as he limped closer.

Before he had time to investigate further, pain exploded in Aestar's back and he tumbled onto the soft, mossy earth. He rolled to one side, barely dodging a hammer-blow from one of the daemon's enormous, rotting fists. 'Fool,' he muttered to himself, climbing painfully into the branches of a tree as the daemon leapt after him.

Alkhor's enormous grin loomed from the shadows, preceded by a torrent of blighted leaves and noxious, fly-laden fumes. 'I can still taste them,' he boomed, allowing his six-foot tongue to flop from his mouth, drooling saliva across his pockmarked chins. 'Your brothers' bones in my gut.' He gurgled with laughter and tugged at a sagging wound in his belly. To Aestar's horror, the crimson innards parted to reveal a grey intestinal loop, stretched around part of a skull. 'Is this your younger brother, or the elder one? Neither have much to say for themselves.' The daemon's laughter became more hysterical. 'I don't know if I can stomach much more of them.'

The daemon's rot oozed across the ground and spread quickly up the tree in which Aestar was perched. The bark mouldered and peeled away and the trunk let out a low creak. Aestar jabbed his sceptre towards Alkhor, wrenching light from the gemstone and hurling it at the daemon.

Alkhor's laughter became a choking cough and as it slumped

against the trees they splintered, dropping the daemon onto its back and sending branches spinning into the air.

As the daemon crashed to the ground, Aestar felt his own perch start to give way. He leapt from the branches, landed on his injured leg and let out an agonised howl.

Alkhor tried to sit and point its battered sword at Aestar, but as it moved more trees collapsed and the daemon fell back, gurgling in annoyance as a branch knifed up through its throat, sticking out through its trembling chins like a horn.

Aestar saw his chance and swung his sceptre like a club, smashing it down into the daemon's face. The silver eagle's head sank easily into Alkhor's flesh and Aestar's magic flared even brighter.

Alkhor began to spasm and thrash on the ground, loosing its sword, shaking the trees with its vast bulk and filling the air with the sound of its fists drumming against the soil.

Aestar nodded with satisfaction as he kicked the sword into the brambles. 'You are not worth one ounce of those you murdered.' He jammed the sceptre deeper and his voice became gentle; pitying, almost. 'Their lights could never be dimmed by such a one as you.' Smoke started to pour from the daemon's tar-black eyes. 'All that they were, all that you destroyed, will be remade anew, and when I face them again I…'

His words trailed off as he sensed movement behind. Keeping the sceptre embedded in the daemon's head, he looked back over his shoulder.

'By the gods,' he cried, feeling the strength go from his legs.

The shadows had spawned a vision: a beautiful noblewoman, with diamond-bright eyes and armour almost identical to his own. She smiled at him and he laughed in shock and relief. 'Who are you?' he cried.

She continued to smile as she stepped closer. 'I am the forest,' she replied.

Aestar frowned in confusion, as he realised that she was not alone.

The noblewoman was accompanied by a creaking, animated grove of wooden daemons, clad in thick, ridged bark and vicious, thorny spikes. Their gnarled flesh was inscribed with spiralling runes and as they approached, they opened their beak-like mouths and revealed long, sharpened branches, like the fangs of a wildcat.

Aestar was speechless with shock. He staggered back, shaking his head and leaving his sceptre embedded in the daemon. He realised that the noblewoman had vanished and where she had been standing there was now another one of the wooden spectres.

Aestar's disbelief grew as the wooden creatures started to sing. No recognisable words came from their knotted throats, just the dry rattle of wind, muttering through the leaves of an old tree.

'Wait,' he said as they jerked and lurched towards him, their song growing more urgent. 'Understand. This creature must be banished. I must kill it, or–' He grunted in shock as the nearest of the monsters pierced his stomach with a branch–like limb.

'I have to destroy its flesh,' he tried to say, but blood was pouring from his mouth. He dropped to his knees, skewered by the branch. 'I must avenge my brothers.'

Countless more creatures flooded from the darkness. They lifted Aestar like a hog on a spit, deaf to his gurgled cries. Dozens more hurried past and punctured the daemon with their twisted limbs, lifting it from the ground with ease. Then, once their victims were secure, they hauled them off through the forest, rushing through the trees with an odd, juddering gait.

Aestar continued shouting as they raced through the forest, begging them to let him finish his work, but Alkhor simply laughed. After a while other beings joined the parade: small, flitting creatures of gossamer and light, creeper-trailing moths and dragonflies with malicious, humanoid faces. Aestar realised that these were the creatures of his imagination – the shapes he had glimpsed in the pool and between the trees. 'My mind has gone,' he croaked, as he teetered on the brink of unconsciousness. His thoughts began to drift as pain and blood loss overwhelmed him. The tiny, luminous beings swarmed closer and he imagined they were the souls of his brothers, come to demand justice. 'I will end it,' he groaned, straining to free himself. 'I promise you.'

The creatures carrying him sensed his movement and jabbed another serrated limb through his armour, piercing his right shoulder and eliciting another howl of pain.

After several more minutes of agonising jolting and lurching, the forest daemons carried their captives into a small, steep-sided valley, with a crimson circle of beech trees at its centre.

Aestar was slipping in and out of consciousness, but as they neared the centre of the hollow he saw that the trees surrounded a dolmen: a trio of broad, black stones, scored with an intricate circular rune. He noticed also that beneath the stones was a deep, ragged hole. It looked as though the earth had exploded, tearing up through the turf to create a trench. He looked over at his enemy and saw that Alkhor was in great pain. The sceptre was still embedded in the daemon's face and the magic bound within it was gradually causing Alkhor to shrivel and diminish. Its grotesque frame had already shrunk to half its former size and its lurid green flesh had faded to a pale, ashen grey.

'I have to finish my work,' croaked Aestar as the creatures lowered him into the hole beneath the stones. 'The daemon's soul will endure,' he said, as he thudded into the grave. 'I must send it back to the abyss.' The creatures of bark and thorn gave no reply and turned their attention to the smouldering dae-mon, dropping it down beside Aestar in the hole. For a second, he thought he might have a chance to grab the sceptre and finish what he had begun, but before he could do so, the tree spirits wrenched the silver staff from the daemon's head and passed it quickly back through their ranks, handling it gingerly with their crooked, brittle fingers.

'No!' Aestar tried to cry, but claustrophobia caused his breath to come in short, shallow gasps. He clawed at the soft earth. 'I have not finished!'

The monsters gave no reply as they formed a circle around the hole and began to sing in the same sinister, creaking voices they had used earlier.

Alkhor dragged its ruined flesh closer to Aestar, pawing him with one of its atrophied, claw-like hands. 'They mean to bind us together.' Flies and drool fell from its mouth. 'They sense your love for me.' The daemon's laughter grew wilder. 'Do you promise to take care of me?'

Aestar whined with impotent fury and tried to grab Alkhor's neck. His strength was gone and he had barely touched the daemon's face before he fell back again.

As the wooden creatures continued to sing, Aestar saw that tendrils of ground-ivy were pouring down into the hole.

'Why don't they just kill us?' he groaned.

The daemon's laughter stopped and it shuffled even closer, so that Aestar could feel its rancid breath on his cheek. 'Can't you hear their song? Killing us would be wrong. It would unbal-ance their blessed idyll.' The daemon laughed again as the ivy spread over its face. 'They're unsure what we are, so they're going to give us to the forest. These old stones have some kind of power. They don't understand it, but they intend to use it as a prison. The words of their song might not be to your–' The daemon's words were cut short as ivy poured into its mouth, but it continued to shake with laughter.

Aestar struggled desperately as the ivy pressed down over his face, but he only succeeded in dislodging the crumbling walls of the hole. Despair gripped him. Whatever the monsters believed, Alkhor would not be bound by a few old stones, whatever magic they contained. The daemon would never age or starve and eventually it would find a way out. Horror thrilled through his veins as he realised the extent of his failure. He tried to scream, but as he opened his mouth soil flooded in and silenced him.

The monsters' song droned on. For a while Aestar could still see sunlight overhead, but then something else started to spread over the hole, plunging him into darkness.

The last shreds of light vanished and Aestar prayed to his gods, waiting for the blessed mercy of suffocation. Unfortunately, even in death his trials were not over. As his life slipped away, Aestar endured one final indignity. His final breath had barely left his mouth when he felt the daemon enter his thoughts and begin to explore, picking through his memories like a crow at a corpse.

WINTER

Gaurach-Dúin
The Season of Ice
Stillness

CHAPTER ONE

Winter was fading. As Sephian ran he felt all the fury of spring, drumming in his pulse. The first breath of a new year was already straining against the cold, filling the trees with hunger; fanning the flames of their wrath. It was a dangerous time to be abroad but Sephian felt no relief in his homecoming. As he hurried through the shifting dark he grimaced, glimpsing the gaudy lights of the Silvam Dale up ahead. It had only been three months since he last saw his home, and the thought of mingling with his kindred again, so soon, filled him with dread.

People. He shuddered, already picturing their ridiculous incantations and their smiling, pointless deceits. He assured himself that his visit would be brief. He would convey his message and flee, back to the mute, honest violence of the trees. More than ever now he craved their company. The great conjunction was approaching: Ostaliss, the Even-Night, when the forest shuddered back into life, filled with dreams of sunlight and blood. What more beautiful, exhilarating moment was there to be alive? He cursed his luck. As the spirits of day and night approached each other, preparing for their passionate, vernal embrace, he would be trapped in airless, enclosed rooms and smoky, crowded halls.

He reached the entrance to the valley and dropped to his knees, weak with pain and exhaustion. He had bound his arm with a poultice of dried leaves and the blood flow had lessened, but his head was still dangerously light. He pressed his palms against the steel-hard ground and muttered a prayer; begging the ghosts of the earth to sustain him a little longer.

After a few seconds, the earth began to shift and roll.

Sephian held his breath as the path closed in around him. Branches cracked and groaned as they crawled over the soil, reaching hungrily for his trembling limbs. Rather than leaves, they were clad in scraps of skin and hair – the remnants of last year's victims. Sephian waited as long as he dared, feeling the first scratch of thorns against his skin, then he lurched to his feet and ran on.

The bloodstained branches reached after him for a moment, grasping and claw-like, then they withdrew into the shadows.

A long, winding greensward led him into the dale, canopied by silver birch trees that gleamed like bones against the darkness. As he passed beneath their naked branches he listened for a voice, a sign that they would forgive him yet another return to society.

He heard nothing and shook his head. Years of watching the forest had honed his instincts. He could feel its displeasure as clearly as the pain of his wound.

He noticed lights pulsing in the shadows: tiny spirits, ignited by the approach of spring. Sephian eyed them with envy, craving the freedom they flaunted so joyously, then, with a sigh, he approached a pale arch at the far end of the avenue. The gateway to his kindred's shame; the realm of the Enchanter, Prince Elatior.

Sentries guarded the gate, silent, sombre and hidden in shadow. They made no move to question Sephian as he entered. He had already walked past them when he realised how odd that was. He had made no attempt to conceal himself. Why did they not stop him, or at least greet him? He paused, looking back at the pale arch, trying to discern the figures that watched over it. Then he shrugged and moved on, hurrying beneath another tunnel of plaited branches and heading for the halls of the prince.

Elatior weaved his spells beneath the roots of a sprawling goliath known as the Wilding Tree. Sephian grimaced as he approached it. What had begun life as a cruel, bristling hawthorn had been neutered and stifled by centuries of brutal charms. Prince Elatior had bound its heart, creating a living, hate-filled citadel; a memorial to his arrogance. Sephian could barely discern a trunk amidst its writhing, bastard growth.

Such conceit, he thought, placing his hands against the tortured bark and looking up through its branches. The Wilding Tree towered over him, brooding and mutant; a vile hybrid of thorn and leaf. Beech and willow had been threaded through its crown and Sephian grimaced at the sight of such cruelty.

In recent years, the Wilding Tree had grown taciturn, nursing its wounds in bitter silence. Only at the culmination of Prince Elatior's most invasive rites would it cry out – cursing its captors with a brittle, outraged voice.

Sephian placed his hands on the knotted wood and smiled. However much the Enchanter might convince himself otherwise, Sephian knew that the Wilding Tree was only biding its time.

A day of reckoning would come.

At the base of the trunk roots fanned out across the earth, framing a gaping hole. There were no steps, just a void in the loamy soil. Sephian approached the hole then paused, noticing that he had gone unchallenged for a second time. 'Arthron?' he called into the shadows. 'Does the dale sleep so heavily? Will no one welcome me home?'

Shadows rippled together like ink in water, forming a tall, slender figure – a hooded sentry with a longbow slung over his shoulder. 'The kindreds have gathered below, watcher.' He spoke in formal, singsong tones. 'The princess is amongst us. She is wearing the shades of the past, in celebration of the coming thaw. The forest is blessed by her radiance.'

There was something odd in Arthron's voice – a stiffness that added to Sephian's sense of dread. He was used to the toadying descriptions of the old princess, but why did Arthron not use his name? Why did he address him as a stranger?

Sephian stepped closer, trying to discern the sentry's face in the gloom, but Arthron shuffled awkwardly and averted his gaze.

'I see,' replied Sephian, confused by the guard's discomfort. He turned back to the hole in the knotted roots and looked down into the darkness, feeling a vague, nameless fear. What was waiting for him down there? He cursed his own ridiculousness. However much he despised it, this abomination was his home. He nodded at Arthron, ignored the sentry's distant gaze, and stepped into the void.

The tree cradled him in the darkness. Sephian had only dropped a few feet before he was caught. Thin, needle-like tendrils prickled against his face, and thick, creaking roots moved beneath him, rolling like waves. He was weightless in the arms of the Wilding Tree. The roots groaned and cracked as they carried him deep below the earth.

Sephian watched vast, hulking shadows roll past him. The magic of Prince Elatior's magi had sunk deep. The tree's roots were barely anchored to the physical world. Strange scenes flickered into view: faces and limbs, trapped into the shifting mass, ghosts of the past. Such distortion of time and nature filled Sephian with sadness. As the roots finally let him go, he hurried off down a gloomy avenue, eager to complete his errand as quickly as possible.

After passing through a slender archway, Sephian stepped out beneath a domed vault of root and thorn. The chamber had been summoned into being over two thousand years ago and over the centuries it had silvered and petrified. He looked up to see frozen veins of starlight snaking through the wood, filling the air with warmth and movement. Golden boughs of dried mistletoe glittered overhead, pulsing with the light of a forgotten sunrise, but, despite all of this, Sephian hurried on, racing through the antechambers, scowling under his hood, disgusted by wonders designed to astound.

He passed through another room, filled with towering columns of roots. They spiralled over his head, twisting into ephemeral, ever-changing statues. Today they had assumed the forms of gods: the snarling, stag-headed lord of the hunt, Kurnous; the laughing trickster, Loec; and the mother of life herself, Isha, wearing a gown of ivy and a circlet of shimmering fireflies.

Sephian swept on into the Tourmaline Hall, a vast chamber of shifting hues, in which hundreds of his kindred had gathered. The air was thick with herb-scented wood smoke and the pungent aroma of roasting game, and there were more fireflies here, drifting through the darkness in delicate cages of silk thread, painting the assembled crowd in columns of hazy light before plunging them back into pools of darkness.

Long, pale faces rippled into view as Sephian hurried past, fixing him with anxious glances and whispering his name behind delicate fingers: sorcerers, all of them, both lowborn and high, and all unwilling to meet his gaze. The few who were unable to avoid him nodded briefly before moving on and edging gratefully back into the shadows.

At the far side of the hall Sephian saw flashes of light. He frowned, unsure what he was seeing. It looked like the flicker of silent, distant lightning, trapped beneath the earth. The flares blinked across a circle of awed faces and Sephian's heart sank. Princess Asphalia must indeed be present. Such a visit was rare, but always induced the most revolting, sycophantic displays. Perhaps this might be enough to explain the strange greeting he had received? Asphalia was adored and feared in equal measure and her strange magic rarely passed without incident. He stepped closer, noticing again how even the most familiar of his kindred shied away from his approach. Sephian had no desire to be part of their games, but such open hostility seemed odd.

Finally, he saw a face that he was sure would not turn away.

'Isére!' he called, conscious of how his voice rang out around the hall. Every conversation faltered as he rushed towards his former lover.

She smiled at his approach, but with little conviction. Her cinnamon locks were plaited with the feathers of a sparrow-hawk and tied tightly back, hanging down between her ivory shoulders and giving her features an oddly severe appearance. Her cool, blue-grey eyes glittered in the shifting light and as Sephian pulled her close he realised that she had been crying.

'Home so soon,' she muttered, after a brief, chaste kiss.

Sephian shook his head, confused by her coolness. 'Why does everyone look at me like a stranger tonight?'

Isére laughed. It was a sad sound. 'What *are* you, if not a stranger?' She shook her head as she studied him. His long, hangdog features were locked in their usual mournful expression. 'Since when did you crave conversation? Surely that one sentence has exhausted your supply of words for at least a year?'

Sephian's frown deepened. 'Does every thought need to be spoken?' He looked around in disgust. 'Is it so bad to keep one's own counsel?'

Isére shook her head in disbelief. She waved at the flickering lights around the princess. 'Do not worry yourself, you're just not the most exciting guest tonight.' She turned away and looked anxiously at a distant silhouette.

Sephian felt his stomach knot as he realised it was her current lover.

'You must learn a little humility,' continued Isére, ignoring his scowl. 'The forest does not revolve around you, however much time you spend praying to it. You may be the Enchanter's favourite watcher, but you are as lowborn as me, Sephian. We still share that much.'

Sephian was too angry to speak for a second. Then he shook his head, trying to rid himself of painful memories. 'I have news,' he said, grabbing a necklace from around his neck and holding it up to her face. It consisted of several loops of gleaming, yellow incisors. 'Five of these are new this evening,' he said, rattling the teeth. 'Harvested less than three miles from this spot.'

Isére frowned. 'Outsiders, three miles from the Silvam Dale?' There was a note of disbelief in her voice. 'Surely a guard would have–'

'It was Tethea's corpse that alerted me to the trail.' His voice faltered as he recalled the scene. 'It took me a while to recognise her.'

Isére's eyes widened. 'Tethea is gone?'

Sephian muttered a prayer and looked up at the vaulted roots of the Wilding Tree. 'Not gone, Isére, *evergreen*. A brave young handmaiden for Isha.'

Isére saw the bloody poultice on Sephian's arm and blanched. 'You're hurt.'

Sephian shrugged.

'You must speak to Princess Asphalia,' she said, surprising him by gently stroking the poultice. Her eyes were suddenly full of pity. 'She will give you an audience, I'm sure of it. You deserve that much.'

Sephian's sense of unease grew. *You deserve that much.* What an odd choice of words. He looked over at the flickering lights. The princess was famously capricious. It was never wise to predict her mood. 'Well, my news *is* important…'

'She will see you,' insisted Isére, leading him across the hall.

The princess was a spent force. Sephian had suspected it before most, but her powerlessness had become an undeniable fact over the last few years. Her decrepitude did nothing to deter the sycophants, though. As Sephian made his way through the simpering crowds, he felt as though he were wading through sap.

As he reached the princess he saw that she was floating several feet above the ground. Her arms were raised over her head and she was surrounded by tendrils of light, and the drifting skeletons of leaves. The dazzling shapes made it almost impossible to discern her outline. Blue wisps of light rippled around her naked body like fire, washing over the faces of her spellbound audience, and painting them with fanciful images of the past. It was an incredible display of power, but Sephian was no more fooled than any of the other spectators. Princess Asphalia was ancient and her power had long since deserted her. Her delusion was maintained by a row of pitiful figures slumped in the shadows – Elatior's most powerful sorcerers, skewered by the tree's grasping roots. Dozens of them, threading their magic through the princess, as their own bodies were slowly being torn apart. It was a gruesome charade, fuelled by terror, but Sephian understood the reasoning. If the princess's happiness were not maintained at all times, Prince Elatior would hear of it. His response would be brief. Brief and bloody.

Despite himself, Sephian was beguiled by the display. Despite their agony, the magi had woven a powerful glamour. He saw diaphanous, rippling pictures of spring and new growth and even the wild hunts of the summer. He noticed with embarrassment that many of the scenes involved him. In recent years, he had become Prince Elatior's most trusted advisor. His calm, earnest determination had earned him the respect of the entire kindred, if not the love. He knew that tales of his tireless wandering had spread even further, to the other kindreds of the forest. As he thought of this, Sephian felt suddenly amazed at the cool reception he had received.

'Princess Asphalia,' he cried, louder than he intended. 'I bring news.'

The princess lowered her eyes and dropped from the air. The lights settled over her sagging flesh as a shimmering cloak.

The assembled crowd turned to face Sephian, but he saw that none of them were surprised by his interruption. They were all expecting him.

'Sephian,' said the princess, turning her incandescent eyes on him. There was a mixture of emotions on her lined, regal face: eagerness, excitement and something else, something quite unexpected.

She's afraid of me, Sephian realised.

'What news do you bring?' she asked, keeping her voice flat and neutral.

Sephian hesitated, still shocked by the fear in her eyes. 'I-I have seen outsiders, Princess, to the south.'

Nervous laughter rippled through the crowd and the princess looked around at her subjects with a wry smile. 'And is that so unusual, watcher?'

Sephian turned on the sneering crowd and noticed how they flinched from his gaze. What do they see in me, he thought? Despite all their fawning and hand-wringing the asrai assembled around the princess were the most noble in the Silvam Dale. Few of them would have even acknowledged one so lowly as him before; now they were cowering before him. What has changed, he wondered?

Realising that the princess was still awaiting his reply, Sephian tried to calm himself and continue, reminding himself that the sooner his message was understood, the sooner he could leave. 'Outsiders have reached the borders of the Silvam Dale,' he announced. 'Cloven ones. Creatures of Chaos. They have already slain Tethea and perhaps others.' He shook his head, shocked by his own words. 'The enemy has followed the secret ways to our home. They have navigated the darkest paths. They have discovered routes that should be known only to us.'

For the first time that evening, Sephian saw surprise on someone's face. The princess's odd expression was replaced by one of confusion. She turned to a figure at her side – an ancient silver-haired mage, clutching a long birch-wood staff. The mage was wearing a cloak of white ermine and a bleached, wooden mask that completely covered her head. The mask was carved to resemble the mournful, heart-shaped face of a barn owl.

'That cannot be,' stated the mage, her voice muffled by the mask. 'No one can follow our most secret ways.' She did not look at Sephian as she contradicted him, keeping her gaze fixed on the princess. 'The watcher knows that better than anyone. The presence of outsiders, so close to your realm, can only be the result of luck.'

Sephian stepped closer and noticed, to his amazement, that the crowd edged away from him, as though his touch might poison them. Incredibly, even the princess took a step back. He paused, losing his train of thought at the sight of such strange behaviour. Then he shook his head and continued, ignoring the white-robed mage and keeping his eyes trained on the princess. 'Your majesty, I have encountered the beasts of Chaos many times but I have never seen them advance with such confidence. Something is wrong. I must speak to the Enchanter.'

The princess looked concerned and seemed about to reply. Then the masked figure leant close and whispered urgently into her ear. Princess Asphalia nodded, and as she listened her fear was replaced by a look of growing excitement and pride. Finally, she turned back to Sephian and beamed at him. Her eyes were blazing with a mixture of sorcery and passion. 'We thank you for your vigilance, Sephian.' She looked at the vast wooden ceiling. 'The gods and I will consider your words.' She waved across the glittering hall to a distant flight of stairs. 'Now you should rest.'

Colour rushed into Sephian's face as he realised he was being dismissed. 'Princess–' he began.

'Please,' insisted the princess, her voice heavy with borrowed power. '*Leave.*'

Sephian felt the weight of her words like a physical blow. He looked around for support but saw a circle of stony faces. Even Isére showed no sign of recognition as he reeled past her. It hardly surprised him to see that the vast crowd had already parted to create a wide path for him.

His desire to leave overwhelmed him. The strange, oppressive atmosphere in the chamber was unbearable. As he marched past the rows of mute faces, he had to resist the urge to break into a run.

'Tears of Isha,' he muttered, emerging from the tree and taking a grateful gulp of the crisp night air. 'What is happening this evening?' He looked up through the dense, evergreen branches of the Wilding Tree and watched the stars wheeling overhead, as though they might give him an answer.

'You should rest, watcher.' The voice came not from the stars, but from the shadows.

Sephian nodded, making no attempt to find Arthron in the darkness. He trod heavily beneath the boughs, feeling trapped in a waking dream. Why had Isére let him leave alone? And where was everyone? The Silvam Dale was silent and dark. At this time there should be countless, irritating lights snaking between the trees and raucous songs echoing between the branches.

Full of confusion and doubt, Sephian wandered the glades and hollows of his home. Then, as quickly as he could, he left the sorcerers of the Silvam Dale and passed back into the wilds of the forest.

He paid no attention to his route, allowing ancient, shifting paths to lead him blindly onwards. His sense of foreboding faded as he yielded to the bewildering embrace of the forest. After just a couple of hours he knew that he was hopelessly, blissfully lost and sat down to rest for a while against the shattered bole of a poplar tree.

Sephian tried to sleep, but his thoughts were restless with images from the Silvam Dale. He was haunted by the nervous glances of his kindred. 'Even the princess,' he muttered, shaking his head and pulling his cloak tighter. To soothe himself, he listened to the voices of the forest – the breeze bustling through the undergrowth, the creak of the leafless boughs, the patter of hungry beasts – but still his sense of foreboding grew.

When sleep came it was a skein of dark omens. First he saw an enormous oak, oozing blood from its thick bark. Then he saw a barn owl, thrashing violently in a cage of stone. Finally he saw his own face, peeling away from his skull to reveal a dark mound of shaded grass, punctured by a long, silver knife.

In the false light before dawn Sephian awoke. A familiar sound was drifting through the forest – a horn blast that sounded like the long, lowing cry of a wounded beast. He peered into the grey, bruise-like void between the trees. 'It can't be,' he muttered. The sound was answered by another, identical note, and then another, until the forest rang with the sound of hunting horns.

Sephian felt his pulse quicken as he climbed to his feet. Spring was still several days away, the Wild Hunt could not be abroad so early; and yet, the evidence was all around him. As the horns grew nearer, animals began to bolt – rats, squirrels, birds and deer exploded from the darkness and scrambled past him.

He vaulted lightly up into the branches of a tree, avoiding the stampede, and peered through the darkness. Sure enough, after a few minutes he began to see movement in the distance – the gleaming white flanks of stallions, smashing through the undergrowth.

'By the gods.' Sephian shook his head as he saw the horses' riders – towering giants with spirals of horn snaking from their ivy-bound hair. Their faces were as pale and beautiful as the moonlight, but their eyes burned with a dark spectral fire.

'The horned riders.' Sephian recognised them immediately

and his voice trembled with awe. 'Priests of Kurnous.'

He watched in stunned silence as they thundered past, but then his sense of awe began to be replaced by the same dread that had driven him from the Silvam Dale. This time, however, it was no vague, nameless fear: he knew exactly what made his breath come in short, sharp gasps.

The riders were coming for him.

Suddenly, everything that had happened that evening made sense. As the drumming of hooves filled his mind, drowning out even his thudding pulse, Sephian realised that *he* was the riders' prey.

The hunt was for *him*.

His excitement at seeing them vanished, washed away on a wave of primal terror. This was the fear he had seen in the eyes of the princess, and all the others too. They knew. The witches of the Dale had been afraid of him because they had seen his fate.

He was marked for death.

He turned and fled, dashing through the trees, leaping from branch to branch, before dropping to the ground and sprinting across the frost. He was a watcher. Even by the standards of the asrai, he excelled in the arts of concealment, but as the riders approached, filling the forest with their dreadful din, he forgot all that he knew, smashing wildly through the paths and glades, as clumsy and noisy as an outsider.

He had glimpsed the riders before, but only from afar. Their haunts were the deeps of the forest, where even he feared to tread. Their domain was as perfidious and strange as anything in the forest and it had turned them into something more than just asrai – daemonic beings with a half a foot in the spirit world.

Sephian felt sure that he knew the reason they had singled

him out. He had failed them by mingling with the sorcerers of the Dale. 'I had to return!' he howled as he ran. 'I had to warn the Enchanter! But I am not like him!'

The drumming of the hooves grew nearer, approaching from several directions, and the horns grew wilder, turning from a deep moan to an otherworldly howl.

As he ran, Sephian snatched a terrified glance over his shoulder. To his horror, one of the riders was already bearing down on him. His speed was incredible and even a brief glimpse was enough to still Sephian's heart. Both rider and beast were glistening with blood and sweat, and draped in the trophies of their previous hunts: scraps of flesh and scalp trailed behind the rider like pennants as he raised his spear and prepared to catch a new trophy. He wore a tall spiked helmet of birch bark, but his ashen face was exposed. His eyes were rolling, feral and dark.

Sephian's fear mingled with another sensation: rage. He had done nothing to deserve the wrath of Orion's guardians. He, above anyone else in his kindred, observed the ancient precepts. He had never so much as stepped foot in the King's Glade. 'You've made a mistake!' he gasped, leaping to safety just seconds before the rider thundered past and slammed his spear into the ground.

Sephian had lived by his wits for as long as he could remember. He had hunted and evaded all manner of creatures in Prince Elatior's name. 'I am not your prey,' he cried, swinging on a low branch and flying back in the direction of the rider. As he hurtled through the air he drew his bow and arrow in a single fluid movement, loosing a shot before vanishing into the trees on the far side of the path.

The rider stiffened in his saddle and let out a cry that had no place in the mortal realm. Sephian's arrow was buried deep between his broad shoulder blades and as he reined in his steed, the horned giant slumped awkwardly in his saddle.

Sephian watched in horror as the rider wrenched the arrow free, without a murmur of pain.

The other riders raced towards him and he ducked beneath a fallen tree, sprinting off down a narrow, icy gulley, knowing that the stallions would be too broad to follow. As he slipped and scrambled through puddles, the horns continued to wail, seeming to come from every direction at once.

A lifetime of wandering had sharpened his senses to an almost unnatural degree. A barely perceptible rushing of air alerted him to another attack and he rolled aside, scraping his skin painfully across a clump of frozen roots, but dodging the spear that whizzed past his ear and thudded into the side of the gulley.

A figure dropped into view, just ahead, and Sephian immediately drew a bead on the horned shape rushing towards him.

Before he had chance to fire, something made him pause.

Rather than hurling his spear, the muscle-bound giant dropped to one knee and held out his hand.

Sephian stumbled and lowered his bow, confused by the hunter's strange behaviour.

He opened his mouth to ask for an explanation, but his words twisted into a howl of frustration as thick tendrils of ivy were thrown around his arms.

Sephian cursed his own stupidity.

He had been tricked.

Gentle hands bound him with more ivy and lifted him from the ground, fastening him to the trunk of a tree. Sephian struggled to free himself but the surrounding branches coiled themselves snake-like around his legs, fixing him firmly in place.

The kneeling giant rose to his feet and stepped closer, looming out of the darkness with his hand still outstretched. Seen close up, the rider was even more unnerving. The dark leaves in his hair were actually growing from beneath his pale flesh and knotting themselves around the slender horns that emerged from behind the birch-bark helmet.

'My leaf-liege,' said the rider, his voice a low growl. 'You do not remember me. I am Atolmis the Hunter. My blood is your sap. My bones are your roots.'

Sephian ceased his struggling and slumped in his bonds, confused. *Leaf-liege*. What does he mean?

Atolmis stepped closer, drew a blunt wooden knife and pulled open Sephian's cloak, exposing his chest.

'Do not be afraid.'

He jammed the knife home.

'Through death, you will live.'

Sephian tried to reply, but hot blood was already rushing from his mouth.

Atolmis's jaw opened to reveal long, yellow teeth.

'Orion,' he growled, punching the blade deeper between Sephian's ribs.

'I have come to make you immortal.'

CHAPTER TWO

Raven-black, Finavar slipped through the dusk. Slivers of star-light lit his way, scattered across the hoarfrost by the skeleton frames of oak, elder and ash. As he dropped from the naked boughs a column of tiny figures trailed after him, glittering playfully in his wake like motes of dust.

Finavar moved in fluid silence, settling on the ground like a dancer. His tall, sinewy frame was almost naked, apart from a long loincloth and a dark cloak bristling with thorns and burs. In his right hand he held a bone-handled sword with an intricately worked leaf-shaped blade and at his belt he carried another one of identical design. His face was hidden beneath the deep folds of his black hood, but as he stood his pale limbs flashed in the moonlight, revealing a network of beautiful, knotted tattoos.

Finavar hummed cheerfully as he studied the frozen earth. He was in a small clearing and the tracks of his enemy were unmistakable. A deep, broad line of hoof prints that marred the frost; a scar in the whiteness, ripe with the smell of corruption.

He flattened himself to the ground, traced a long, elegant finger over the tracks and mouthed the words of a song. Then he nodded. 'Thirty or so, at most.' There was no fear in his voice, only excitement.

'Perfect.'

Finavar's words scattered his glittering entourage like a bank of fog. As the shapes billowed around him their miniscule forms caught the light and were revealed in more detail: some were spiny and ridge-backed, some were scaled and serpentine, but all were hazed by a blur of gossamer wings.

Finavar paid them no heed as he stood and looked around the clearing. His gaze came to rest on pair of small, slender shadows that had followed him from the trees: a pair of polecats that circled him with liquid, snake-like grace. 'Mormo. Mauro,' he said, bowing with mock solemnity.

The creatures looked up thoughtfully at him but gave no reply, so he continued exploring the clearing. A few feet away there was a broad, stag-headed oak, as hunched and fierce as an old boar. He stepped towards it, raising his sword as he approached the trunk. He muttered a short poem, pressed the blade carefully between the ridges of bark, then drew it back and pressed the metal to his lips, closing his eyes as he savoured the taste of the thick sap. His tall frame stiffened as the tree's essence mingled with his own. He tilted his head back, revelling in his growing strength, and as he did so his hood fell away, revealing a bright, youthful face and a tumble of dyed orange hair.

Finavar's almond-shaped eyes flickered as the sap spread through his body. All along his pale limbs, the tattoos rippled and flowed, as through caught in a spectral breeze. He rolled his shoulders beneath the cloak, delighting in the sensation. Then, after carefully blocking the tree's wound with a sliver of bark, he turned on his heel and sprinted from the clearing.

The outsiders had left a trail of destruction in their wake. Finavar's lip curled at every broken bough and splintered root. He was still young – barely sixty summers old – but he was experienced enough to know that this was unusual. Even the most lumbering brutes tried to disguise their passing, but his current prey seemed happy to be found. It was as though they were announcing their presence with a proud, guttural roar.

Fools. Did they not realise the forest was waking? Had they forgotten that spring was just days away? Once the trees had shaken off their slumber, nothing would be safe.

I must act fast, Finavar decided, before the trees rip them apart; or Thuralin spoils my fun with some tedious words of wisdom. I will be ruthless. I will be decisive. He felt a rush of joy. He knew his kinband would follow. There was adventure here. His face lit up in a smile. What else mattered?

Finavar whistled as he ran: a low, musical trill that received an identical reply from somewhere to the east. As he passed through glittering hollows and frosted glades, Finavar vanished and reappeared, as fleeting as a tree spirit, with Mormo and Mauro racing after him like a pair of extra shadows.

He emerged into a narrow, moonlit valley and crouched at the confluence of two frozen streams, sniffing the air and trying to gauge the mood of the trees. There were paths in the forest, but they could rarely be trusted and never looked the same twice. Finavar, like the rest of the asrai, had learned to hear the voice of the forest and he closed his eyes for a second, listening to the trees. Then he peered at the trail of hoof prints he was following.

'The enemy paused here,' he said, as the two polecats snaked out of the trees and climbed up onto his shoulders. 'They waited by the edge of the frozen water, then hurried on, leaving that channel of shattered ice that leads to the trees on the northern bank.' As the polecats edged closer to his face, following the direction of his gaze, Finavar frowned. 'They took just the route I would have chosen if I was seeking the fastest way home.'

Without looking up from the ice, he sensed movement further downstream and heard a soft exhalation of breath. 'Tired, Caorann?' he asked, keeping his gaze fixed on the tracks and barely raising his voice above a whisper.

The figure downstream let out a deep bark of laughter. His attire was as primitive as Finavar's – tattoos and a loincloth and little else – but that was where the similarity ended. He was almost a foot taller than Finavar, with a broad, powerful chest and arms like knotted steel. By the standards of his kindred, he was a giant. He wore no cloak, but his long hair was just as oddly coloured as Finavar's – a mass of greasy blue locks that hung down around his large, prominent jaw. 'Only of your humour, Fin,' he grunted. 'But I'm quite happy to wait as you catch your breath.' His tone was severe, but he could only keep his face straight for a few seconds, then his face cracked into a broad grin.

Finavar laughed and looked up to study his friend's face. Nobody called him Fin anymore.

'They made straight for our halls,' said Caorann, following Finavar's gaze and guessing his thoughts.

Finavar nodded and peered across the shattered ice, rising to his feet with a pout on his face.

'Coincidence?' suggested Caorann, resisting the urge to comment on his friend's ridiculous expression.

Finavar shrugged and continued pouting. As he raised his voice to address someone else, his words took on a mocking tone. 'And what do you think, Thuralin?' He lifted his gaze to the far side of the stream.

A third figure emerged from the shadows. He was as wiry as the first two, and covered in the same circular tattoos, but his demeanour could not have been more different. Where the others were lithe and clear-eyed, Thuralin was stooped and saturnine. He had a crumpled, heavily lined face and a thin-lipped, down-turned mouth. The right side of his face was a silvery mass of scar tissue, clearly the result of a terrible burn, and the left side was hidden behind a featureless wooden mask. His left arm was as crooked as a withered tree and his one visible eye glared out from folds of sallow skin.

He looked appalled by the world.

'They travel through the forest as easily as we do.' His voice was a rattling wheeze. He dropped awkwardly to one knee and grabbed a handful of rotten leaves. They oozed dark fluid as he squeezed them in his fist and tilted back his head, allowing the liquid to pour into his mouth. After a while he opened his eye and rose back to his feet. 'They are moving fast, too. Left unchecked, they will reach Locrimere within two hours.'

Finavar replaced his pout with a smirk. 'Left unchecked?' He turned to Caorann with his eyebrows raised.

Thuralin's mouth continued to hang down, but his eye glittered. 'Alhena will doubtless be with them by now, after you gave her such a long leash, but with luck she might keep her distance until you arrive; as should the boy. You have time to gather aid before you join them.' His voice dropped even lower. 'That would be *my* advice. Lord Beldeas would–'

'Lord Beldeas,' said Finavar, clanging his blades together, 'is a fool. We cannot rely on him. We are more than enough, Thuralin. There are no more than thirty of them. There are *five* of us. Besides, we must strike fast, or your daughter will butcher the lot of them before we can even draw blood.'

He clutched a strand of rat's hair, plaited into his own, and stared at Thuralin, daring him to argue. Then he sprinted across the ice, moving so lightly that his feet left no mark.

Caorann paused long enough to give Thuralin an awkward shrug, then he vanished too.

Thuralin hesitated, stroking his scarred face and glaring back towards Locrimere. For a moment it seemed that he might head off in the opposite direction to the others, then he shook his head and undid a small leather pouch slung around his neck. He took out a handful of seeds, fixing his gaze on the stars overhead. 'How can I endure this fool? Even for the sake of my child?'

He moved his mask aside, revealing a drooping mess of scar tissue. Then he shoved the seeds into his mouth and closed his eyes. After a minute or so his shoulders relaxed and the pained expression dropped from his face. 'I must. He is her best hope. When I am gone…' The thought was too awful for him to finish.

With a final shake of his head, he moved his mask back into place and raced after Finavar.

Finavar felt the rat's speed mingling with the strength he had borrowed from the oak. The shackles of his flesh fell away as he joined his spirit with the forest. Wintry boughs passed by in a grey-green blur and as he ran he adopted the grace of a rodent, dashing through the undergrowth. Within twenty minutes he reached his prey and, without pausing, he swung himself lightly up into the branches of an oak tree and looked down over a broad clearing.

The sight that greeted Finavar filled him with nausea. He had hunted outsiders on countless occasions, but their presence never failed to shock him. It was not their appearance, so much; the forest was home to creatures far stranger than hulking, bull-headed oafs. No, it was something far more profound. Their thick hides stank of disease and sweat, but they were empty; as hollow as a piece of rotten bark. However bestial they might appear, with their cloven hooves and their greasy manes, these children of Chaos were nothing more than a void – a wound in the forest's soul.

Finavar sneered as he watched them. The leader was enormous – a scarred minotaur with human skin draped over its back and head, so that a screaming man's face was stretched over its massive brow. Blood-streaked thighbones were dangling from its belt and as it moved they filled the air with a gruesome clattering sound. It hunched over what looked like the broken stump of an old tree and Finavar crept out further to see what it was doing.

It was grunting and snorting, as though in conversation with something.

The last traces of daylight had sunk beyond the horizon but the scene was picked out by the light of the twin moons and as the minotaur moved to one side, scratching angrily at its leathery neck, Finavar glimpsed a flash of light on the stump. It was pale spectre; a tiny glimmering spirit, crouched on a lichen-covered stone. He pouted again. The rock was carved with a circular design.

Finavar turned and looked questioningly at the radiant shapes hovering behind him. The spirits had followed him from the first sign of impending violence, as eager as ever to see bloodshed. One of them drifted closer: the skeleton of a tiny serpent, a slender opalescent chain, with a leering cadaverous grin and a filthy rosehip helmet. It shone with a faint lunar glow, as did its mount – a tiny, flittering wren.

The tiny serpent sneered back at Finavar, baring its needle-like incisors and brandishing a rose-thorn sword with its tail.

'What's this, Gole?' whispered Finavar, pointing at the light beneath the minotaur. 'Do your brothers betray their own home now?'

The serpent cursed, undulated violently and waved its thorn-blade in Finavar's face, but then it steered the wren higher and studied the scene below. As it watched the exchange the pale fire in its eye sockets pulsed brighter. It waved its thorn-blade at the other spirits and they flew to its side, flickering nervously through the air as they watched the minotaur. They were clearly as confused as Finavar and immediately began quarrelling with each other in their shrill, rippling language.

Seeing he would get no useful answer, Finavar raised a finger to his lips and let out a musical fragment of birdsong. He received a reply from half a mile south then, over the next few minutes, he heard several other identical calls, each one coming from a little further away. He nodded in satisfaction, then, as the vile creatures below prepared to move on, he allowed himself to fall from the branch.

Finavar landed with mock clumsiness in the undergrowth and there was an explosion of snarls as the beastmen whirled around to face him. The minotaur towered over the others, but they were all hulking brutes. Their torsos were covered with scars, filth and blood, and their snouts quivered with excitement as they formed a circle around Finavar. Some were bull-headed, like the minotaur; others had curled, spiralled, ram's horns coiled around their heads, and some resembled hunched, goat-legged humans, with crimson skin, straight black horns and mouths crammed full of fangs. They were all as scantily clad as Finavar, but where his flesh was pale and lithe, these creatures were hulks of knotted, oversized muscle, covered in greasy, tangled fur. As they huddled closer, raising crude, vicious-looking axes, Finavar saw hunger burning in their blood-red eyes, but they did not attack. They roared and churned the earth with their hooves, waiting for the minotaur to make the first move.

The towering creature barged through the crowd and Finavar grimaced; to see the monster in such close proximity made his head pound. It was over eight feet tall and had thick plates of spiked, hammered iron strapped around its enormous arms. Its massive, bovine head was hung low between grossly oversized shoulders and as it approached, the stench of decaying meat poured from its jaws.

The minotaur glared at Finavar with tiny, crimson eyes, then it raised its battered axe and let out a guttural roar, scattering birds from the trees and spurring its warherd into action.

As the monsters charged, Finavar turned and fled, sprinting down a frosty, leafless avenue.

The creatures thundered in pursuit and behind them came the minotaur, stomping heavily through the trees and bellowing as it realised its warherd were being led away from their original path.

To Finavar, their pursuit was as slow as ivy climbing a tree. He could easily have outrun them, but as the monsters crashed clumsily through the glades and gulleys, he made sure never to race too far ahead. Gliding wraith-like between the trees, he taunted them with snatches of song, leaving a trail of sinister melody that echoed around the glittering boughs, mocking their lumbering, awkward pursuit. He grinned as he considered the aptness of his words and the delicate phrasing of his melody.

> *Trail a tale of shallowbrains,*
> *Cumbrous, rank and doomed;*

> *Lead the dance of Everwood,*
> *And leave their bones entombed.*
>
> *Sing a song of jobbernowls,*
> *Clumsy, fat and slow;*
> *Feed them to the Everqueen,*
> *The creeper and the crow.*

After a few minutes the minotaur ceased its pursuit and bellowed furiously at the others to return, but Finavar's song had driven them to such a frenzy that they were deaf to anything else. As the path grew narrower and more difficult, they started to pant and cough, stumbling over roots and reeling from jagged branches, but they would not stop. They could not allow this dancing, infuriating wraith to escape. The more difficult the pursuit, the more incensed and determined they became, howling and grunting as Finavar skipped down a gloomy network of avenues.

After another ten minutes of furious pursuit they emerged into a clearing – a circular patch of scrub and gravel that ended at a rocky outcrop, looking down over a sheer-sided drop that plunged sixty feet or more down to the valley below.

Finavar came to a halt at the edge of the drop and, with no place left to run, turned to face the beastmen.

They lumbered from the trees, panting and trailing their axes through the frost, but at the sight of their prey, stranded at the cliff's edge, they howled in delight, raising their battered weapons and thundering their hooves against the frozen earth.

Finavar calmly drew his blades and adopted a low fighting stance, still grinning as the monsters approached. His smile was not directed at the beastmen but beyond them, to four slender figures stepping silently from the shadow of the trees.

The beastman closest to Finavar, one of the crimson-skinned

monsters with a humanoid face, noticed the direction of his gaze and looked back over its shoulder, but before it had time to roar a warning Finavar's kin began their dance.

Caorann and the others waltzed towards the monsters with astonishing speed, flipping and spinning through the air so gracefully that the beastmen seemed to be surrounded by spirits rather than mortal foes.

The brutish monsters tried to defend themselves with slow, lunging axe blows, but the shapes surrounding them were as vague and intangible as the winter breeze. As they danced, they picked up the tune of Finavar's song, and as the bewildered beastmen lurched and stumbled, trying to grasp their attackers, the haunting melody swelled in volume.

The bloody dance did not last long. Finavar joined the lethal storm of flashing blades and, one by one, the beastmen dropped to their knees, clutching at cuts that erupted all over their bodies – deep, lethal wounds that seemed to appear from nowhere as the singing figures spun back and forth.

As the last of the monsters fell, Finavar was left to fight alone. The others had backed away, lowering their blades and watching his acrobatics in mute wonder.

Finavar performed a final, beautiful pirouette and sliced his sword through the last monster's neck, sending its head spinning off the edge of the cliff.

'So few!' cried one of the dancers, leaping forwards and hacking at the dead bodies. Her head was shaven apart from a long, plaited ponytail and the combination of shaven head, blood-splattered face and furious snarl made her a fearsome sight.

Caorann grimaced at the gruesome display, but Finavar laughed. 'You have them on the run, Alhena! Just a few more blows!'

Alhena was so consumed by bloodlust that she did not hear.

Seeing that there would be no more sport, she crouched next to the bodies, drew a long knife and began to scalp them, whispering furiously to herself as she hacked and sliced.

After a few minutes, she noticed that she was being watched and stood up, wiping the gore from her cheeks. Her eyes were wide and glittering, as though on the verge of tears.

Finavar looked at her in wonder and she glared defiantly back. She was like a tightly stretched vine; always just on the verge of snapping. Her eyebrows were drawn up from her brow in a furious V and her ponytail was matted with blood. As she looked around at the others, she silently dared them to question her actions.

Finavar looked away and noticed that Thuralin was staring at the bodies, muttering under his breath. Finavar waved at the steaming corpses. 'Do you still believe that we should seek aid?' He laughed again. 'Perhaps they're only playing dead?'

Finavar's brother approached. He was a slight, earnest-looking youth named Jokleel, barely out of childhood. He flashed a pleading glance at Finavar then turned to Thuralin. 'What troubles you?'

Thuralin continued staring at the corpses in silence for a while, but the rest of the kinband waited for him to gather his thoughts. His agility might be gone, but only Finavar doubted his wisdom. He shook his head. 'I'm not sure.'

Thuralin coughed so violently that his whole body rocked with the force of it. Then he tried to continue in a strained voice. 'Something is odd. I cannot...' His words trailed off as he noticed how closely the others were watching him. Even Alhena stopped to look anxiously at her father. He managed to stifle his cough and his face dropped back into its habitual scowl. 'You do not want to hear my counsel,' he muttered, turning to Finavar.

Finavar shrugged. 'I know it anyway. You are alarmed that outsiders could beat such a direct path to Locrimere. You think we should rush home and raise the alarm.'

Thuralin's scowl deepened. 'You have skill with a blade, Finavar, I grant you that, but you do not see what's in my head.'

Finavar laughed. 'Thank the gods.' He turned away and nodded to the bloody remains. 'Prepare the bodies,' he said. 'The forest is waking. It will find nourishment even in these vile creatures.'

Caorann nodded and started hurling corpses into a pile, his huge frame making light of the work. The others joined in, but after a few minutes Alhena paused and raised her hand for silence.

Caorann and the others dropped the corpses and drew weapons.

'There are more of them,' whispered Alhena, turning to her father.

The others remained silent, listening carefully. After a couple of minutes they nodded, recognising the clumsy, arrogant sound of outsiders gouging their way through the forest.

Thuralin gave no reply, so Alhena turned to Finavar.

He gave her a nod and her eyes lit up. She bounded up the trunk of a tree and peered out through its branches.

'By Loec,' she gasped, looking back at Finavar with a shocked expression. 'You should see this.'

Finavar and the others dashed across the clearing and climbed the tree, following the direction of her gaze.

Half mile to the east, a vast column of dun-brown shapes was carving its way through the trees. There was no mistaking the fact that they were outsiders. Their brutal weapons glinted in the moonlight as they snaked through the forest and some of them carried blazing brands, the light of which picked their grotesque forms out of the darkness. As the flames flickered across the column of figures, they revealed glimpses of humanoid and animal forms: men with the heads of goats and bulls and others that were a hybrid of man and horse, carrying long, barbed spears. Further back, half-hidden in the darkness, there were other shadows – things so immense that they towered over the trees.

Finavar shook his head and let out a low whistle. 'They show some nerve, marching through the forest on the eve of spring.' He turned briefly to the surly figure at his side, expecting a comment.

The old cripple remained silent but Jokleel gripped his brother's arm. 'Look where they're heading.'

Finavar's smile faltered as he realised which valley the outsiders were making for. They were headed back towards the home of his kindred. They were headed for the blessed halls of Locrimere.

'We must move fast,' he said, feeling a thrill of adrenaline as he realised the significance of the situation. 'We have to stop them.' His voice quivered. 'Imagine what could happen if such an army stumbled into Locrimere.'

Caorann dropped to the ground and let out a booming laugh, amazed by Finavar's daring. 'Just the five of us, Fin?' He looked around at the others to see how far their respect for his old friend would take them.

'He's right, father,' snarled Alhena, flexing her fingers at the thought of more violence. 'We could lead them in a dance they will never forget,'

Thuralin looked horrified. 'Have you forgotten *everything* I taught you? You are a shadow-dancer, not some meat-headed human. You do not charge headlong at your foes like–'

'We will do this,' interrupted Finavar, mirroring Alhena's

wild stare. 'I order it.' He dropped to the ground and looked defiantly at the old wardancer.

Thuralin glared back.

'I know what you're thinking,' said Finavar. 'You think we should run back to Locrimere with our tails between our legs and pray that Lord Beldeas will be interested in our story. You think we need to swell our ranks before tackling such a host, but you are wrong.' Finavar's face filled with elation. 'We are the ones to stop them. And we will stop them now.'

Thuralin looked around for support, but the others were staring at Finavar with undisguised admiration. 'There are five of us,' he muttered.

'Make for Locrimere then,' said Finavar, waving at the trees. 'I want no reluctant allies. I did not recruit you, Thuralin. You practically begged me to take you and your daughter under my wing. You can leave at any time.'

Before Thuralin could reply, Finavar waved in the direction of the beastmen. 'Perhaps word of an army this big might drag Lord Beldeas from his halls.' He sneered in disgust. 'Somehow I doubt it, but if you *do* manage to free him from Ordaana's clutches, tell him that I am his most loyal servant.' Finavar's voice was full of scorn. 'Tell our noble warden that I will keep the enemy from his glades, while he indulges his lunatic wife.'

Thuralin winced at the mention of Ordaana. Then he shook his head and held out his good hand to his daughter. 'I made a mistake,' he said, his words thick with phlegm. 'We would be safer travelling alone than with this clown.'

Finavar laughed.

Alhena blushed and stepped back, lowering her gaze.

Thuralin stared at her in shock. 'You would defy your own father to indulge the whims of this...' His words trailed off as he glared at Finavar.

Alhena kept her gaze fixed on the ground and tried to sound nonchalant. 'I'll find you, father, as soon as we are done.'

Thuralin stared at her for a few more seconds. Then he shook his head and limped off through the trees.

Finavar barely noticed him go, gazing into the distance with his eyes gleaming. 'Take different paths. We cannot risk failure. We cannot risk letting this army arrive unannounced. Imagine such a thing – outsiders, marching right into the heart of Locrimere, tainting our most sacred groves with their foul stink.' He lowered his voice. 'The safety of the kindreds is in our hands.' He drew his twin blades and stared at them, trembling with excitement.

Alhena looked tormented as she watched her father leave and started to follow him, but then she stumbled to a halt. 'I will find you, father,' she called.

'But Fin, what about this?' asked Caorann, nodding to the mound of corpses.

Finavar shrugged. 'Whatever happens is meant to happen. Fate has determined that the bodies will remain on display – as a warning, perhaps.'

He raised one of his leaf-shaped blades and pointed it at the distant valley. 'The forest will take what it needs. We have work to do.'

CHAPTER THREE

Dawn arrived, dripping pale fingers of light through the branches, and still the torture continued.

Sephian slipped in and out of consciousness as the riders worked at his torn flesh. The pain was like nothing he had ever endured, but his captors had somehow managed to keep him from the quiet mercy of death. The one who had spoken, Atolmis, seemed to be a shaman of some kind. As he gouged runes into Sephian's chest with his thin wooden knife, he growled commands at the other riders and muttered dark, meaningless rhymes. Even if he hadn't been bewildered by the pain, Sephian could not have understood him. The words were familiar, yet strange, like an elaborate, obscure dialect of the asrai tongue, mingled with a mixture of animal grunts and odd moaning chants.

Every now and then, Atolmis would cease his ministrations and peer into Sephian's face. At these moments, Sephian felt as though he was trapped in a nightmare. Atolmis's face was similar in some ways to his own, but in other ways it was hideously transformed. The rider's head was almost twice the size it should be and strands of living ivy were wrapped in spirals beneath his pale skin. Even the tall birch-bark helmet that framed his face had merged with his scalp, spreading tiny roots that bulged and snaked beneath his thunderous brow.

'What are you doing to me?' groaned Sephian as Atolmis summoned the other tall figures to approach. They were carrying bundles of sharpened sticks that flashed ominously in the morning light.

Atolmis paused and brought his face closer. His eyes were death-deep pools of hunger. They had no whites or irises, just a pair of enormous pupils flecked with shards of crimson. As he breathed over Sephian, the struggling waywatcher gagged on a heady aroma of potent herbs, ripe berries and raw, bloody meat.

'My lord,' said the giant, managing to suppress some of the wildness in his rumbling voice. 'We are preparing you for the great conjunction.' He stretched out one of his fingers, pointing a long, curved talon at the approaching figures. 'Olachas, Karioth, Ilaruss and Sélva are going to dress you for spring.'

As the other horned riders approached the blood-drenched tree, Sephian moaned in horror. Then he was a sacrifice. He closed his eyes and begged for unconsciousness to take him. They were preparing the way for Orion. They were feeding this sacred tree with his blood.

The riders pressed closer, and gently pulled opened the knife wounds made by Atolmis.

Sephian screamed as they used the sharpened sticks to thread leaves and roots beneath his skin, working at his flesh like industrious tailors. He tried again to wrench himself from the trunk of the tree, but the ivy was like iron. Just as he thought the pain could get no worse, Atolmis placed a garland of holly and mistletoe around his neck and began forcing the berries into his flesh, stabbing the fruit into his skin with his long, ridged talons.

Finally, amidst all the pain, Sephian began to guess the truth.

As the riders tore at his flesh and planted their gifts beneath his skin, he could hear nothing but deference in their voices. Most of what they chanted was gibberish, but over and over he heard the words *Orion* and *King*.

At first, Sephian had thought his ordeal was the result of some terrible mistake, but as the fruit's flesh mingled with his own, other ideas began to form. The pain in his limbs remained, but deep in his chest another sensation began to grow: a burning heat that was oddly pleasant. It felt like the midday sun, beating down on his exposed heart.

He looked down at his ruined body, forgetting the pain for a moment. The horned riders had peeled back whole sheets of his skin, leaving his veins and organs exposed, but they did not stop there. As his skin hung down around his legs, they sewed strands of mistletoe around his viscera and sheathed his organs with ivy leaves, chanting and grunting to themselves as they worked.

Sephian realised that the pain was becoming oddly bearable. In fact, the burning in his chest was almost exhilarating. He ceased his screaming and relaxed his body, allowing the horrific mixture of sensations to wash over him.

Atolmis paused for a second, noticing the change. His lips curled back in a feral grin, revealing teeth that were as long and ridged as his talons. 'The King is stirring,' he growled, then he returned to his work with even more enthusiasm.

Sephian did not even notice this last comment. Something was beginning to happen.

As his thoughts centred on the sensation of sunlight in his

chest, memories began to surface in his mind. Memories that were too varied to belong to just one life, yet they were all undeniably his. He pictured himself leading the horned riders in a glorious hunt. The memory of it filled his tattered flesh with vigour and he ached to be free of his bonds so that he could relive the chase. To his dismay, the images faded as quickly as they came. But when he looked once more into the black, rolling eyes of Atolmis, he saw that they were not strangers. This daemonic being was not his killer, but his servant.

Atolmis continued to grin. 'Patience, my lord.' He nodded at the white-clad branches that surrounded them. 'Winter is dying. Soon we will ride.'

The butchery of his flesh had taken no more than an hour, but as Sephian drifted into oblivion, he felt as though whole lifetimes had passed. With his last vestiges of wakefulness, he was vaguely aware that Atolmis and the others were loosening his bonds. He imagined that he would rise, powerful and king-like, from the wreckage of his body, but he tumbled to the ground, as feeble as a newborn.

The riders lifted him carefully from the blood-soaked earth and placed him on the back of one of their horses. Then he knew no more.

CHAPTER FOUR

As Finavar ran, a late snow began to fall, tumbling gently from the ink-black sky. It settled on the frosty ground and glittered on the hood of his barbed cloak. He smiled as the flakes needled his skin and then he thanked the forest for its benevolence – not only had it graced him with cool, invigorating snow, it had also provided a guide. Up ahead, a nightjar was gliding through the treetops, a sombre, long-tailed ghost, pausing only to catch the odd moth as it headed off to investigate the disturbance to the east.

Fast as he was, Finavar could not keep up with his guide for long, but even once the bird had disappeared from view, Finavar continued following its haunting song as it drifted down into the valley.

Later on, he would make excuses for his lack of prescience, telling himself that the song of the nightjar had beguiled him in some way, but the truth was simple: he was hurrying, blinded by his excitement, and his enemy was patient.

He saw the axe seconds before it bit and he managed to leap

aside, but the shock of the attack unbalanced him. With uncharacteristic clumsiness he caught his cloak on a low-hanging
branch and stumbled. He rolled painfully across frost-hard roots
and slammed into the trunk of a tree, shaking a cloud of snow
from its branches. His blades slipped from his fingers and spun
off into the darkness. Mormo and Mauro vanished into the
undergrowth.

The minotaur strode forwards with a thunderous bellow, consumed with bloodlust at the sight of its fallen enemy. It grabbed
Finavar by the throat and lifted him easily from the ground,
slamming him against the tree trunk with such force that Finavar's breath exploded from his lungs.

Finavar drew his knife and plunged it deep into the monster's
exposed chest. Its hide was so thick that he could barely drive the
weapon home, but he forced with all his strength and waited to
see the creature fall.

The minotaur paused for a moment, lowering its massive,
horned head to study the blade. Then it snorted, wrenched the
knife free and hurled it to the ground.

Finavar struggled to escape, but the minotaur's iron-like grip
defeated him and he cursed bitterly as the monster drew back its
axe for another blow.

Blood rushed from the minotaur's head as a gleaming, leaf-
shaped blade sprouted from its brow.

The monster tightened its hold and Finavar felt something give
in his throat. Then the minotaur's head snapped backwards as
the blade was removed and the beastman reeled away from the
tree, dropping Finavar to the ground with a pained grunt.

'Sorry,' said Alhena with a sarcastic smile, stepping back as the
monster toppled to its knees. Then she flipped gracefully through
the air and landed a few feet away, after jamming her sword in
the minotaur's throat. 'I realise you were only toying with it.'

Finavar gasped as he climbed to his feet. There was a deep, grinding ache in his left shoulder but after rolling it back and forth he decided there was no break. He grimaced and as he slumped against a tree he considered how odd Thuralin's daughter was. She had just saved his life, but her snarl was almost as worrying as the minotaur's.

Alhena's eyes remained staring and wild as she approached him, but she softened her expression slightly. 'Let me see,' she said, stepping closer and placing her hand beneath Finavar's black cloak. She was not gentle and he grimaced as she prodded the injury. 'Painful, but not fatal.' She withdrew her hand and looked at the still twitching hulk of the minotaur. 'It could have been worse.'

Finavar wondered at her skill. Thuralin might have raised a monster, but she was a monster of incredible grace. He gave her a nod of thanks and staggered off through the snow, looking for his swords.

Alhena returned to the dead minotaur and wrenched her weapon free. Then, after a moment's thought, she stabbed it back into the open wound with a string of vile curses. After removing the blade for a second time, she scoured the surrounding trees for signs of any other assailants. 'Strange, that it would stalk you like that. Outsiders rarely show such cunning.' She sneered at the slumped remains of the minotaur, still trembling with rage.

Finavar looked up at the network of leafless branches; pale fingers, stretched over a void. '*Everything* seems strange this evening.' He winced as he rolled his shoulder again, then dashed back into the trees. 'Come, Alhena, we are neglecting our guests.'

* * *

As they headed down into the valley, they took different paths. Alhena passed ahead of the invading army, swinging and vaulting through the treetops and circling around to their left flank; Finavar, meanwhile, moved silently down past the whole deafening horde, until he reach the whelps and curs of the rearguard. Once there, he began to scatter little snatches of song in the darkness, planting odd lilting phrases at the edge of the beastmen's hearing as he dodged between twisted, ancient yews.

At the sound of his voice, some of the monsters began to falter, baring crooked fangs at the shadows and howling in annoyance at the ghostly presence that moved around them.

Finavar felt a thrill of excitement as he realised the scale of the invasion. He had never seen such an enormous host: a lumbering, galloping legion of mismatched animal parts, smashing carelessly through the trees, filling the forest with noise and stench. The momentum of the beasts' charge was such that even his most mocking, eloquent phrases could not halt their advance. Every time his words caused a monster to pause, some hulking overseer would grab the straggler by the throat and hurl it forwards, bellowing furiously at any sign of delay.

'What would drive them on like this?' he whispered, swinging higher up into the trees, hoping for an answer. Up at the head of the column, he thought he saw a possible explanation: a flicker of light, dancing in and out of the shadows and occasionally alighting on the shoulders of an enormous brute marching at the head of the army.

That must be their leader, thought Finavar, peering at the distant figure. It was even more heavily muscled than the rest of the horde and its ancestry seemed to be a grotesque, Chaos-spawned muddle of man and boar. As it looked back over its army, Finavar saw its face: a blunt, bristled snout, a pair of crooked tusks and a low, heavy brow, topped by a foot-long horn that curled up from a shaggy mane. Like most of its followers, the mutant's legs were hoofed and goat-like, but its chest was bull-broad and clad in thick iron chainmail and crudely hammered plates of brass and copper. As the other beastmen lumbered through the forest, this rattling hulk of metal and fur roared commands at them, spraying drool and blood across an enormous double-headed axe.

How does it know its way? wondered Finavar, swooping silently through the branches and alighting on the next tree. He could still make out a tiny wisp of light drifting ahead of the column and he turned to look suspiciously at the spirits that were still trailing after him. Gole, the skeletal, wren-riding serpent, sneered back at him.

Finavar's thoughts were interrupted by the sound of Caorann singing. His voice was as clear as a woodlark and as it drifted from the shadows Finavar could not help but smirk, knowing what a brute his friend was. He saw him briefly, slipping in and out of the trees, teasing the outsiders. His coils of blue hair marked his passage, but his movements were so fast that even the most skilled marksman would have found it impossible to track him.

Boar-face paused, raising a spiked fist as it scowled at the trees ahead. The forest erupted with the sound of clattering armour and belched roars as the whole army ground to a halt.

Finavar smiled as he heard another, equally beautiful song, drifting from the trees to the left of the beastlord. 'Alhena.'

A third song rang out from the forest to his left, just a few feet away from beastmen. 'Jokleel,' he gasped, delighted by his brother's daring. Caorann had always doubted the boy. He thought he lacked the killer instinct required to serve Loec, but here was proof to the contrary. Jokleel was moving as fast and fearlessly as any of them.

Finavar's heart filled with pride and he leapt through the trees in the direction of his brother's song, but before he had gone far, boar-face let out a furious howl. A slender, fast-moving shape had waltzed from the trees; a blur of silver blades that immediately vanished from view, leaving a pile of bleeding beastmen sprawled in its wake.

Finavar nodded, amazed again by Alhena's furious skill. He felt more certain with every day that he was right to shelter her. Thuralin was a tedious old fool, it was true, but he would put up with any amount of grumbling to have Alhena at his side.

On the far side of the army another shape spun into view. Finavar recognised Caorann's vivid blue locks as he flipped and danced from the trees, mocking the creatures with a song about their empty skulls.

As the outsiders charged furiously at Caorann, they failed to notice that Alhena had appeared again, hacking wildly with her blades and accompanied now by Jokleel.

By the time Caorann vanished back into the whirling banks of snow, still laughing and singing, the rest of the kinband had butchered a whole swathe of the army and were already racing back towards the shadows that spawned them.

As he hurried to join the fun, Finavar added his own voice to the chorus, finally causing some of the monsters to break ranks and lumber after him.

The column started to break up. The monsters whirled and flinched from the shadows, bewildered by songs that came from every direction. 'We can take them all,' cried Finavar, laughing as he ran, with no idea if he was right.

He stumbled to a halt, and crouched beside a clump of snow-draped hawthorn bushes. 'What's this?' he gasped, staring in shock at the leader of the army. The hulking creature had raised its axe and pointed it at the trees, and the weapon was draining thick worms of mist from the branches. Banks of the stuff rippled through the air, shimmering with inner fire as it seeped into the trees.

Finavar had never seen beasts of Chaos wield this kind of sorcery. 'That's the work of a spellweaver,' he muttered, lowering his blades.

His dismay grew as the horned monster wrenched back its axe, like a fisherman hauling in his catch, and dragged Caorann into view.

To Finavar's horror, his friend was tightly bound by the tendrils of mist. As the beastlord heaved back his axe, Caorann bounced and rolled across the frozen ground, cursing, unable to free himself.

Finavar, Alhena and the boy immediately dropped into view and sprinted towards the vapour. Their smiles and songs were gone, replaced by silent rage.

Before any of them could reach the scene, boar-face strode towards its struggling prey and hacked down with its axe.

As the monster struck, the strange mist evaporated, releasing Caorann from its grip.

Freed from his bonds, Caorann tried to dodge the blow but, agile as he was, there was not enough time.

The axe sank deep into his shoulder, pinning him to the ground with a dull *thunk*.

Blood gushed from the wound and Caorann blacked out, slumping back onto the ground as the beastlord yanked the blade free for a second strike.

Before Caorann's kinband could reach him the rest of the army intercepted them.

Now that the asrai were drawn out into the open the

monsters had the advantage. They howled victoriously and rolled towards them like a wave of fur, horns and battered iron. Only Finavar managed to break through. He flipped up over their heads in a bewildering series of twirls and rolled to a halt beside his wounded friend.

The boar-faced one let out a grunt of laughter, towering over Finavar and levelling its axe at his head. Mist slipped from the blade but before the monster could complete its spell it snorted and dropped the weapon, backing away in confusion.

As the monster reeled backwards, two small shadows dropped from its arm and scattered into the darkness.

Finavar muttered thanks to Mormo and Mauro and hefted Caorann onto his shoulder, cursing his friend's weight as he sprinted for the trees.

Dozens of the outsiders were busy with Jokleel and Alhena but plenty remained to block Finavar's route to safety. He lashed out as he ran, but, encumbered as he was, his movements lacked their usual grace.

One of the red-skinned humanoid creatures dodged Finavar's sword and slammed a brass-studded mace into his stomach.

Finavar's breath exploded from his lungs and he crashed to the ground, sending Caorann rolling across the churned earth.

The monsters surged forwards, but as Finavar clambered to his feet they dropped to their knees, clutching at their chests and throats.

Without pausing for an explanation, Finavar hauled Caorann back onto his shoulder and continued racing back to the trees. As he ran, he felt the breath of arrows, whistling past his face and slamming into his assailants.

'Thuralin!' he gasped, reaching the cover of the trees and glimpsing a scarred face glaring out at him from a dark, thorny gulley.

The old wardancer replied with another wave of grey-flecked arrows. Dozens of them flew from the trees, slaying everything that tried to follow Finavar into the forest.

CHAPTER FIVE

Sephian rose through an ocean of dreams. He watched seasons come and go in the blink of an eye, dragging lime-green shoots from the ground, filling them with life, twisting them into beautiful copper-coloured blades and then scattering them across the ground. He saw this cycle, repeated endlessly, at ever-faster speeds until the world became a blur of birth and death. Finally, just as he thought he could bear it no more, the blur became a point of light, and at the heart of the light was a female face: Isha, the mother of everything. In a moment of heart-pounding revelation, Sephian realised the whole forest was nothing but a single bead of dew, glittering on her freckled cheek. As he strained to see her more clearly Sephian felt he was on the brink of an even greater revelation – something that concerned himself and black rocks, rearing up from snow. His elation vanished, replaced by a terrible guilt, and he reached out with his mind, edging closer to an explanation.

The light grew brighter and the revelation vanished. Sephian awoke with a hoarse groan. He could remember nothing of the dream, except the awful sensation of guilt. 'What have I done?' he gasped, filled with horror.

'So many things,' growled a voice from somewhere.

Sephian remembered the daemon riders with a shiver of fear. Their horned shapes were up ahead in the shadows, mounted on their gleaming steeds. They had bound him to another piece of wood, attached it to their stallions by thick strands of ivy and were dragging him through the forest. Every jolt sent explosions of pain through his shredded flesh.

'How am I alive?' he gasped, looking down at the bloody mess that had once been his body. Along with the ivy, the riders had sewn oak leaves into his skin. The leaves had been preserved somehow and they were as dark and glossy as if it were still midsummer. Little of his torn skin was now visible. The areas not covered by leaves had been clad in the same spikes of birch bark that adorned the riders' heads.

Sephian squinted through blood-filled eyes at his captors. They were silhouetted against a shimmering glare, shining from somewhere up ahead. As they turned their proud, horned heads to look back at him, they scattered silver blades of moonlight across the ground.

'Not far now,' growled the same voice, and Sephian recognised that it was their leader, the one called Atolmis.

He looked past the riders to the light and realised it was this that had dragged him from his dreams. At the memory of his dream he felt another rush of guilt, but as he tried to recall the reason for his shame, the dream slipped even further from his grasp.

The riders came to a halt in a grove of linden trees, gathered at the foot of a steep escarpment. The leafless trees were standing like tall, stately guardians around a wide, moonlit pond. The water was utterly still and so brightly lit that it resembled an enormous silver coin, hidden in the forest by a celestial miser.

Atolmis and the other riders dismounted and approached their groaning prisoner. When they were just a few feet away, one of them paused and handed something to Atolmis. Sephian strained to see what it was, terrified to discover what new agony he must endure. The object was a red, misshapen ball of some kind.

'An oak apple,' he muttered, as the moonlight revealed it more clearly.

Atolmis gave no answer as he stepped closer, but began to chant a simple poem instead.

Sephian heard only snatches:

> *Ebb and tide,*
> *Drifts away.*
> *Heath and bough,*
> *Must decay.*
> *Flaxen hair,*
> *Turns to grey,*
> *Every life,*
> *Has its day.*

There was another flash of pain as Atolmis leant over Sephian and shoved the oak apple into a wound in his chest. The pain no longer had any meaning to Sephian. His scream was mere force of habit. The pleasing warmth growing in his chest had eclipsed everything else and it grew even more intense as Atolmis jammed the new, wooden heart into place.

The other riders loomed over him. Their long, wild faces filled with eagerness as they placed their hands over Atolmis's, covering Sephian's chest with their enormous, clawed fingers and joining in with the droning chant. Then, at a nod from

Atolmis, they freed Sephian from his bonds and carried him to the edge of the pond.

'We have seen you, my lord,' said Atolmis, as they reached the broad expanse of ice. 'Now the forest must sanction your birth.'

Sephian shook his head in confusion, but the blood loss had left him too weak to answer and he could do nothing but groan as Atolmis gently laid him down on the ice.

Strands of ivy were still wrapped around his shoulders and arms, and Atolmis hurled them across the pond, to be caught by the other riders. Then he took a spiralled antler from his belt and blew into it. The horn blast echoed around the grove and the riders hauled the ivy, sliding Sephian out across the ice.

He had gone no more than a few feet when it exploded beneath him and he dropped, tumbling voicelessly into the freezing depths.

For a long time, Sephian moved through the void without any sense of direction. He tried to keep his mouth closed and hang onto his last gasp of air, but as he let it escape, he realised that he was far too cold to be alive anyway. Rather than pain, or bitterness, he felt an overwhelming sense of disappointment. He was, after all, nothing more than a sacrifice.

He called himself a fool for suspecting anything else and waited for the end.

After a while, Sephian had the strange sensation that, rather than falling, he was now rising through the water. A silvery, undulating ceiling appeared over his head, glinting with moonlight.

I'm returning to the surface.

He saw rippling figures, passing back and forth on the other side.

The riders.

Then, as he moved closer, he saw that the shapes were too varied to be his captors – some were lithe and small, while others were great, slow-moving hulks. They were animals of some kind. He glimpsed tawny-coloured wings and broad, dappled hides and even the antlers of a great, ivory-coloured stag.

Sephian broke the surface of the water with a gasp and felt warmth washing over his frozen skin. He kicked his legs, feeling oddly invigorated. Without pausing to study his surroundings, he swam quickly across the pond, climbed out through a clump of weeds and stepped up onto the grass.

He was back in the same moonlit clearing, but everything had changed. The ice had vanished, replaced by clouds of frothy green linden blossom and rippling, flower-strewn grass.

Sephian gasped in confusion. In the few minutes he had been in the water, spring had arrived. No, he realised, as the linden blossom began to fall and carpet the grass with petals, *it's already summer*. Sephian shook his head as a whole summer passed before his eyes and the leaves began to wither and bronze.

'What is this?' he muttered. Only then did he remember the animals he had glimpsed from beneath the water.

He whirled around, turning his gaze from the shifting seasons back to the pool. As autumn became winter and returned, full circle, to spring, the twin moons remained motionless in the sky. Whole years were passing in the space of a single evening. The beasts he had seen were still there, he *thought*, but now that he had emerged, they were little more than shadows, drifting amongst the tall, smooth trunks of the linden trees.

Sephian stepped towards the shadows and then paused, remembering that his body had been torn apart by the riders. He looked down and saw, to his amazement, that his body was whole again. His naked flesh was almost entirely unmarked. In fact, he realised, he felt better than ever. Only one sign of his torture remained. The oak apple sunk deep in his chest was just visible beneath his skin. He gently tapped the hard, knotted canker, feeling no pain.

'I could return to the trees,' he muttered, suddenly remembering his eagerness to be alone. 'The riders are done with me.' He felt a rush of excitement. 'I will never go back to the wretched Silvam Dale.'

'Listen: he serves himself,' whispered a quiet voice, 'no one else.'

Sephian flinched at the sound. The voice was sibilant and full of derision. He stared at the shadows, but as the trees rippled and creaked in the breeze, the shapes remained impossible to make out clearly. He thought he saw a stag, but as he squinted into the gloom it seemed to change into an enormous boar. The other shadows were just as confusing: a pair of colossal wings fanned out from a long serpentine lizard of some kind, or was it a squat, glowering toad?

As Sephian staggered back towards the pond he glimpsed a whole menagerie of other creatures, eagles, wolves and deer; but they all morphed into something else as he tried to examine their details.

'The auguries cannot lie,' replied another voice. The words were high-pitched and musical and as they zipped through the air, they caught falling leaves and spun them around, before they turned to snow and then a gentle spring shower.

Sephian followed the sound and for a second he saw a blond-haired child, no more than eight or nine years old, with golden, sparkling eyes and copper-coloured leaves in his hair. The child skipped through the moonlight, watching him with playful, mischievous eyes, then vanished, merging with the other shifting shapes that filled the grove.

'Prophecies can be interpreted in many ways, Zephyr, you know that.' This third voice was a low, rolling belch that shook the ground, giving the impression that its owner was a creature of enormous weight. 'I sense that something is wrong. There is a cloud hanging over his future: a secret.'

Sephian whirled around, unnerved by the feeling that he was on trial and trying to make out this new speaker. For a second, he made out a toad the size of a small hill. Its pale pink skin resembled old leather and was covered in hundreds of wart-like lumps, but its eyes glittered youthfully as it met Sephian's gaze. Then it shuffled back into the dark and rippled into something slender and winged before vanishing from view.

Sephian felt a cool breeze rustle through his hair as the childish voice piped up again. 'After all that bloodshed, he lives.' Sephian felt the wind brush against the oak apple embedded in his chest. 'And he has the fruit of the Sorrow Tree filling his veins. Why waste our time, Merula?' Sephian glimpsed the child again, drifting through the boughs of the linden trees. 'The riders have chosen him. We could be away by now.'

There was another low, rumbling belch, but this time there were no words, just a thunder of disapproval.

'Patience, Zephyr,' replied the hissing, quiet voice, still dripping with menace. 'We have been lied to before. Just ask Drycha. This one cares only for solitude and freedom. He has no interest in our welfare. If Tanos were here, he would incinerate such a mewling wretch.'

Sephian turned in the direction of the whisper and saw a shifting column of mist, drifting towards him. The light changed and he saw, quite clearly, a small, wizened figure, wearing the mist as a cloak. He was hunched and frail and the face within his drifting hood was oddly mobile. His features were mostly hidden in shadow, but Sephian caught a glimpse of white, sightless eyes as the figure became vapour once more. Before he vanished, Sephian noticed that he was leaning heavily on a staff. The staff was topped with a lump of black, polished stone and the fingers resting on it seemed far more undulating and numerous than they should be.

Sephian sensed a towering shadow, spreading like branches over his head.

'The Wrach is right,' stated a fourth voice. This sound was strong, booming and full of pride. It echoed from every direction, louder than any of the previous speakers. 'We can be sure of nothing. The great drakes no longer deem us worthy of their time, but we do not need Tanos to recognise a weakling. How can someone who was caught so easily be powerful enough to rule such scattered folk? Sativus, what do you say? Do you see this "cloud" over his future?'

There was a thud of hooves and a flash of white antlers, somewhere to Sephian's left.

'His heart is a windfall, taken from the foot of the Sorrow Tree,' replied a clear, noble voice. 'Who but Orion could survive such a thing? The riders' auguries have never lied. What do you think, Amphion?'

'He is weak,' replied another voice from the branches; a thin, cruel screech. 'Just like all their kind.'

This latest accusation came from a drifting mass of amber light. At first, it was as intangible as all the other creatures but as it spoke it started to take form. Sephian glimpsed something huge and avian, with four enormous wings, clad in feathers of fire. Briefly, the bird met his eye and Sephian winced. Its eyes burned with a hatred so fierce it took his breath away.

Sephian turned away, full of panic. These beings, even more than the riders who caught him, were everything he aspired to be. Even half-glimpsed it was clear that they embodied all the timeless beauty of the forest. Their voices were laced with wild power and they shone with the light of Isha. They, more than anything else, were fragments of her being.

'I can be whatever you need me to be,' he cried, desperate to please them. This was not the deluded sorcery of the Silvam Dale – this was the very soul of Isha, he was sure of it. This was the true heart of the forest. 'What do you ask of me?' he cried.

The voices fell silent and the shadows vanished, slipping back beneath the trees.

Sephian staggered around the grove, peering between the trunks. 'Wait,' he moaned. 'Don't leave.'

To his enormous relief, he saw a flash of white and heard the clear, noble voice ring out again. 'He hears us. Who else but the King could sense our presence?'

Sephian flinched as he sensed an enormous shape looming over him. He thought for a moment that a tree was falling as the booming voice rolled around the grove.

'Nonsense. I have often made myself known to the Queen's court, Sativus, as I know you have.'

A powerful white stag trotted into view, abandoning the shadows and revealing itself fully to Sephian. It was over eight feet tall and its white, twisted mass of antlers stood even higher, like a gleaming ivory crown. It turned a pair of shining, amber-flecked eyes on Sephian.

'Until now, I had not chosen to reveal myself and yet he heard me just the same.'

Sephian dropped to his knees, astounded by the majesty of the stag. 'My lord,' he whispered. 'I do not know who you are, I–'

'Do not kneel,' said the stag, with obvious distaste.

Sephian did not see its mouth open, but he knew the creature had spoken.

'It is not becoming for a king,' it continued.

The golden-skinned youth appeared at the stag's side and grinned at Sephian. 'Listen to Sativus,' trilled the boy, before spinning off around the grove. 'You will need to assume the correct mantle, if you wish to rule.'

Sephian watched the boy's dance for a moment, trying to think of a suitable reply, then he saw another pale, four-legged shape approaching. This one was smaller than the stag, and as it padded through the bracken he realised it was a wolf; a wolf that looked as cool, grey and serene as a piece of ice.

'The forest needs a king,' it said, stopping a few feet away, 'not another pompous noble. Can you wield real power?' It revealed its teeth in a snarl. 'Are you a *hunter*?'

Sephian climbed to his feet and saw that dozens of creatures were now emerging from the trees, no longer making any attempt to conceal themselves. Some resembled animals he could recognise – deer, wolves, bears, otters and eagles – but others were stranger. He saw the hooded, blind figure with the writhing flesh and the golden youth with the autumn leaves in his hair, but there was also some kind of horned snake and a group of towering, confusing shapes, assembled from the boughs of twisted trees and bristling with sharpened leaves.

'Are you a hunter?' they asked, speaking with one voice.

Sephian nodded eagerly in reply, not sure what they were asking of him, but desperate to please them. 'I will do anything,' he gasped.

As they formed a circle around him and began to shepherd him back into the pond, he heard the doubt that still remained in many of the voices and it filled him with pain – a pain far greater than anything he had endured at the hands of the riders.

He tumbled back into the water, feeling weeds dragging at his calves as the stag, Sativus, trotted out after him.

'You must be strong,' it said, lowering its head as Sephian sank beneath the surface; studying him calmly down the length of its long, glossy face. 'If you are Orion, be fearless.'

CHAPTER SIX

'Lord Beldeas, you have surpassed yourself.'

The voice came from a tornado of spiralling shapes. Thousands of glittering, pewter-coloured moths were fluttering through the air, creating a shimmering statue – a thirty-foot likeness of a beautiful asrai noblewoman. Her face was delineated in perfect detail, with high angular cheekbones and a disdainful sneer. She looked down over a grove of moonlit yew trees with hooded, pitiless eyes.

An asrai of more normal proportions stepped out in front of the display. Lord Beldeas wore long, jade-coloured robes, embroidered with delicate copper thread, and his regal brow was crowned with a circlet of copper hawthorn leaves.

'But what will *she* think?' His words were soft and considered. He clasped his hands together and stepped into the light, so that the moths were spinning and dancing around him, buffeting his fine, white hair. Even by the standards of asrai nobility, Beldeas was painfully thin. His shrewish features nestled beneath a large forehead and his cheeks were so drawn and sunken that he resembled an animated corpse.

'I have never seen such an eloquent declaration of love.' Lord Beldeas's advisor, Hauran Quillwort, shook his head as he studied the display. Quillwort was as tall as Beldeas, but he seemed even more so, due to an elaborate collar of knotted ash that rose above his head. Unusually for an asrai, his glossy black hair had been cropped into a neat bob and his face was delicate, or even pretty, with sensuous, full lips and an expression of mild, theatrical surprise. His robes were the same shade of green as his lord's, and as he neared the moths their radiance shimmered across his chest, revealing an impressive collection of silver and gemstones. 'Before the incident, Lady Ordaana was fascinated by nature, in any form. I'm sure this incredible art will remind her of her past – and her love for you.'

Lord Beldeas shook his head. 'I have no idea what fascinates her now. Neither do I understand this sudden change of heart.' He shrugged. 'But if we are to appear at Ariel's court, I will not look like a fool. I must make some attempt at reconciliation.'

He sighed. 'Of all the things she has done though, this is the most perverse.' He turned to Quillwort. 'Surely the past should be left to its own devices? She has her life and I have mine. How does she imagine we can resurrect such dead love?'

Quillwort smiled. 'A gift like this is sure to smooth over any indiscretions. If there is to be a reunion, then you have–'

'I appreciate your advice,' interrupted Beldeas, 'as ever, but really – so much has happened. How can she expect us to become what we once were?'

'What exactly has she requested?'

'That we attend the festival of Ostaliss, Quillwort, and stand together, smiling, before the Queen, and her Consort-King, while their entire court sniggers at us. She wishes me to act as though we are lovers again – as though our union is as vital as it was all those centuries ago, before her "accident".' He shook his head. 'What does she hope to gain?'

Quillwort looked to the south, towards Ordaana's ruined grove. It was impossible to see the damage from here, but all of Locrimere knew the harm she had caused. Tales of death and madness had a habit of lingering.

'Lord Beldeas, perhaps she really does wish to repent and begin again. You are both highborn, my lord. The statutes of marriage must bend to your will, not the other way around. Ordaana will understand that even your most recent indiscretions are quite natural for a person of such magnificence.' Quillwort waved a bejewelled hand at the trees. The heart of Lord Beldeas's kingdom stretched up around them in enormous spirals, like the coiled leaves of a colossal fern. They were standing at the centre of a whole city, consisting solely of green, looping towers, and, even now, hours before the dawn, hundreds of lantern-carrying figures could be seen, moving up and down its bewildering curves. Locrimere was one of the largest kingdoms in the forest, home to thousands of asrai. From this distance Beldeas's subjects looked like tiny embers, drifting through the mile-high towers of their home.

'You are surrounded by such adoration,' continued Quillwort. 'How can you be expected to refuse every offer of devotion? All of Locrimere loves you, Lord Beldeas. One misstep is completely understandable, and Lady Ordaana will realise that. She was nothing before she became your bride. Without you by her side, she could never have stepped foot in the court of the Queen.'

Lord Beldeas shrugged. 'Of course, you are right, Quillwort. But you are not, thank the gods, female. We will never fully understand what goes on in Ordaana's mind. For all these centuries she has refused to speak to me, never mind attend Ariel's court together; now she wishes to return and act as though nothing has happened. There must be some reason. She must hope to *gain* something.' He coughed awkwardly. 'And besides, my own situation is more complicated than you might realise.'

Quillwort allowed himself a brief smile, but as Beldeas looked up at him, he adopted a concerned expression. 'My lord?'

Beldeas scratched at his skull-like head. 'Well, it is nothing of significance. Do you remember the servant you brought back from the Pine Crags, the one with the beautiful singing voice?'

'Yes?' Quillwort dropped his voice to a conspiratorial whisper. 'What of her?'

Beldeas raised an eyebrow.

Behind him, the moths, forgotten for a moment, began to drift. Within seconds, the floating sculpture lost an elbow and a section of its left forearm. The diaphanous creatures began to spiral off into the night, like scraps of silver leaf against the black vault of the heavens.

Quillwort placed a hand over his mouth to hide another smile. Once he had calmed himself he removed his hand and stepped closer with a concerned expression on his face. 'You don't mean…?'

Beldeas nodded.

Quillwort flinched as moths fluttered in his robes and hair. 'Well, what of it?' He batted away some of the moths. 'You cannot blame yourself. I have no doubt that she threw herself at you. Your love for your people is well known and it would have been cruel to spurn her. And besides,' he placed a hand on his lord's arm, 'what could Lady Ordaana expect? After all these years? You weren't to know she was planning a reconciliation.' He looked up at the crumbling sculpture. 'And if she wishes to begin again, this present is easily enough to atone for your recent indiscretion.'

'Do you think so?'

'Of course.'

Lord Beldeas nodded. 'You're right. After all, she has crimes of her own to consider. This should be penance enough.' He turned his attention back to the statue and began plucking currents of magic from the air. As he snapped his wrists and fingers, the moths drifted back into position, recreating the beautiful image. As he worked, he began to smile, but after a few minutes he frowned and gave his advisor a quick glance. 'Why did you ask to see me?'

Quillwort frowned. He seemed genuinely confused. 'I...' He pursed his lips and clapped his hands together. 'What was it, Quillwort?' he asked himself. 'Ah, yes,' he said with a shrug. 'It was nothing important.' He waved vaguely in the direction of Locrimere's spiral towers. 'Do you remember the young orphan, Finavar?'

Lord Beldeas nodded vaguely, without ceasing his work. 'Yes. Something of a joker isn't he? *Talented* though, from what I hear, despite being from,' he paused, unable to completely hide his distaste, 'the lower orders.' He laughed. It was a soft, mirthless wheeze. 'Isn't he the bard who calls himself a prince?'

'Indeed, my lord. Or at least his followers do and he does nothing to dissuade them. They call him the Darkling Prince.'

'Yes, that's it.' Beldeas shook his head in disbelief as he moved the final few moths into place. 'Just because he wears some kind of fancy cloak. I have the utmost respect for our song-smiths but, however skilled they might be, art is no substitute for noble birth. People are so easily impressed by fripperies and tricks.' He stepped back to admire his handiwork. The statue was, if anything, even more impressive than before, but Beldeas frowned again. 'Why are we discussing this person?'

Quillwort shrugged. 'If it were left to me, my lord, I would never have troubled you with such a thing, but Eremon insisted I interrupt you.'

At the mention of his most senior captain, Lord Beldeas raised his eyebrows. 'I see. Eremon. What exactly did he want you to interrupt me with?'

Quillwort spoke quickly, sensing he had exhausted his master's patience. 'Finavar and his little clan have returned from the borders. They encountered outsiders while they were travelling home – mutants of some kind; servants of the Chaos gods.'

Lord Beldeas looked up at the sky. The twin moons were almost directly overhead, sending shafts of light down through the twisted branches. The light fell on a cloak, folded on the grass at the far end of the grove. 'She will be here soon,' he muttered, smoothing down his gleaming white hair and flicking a leaf from his robes. Then he remembered his advisor and paused, looking irritated. 'Yes. Outsiders, you say.' He gave Quillwort a thin, insincere smile. 'Do I *really* need to be bothered with such a thing, when I have so much on my mind already?'

Quillwort clasped his hands to his chest and closed his eyes, looking mortified. 'I beg your forgiveness, my lord. Apparently, the outsiders were travelling in greater numbers than usual and they were making straight for Locrimere.'

Beldeas looked at Quillwort, maintaining the same frozen grin. 'And?'

'Eremon had an idea that you might want to lead the kinbands out to deal with them.

Lord Beldeas shook his head and looked back at the spinning mass of moths. 'Ride to war? *Now*?' He shook his head. 'I am hardly one to shirk from my duties, Quillwort, but really, I think such a small matter could be dealt with by Eremon.'

'Of course, my lord, I understand completely.' Quillwort began to edge away, then paused, cringing like a scolded dog. 'There was just one other thing...'

Lord Beldeas's smile finally began to falter and some colour crept over his skeletal face.

'The orphan, Finavar, almost lost one of his friends in the encounter – someone called Caorann. Apparently he was terribly wounded and Finavar holds himself responsible. He has asked to lead the kinbands into battle, at your side, so that he may repay the monsters for what they have done to his friend. Eremon and I both told him it was ridiculous to think that such a lowborn could lead–'

'By the gods, Quillwort,' snapped Lord Beldeas, his soft tones finally gone. 'What do I care who fights and who doesn't?' He took a deep breath and held it, then exhaled slowly. When he spoke again his voice was under control and the hideous smile had returned to his face. 'Ordaana wishes to reignite our marriage and attend the rites of spring. She wishes to *speak* to me, Quillwort, after all this time. Much as I would love to spend my time dealing with this border skirmish, I really think I will have to remain here.' The colour drained from his face and his voice grew softer. 'If Eremon is no longer able to deal with military matters by himself, ask this Finavar character to lead the kinbands.'

Quillwort laughed, but then realised that his master was being serious. He hesitated at the edge of the grove. 'Let a fatherless lowborn lead your armies?'

'You should know by now, Quillwort, that I have faith in *all* my subjects, whatever their parentage. And you are always telling me what an incredible warrior he is. Let him have his revenge.' He raised his hands in a pleading gesture. 'And let me finish my work.'

Quillwort shook his head in confusion and opened his mouth to reply, but after seeing the dangerous gleam in his lord's eyes he shrugged and backed away. 'Of course,' he muttered, disappearing into the dark.

Lord Beldeas stood for a while, keeping a sickly smile on his face as he watched Quillwort leave. Then, when his advisor had vanished from view, he took a deep sigh and turned back to his living, floating piece of sculpture. Despite all the distractions, the statue now resembled Lady Ordaana once more. He smiled in satisfaction. He had captured just the right expression of bitter contempt. 'Could we *really* begin again?' He sat cross-legged on the grass and waited for the real Ordaana to arrive. 'There were, after all, only a couple of indiscretions on my part. I will assure her she need never doubt me again.'

His thoughts began to wander as he remembered the pretty young servant from the Pine Crags. After a few minutes, a mischievous smile spread across his face as he recalled his most recent dalliance. He relived the encounter in his mind, running his fingers across his sunken cheek and closing his eyes with a gentle sigh.

Beldeas was so lost in his lurid memories that he did not notice his wife entering the clearing, a few minutes later. The real Lady Ordaana was even more beautiful than the likeness drifting overhead. Her hair was a gleaming sweep of silver, framing a delicately sculpted, angular face, high cheekbones and an arched left eyebrow that gave her a permanently quizzical expression. Ancient, aristocratic lineage shone through her ivory skin and her long, graceful neck was accentuated by a shimmering chain of silver, ending in a locket bearing the symbol of Locrimere: a pair of knotted black yew trees. She studied Beldeas for a few minutes from beneath heavy, lidded eyes then looked at the moths in utter disbelief. Her husband was rocking gently back and forth with his eyes still closed. Ordaana saw the cloak, folded neatly beneath the sculpture, and took it with a nod of satisfaction. She paused, on the verge of speaking to her oblivious husband, then she reconsidered, tucked the cloak under her arm and slipped silently back into the trees.

'He's a child,' she said, speaking in hollow, icy tones. She was addressing a tiny wooden spectre following her through the undergrowth. It was a twitching bundle of thin, stick-like limbs that clicked and snapped as it hurried through the forest. Its movements were as clumsy and spasmodic as a marionette and its head resembled a tall, wooden skull. As it lurched and clattered in the wake of her robes, it pulsed with a faint light.

'Children do not have such appetites.' Its voice was the sound of branches, creaking in the wind.

'True.' Ordaana looked pained. 'If he was not so concerned with his own desires he might have understood my actions. All the forest knows how shamefully I was slighted, apart from him; apart from my own husband. Even after all these years he has never once enquired what drove me to such despair.'

The spirit giggled as it lurched after her.

Ordaana marched on through the darkness until she came to the borders of her private groves. It was easy to see where her realm began. It was a black desert in the heart of the forest. Where trees had once stood, there was now a rippling, flinty mess of dust and scorched stumps. In some places there were still thin trails of smoke drifting up towards the stars, a constant reminder of Ordaana's violence.

She was blind to the desolation and strode on, heading for the single, enormous yew that remained standing at the centre of the clearing. Its bark was little more than charcoal, but Ordaana's sorcery had kept the tree roughly intact. Pale light was leaking through cracks in its trunk, and slender figures could be seen moving inside.

'Leave me,' said Ordaana as she entered. Her voice was quiet but dangerous, and her guards scattered into the night, bowing as they fled. She paid them no heed and climbed down a wide spiral stair into the network of chambers beneath the tree.

The passageways were littered with the evidence of her rage: piles of black ash that had once been beautiful gowns, and charred limbs of furniture, reaching from the ground like the remnants of a cremation. There were items of ruined jewellery too: diadems and crowns, warped by immense heat into odd, ugly shapes that glittered in the lamplight. All of it was coated in a thick layer of ash.

Ordaana paused at the sight of a necklace, miraculously intact amidst the carnage. She stooped to pick it up and her sneer grew even more pronounced. The necklace was a delicate cord of gold chain, designed to resemble a sprig of mistletoe, with pearls in place of the berries. It was small enough to fit a child. As she stared at the necklace, tears glittered in her eyes. Then, a sapphire glow pulsed between her fingers and the metal began to slump in her palm. As the light grew, her hands began to tremble, scattering molten gold from her fingers.

Her twig-limbed companion let out another giggle and clattered quickly back towards the stairs.

'When will I forget you?' gasped Ordaana, hurling the liquid remnants of the necklace down the passageway, engulfed in a column of blue fire. Flames and liquid metal exploded across the wooden walls and Ordaana's elegant frame was wracked by a fit. 'When?' Her back arched and a whine slipped through her clenched teeth. The light flared in her eyes and spread across her alabaster skin, covering her limbs with crackling energy. An anguished moan slipped from her lips. 'How can I live?'

'Because you must,' came a voice from the darkness. The words were soft, and kind, and they seemed to come from every direction at once.

Ordaana froze. Her fit passed as quickly as it came and the light vanished. She crouched low to the ground, peering into the shadows between the lanterns. 'You came back,' she whispered, wiping away her tears.

'We made a pact, Ordaana. Where I come from, such things are not taken lightly.'

'Where are you?'

'Close by, as always.'

Realising which direction the voice was coming from, Ordaana hurried down the passage, skipping lightly over her ruined possessions and stopping in front of the shattered remnants of a door. 'Here?' she hissed, touching a clump of dusty cobwebs.

She snatched back her hand as the webs began to ripple and shift. It was as though a breeze was tugging at the threads, but there was no breeze this far beneath the tree.

'I see you!' she whispered, as the web assumed the shape of a lordly, handsome face.

The shimmering face smiled. 'And you will never know what that means to me, Ordaana. After all these long centuries of imprisonment, I had given up hope of being seen by anyone – let alone one of my own kind.'

Ordaana placed her fingers gently on the web, her eyes filling with tears. 'You must think me so heartless, Aestar.' Her sharp, perfect diction faltered as she caressed the face. 'I am so concerned for myself, I never once asked about your suffering. To be bound, beneath the earth, for all these years. I cannot imagine how you have remained so sane.'

The web shook its shimmering face, sending dozens of shiny

black spiders scuttling into the darkness. 'I carry within me the vision of my entire people. Every Ellyrian song, every Sapherian poem; they are as much a part of me as my own heart. Those epic rhymes preserved my soul until...' He stumbled over his words, seemingly overcome with emotion. 'They preserved my soul until your despair cracked my prison walls and gave me the one thing I had forgotten: hope. If not for your grief, I would still be alone, silent and undiscovered beneath the roots of these ancient trees.'

Ordaana traced a finger over the billowing face. 'Let me find you, Aestar Eltanin.' She breathed his name like a prayer. 'Tell me exactly where you are imprisoned. You have seen the power I wield. I could lift the curse that binds your–'

'No!' snapped the voice. For a moment the gentle tones vanished, replaced by something harsher, something more desperate. 'No,' repeated the web, a little softer. 'I am too weak. It would be the end of me. Your rage has created a link between us – a hairline crack in the walls of my prison – but you could never fully uncover me. And even if you could, it would mean my doom. I would be revealed to Ariel and she would destroy me. She would not let me survive a second time.'

'But why? You represent all that is most noble in us. You and your kind are our ancestors. Why would the Queen wish you dead?'

'For the same reason she imprisoned me, all those years ago. I know the truth. I have seen your doom. This forest will fall and your people will fail. Unless you return to your real homeland, the asrai will be no more.'

At the thought of the Queen, the pain returned to Ordaana's face. 'Ariel is *deluded*.' She spat the word out, like a piece of bitter fruit. 'But why would she ignore your warning? She cast me aside, but I do not believe she would see her own people die.'

The web shivered and the face faded from view for a moment, before returning with even more clarity, revealing a pained grimace. 'I once thought the same, but I was wrong. She will heed no warning; not if it might drag her people away from her rule. She is jealous, Ordaana, and terrified by the idea of sharing power. She would never allow me to speak openly. That is why we must continue what we have begun.' He lowered his voice. 'It is difficult work, Ordaana, I grant you, but it is the only hope the asrai have left.'

Ordaana's hand faltered and fell away from the web. She looked down at the floor, her eyes wide. 'But it is so dangerous, Aestar. To sacrifice Locrimere, just so that–'

'So that your people might *survive*. It is a small price to pay if we are to unseat Ariel. Think what she did to you, Ordaana. Think how she cast you aside, on the slightest whim. What does that tell you? Every action reveals a part of the soul.'

Ordaana's anguished expression returned. 'The Queen is a liar.' She trembled as she recalled the ease with which Ariel had turned her back on years of devotion. The ghostly fire returned to her flesh as her mind slipped back through the years. 'How could she have said those things? How could she call me unsuitable? After everything I did for her.'

'Because her heart is a thorn bush, Ordaana. Perhaps she was once one of us, but what is she now? She is a monster and we must unseat her.'

'But is this really the only way? To involve such creatures?'

'Only for the briefest time, believe me.' The web shimmered with silver light and the whole passageway filled with ghostly images. Crumbling, ancient stones rippled across the wood, huddled in gloomy, hidden groves. 'There are secrets down here, Ordaana. I have not wasted my time. All these long centuries I have been searching. No one else knows the locations of these old sites. No one else could tap into this web of power. As those beasts follow your guidance, they will begin to wreak havoc and reveal just how powerless the Queen really is. Then, with my help you will become more powerful than anyone the kindreds have ever known. As Ariel falls, you will rise. You will become the true sovereign of your people. You will be the one to crush the enemy and lead the asrai from the ashes of the forest. With me by your side *you* will lead this lost nation back into the welcoming arms of its true home, Ulthuan. You will go down in the annals of history as the glorious Queen Ordaana, who managed to reunite the children of Asuryan!'

At the mention of the Creator God, Ordaana's eyes flashed with pride. She raised her chin and closed her eyes. 'Can it be true?' she whispered, as the flickering lights washed over her skin. '*Queen* Ordaana. I have always felt I was destined for some great purpose – that I had some great deed to perform. Beldeas may have failed me, but now I see the true path.' She opened her eyes to reveal that they were bright with tears. 'Ariel has brought this on herself. I loved her more than she could ever know. No handmaiden ever served a queen more faithfully. Whatever I did…'

She looked around at the blackened remains of her home and her voice faltered. Her hands began to shake again and she turned her gaze to the floor. Her voice dropped to a horrified whisper. 'I did a terrible thing, Aestar Eltanin. I created such imbalance. How could I ever pay for such a crime?'

'This is your chance to atone. Don't you understand? This is your chance to redress the balance. I have seen more than you know, Ordaana. I *know* what happened here, but fate has thrown us together. With me by your side you can save your entire race; what is one crime when placed against such an act of heroism?'

Ordaana looked up. Tears were now flowing freely down her face, but the glimmer of hope had returned to her eyes. She gently stroked the glittering web. 'Perhaps you are right. And besides, if I had remained by Ariel's side, if I had committed no crime, I would never have known you, Aestar Eltanin.'

'Our meeting was fated.' The web undulated and revealed a sombre, stern face. 'But there is just one risk to be removed, Ordaana; one final canker.'

She nodded, slowly. 'Orion.'

'Orion. Remember what we agreed, Ordaana. This will be the hardest trial of all, but there is no other way. Show me the blade.'

Ordaana drew a silver knife from her robes and peered at its long, serpentine blade. The metal had been engraved with a series of strange-looking symbols, as Aestar had instructed. She held it up to the web. 'I will remember.'

For a while she seemed to be in some kind of trance, staring at the knife as though it contained her entire future. As she watched, strands of the web rippled around the blade, covering it in luminous tracery. The glyphs shimmered and the weapon began to ring, like crystal tapped with a spoon.

A clattering sound interrupted Ordaana's thoughts.

The lights died and the handsome face vanished, leaving nothing more than a dusty spider's web.

Ordaana whirled around, levelling her knife at the shadows and disguising her fear as outrage. 'Who dares to bother me?'

A spindly, foot-high figure lurched into view, clicking and clacking as it approached. It answered with a nervous giggle.

Ordaana lowered the knife, sighing with relief. 'Death's-head.'

Then she turned back to the web and held her palm against it for a second, knowing the face would not return. There was no need. She knew what to do. For the first time in centuries she felt hope. Could there really be a way to ease her guilt, or at least to atone?

'Come,' she snapped, waving her knife at the twitching bundle of sticks. 'We have work to do. The creatures have almost reached the next stone. You need only lead them a little further.' She caught her reflection in the blade of the knife and paused, surprised by the passion in her own face. 'Then you must bring them here.'

'Locrimere could burn down around his ears without him noticing,' laughed Finavar. His eyes were wild and his sinewy frame was covered in mud and fresh scars. 'Why do you make excuses for him? You know he sees nothing. Nothing beyond the nearest pretty face, that is.'

He was standing in a large chamber, constructed from a single enormous leaf curled around itself in a long spiral to create a tunnel-shaped guardroom. The chamber was at the foot of Locrimere's southernmost tower and the view from its lower end revealed the bare treetops of the surrounding forest. Finavar jabbed his finger at them. 'The creatures were headed straight for our home.' He stared at the captain of Locrimere's Guard, still grinning. 'Do you understand? Something is *leading* them here.'

Eremon's face had clearly never had to endure the indignity of a smile. His crude, heavy features could have been chiselled from a piece of old granite. They were little more than a collection of harsh, brutal lines centred around a heavy brow and a pair of dark, brooding eyes. He showed no flicker of emotion as he surveyed the wardancers, other than perhaps a slight curling of his thin lips.

One of his guests, a ferocious-looking girl, was draped in fresh, bloody scalps. There was a constant dripping sound as blood pattered from the scalps onto the glossy green floor and Eremon shook his head in disbelief. She looked feral. All of them were covered in wounds of some kind, but no trace of sympathy stirred in him, except perhaps for the old cripple. He might once have been a figure of some dignity. Despite his terrible deformity he was attempting to hold himself with pride and carried a bow of the most incredible, delicate workmanship. He had his head down, trying to keep his face hidden, but Eremon could still see a faint yellow tinge to his mutilated face. Zeuzera, he guessed, with a mixture of disgust and sympathy. He has numbed his pain with fern seed. He will not survive long.

Most offensive of all though, in the captain's eyes, was Finavar himself. Even his long, thorny cloak offended Eremon. The lowborn youth wore it as though a few yards of barbed black cloth were enough to confer royal status. He grinned from his hood with his chin raised and absolutely no trace of respect. If you surround yourself with such rogues and villains, thought the captain, decent folk will soon begin to see you for what you are. I will *teach* you your place, Eremon thought, feeling his blood pounding in his ears; skilled or not.

'That is not possible,' he replied, keeping his voice calm and level. 'Our halls are hidden from all outsiders. You must be mistaken.'

Finavar threw back his hood and raised his voice. 'You are not listening to me, Eremon! They were being led straight towards us.'

Eremon tensed at the young lowborn's tone, but he waited for a few seconds before replying, determined not to raise his voice. Once he felt calm enough to speak, he said: 'Are you saying that one of our own kin is leading creatures of Chaos to Locrimere?' The captain managed to suppress the rage in his voice, but not the ridicule. 'Do you seriously expect me to believe such a thing?'

'Believe what you like, but the evidence is here!' Finavar jabbed a finger at the blood that covered his scarred chest. 'Caorann is almost dead!' His grin faltered as he recalled his friend's pain. 'He is a master of the shadow dance; a dutiful servant of Loec. Do you think such a warrior falls easily?'

The captain spoke over his shoulder, addressing the row of guards standing impassively behind him. 'Quite the opposite, Finavar. I am intrigued to know more. If this invading army is as impressive as you claim, why would you decide to lead one _tiny_ kinband against them?' He looked back at Finavar with an exaggerated frown. 'Five of you, against a whole army? That seems reckless, even by the standards of the famous Darkling Prince.'

Finavar held the captain's gaze. 'On any other day we would have taken them.' His voice cracked. 'Caorann should never have fallen, but the creature leading them was communing somehow with the forest.' Finavar shook his head, confused by his own words. 'It was wielding the power of our own magi. I have never seen such a thing.'

The captain's chest swelled as he considered the rabble arrayed before him. Then, after a few seconds he shook his head. 'I have heard tales of your arrogance, Finavar, from many lips, but I am still surprised to see it for myself.' He strode forwards, finally letting his calm mask slip, and jabbed his finger into Finavar's slender chest. 'How can you dare march in here with this group of,' his voice became a growl, '_outcasts_, and ask to lead our kindreds to war? Have you forgotten who you are?'

As soon as the captain approached Finavar, Alhena drew her blades and gave him a ferocious glare.

After a second's hesitation, Jokleel and Thuralin did the same.

Immediately, the guards arrayed behind Eremon lifted their longbows and trained arrows on the bloody rabble.

'I know who *I* am, Eremon,' snapped Finavar, blind to the impending violence. 'A guardian of the forest. But what exactly are you? Other than the lackey of a fool.'

Eremon closed his eyes and took a deep breath. Then he stepped back and indicated that the guards should lower their bows. 'There will be no bloodshed here.' His voice was calm again. 'I suggest you leave, Finavar,' he said, looking at Alhena's wild face, 'and return in better company.'

'You are as blind as Beldeas!' cried Finavar. 'And as deranged as Ordaana.'

At the mention of Ordaana, Eremon drew his sword, muttering a bitter curse.

'Wait!' cried a thin voice.

The guards parted, allowing Quillwort to enter. His elaborate, winged collar quivered as he dashed across the room and placed a hand on Eremon's sword.

Eremon stepped back and lowered the blade, embarrassed by his display of emotions.

'I have spoken to our father, the warden of Locrimere,' announced Quillwort, flinging his bobbed hair back from his face. 'He has deemed it appropriate for Finavar to lead *some* of our kinbands out of Locrimere. His heart is filled with pain at the thought that outsiders might stumble across our most holy glades. His work consumes him, but he assures me that he will not rest until he hears that these vile interlopers have been slain.'

Eremon was unable to hide his shock. 'Are you sure? Was that *really* Lord Beldeas's intent?' He looked at Finavar and the colour drained from his face. 'Are we really to entrust our defence to such a rogue?'

Finavar ignored the captain and grabbed Quillwort's forearm. 'It will be done. No trace of their foul stink shall reach these borders.'

He turned to his friends and the grin returned to his face. 'We will repay them tenfold for what they did to Caorann, I promise you.'

CHAPTER SEVEN

'He has returned.'

As Sephian clambered from the ice, he recognised the deep growl of Atolmis, welcoming him back to the sharp, damp air of a dying winter. Before the horned giants could reach him, Sephian drew himself erect and tried to adopt an imperious glare, remembering something about needing to assume a mantle. As he did so, his limbs erupted with pain. He gasped and stumbled and saw that his flesh was once more hanging in shreds. He was robed in a sticky mess of thorns, blood and oak leaves and the strength he had felt while talking to the beasts had vanished.

Atolmis and the others caught him as he fell and stopped him crashing to the icy ground.

'I knew you from afar, my king,' rumbled Atolmis, bringing his terrifying face close to Sephian's. 'And I knew the forest would recognise you.'

'But they thought me weak,' gasped Sephian, daring to meet Atolmis's immemorial gaze. 'The wolf, and the child and the other things.' He pulled the giant rider closer, his voice full of urgency. 'I must convince them. Do you know them?' Somehow, even after all the dreadful things Atolmis had done to his flesh, Sephian felt as though he could trust this black-eyed giant. He saw that all the pain inflicted on him was the price he must pay: a rite of passage that would enable him to join the radiant beings he had seen through the ice.

The embers in Atolmis's eyes flared for a second, but he shook his head. 'I do not know them. I will never see what you have seen.'

Sephian whimpered as the riders lifted his limp, dripping body from the edge of the pool and carried him towards the patiently waiting stallions.

'I must prove myself,' he muttered, but as pain and delirium overcame him, he realised he was already forgetting what he had seen on the other side of the water.

'Spring is coming,' said Atolmis, as they rode away from the grove, making for the heart of the forest. 'It is time you returned to your home.'

'The Silvam Dale?' gasped Sephian, his voice full of horror.

'No,' replied the giant, 'the King's Glade.'

To a casual observer, the clearing would appear a little odd perhaps, but nothing more. The circle of oaks at its centre might look a little too sprawling and labyrinthine. The quality of the light might appear strange. The shadows did not quite correspond to the movements of the plants and trees, rippling across the matted thicket with a life of their own; looming and fading as though thrown by invisible dancers.

But Sephian was a spirit in flux.

He was a liminal soul, hung between two worlds, and he now saw *everything* more clearly. The trees blazed with golden fire: veins of sunlight that threaded through the bark, tracing the outlines of hunters and bounding, wild-eyed animals. As Atolmis led Sephian further into the King's Glade, he gasped and dropped to his knees.

He was in the company of gods.

The figures standing beneath the golden boughs resembled Atolmis and the other riders, impossibly tall and lashed together by thick, knotted muscle, but they were something altogether more wonderful and terrifying. They towered over their high priest, Atolmis, and their heads were crowned with enormous, ridged antlers, almost indistinguishable from the twisted, glittering branches behind them. Their lower legs resembled the hindquarters of stags, with thick, battered hooves, and their broad angular muscles seemed carved from slabs of mossy wood. Their whole bodies were tinged a pale, arboreal green, engraved with serpentine spirals and, despite the winter chill, their broad shoulders were garlanded with spring flowers: beautiful foxgloves and bluebells that quivered in the breeze. They each held a tall, ivy-bound spear, and hanging in the centre of their chests was an emerald: a flawless green sphere, surrounded by leaves of glinting brass.

Sephian struggled to hang on to his sanity as he looked at each of the faces in turn. Here were the long centuries, laid out before him. Here were the kings of a dozen ages, come to pass judgement. Each of the figures was filled with a majesty so feral that Sephian's body shook as he tried to meet their gaze. These beings were the soul of the forest, just like the beasts he had seen beneath the pool. Their faces resembled those of the asrai highborn – long and noble, with tall, leaf-blade ears and wide, thoughtful eyes – but these beings were no mere mortals. As the lights rippled across the clearing, they passed through the green-skinned gods like smoke. Sephian realised that he could even see trees through their flesh. They were spirits. They were the ghosts of the Wild Hunt.

'Orion?' he breathed, hardly daring to speak the name.

The answer was immediate: a hoarse, rumbling growl that came from all their throats at once. 'Soon,' they answered. 'Spring is coming.'

Tears rolled freely down Sephian's face as the ghosts of Orion began to sing. Their voices rose and fell in a deep, bewildering chorus, filling his head with tales of their doomed, magnificent lives. As they sang, flames bled from their skin, filling the glade with dazzling light, until it seemed as though a constellation of stars had fallen from the heavens.

CHAPTER EIGHT

Dawn came to the forest, revealing a crust of silver frost and a pale, hooded figure. Finavar was crouched in the sparkling fork of an old ash tree, running his fingers over the branches, tracing the outline of tiny buds. Spring was just days away and his spirit soared as he considered what that meant. Soon the forest would be draped in green, preparing the way for Orion.

Finavar closed his eyes for a second, trying to picture the King in all his terrible glory, wondering if this year, finally, he might catch a glimpse of him. Then pain drew his thoughts back to the present. Several of the buds had latched, leech-like, onto his hand, drawing dark jewels of blood from his skin. He snatched his hand free, sucked at the wound and spat out the blood. Most of the trees carried some kind of poison. Finavar had learned long ago to take no risks.

He eyed the tree suspiciously for a moment, waiting to see if would do anything else. Then he rose to his feet and whistled. After a few minutes a pair of small, sinuous shapes rushed up the tree. The polecats looped once around the trunk, ran along his arm and settled in the folds of his black, spiny cloak. He smiled as they nestled against his body for warmth. 'Mormo and Mauro,' he whispered, 'most perfect of guides. I have need of you again this morning.'

He placed two fingers in his mouth and whistled a long, trilling note.

Even before the echoes had faded, the forest around him sprang into life. Hundreds of lithe, blue-grey figures slipped through the trees. Despite their numbers the asrai advanced like a gentle breeze, rippling through the leaves with such grace that not a blade of grass was flattened by their passing.

Finavar grimaced at the sound of wood breaking above him. He turned to see his friends waiting patiently in the upper branches. They had surrounded him in silence, apart from Thuralin, who was scowling at his own clumsiness.

'The kinbands are at your command,' breathed Alhena, her eyes glittering with emotion. 'Lord Beldeas has trusted you with the safety of his entire kingdom.'

Finavar laughed. 'Ignore the drivel that falls from the mouth of Hauran Quillwort. I do not know how this has come to be, but it is certainly not because Lord Beldeas has any trust in me.'

'The Warden of Locrimere is a fool,' agreed Thuralin, with surprising vehemence. 'He is more concerned with matters of the bedchamber than matters of war. It has always been the same. He is a degenerate rake. He has no interest in his duty. I would imagine *that* is why we have been given this chance.'

Alhena nodded, used to hearing her father's bile when discussing Lord Beldeas. 'It is that spineless worm Eremon that I despise. If he is so high and mighty, why does he do the will of such a fool? Where is his dignity? He must know that Beldeas does not care what happens to Locrimere.'

'Eremon is far from spineless,' said Thuralin, glaring at his daughter.

Finavar gave Jokleel a wry smile, amused by the old warrior's sour tone.

As always, his brother's gentle manner was a sharp contrast to the charged emotions of the others. There was a reptilian slowness to his gaze; an odd languor to his words. He whispered a prayer and took Thuralin's hand, gently removing it from his featureless mask. His wide blue eyes were full of compassion. 'I feel your pain, Thuralin. Perhaps if you told us something of your past, I could help?'

Thuralin shrugged off Jokleel's grip and sneered at him. 'My past is my own, boy.'

Alhena scowled at Jokleel with as much fury as her father.

'Are you ready for this, Thuralin?' snapped Finavar, noticing the hurt in his brother's eyes. 'They will not find the trail without us. Are you with me or not?'

Thuralin blushed furiously and his voice grew even more hoarse than usual. 'I am ready.'

'Good.'

Finavar squeezed his brother's shoulder and gave him a reassuring smile, knowing he would be tormented for days by the thought he had upset someone. Then he dragged Mormo and Mauro from the warmth of his cloak and held them up in his palms, placing a kiss on each of their heads. 'Take us to the largest of them.' He held the polecats close to his face and whispered. 'Take us to the one with the face of a boar. Let us teach it what happens to the enemies of our friends.'

The polecats stared back at him with stern, thoughtful

expressions; then they hurried from the tree, vanishing quickly into the shadows.

The asrai advanced in silence. They were dressed in sombre hues to match the colours of the fading winter, and they moved with almost as much grace as the Darkling Prince himself. Even perched high in the trees they were invisible, merging seamlessly with the leafless branches and the cold, hard sky.

The lurching horrors below had no inkling of the impending attack.

Finavar vaulted to the top of a tree, surveying the scene with satisfaction. The dancers of Locrimere had come equipped with bows and they had already picked their targets. Now they were waiting patiently for his signal. However this strange situation had come to be, there was no denying that he now commanded a force larger than he could ever have imagined. Finavar felt a rush of excitement, elated to be at the head of such an army; then he remembered Caorann and his grin faded. His lack of caution had almost cost the life of a dear friend; still might, he realised, remembering the severe expressions on the faces of the healers. He looked back through the trees at the remaining members of his kinband. Like the others, they were waiting silently for his order to attack. No one seemed to doubt his ability. Even old Thuralin was watching for his lead. 'I will make them pay, Caorann,' Finavar whispered.

He pulled his hood low over his mass of flame-coloured hair and crept out further on a branch, intrigued to know why the outsiders had paused. The largest of them – the one with the boar-like snout – had stooped over a hulk of mossy stone and was conversing with something.

Wisps of fog were drifting through the air, filled with glittering, ember-like spores. Finavar rose carefully to his feet and leapt silently into the next tree. From here he could make out a tiny, spindly stick figure, moving through the mist. He was still too far away to make out any details, but he was sure it was a spirit of some kind. No mortal creature would move so oddly. It had a head like a gleaming, elongated skull and its twig-like limbs glimmered with pale fire – quite unlike the sparkle of the frost. Once again, Finavar felt a twinge of doubt. How had an outsider managed to turn one of the forest's own spirits into a servant?

The twig-thing nodded and leapt from the stone, dashing back into the undergrowth with a clicking sound.

The leader of the outsiders backed away from the rock and turned to face its grunting horde. It lifted its enormous double-headed axe and let out a guttural belching sound. The cry was so loud that a cloud of rooks and crows erupted from the trees, circling up into the pale sky with a series of peevish caws.

Finavar felt a dull rage building in his chest as he studied the creature that had mutilated Caorann. Then he frowned. It looked even more powerful than he recalled. Its armour-clad bulk towered over the other outsiders and there was something else odd: the ghostly light that shone from the tiny wooden spirit also illuminated the beastman's mantle of fog.

'Is it part of the forest?' whispered a voice in his ear.

Finavar turned to see that Alhena had crept up beside him.

'Magic is bound to its flesh.' Her voice trembled with a mixture of confusion and outrage. 'How?'

Finavar felt a rush of pride. Alhena deferred to him so naturally now. When Thuralin had first emerged from the forest, his daughter had glared like a savage; now she addressed him like a brother.

He looked back at the roaring creature. He could not deny that it seemed different from the beasts of Chaos he had seen before. 'It has something to do with that spirit,' he muttered. He looked around the branches of the tree and laughed quietly to himself. As he expected, the promise of an impending battle had won him a spectral entourage of his own. A cloud of tiny, sparkling faces peered back at him through the branches.

He recognised the one called Gole and summoned it towards him. The skeletal serpent was no bigger than Finavar's hand and it hesitated for a few minutes, snapping the reins of its winged mount and baring its teeth. Then after a while intrigue got the better of it and it flew closer, alighting on a branch near Finavar's head. It babbled and squeaked at him in its own strange tongue; then, seeing his blank expression, it reluctantly spat out a few words he could understand.

'Name of Death's-head,' it hissed, writhing uncomfortably in the morning light.

'What?'

'Name of Death's-head,' it repeated, waving its rose-thorn sword at the scene below.

Finavar nodded eagerly, surprised that the spirit was being so helpful. 'The largest of the outsiders is called Death's-head – the one with the face like a boar?'

The spirit howled in annoyance, screwing its face into a furious grimace. The sound that emerged was no louder than a squeaking hinge, but Finavar looked anxiously at the enemy to see if they had heard.

The creatures were still unaware of the rows of arrows trained on them, so Finavar turned back to Gole and held a finger to his mouth. 'What do you mean?'

The spirit waved at its radiant, gossamer flesh and then

waved at the stump near to the leader of the beastmen. 'Name of Death's-head.'

Finavar shrugged and turned to his brother with an exasperated expression.

Jokleel rocked back on his heels and allowed his eyes to glaze over. He reached out to Gole and muttered a soft prayer. The venomous little thing glared back at him.

For a few seconds, Jokleel was oblivious to everything but the spirit. He repeated his prayer several times until it became a kind of moaning plainsong. Finally, he focused his gaze back on his brother.

'I understand,' he said. 'Gole is saying that the outsiders are being led to Locrimere by something called Death's-head.'

'Of course.' Finavar nodded, remembering the stick-thing's elongated skull. His face crumpled into the same childish pout he always wore when he was puzzled.

There was an explosion of noise from the gulley below.

The boar-faced creature had climbed up onto the tree trunk, raised its axe over its head and filled the clearing with drifting mist. As the fog washed over the surrounding forest it flickered with light, revealing the rows of asrai, crouched amongst the trees.

At the sight of their enemy the mutants launched into action, hurling spears and axes and charging through the undergrowth.

The asrai loosed their arrows but the element of surprise was gone and several of them tumbled from their perches, clutching wounds.

'Not again,' hissed Finavar, drawing his twin blades and turning to the other wardancers. 'Keep the others off me while I put an end to that creature's tricks.'

He leapt from tree to tree, dodging past the archers as they fired into the grunting ranks below, making for the creature at the head of the column.

Even without the element of surprise, the asrai were terrifying. Their limbs blurred as they fired arrow after arrow with incredible precision. The air filled with a lethal, glinting rain, and whole rows of the beastmen dropped to their knees, pierced by dozens of feathered shafts.

Finavar paid no attention to the carnage erupting around him and stayed focused on his target. The enormous brute towered over the other creatures and the single great horn that curved up from its brow made it easy to follow, even as the army broke into a confusing mass of struggling shapes.

There was a sudden, blinding flash of light and Finavar stumbled.

He reached out blindly and managed to grab a low branch, muttering a prayer of thanks to Loec as he did so. For a few seconds he was hanging in full view, blinded by the glare. Then the light faded and he saw that it was the mist, pouring from the axe of his prey.

Cries rang out as the fog settled around the archers and scorched into their skin; then the monster slammed its axe down into the trunk, dragging its captives from the trees and sending them crashing across the frozen ground.

Finavar cursed as dozens of his kin tumbled into view, cocooned in the monster's magic and powerless to defend themselves as the other beastmen bore down on them. Finavar looped back up onto a branch and continued racing towards the source of the fog with the other wardancers close behind him. All around them, archers were being wrenched from the trees and slammed down onto the ground. The clearing was already becoming clogged with the dead of both sides. 'By Loec,' he said, 'I will see this creature dead!'

He dropped from the trees and began sprinting through the carnage, moving so fast that the monsters barely registered his passing. The archers on the ground were trying desperately to defend themselves but the beastmen were in a frenzy: axes fell, horns gored and hooves stomped as they saw a chance to finally lay hands on their elusive foes.

Light flared again and Finavar stumbled to a halt, blinded.

Lumbering shapes loomed over him and he lashed out with his blades, leaping into the air and arching his back in a graceful dance of death. He felt the swords bite, slicing through armour and bone and filling the air with blood, but as his attackers fell away, more rushed to replace them.

Finavar dropped into a crouch, surrounded by a wall of leering faces.

The beastmen lunged and hacked, but Finavar slipped between their blows, leaping onto the shoulders of the first attackers and spinning over their heads in a blur of sharpened metal. Even his barbed cloak acted as a weapon, slashing the faces beneath him as he somersaulted through the battle.

Finavar looped and tumbled, lunged and dived, but it was not enough. As the mist continued to flood the trees, more of the asrai tumbled into view and fewer arrows thudded into the beastmen. Seeing a chance for butchery on a grand scale, the monsters bellowed and tore into their dazed attackers. Finavar whirled around and made for the leader, flipping and vaulting across the crowds.

As he landed before his prey, Finavar saw that the monster was readying its weapon for another burst of sorcery. The blade of the double-headed axe was blazing as it leeched magic from the moss-covered trees.

Before the brute could unleash its spell, Finavar dived through the air and brought both his blades down towards the beastman's face.

The creature was fast.

Finavar's blades clattered against its axe and the weapon shed its power, throwing Finavar back with a thunderclap.

Finavar found himself sprawled supine on the ground, his ears ringing from the blast.

The monster loomed over him, hefting its axe back for another strike and shaking its pig-like head. Blood and drool sprayed from its tusks.

Finavar rolled aside as the axe sank into the earth and lashed out with his one remaining blade. The sword clattered harmlessly across the monster's chainmail and Finavar backed away, readying himself for another lunge.

To his delight he saw the other three wardancers whirling around him in a circle, holding back the rest of the beastman army with a flurry of sword strikes and kicks. Alhena was delirious with pleasure, grinning as she hacked and lunged. The boy fought with less enjoyment, but no less skill, severing throats with a mournful ballad on his lips. Thuralin grimaced as he fought. Every jump and strike caused him obvious pain but Finavar was surprised to see that he killed more than any of the others. His ruined arm was strapped uselessly to his chest and his moves were a crude imitation of their beautiful waltz, but he moved with a cunning economy that bewildered his opponents. Between the three of them they quickly cleared a circle in the centre of the battle, leaving Finavar free to engage his foe.

The hulking, boar-faced creature saw that it was suddenly alone with Finavar, but made no attempt to lunge at him. It held its axe aloft instead, catching the threads of mist that were still spiralling from the trees.

Finavar flipped across the ground and spun into the air, slashing his sword at the monster's wrists.

It wrinkled its snout and laughed.

Light bounced off the head of the axe and knifed into Finavar's eyes, so that his blow went wide and he crashed back down to earth with an explosion of breath.

Finavar rolled clear, dodging another axe blow, and howled in frustration, springing back up with such force that he knocked his opponent from its feet and sent them both rolling back across the space cleared by his kinband.

The creature smashed the haft of its axe into the side of Finavar's head and blood exploded from his ear.

He rolled away, spitting curses.

As Finavar rose woozily to his feet, Thuralin cried out in a strained voice. 'We are being slaughtered!' He ducked beneath a spear thrust, downed another two beastmen, then whirled to face Finavar. 'Show some sense, boy! The sorcery has undone us. It's a massacre!'

Finavar shook his head furiously, enraged that the old warrior would speak to him in such a way. 'That's not possible,' he spat, but as he looked back at his opponent he saw that the creature was still hurling and dragging great nets of fog from the trees, wrenching dozens of archers from the branches and scattering them at the feet of its army.

'I almost have him,' he gasped, diving at the mutant again. As before, the monster's magic pulsed from its blade as he neared it, sending Finavar's sword strike wide and leaving him sprawled on the ground.

'Finavar!' cried Jokleel, as the wall of beastmen finally broke through their defence and flooded the space they had cleared for him. The gangly youth flailed desperately with his swords, losing his footing as the numbers overwhelmed him.

The sight of his brother in danger caused Finavar to panic. He fumbled his blades, dropping one of them. He stooped and caught it before it hit the ground, but when he looked again there was no sign of Jokleel.

He saw Thuralin tumble past him, fending off blows as he made for a scrum of figures.

Finavar gasped, only realising that he had been holding his breath when he saw Thuralin drag his brother to safety.

The old cripple glared at Finavar through the mayhem, shaking his head as he defended Jokeel.

Finavar looked around and spotted Alhena. She was clearly unaware that the tide was turning. As the enemy flooded over them she continued smiling; stabbing, kicking and biting the monsters as they crushed against her.

'We must fall back,' gasped Thuralin, hauling Jokleel to Finavar's side.

'We must *not*!' cried Finavar, throwing himself again at the boar-faced shaman.

This time there was no need for magic. The crush of bodies was now so great that Finavar could not even reach his opponent. He stabbed and punched furiously, but the beastmen were tumbling over each other to attack him and he found himself unable to do anything but fight for his life. As he whirled around, parrying and lunging, he realised he could no longer even see the other wardancers.

'Jokleel!' he cried.

'We must retreat,' came a hoarse reply from somewhere to his left.

Finavar tried to see through the melee but it was impossible. Blood, iron and fur filled his vision.

'Father!' cried another voice.

He realised it must be Alhena and grimaced. He saw a brief glimpse of her lowering her blades and dashing to Thuralin's side, her face filled with concern, then she vanished in the crush.

An image of Caorann's terrible wound flashed into Finavar's mind. His kinband followed him with utter devotion. He knew that as long as he fought, they would never flee. He rolled across the ground, sending a row of beastmen to their knees, then flipped back over his shoulders and landed on their backs, trying to get a better view.

His heart sank as he saw what had become of his great opportunity. The forest had become an abattoir. Strands of glowing fog were still dripping from the trees and most of the archers had been dragged into view. Hundreds of them lay dead or dying at the feet of the beastmen.

The creature with the face of a boar was now several dozen feet away, laughing and snorting as it continued to haul in its catch. It caught Finavar's eye and snorted with disdain, holding up a struggling victim.

The crowd swelled again and Finavar fell backwards, losing his remaining sword as the monsters tumbled on top of him.

A female scream sliced through the din.

'Retreat?' The word slipped into Finavar's head like a criminal. 'I cannot,' he whispered, picturing the mocking sneer on Eremon's face. He hauled himself up through the press of bodies and wrenched a crude, jagged knife from the hands of a corpse.

There was no sign of his kinband and, to his horror, Finavar saw that hardly any arrows were coming from the trees. Some of the archers were bolting from the clutches of the beastmen, dashing back into the trees, clutching terrible wounds.

He leapt and punched back the way he had come, looking for a sign of his friends but seeing none. Then, at the edge of the trees, he paused and looked back. The monsters were making no attempt at pursuit. The boar-faced giant was already leading them back on their original path. Flushed with victory, the creatures began roaring and howling as they smashed through the trees in the direction of Locrimere.

Finavar remembered the name Caorann had given him. 'Face me!' he howled, leaping onto the shoulders of one of his attackers. 'I am the Darkling Prince!'

Before the monster below him could act, Finavar had leapt onto the shoulders of another beastman. He raced lightly across the battlefield, dancing from shoulder to shoulder as easily as if he were crossing the stones in a river.

Up ahead, the boar-faced monster paused and looked back in surprise; it was clear that it had considered the battle over. It barely had time to recognise that, as he ran, Finavar had hurled his borrowed knife, sending it spinning and flashing across the rows of horns, shields and battered helmets.

There was a thud as the blade sliced neatly into the sorcerer's brow. The knife sank to its hilt and sent the snorting giant stumbling back into its guards.

For a few seconds an odd silence descended on the scene as the beastmen watched their leader stumbling backwards with a confused expression on its face.

Then the brute collapsed, hitting the ground like a felled tree.

For a few more seconds the beastmen remained motionless, looking at their dead leader in stunned silence.

Finavar took advantage of the pause and turned to the trees. He was still standing on the shoulders of a beastman as he raised his arms to the morning sun.

'Guardians of the forest!' he howled with a broad, bloodsplattered grin. 'Defend your home!'

The outsiders finally lurched into action, but by the time any of them thought to reach for Finavar he was gone – spinning gracefully across the battlefield, landing kicks and punches as he went.

At the sound of Finavar's call, the asrai turned to see that the pulsing mist had vanished with the fall of the creature that had been wielding it. A smattering of arrows began falling again. Within seconds the smattering became a shower, then a storm as they returned in force.

Hundreds of the beastmen began dropping to the ground as they saw the full, untrammelled force of the asrai archers.

A long, undulating whistle drifted through the carnage and made Finavar's grin even broader. He bolted for the trees, climbed the first one he reached and peered out across the canopy of leafless branches. Seeing nothing, he raised his fingers to lips and let out an identical whistle.

Far in the distance he saw a flash of pale skin and raised his fist in salute 'Alhena!' he cried. She was too far away for him to see if she was wounded or not, but if she was still able to scale trees, he doubted she was too badly hurt.

Another whistle and then another rang out and Finavar was so overwhelmed by relief that he almost wept. Thuralin and Jokleel had survived the bloodbath too and were racing back towards him.

He embraced his brother, realising how close to death he had led him.

After a moment he looked up and saw that Thuralin was glaring at Alhena.

'You lowered your guard,' he said, his voice trembling with fury.

Alhena hung her head in shame. 'I saw you fall.'

The mention of his weakness seemed to enrage the old warrior even more. 'You *must* remember what I taught you!' He was on the verge of saying something else, but his fury turned into a violent cough. 'I will not always be here to remind you,' he managed to say eventually.

Finavar looked at him in silence, recalling how well he had fought. Then he turned and nodded at the grey-clad shapes moving past them. The asrai were revelling in the chance to avenge their fallen kin, firing into the mass of struggling beastmen with incredible speed. 'We're missing all the fun,' he said, managing a tentative smile. 'I'm sure even Eremon wouldn't begrudge us a bow or two.'

The others did not manage to return his smile but they nodded and gathered weapons from the fallen, then joined the attack, firing with almost as much accuracy as Eremon's archers.

As the morning sun crept higher, the slaughter continued. Seeing they could not escape, the beastmen lumbered into the trees, trying to find their invisible attackers. But as they entered the forest, they found themselves bewildered by the shadows and dazed by snatches of gentle music.

For nearly an hour the archers poured death down on the outsiders and Finavar's strength began to fade. Some of the soldiers were beginning to exhaust their supply of arrows and many of them were bleeding from their fingers. He noticed an archer spying eagle-like from the top of a sycamore tree, and climbed up towards him.

'Surely there cannot be much more of this,' he said. 'How many do you see? When do they end?'

The archer lowered his bow and looked down at Finavar. His face was drawn with exhaustion and there was fear in his eyes. 'There *is* no end.' He waved for Finavar to approach.

The treetop was slender and Finavar had to climb with care. Once he was settled he peered out into the growing light. From this height he could see the whole length of the valley surrounding Locrimere. At first he thought the sunrise was playing tricks on him. It looked as though dozens of new rivers had burst their banks and were flooding down from the Grey Mountains.

He pulled his black hood lower to shield his eyes from the glare. 'Is that... Is that an army?' he gasped.

The archer nodded. His voice was hollow. 'An invasion.'

Wounded, she thought, as a voice rang out through the trees. It was a pitiful, whining plea that filled her with disgust. She shifted through various forms, becoming a hawk for a while, gliding over the frozen boughs, then a ferret, bolting across the ice. Finally, at the sight of her prey, she dressed herself in pale, naked skin, long, glossy locks and a smile warm enough to melt the frost.

'Who's there?' gasped the fallen warrior, spitting blood and peering into the shadows. He reached around for a weapon as she approached, clearly too weak to stand. His longbow was lying in pieces at his feet, as broken as his body, so he began scrabbling in the leaves for something else to use, but when he saw who was approaching he froze, shaking his head in amazement and forgetting his weapons. He studied her long, sylphic body with undisguised admiration. 'What kind of death is this?' His voice was a hoarse whisper as he sat up against a tree and wiped the blood from his eyes.

One of Ariel's runts, she thought, stooping down next to him and stroking his bloody brow. Felled by the creatures from the north. Clogging these old roots with his worthless, foreign blood.

The wounded archer closed his eyes, soothed by her gentle touch. As she took him in her arms, the morning shone through her flawless *skin and flooded his grateful eyes.*

'So beautiful,' he sighed, leaning closer for a kiss.

As his mouth pressed against hers he froze. Rather than the soft, yielding lips he expected, he found himself kissing cold, rough bark.

He turned away in disgust, spitting moss onto the ground and trying to pull away.

Her grip was as hard as oak.

'What are you?' His dreamy expression was replaced by a terrified grimace as he saw her true, gnarled features.

'I am the forest,' she replied softly, snapping his neck like a piece of kindling.

CHAPTER NINE

'The Darkling Prince! I cannot believe this. Have you heard? They are all singing his name!' Eremon's upper lip curled in a sneer. 'They say he's a hero.' He paused halfway across a broad, grassy amphitheatre and looked down over Locrimere's most sacred place: a deep, sombre lake; a placid jewel known to the asrai as the Idolan. After a few moments he sighed and turned from the water to the figure at his side. 'To hear them talk, you'd think he'd *won* a battle, not fled from one. And all this rubbish about vast numbers and lumbering giants is clearly an exaggeration. This is all just another one of his ridiculous tales.'

Hauran Quillwort smiled awkwardly. 'From what I hear, he only agreed to draw back when there was no other option. The kinbands exhausted every arrow and spear, so they were clearly fighting *something*. Finavar and his friends remained to fight alone for as long as they could.'

Eremon shook his head in disbelief. 'Please, Quillwort, tell me that you at least are not enamoured by this knave.'

Quillwort looked around to make sure they were not being overheard. It was late afternoon and the folk of Locrimere were already at play. Spring was starting to break through the late winter chill and the asrai were in celebratory mood. Most of them wore flowers in their hair: the tiny petals of cowslips and forget-me-nots, woven into their matted locks. The air was still sharp enough for Quillwort's breath to trail behind him in a glittering cloud, but most of Lord Beldeas's subjects were scantily clad, or even naked, and they carried no weapons; safe in the haven of Locrimere's innermost sanctuary. Other than during festival rites, no blood had ever been spilled on the shores of the Idolan and few imagined that it ever would be. Quillwort saw nothing but joy in the eyes of his kindred. Laughing, dark-eyed musicians serenaded groups of ivy-clad dancers who sang and whirled in time to the music, tumbling through the long grass, drinking heady fruit wine and practising rites that would soon be seen across the whole forest. The festival of Ostaliss was only days away. Soon the spheres would align for the Even-Night. The Queen would emerge once more, shrugging off a winter-long slumber to embrace her immortal beloved: her Consort-King, Orion.

Quillwort forgot Eremon's question for a moment as he gazed at the bucolic scene. Then he looked back at the captain's scowling face and recalled the ignoble task allotted to them. 'Heroes do not last,' he replied, with sadness in his voice. 'Especially those born without the advantage of noble blood.' He leant closer to Eremon and lowered his voice. 'Finavar cannot hinder our plans. In fact, if his story is true, then he may even be of help. Beldeas and Ordaana have already left for the rites of spring.' He smiled and tapped the hilt of Eremon's sword. 'While they rekindle their love and welcome Ariel and Orion to the Council Glade, who will be defending Locrimere?

Who will lead us to victory? You, Eremon. We should pray that Finavar's story *is* true.'

Eremon looked doubtful, but made no attempt to interrupt.

'And then, if an unexpected tragedy deprives us of our Lord and Lady, your claim to the throne will be irrefutable. The saviour of Locrimere will become the Warden of Locrimere. Who could question such a decision?'

Eremon rubbed his scarred jaw and considered his friend's words. 'Perhaps.' He lifted his chin. 'It *is* crucial that I am not seen as some opportunist. I must be the kind of noble leader we have been lacking. I do not want it thought that I am merely taking advantage of Beldeas's misfortune.'

Quillwort looked down at a knife tucked into his belt and frowned. 'We have to *engineer* his misfortune first.' He shook his head, trying to vanquish the unpleasant image he had conjured. 'Noble is exactly how you will be seen, Eremon. Nobody can doubt your suitability. After all these centuries of misrule, you will be heralded as a hero. Finally, Locrimere will have the leader it deserves.'

The sneer returned to Eremon's face. 'I can prove nothing while that wretched villain is being hailed as our saviour.' He looked into the middle distance. 'They would probably consider him a more suitable replacement for Beldeas.'

'He is a fatherless orphan.' Quillwort smoothed down his robes and looked at the figures dancing nearby. 'Only you can lead Locrimere as it should be led, in the way Beldeas has so miserably failed to do, but you will need the love of his people. And that might not happen while this ridiculous bard is dazzling them with his so-called wit.'

'Then what do you suggest?' Eremon's voice was brittle.

'Let him go. Let him run his pointless errand. Anything. Just make sure you have Locrimere to yourself when these beasts attack. If he thinks he can just waltz into the Council Glade and address the King, let him try. Think of the outrage he will cause. Let everyone see what an ill-mannered lowborn he is, while you remain here and face the enemy with dignity. Once you are victorious, no one will question your right to rule; Finavar, meanwhile, will be disgraced.'

Eremon raised his eyebrows. 'You have a talent for this. I must remember to keep you close when I become the Warden of Locrimere.'

Quillwort paled. 'I do not enjoy this deceit. What I do, I do for Locrimere.' He tapped his chest so fiercely that his jewellery rattled. 'My heart is pure, but I have put all my hope in *you*, Eremon, not this dancing jester. It will take a person of dignity to rid us of Beldeas and his poisoned wreck of a wife. *That* is the reason for all these lies, Eremon. I do not make a habit of betrayal.' He clasped his hands together, clearly distressed. 'I am not proud of what we are doing.'

Eremon gave a slight bow. 'Forgive me, Quillwort. I did not mean to make light of your sacrifice.' He threw back his broad shoulders, shrugging his leather armour into place. 'I know you would not dirty your hands if there was any other way and I understand your pain, but you *should* be proud. The safety of Locrimere is in our hands. Consider what an honour that is.' He nodded to the guardhouses, hanging above the far end of the meadow. Finavar and his kinband were already gathered at the edge of the Idolan, waiting to hear Eremon's decision. 'Let us send this fool on his ridiculous errand. Then I can begin to make my mark.'

CHAPTER TEN

Ordaana stumbled through a veil of shadows, taunted by distant laughter. Strange music echoed through the trees: low, mournful horns and the glacial tinkling of harps, a bewildering jumble of melodies that spiralled and rose, without the slightest trace of discord. If her purpose were not so dreadful, Ordaana would have tumbled into the arms of the forest and wept for joy. She was nearing the Oak of Ages: the verdant heart of the Queen's realm. This was the core of the forest's power, where nothing remained solid or fixed. As the equinox approached, the spirits became wilder and stranger than ever. Dark, spectral figures called to her from under every bower, tantalising her with glimpses of impossible, beautiful futures. If not for her desperate errand, Ordaana would have gladly answered their call, happy to lose herself in Ariel's strange halls. What bliss it would be to dance with the spirits of the Council Glade, and forget her past. But Ordaana's determination was even more potent than her shame. All the grief in her soul drove her on, through the beguiling visions, through the noble trees, through the spiralling notes, all the while clutching a long, rune-covered knife to her chest.

For hours she searched, tearing her robes on centuries-old thickets and numbing her feet in long-forgotten brooks. Finally, she dropped to her knees and cursed. Standing in front of her was a stunted, wizened-looking hawthorn bush, and crumpled in its roots was the rotten corpse of jackdaw. 'I *have* been here before,' she groaned. She could not be mistaken. One half of the jackdaw's face had shrivelled away to reveal an empty eye socket and Ordaana could not mistake the way it seemed to be winking at her.

'Where do I go?' she moaned, her voice full of panic. The highborn of the forest were already gathering to welcome Ariel and Orion. Beldeas would be too busy flirting to notice her absence, but others would soon start to talk. She must return before the priests of Kurnous emerged to honour their Chosen One. If she were absent for the start of the observances, the whole of Ariel's court would wonder why. She looked up at the stars for guidance but it was useless. This close to the Oak of Ages, time itself became merry, waltzing and swooning like an intoxicated youth. The heavens were a confusing mess of stars long forgotten and stars yet to be born. 'Aestar Eltanin,' she whispered, 'guide me! I need you!'

There was no reply and Ordaana stretched out her fingers in a furious spasm. Blue light began to drip from her hands, catching like flames in the lemon-coloured folds of her gown. 'Guide me!' she groaned as her magic crackled through the grass and merged with shifting gloom.

A wet cracking sound caused her to pause and look back at the old hawthorn bush.

She grimaced in disgust.

The maggots burrowing through the corpse of the jackdaw

seemed to have been affected by her rage. They were wriggling and bubbling beneath the bird's feathers, causing it to jerk and twitch.

She shuddered at the repulsive sight. 'Perhaps this way,' she wondered aloud, turning to face a tunnel of lichen-clad trees, but then she shook her head, full of doubt.

'Ordaana.'

She froze and sighed with pleasure. The voice was rasping and strange, but unmistakable. 'Aestar!' She looked around at the trees for a cobweb or some other drifting shape that might reveal his face. 'Where are you?'

'Down here,' came the reply, and Ordaana realised that the rotten jackdaw had climbed to its feet and was staring at her with its single clouded eye.

She recoiled in disgust, struggling to believe what she was seeing. Could her noble guardian really appear to her in such a foul guise? 'Aestar?' she whispered, stepping gingerly back towards the teetering lump of bloody feathers.

The tiny corpse hobbled towards her. As it moved, its little bones cracked and popped, shedding gobbets of dark, clotted blood. 'Don't you recognise me, Ordaana?' The dead bird tilted its head on one side and fixed its milky retina on her. 'Surely a little decay is not enough to confuse you?'

Ordaana dropped to her knees, shaking her head fiercely and shuffling towards the twitching jackdaw. 'No, of course not, Aestar, but I would not have associated you with...' Her voice trailed off and she shrugged awkwardly.

'There is beauty in everything, Ordaana. You should know that.' The jackdaw lifted its misshapen head, revealing the oily, shimmering feathers of its breast. 'Death is as much a part of the forest as anything else. It is simply an agent of change.'

'Of course.' Ordaana amazed herself by blushing. If anyone

else had spoken to her in such a way, she would have been outraged, but Aestar was so dignified and noble she hated to think she could have disappointed him. 'I was confused.' She waved at the shifting pall that surrounded them. 'Ariel's magic is muddying my thoughts.'

The jackdaw continued looking at her in silence for a moment. Then it turned and nodded its head, indicating the avenue of trees that Ordaana had almost headed down earlier. 'You are almost there, child. Just a few more minutes and you will reach the oak.' The bird let out a ragged, cawing laugh. '*Then* you will be confused. And I cannot help you there. I will not be able to approach such a place. My eyes were not made for such visions.'

'Almost there!' she gasped, leaping to her feet and approaching the trees. 'And then I just need to pierce the shadow, is that right?' She looked back at the hawthorn bush and saw that the bird was lying on its side again, exactly as it was when she first saw it. 'Very well.' She gripped the knife even more tightly and hurried on through the trees. After a few minutes she heard voices and snatches of music coming from up ahead. Many of the voices were familiar and she realised she was approaching the Council Glade from behind. Soon she would see the Oak of Ages in a way few others had ever done, from the direction of the Queen's most secret glades.

A sound rang out through the trees: the crunch of hooves grinding into frosty soil.

Ordaana gasped and drew out the cloak she had demanded from Beldeas. The stitches rippled as she threw it over her shoulders, then they rose out of the cloth, forming a spiralling mesh of leaves, enveloping her so completely that she merged seamlessly into the undergrowth.

As the last of the leaves fell into place, a terrifying figure rode into view. A seven-foot giant, smeared in blood, human scalps and animal hides. He was riding bareback on a beautiful white stallion and his head was crowned with a pair of thin, spiral horns.

Ordaana knew the rider by name: Atolmis the Hunter, High Priest of Kurnous, immortal equerry to the King. She felt a rush of terror as she realised how close she had come to being discovered. Of all the beings in the forest, none would judge her actions more harshly than Orion's own guardian. A vision flashed into her mind; a memory of the last time she saw Atolmis. It was the heart of the summer, and the Wild Hunt was abroad. Atolmis was riding at Orion's side. Both of them were draped in wreaths of flowers and robes of oak leaves, and both of them were drenched in blood, trailing their terrified victims behind them in a dreadful, screaming mound. Atolmis was laughing hysterically, surrounded by pale, spectral hounds. Ordaana shuddered, bringing her attention back to the present, but unable to fully escape the memory of the hounds, snarling as they tore through the undergrowth.

Atolmis reined in his horse just a few feet from Ordaana, scouring the trees with his enormous black eyes. His pale features were covered in fresh, ritualistic scarring, and thin trails of blood ran down his face like a grille. 'Olachas,' he said, looking directly at Ordaana, his voice a low growl.

She heard the sound of another horse approaching and held her breath, terrified that she might fall back on a branch and reveal her presence.

The second rider's horse passed within inches of her trembling arms and came to a halt next to Atolmis. He was equally wild-looking, but his reply was a calm rumble. 'The Silver Glade has been searched by Sélva. Karioth has scoured the eastern meadows.'

Atolmis looked up at the whirling heavens. 'He is the Chosen of Kurnous, Olachas. We have never been mistaken.'

Olachas frowned. 'Of course.'

Atolmis nodded. 'Of course.' But as they rode from the clearing, Ordaana noticed that beneath his heavy brow, his eyes were full of doubt.

He senses something, she thought, with a thrill of pride. The riders' auguries have foreseen the success of my curse, but Atolmis is too arrogant to question his own judgement.

Once she was sure the riders had gone, Ordaana removed the cloak and the leaves became stitches once more. She hurried on down the avenue of trees. After a few minutes she saw a mountainous shape looming out of the shadows. Seen from behind, the Oak of Ages resembled a wall of shifting images. It was impossibly broad and, after thousands of years of ritual and magic, it bore little resemblance to a tree. Perhaps to the eyes of an outsider, it might have appeared as a hulking mountain of root and branch, but Ordaana, like the rest of the asrai, was part of the forest, and her soul was inextricably bound to the strangeness at its core.

As she approached the kindreds' most sacred totem, Ordaana saw all life displayed before her. The tree's roots were a bottomless pit, crawling with every spirit that had ever tumbled from the mortal realm; vast armies of lost souls stared up at her from an inky void, a host of drawn, ashen faces, filled with loneliness and regret. Rather than a trunk, Ordaana saw the entire world: oceans and mountains and scorched desert plains, spiralling around each other in an endless dance of death and rebirth. In place of a crown, the tree bore the slowly spinning heavens.

The faintest shadows of gods and daemons cavorted in the branches, dazzling Ordaana, even in their most subtle forms.

She had witnessed the sight before, but always in a crowd, at the height of a ceremony, in the heart of Ariel's procession. Seeing from this new vantage point, without the guidance of ritual and prayer, Ordaana was quite overwhelmed, dropping to her knees and forgetting all about her vile errand. She saw a hammer of moonlight, pounding against an enormous anvil, filling the grove with flashes of lightning. 'Vaul,' she breathed, recognising the long, anguished face of the weaponsmith, as blind and dazzling as the stars exploding beneath his hammer.

Next Ordaana saw a shade of the Loremaster, Hoeth, poring over his forgotten texts and reading the impossible language of the heavens, devouring wisdom with bottomless, ancient eyes. Moving behind the Great Scholar was a dark, undulating figure; lithe and graceful, tripping through the vaults of the tree with a devious smile. 'Loec,' she breathed, 'the Shadow Dancer.' He rolled and flipped gleefully through the heavens, as light as a falling comet, illuminating a vast pantheon of gods and demigods. Ordaana shook her head in wonder, unable to name even half of the spectral figures moving through the tree's upper branches.

Finally, as she lay on the grass, utterly overcome, she saw a being so dazzling that even the other gods faded into insignificance. What she had at first mistaken for the spiralling arms of galaxies, were actually the all-encompassing wings of a phoenix. 'Asuryan,' she breathed. As she spoke the name of the Father God, Ordaana suddenly remembered the noble face of Aestar. Along with his face came all her other memories and Ordaana snatched her gaze from the tree, desperately trying to drag her thoughts back to the Council Glade.

She sat still for a moment with her eyes clamped tightly shut. Without the distraction of the tree, she noticed sounds, emerging from the other side of its enormous trunk. Hundreds of voices were drifting through the trees, all of them full of excitement and anticipation. 'The opening ceremony is about to begin,' she gasped, opening her eyes and scouring the grass for her knife. The glinting blade was still lying next to her, so she snatched it from the grass and rose to her feet. 'I am almost out of time.'

Ordaana hurried around the trunk, keeping her gaze fixed on the grass, so as not to be distracted by the beguiling visions overhead. As she went, she replayed Aestar's instructions through her head and silently mouthed the words he had taught her back in Locrimere. After a few minutes, she reached her goal: an oily pit of darkness, directly behind the tree, thrown by the light of the twin moons. On the far side of the oak, the voices were growing louder and more frenzied. She heard the clanging of gongs and the sound of harps being tuned. The highborn were almost assembled, ready to welcome their king and queen, but she remained calm, crushing the panic that threatened to overwhelm her. Of all the asrai present, only she knew the truth. Only she could lead them back to their true home. The thought gave Ordaana courage as she stepped deeper into the darkness and raised her knife.

'In the heart of the shadow,' she whispered, reciting Aestar's instructions, 'where light never falls.'

She plunged the blade into the tree's shadow. As she did so, she uttered a long, garbled incantation. The knife sank deep into the muddy earth, but there was no obvious effect. Ordaana wondered if she had remembered the words correctly. Then, as she peered anxiously at the ground, she noticed it was starting to ripple around the silver blade. It was as though the patch of soil around her feet had become a miniature, windswept ocean. She nodded, feeling a strange mixture of pride and foreboding.

The sound of hooves drummed through the trees and Ordaana gasped, pulling her cloak back into place. To her horror she saw that the blade was clearly visible, glittering beneath her cloak of leaves. She tried to draw it from the ground, but it was stuck fast. She tugged desperately at it, remembering what Aestar had said: the success of the curse would depend on its secrecy. Still, the knife would not move. Tears of rage and frustration welled up in Ordaana's eyes. The cloak's magic would only work if she remained absolutely still, but she needed to assume her place at Beldeas's side.

Atolmis entered the glade. He was looking in Ordaana's direction but, rather than approaching her, he dismounted and dropped to his knees, lowering his horned brow in a prayer to the figures moving overhead.

To Ordaana's delight, the ground beneath the knife suddenly opened, mouth-like, and swallowed the blade. The metal flashed once, then sank deep into the ancient soil. By the time Atolmis had finished his prayers and started towards her, there was no trace of her curse.

Atolmis moved on, unaware of her presence.

Ordaana backed carefully away and slipped into the trees, disappearing from view just seconds before the pale lemon of her dress became visible once more. She raced through the forest, knowing that her time was almost up. The dawn was just seconds away. Ariel and Orion were about to emerge and greet their adoring subjects.

Ordaana's pulse began to race and she was sure she could already catch the scent of blood on the air.

Spring had come.

SPRING

Éorann-Ostallis
Quickening
The Season of Birth

CHAPTER ELEVEN

Orion became aware of sound, before anything else: hundreds of voices, chanting his name. They were singing glorious ballads and long, rousing epics, describing his past in glorious, extravagant detail.

He smiled in the darkness.

As their adoring syllables caressed his formless limbs he felt them start to solidify and grow. He sighed with pleasure as broad muscles spread across his chest and back. Tendons snaked around them like ivy, and his spine stretched and grew, creaking like old bark as it snapped into place. He felt his scalp burst as hard, shoot-like horns slid through his skin, spiralling up from his head to form wide, tangled antlers. For a long time, centuries it seemed, he revelled in the sheer visceral ecstasy of birth, stretching and flexing his limbs.

Then, as the coils of his brain formed and ignited, he remembered another name: Sephian. Orion's pleasure faltered as he recalled a vague sense of shame. Had there had been some suggestion of weakness, some implication that he was not fit to rule?

As Orion's features tumbled into position he opened his mouth and howled in defiance. He called out with such animal rage that his dark, arboreal womb shook and splintered around him. The chorus of voices faltered and the music ceased, but still Orion roared. 'I will show you power!' he bellowed, railing against his unknown accusers. His freshly formed body shook with wrath.

'I will teach you to kneel!'

As Orion roared, his fury spiralled. The sound of splintering wood merged with another noise. At first Orion thought it was his own booming roar, but soon he realised it was hounds, dozens of them, joining their wild clamour to his. It was a fierce, hungry sound that filled his quickening heart with joy.

'Orion,' said a voice in his ear. The words were soft, but somehow managed to drown out the din he had raised in the dark.

He turned to one side, delighting in the feel of his thick, tendon-wrapped neck.

His roar faltered and ceased as he looked into the eyes of a god.

The shape beside him was incandescent: a mantle of shifting stars, draped around a shimmering face. Orion flinched and closed his eyes, blinded by the light. 'Isha,' he said in a low growl.

'The forest is us,' said the voice. 'We are the forest. You have nothing to prove.'

Orion tried to look again and found the stars were already fading, revealing a face less celestial, but no less beautiful. Before he closed his eyes, he glimpsed pale, flawless skin, high, aristocratic cheekbones and a sad, distant gaze.

'Ariel,' he said, correcting himself. Even meeting her eyes so briefly was enough to send his thoughts tumbling into the past. Ariel. His queen. In an instant he saw all the long centuries they had shared. He saw a passion that had spanned thousands of years, born of innocent youth. Their love had so intoxicated them that they embarked on an adventure neither of them understood. As he took her hand, so familiar and dear, Orion remembered the true weight of his crown. Ariel's immortality was bound to the forest. Without these ancient trees, she could not exist. If he failed her, if he lacked the power to enforce her rule, she would die. He felt his pulse beginning to pound as his fury returned but, as he opened his mouth to roar, Ariel silenced him with a soft, lingering kiss.

For a second, Orion resisted, torn between lust and a desire to answer the baying of the hounds; then he threw his arms around her, abandoning himself to a new kind of ecstasy.

For a long time Orion forgot everything beyond the darkness and Ariel, but finally, as their passion faded, he realised that the voices outside had returned and multiplied. Hundreds were chanting in unison now, their voices as wild and unhinged as spring itself. Orion knew what was waiting for him, beyond the dark, and his newborn flesh tingled with anticipation. He was old and new; a mewling pup and wizened crone. He had lived for thousands of years and he was about to be born for the first time.

As the chorus spiralled into a rousing crescendo, Orion felt Ariel take his hand and lead him forwards. At first they were stepping through the heavens. Orion looked down and saw his hooves, treading lightly across the cosmos. Comets and stars folded in his wake as he followed Ariel in a celestial dance. Then he felt ground beneath his hooves, a soft, pungent carpet of rotting leaves that oozed and squelched beneath the weight of his mortal flesh. As they walked, Orion saw light pouring in through a hole in the void: an enormous gateway that allowed the morning to wash over him, bathing his body in warmth and light. The sensations felt utterly new and Orion sighed with pleasure, turning to see Ariel at his side. As the darkness fell away, he saw that his queen was an impossible beauty: a mixture of warm, mortal flesh and glimmering insubstantiality. She was naked, but her hair trailed around her in such a bewildering web of gold and silver that it was impossible to make out her true form. He noticed two tall shapes rising up from her shoulder blades and realised that they were the fluttering, tawny wings of a hawk moth. She caught his eye and gave him a shy smile, before nodding at the archway ahead of them.

Orion followed the direction of her gaze and saw figures moving through the glare, framed by the archway. He felt a rush of impatience and hurried forwards, dragging Ariel after him.

She laughed, softly, squeezing his hand as they stumbled out into the light.

The music ceased and silence descended, broken only by the sound of Ariel, laughing quietly.

For a second, Orion was blinded by a crimson sunrise. He grunted in confusion, holding his hands up before his face. Then his eyes grew accustomed to the bloody glare and he saw that they were standing on a wide, grassy dais, at the centre of a circular clearing, surrounded on all sides by enormous oak trees. The dawn light was bleeding through the branches, reaching across the lawn and washing over hundreds of nobles. The highborn of the forest were spread out around the dais, standing beside rows of scented balefires. The flames went untended as the asrai stared up at the beings they had summoned.

Orion began to understand Ariel's mirth as he surveyed his subjects.

They were terrified.

Every single face was white with fear. The lords and ladies were draped in their most beautiful spring finery: robes of the palest lemon and dresses the colour of new-sprung leaves that flapped and drifted in the morning breeze. Their trailing locks were plaited with bluebells and their wooden, splinter-like crowns blazed crimson with the fire of the rising sun. But, despite all of this, they resembled nothing more than quaking vermin, cornered by a hound.

Orion started to laugh. He was delighted to find that his voice was a rolling, powerful roar that caused the asrai to cower even further away from him. Some dropped to their knees and all averted their gaze. As his body shook with the pleasure of being alive, Orion looked down at himself. The memory of Sephian's shredded, bloody skin faded as he saw what he had become. His body looked as though it had been carved from the tall-est, most venerable oak in the forest. His hindquarters were broad and powerful and ended in enormous, ridged hooves. His chest was clad in thick, angular muscles and his whole body was tinged a beautiful lichen green. He looked back and saw that he and Ariel had emerged from an oak that towered over the others. Its shape was hard to define and it seemed to shift from his gaze, as though it were not entirely enamoured of the material realm. Orion knew which tree he was looking at and suddenly he felt all the glory and power of his new life. He let go of Ariel's hand, raised his fists to the fading winter's light and howled.

As Orion's cry echoed around the forest, the balefires gut-tered and danced and a fierce breeze struck up from nowhere, sending several of the asrai stumbling to their knees. The roar swelled in volume and Orion realised he did not wish it to ever stop: he would drive the world to its knees with one, endless, life-affirming howl. As he filled the forest with noise, Orion felt his heart pound with a nameless, wonderful fury.

'Listen,' said a voice in his mind. The words were no more than a whisper, but they cut through Orion's cry and caused him to pause. He recognised the gentle tones and ceased his cry, turning to see that Ariel was still smiling at him.

'They are welcoming us,' she said.

Orion looked back at the cowering asrai and realised that one of them was reciting some kind of poem. He was a pale, delicate-looking youth, dressed in worn, rust-coloured leather. The name Khoron Belidae popped into Orion's mind and he felt that this was someone he disliked; an artist of some kind, whose florid, flamboyant tone was already starting to irritate him.

'Bidden but never bound,' recited the fey-looking noble, 'we implore thee, our most sacred mirrors of Kurnous and Isha, that thou seest the loyalty in our bosom and that thou seest the hunger in our souls and that thou seest the joy in our welcome and that thou seest the blessing in our gifts. Both mortal and divine, we beg that you deem us worthy; that you abjure the mystical realm and, for a brief season of...'

Orion shook his head at the ridiculous, pompous youth, so clearly in love with his own voice. He pictured himself in simpler times, racing through the trees with his young lover at his side. There had been no elaborate rituals then; no nauseating, tousle-haired poets. 'How did we get *here*?' he said, turning to Ariel with a bemused expression.

'That's what you always say,' she replied, with another gentle laugh.

Orion frowned and looked at the other nobles.

Many of them had backed away to the far side of the clearing and some were crumpled on the ground, terrified by the ferocity of his howl. As the echoes faded, and Khoron Belidae droned on, they climbed nervously to their feet and edged back towards the King. Orion realised that many other faces were familiar to him. They peered back at him from the past and present; from countless ages of the world, the dutiful subjects of his endless reign.

He saw an old spellweaver, her eyes clouded by age. She was one of the few who had not abandoned her place by the fires and he realised it was because her sight was gone. Princess Asphalia, he thought with a shock, remembering the clear-eyed beauty she had once been. He looked to her side and saw her husband, Prince Elatior – the one they called the Enchanter. Despite the terror he must be feeling, Elatior looked just as Orion remembered him: gaunt, immobile features with lidded, disdainful eyes. There was something vague and insubstantial about the Enchanter. The morning light shone through him, as though he were a figure painted on canvas, rather than a corporeal being of flesh and bone. He and his wife were drifting a few feet from the ground, shrouded in tendrils of rippling light. Sprawled around them were their servants and slaves, whimpering into their robes. Orion felt a vague sadness at seeing Asphalia so diminished and turned his gaze elsewhere.

On the other side of the clearing he saw another familiar face: a low-browed, powerful-looking warrior, with a broad, bare chest and thick bronze torques coiled around his biceps. The torques had been cleverly wrought to resemble eagle wings, sweeping up from his arms, but the most striking thing about him was the ritual scarring that covered his face: deep, circular grooves that spiralled down from his forehead and surrounded his eyes, adding to his ferocious appearance.

'Prince Haldus,' growled Orion, glimpsing memories of the warrior in battle, riding an enormous bird of prey. 'A rider of hawks.'

As he studied Prince Haldus's intricately scarred face, Orion recalled the name of the warrior's home, way up in the Pine Crags: Arum Tor. He was about to call out, and demand that the warrior introduce himself, but then he noticed something odd. Behind the warrior from Arum Tor was another pair of familiar faces. They were dressed in pale yellow robes edged with intricate copper thread, and they wore expressions of the most absurd haughtiness. Lady Ordaana, he recalled, fixing his gaze on one of them. Her robes were dishevelled and torn, but it was not that Orion found strange; most of the celebrants bore some sign of their night-long excesses. No, it was something else he found odd. She had the most curious expression on her face. Whilst everyone else was either staring at the ground in fear or peering anxiously at him, Lady Ordaana had her eyes locked on the glittering vision at his side. She was staring at the Queen with the most intense passion.

Orion stepped forwards, causing several nobles to gasp and scramble away. He intended to summon Ordaana to his side when yet another familiar face caught his eye.

He laughed as he realised it was Atolmis. It seemed absurd that he had recently been so afraid of the horned rider. Atolmis managed to briefly meet his master's eye, looking up at him with an expression of awe and pride. He towered over the assembled nobles, but Orion, in turn, towered over him.

'You will grow stronger yet,' said Ariel, speaking inside his head once more. 'Come midsummer, and the great conjunction, you will become something more. You will return here to claim your weapons and begin the Great, Eternal Hunt.' Her voice was full of pride. 'Even the forest will not hold you.'

Orion closed his eyes and let out a long, rumbling sigh of pleasure, picturing all the glories that lay ahead of him. Then looked back at Atolmis, and remembered how he had transformed him. He strode forwards and grasped Atolmis's shoulder. Then, after a moment's thought, he took his spear.

Atolmis shook his head and rose to his feet. 'My-my lord,' he stammered. 'Such a weapon is not worthy of you.'

Orion nodded. 'It is worthy.' He tightened his grip on Atolmis's shoulder and stared at him in silence. Then he turned away and noticed a pair of tall, serpentine thrones, made of knotted roots, placed beside the Oak of Ages. He thudded across the grass and slumped in one of them, still cradling Atolmis's spear.

Ariel followed and sat beside him. Then she nodded at the huddled crowd, indicating that the rites could continue.

After a few minutes musicians emerged from the trees, plucking hesitantly at harps and breathing lightly across their flutes. Being careful to avoid Orion's thunderous gaze, the bravest of the highborn crept forwards and knelt at Ariel's feet, proffering gifts of honey and wild flowers and hanging delicate wooden beads across the arms of her throne.

Seeing that Orion made no move to attack, more of the asrai returned from the trees, joining drums and voices to the odd, lilting tune. As Ariel's sad smile washed over them, the highborn grew more confident and soon they were whirling back and forth across the grass, pounding their drums with wild abandon and leaping across the balefires.

As the sun rose slowly into the sky, the birds of the forest joined their voices to the celebrations and Orion remembered what it was to be warm. For a while he watched the dancing and the rituals with bemused indifference, happy to know that the Queen was being worshipped as she had been for countless centuries. Her handmaidens had emerged from the trees – sylph-like mirrors of her splendour, who fussed and fawned over her golden limbs, adjusting her tresses, whispering secrets into her ears and causing her musical laughter to ring out across the clearing. She saw Orion watching and smiled back at him, pursing her lips as though they were sharing a private joke.

Orion's attention drifted and he let his gaze wander over the weapon in his hands. As he studied the grain of the wood, a face suddenly drifted into a view – a scene from a half-forgotten memory. The face was as pale and gnarled as the birch wood and, as it grew in his mind, Orion felt a terrible dread, welling up from the core of his being. The sound of the singing faded away as the ashen face glared back at him, filled with scorn. Who is it? he thought. Who doubts me? As his panic grew, Orion hunched over the spear, gripping it so tightly that it began to splinter and crack.

Ariel looked over at him and her smile faltered. She moved her handmaidens aside and leant towards her king. 'Orion, my love?'

Orion did not hear but kept glaring at the spear. A low growl rumbled up from the depths of his chest. Who is it?

Then a single voice rang out through the din of the spring rites. Orion's sharpened senses picked out two words amongst thousands; two syllables that caused him to sit up in his throne: 'the Wrach'. The name released a torrent of images into Orion's mind. He pictured the creatures he had seen on the far side of the frozen pond, all the strange beings that had found him so badly wanting; the blind old man, wreathed in fog, called the Wrach was just one of them. Orion's stomach knotted as he recalled the child with autumn leaves in his hair; the lumbering, wooden giants; the revolting toad; the stag; the serene, doubting wolf; all the lords of the forest; all the bestial judges that doubted his strength to rule. As he remembered their scornful faces, their terrible accusations flooded his ears. 'There is a cloud hanging over his future,' said one voice. 'He is weak,' said another. Orion's panic grew. If he failed, Ariel's rule would end. She would die. He was sure of it. All those centuries they had shared would mean nothing. Their lives would wither and fade. He had to prove the creatures wrong. He had to prove his strength. He lurched to his feet, his heart pounding as he jabbed his spear at the crowd, scattering handmaidens and nobles as he lurched across the grass.

'Who said that?' he howled.

The light in the clearing dimmed and a strange groaning sound came from the surrounding trees.

The asrai stared at Orion in abject terror and even Khoron Belidae ceased reciting his endless poem.

Ariel's handmaidens turned to her with questioning glances, but she looked just as confused as anyone else present. She leant forwards with a question on her lips but before she could speak Orion roared again.

'Who said "the Wrach"?' Orion's enormous body shook with rage and several nearby branches cracked and splintered. The light dimmed even more and a deep, creaking rumble came from beneath the ground. Some of the nobles began bolting for the trees. Others dropped back to their knees, terrified of the daemonic being in their midst.

Only one figure remained standing, unbowed by the strange pall that had flooded the clearing. It was a stranger; tall and lean and clad in a long black cloak. As the nobles scattered around him, he waited in silence, dark and gaunt as a crow.

Orion fixed his blazing glare on the youth. His senses seemed already to have passed beyond the merely physical and he knew immediately that the stranger was not of noble blood. He was a common bard and should never have been admitted to the rites of Ostaliss – not without an invitation from the Queen. Orion sensed a mystery in him. Why did he stare back so proudly?

'You?' bellowed Orion, thudding across the grass and jabbing the spear at the hooded figure.

The bard staggered under the weight of the question.

'Who are you?' demanded Orion.

As Orion approached, the stranger could not hold his gaze and was forced to lower his head. 'My lord,' he replied, his voice trembling. 'I am Finavar. I am... well, that is... in Locrimere they call me the Darkling Prince.'

Orion heard a gasp from his right. He turned to see the couple he had noticed earlier. Lord Beldeas and Lady Ordaana dropped their looks of haughty disdain and replaced them with expressions of stunned disbelief.

'Did you bring *this* to the Queen's glade?' he asked, rounding on them.

Lord Beldeas's eyes seemed to hide beneath his vast expanse of forehead. 'My lord, I-I...' As he tried to face the demigod looming over him, Beldeas's reply became a stream of incoherent apologies.

'Lady Ordaana?' said Ariel, gliding across the grass and taking the hand of her former handmaiden. She pulled Ordaana close, her face full of affection and surprise. 'Is it really you? I did not see you, hiding back here.' There was pity in her voice. 'You have returned, after so many years.' She squeezed Ordaana's hand. 'They told me of the fire.'

Ordaana's usual refinement and poise abandoned her. Her flawless skin flushed pink and she attempted an awkward smile that did not suit her angular features. 'My queen,' she said, managing at least to maintain her crisp, icy diction. 'After what happened, I did not know if you would care to see me.'

Ariel closed her eyes for a moment, before throwing her arms around Ordaana's tall, brittle body. 'My love does not fade so easily, Ordaana.' She glanced back at the handmaidens crowded around the root thrones. 'You may not be my hand-maiden, but you will always be my friend.'

Ordaana looked over at the handmaidens. Her gaze rested briefly on one in particular: the Queen's new favourite, Laelia. 'Thank you,' she replied, not quite managing to hide the pain in her voice.

Ariel frowned and was about to say something more when Orion interrupted.

'Who *is* this?' he demanded, grabbing Finavar by the shoulder and hauling him closer.

Seeing that her husband was still unable to speak, Ordaana replied for him, keeping her gaze somewhere near Orion's blood-splattered hooves. 'He is not here by our bidding, I assure you, my lord. I can only imagine–'

'Eremon allowed me to come,' exclaimed Finavar, with his hood trapped in Orion's enormous fist. He tried to look at his king, but one glance at such close quarters made his head pound. To his horror, he realised that blood had started rushing from his nose and ears. He turned to Lord Beldeas with a pleading expression. 'He agreed that my message was urgent enough to warrant the interruption. We need help. Locrimere needs help.'

Lord Beldeas turned to his wife, horrified that he might be associated with someone who had earned the wrath of Orion. 'I assure you we have nothing to do with this insolent rogue,' he said, facing Ordaana as he spoke, unable to address the magnificent beings looming over him. He clasped his hands together. 'The name is familiar, but I would *never* have summoned him into the presence of your majesties; not during the rites of the Even-Night.'

Finavar wiped the blood from his face and shook his head. 'Eremon needs help.' He raised his voice, sure that the great

Orion would help if he could just make him understand. 'The cloven ones are marching on Locrimere, my king. It is a host greater than anything I have ever heard of. Eremon cannot hold them alone, but if you were to lead the Wild Hunt against them, they would be destroyed.'

The colour drained from the faces of Beldeas and Ordaana. Finavar's breach of court protocol was horrific. How could he think to advise his king?

'Ridiculous,' said Ordaana, raising her chin. 'A few goat-headed outsiders are no threat to Locrimere.'

Orion stooped so that his face was just inches from Finavar's. 'What do you know of the Wrach?' he asked, ignoring Finavar's talk of invasion.

Finavar struggled in Orion's grip, straining to avoid the King's dreadful gaze. 'Eremon, the captain of Locrimere's kinbands, allowed me to bring you this news. He cannot stand against such numbers.' He looked over at Beldeas again. 'They are already tearing through the southern glades. They have some kind of–'

Orion stood up straight, grabbing Finavar by the throat and lifting him from the ground. 'The Wrach,' he said, his voice low and dangerous.

Finavar gasped and began to cough up thick gobbets of blood. Beldeas and Ordaana backed away, trying to distance themselves from their subject.

'I needed to reach you fast,' groaned Finavar, trying to stretch his face away from Orion's. 'I knew that only you could help.' Finavar waved back towards the trees. 'My brother advised that we take the Dark Paths.'

Orion nodded. He was aware that the bards of Loec had their own routes through the forest; some safer than others.

'We travelled by the Tenderfoot Way.'

Orion gave no sign of recognition, so Finavar continued, still trying desperately to avoid his gaze. 'Such paths are hazardous. One may travel leagues and still emerge on the day after you entered.' He paused. 'Or three centuries earlier.'

Orion tightened his grip on Finavar's throat.

'The Wrach is also known as the Blind Guide!' exclaimed Finavar, kicking his legs wildly. 'He leads where sight is no use.' His voice became a thin croak. 'He has a piece of stone for an eye. It leads him through the forest.'

Orion stared hard at Finavar and lowered his voice, recalling the milky irises of the figure beyond the pool. 'The *Blind Guide?*'

Finavar tried to nod, seeing that he had finally caught Orion's attention. 'His eyes... are... They are... as white as pearls.'

Orion remained motionless for a moment, with Finavar still dangling from his grip. Then he nodded and dropped him. 'Show me.'

Finavar thudded onto the ground, clutching his neck and coughing violently.

Ariel stepped to Orion's side. 'The celebrations have only just begun.' She placed her hand on Orion's arm and smiled. 'Who is this Blind Guide, that would take you away from your queen?'

Orion backed away and lifted his chin, looking at Ariel down the length of his regal nose. 'There are spirits in the forest who would deny our rule.' His eyes blazed. 'I will return, as soon as I have proven myself.'

Ariel's smile faltered. 'My love, what do you mean? The trees are full of spirits. They are as much a part of us as we are of them. You do not need to prove anything.'

Orion nodded at Finavar and the youth clambered to his feet, staggering off towards the trees, still coughing and spluttering.

'I will return as soon as I can,' repeated Orion, refusing to meet the Queen's gaze and storming off into the forest.

As he shouldered his way through the low-hanging branches, Orion tried to keep his gaze fixed on the slight figure of Finavar, bounding through the trees ahead of him, but he was haunted by visions of the beasts beyond the pool. They crawled from his memory and watched him from the branches and scrub, whispering accusations and sneering at him. They looked so real, so hateful, that Orion began to snarl and lunge as he ran, struggling to believe they were illusions. Finally, smashing through the bracken, he saw an even stranger vision: himself, bloody, but proud and clutching what looked like a piece of dark, raw meat – a glistening red lump, trailing a cluster of pale, artery-like tubes.

Amongst all the strangeness of the morning, this latest vision did not even seem odd, but the defiance Orion saw in his own eyes filled him with determination. 'You are bound for glory,' the other Orion seemed to be saying. 'You cannot fail.' He nodded at himself and picked up his pace, fixing his stare back on the hooded bard, allowing the beasts to fade and wither back into the shadows.

After a while he heard horses and began to smile. As his riders approached, thundering through the trees to his side, Orion realised that only two things mattered.

He was alive.

He was hunting.

Finavar scrambled back through the trees, coughing and spitting blood as he staggered through the undergrowth. 'What have I done?' he muttered, hearing the sound of Orion behind him. After a few minutes he paused and leant against a tree, plucking up the courage to look over his shoulder. Orion was still there, striding after him, his twisted antlers tearing through the branches and his hooves pounding across the quickly thawing earth.

Finavar clutched his shock of dyed hair as he saw other shapes emerging from the gloom: huge, ivy-clad riders, with tall birch-wood helmets and spiral horns, riding pale stallions. 'By the gods, Fin,' he muttered, lurching on through the trees. 'Orion.' He laughed in amazement. 'I am leading the King to war.'

Finavar picked up his pace, keen to impress Orion with his skill. As he ran, he let out a low whistle. After a few minutes he glimpsed a pair of small, dark shapes, dashing through the undergrowth ahead. He grinned with bloody teeth. 'Find the others,' he called. 'Take me back to the old stones.'

Orion and his riders followed Finavar for the rest of the morning, maintaining an ominous silence. The only sound was that of hooves and breaking wood.

Finally, Finavar leapt down into a small rocky crevasse ending in a jagged cluster of stunted hawthorn trees. The sun was now directly overhead and as he scrambled down the slope, Finavar watched Mormo and Mauro race across the rocks and halt beside a group of figures huddled in the shade of the trees. At the sight of Finavar's guides, they leapt to their feet and hurried out into the sunlight, drawing their swords and calling his name.

Alhena moved the fastest, her face taut and fierce. Next came the boy. This far from Locrimere, his brother seemed more childlike than ever, with his anxious eyes and small, delicate face. Behind them came Thuralin, limping across the rocks and wearing his perpetual, crumpled scowl.

Alhena stopped a few feet away from Finavar and cursed as

she saw the blood smeared across his face. Then her mouth dropped open as she saw the figures that had appeared at the edge of the crevasse.

'The Wild Hunt,' she muttered, allowing the tips of her blades to clatter against the ground.

'Stand aside!' cried Finavar, as he hurried past. 'Hide yourselves.' He clapped his brother on the shoulder and grinned at him. 'Orion is amongst us!' Then he shoved him towards the slope.

The blood on his face, and the towering figures riding down the slope behind him were more than enough warning. Jokleel and the others scrambled up the incline and hid themselves from view as he charged on towards the clump of trees.

Finavar stumbled to a halt, looking at a cluster of sun-bleached stones. He grimaced as he studied them. To travel by the Dark Paths had been his brother's idea, and it was the boy who had known about the stones. Finavar shook his head. There was something odd about Jokleel. There was an old wisdom in those, large, thoughtful eyes; a wisdom Finavar had never quite understood. When Jokleel explained that the stones were portals of some kind Finavar had not even thought to doubt him, or wonder how he knew such things.

The sound of voices dragged Finavar back into the present. The riders had dismounted and, along with the King, they were marching down the gulley towards him.

Finavar hurried on, making for the tall, crooked dolmen: an enormous slab of granite, supported by two others, forming a window onto the trees at the far side of the gulley.

He came to a halt beneath it and lowered his gaze, feeling his pulse start to pound as the riders approached.

He felt Orion's presence looming over him as the horned giant stepped beneath the dolmen. The King had to stoop to fit his antlers beneath the slumping capstone. The sound of his breathing echoed between the stones.

'The Wrach lives here?'

Finavar cowered from Orion's rumbling tones, noticing as he did so that his friends were peering down at him in disbelief from the top of the incline.

'This is where the Wrach left us,' he gasped, finding it suddenly hard to breathe. 'These stones are one of the gateways to his paths. He has a key – a black stone that he keeps on the end of a staff.'

Orion said nothing for a few seconds, scraping one of his talons across the rounded, dusty stones. The sun was beating fully on them now and it was possible to make out the remains of a circular inscription: an ancient hieroglyph of some kind, depicting branches knotted together in a thick wreath. Orion sighed. It was a heavy, growling sound that could have implied pleasure or irritation.

'Torr-Goholoth,' said Atolmis, removing his wooden helmet and stepping beneath the dolmen. Like Orion, he had to stoop, but rather than irritation, there was a note of excitement in his voice. 'That would make sense.'

Orion turned to face Atolmis. 'You know this place?'

Atolmis frowned, momentarily confused by his lord's ignorance. Then he recalled that Orion was effectively a newborn. 'There are many such standing stones buried in the forest. Naieth, the Queen's prophetess, sometimes speaks of them. She refers to them by an old name, the Sínann-Torr, but in truth I think even she knows very little about them. They are hard to find, and old; older even than our own waystones. Naieth says they are older than the forest itself.' Atolmis shrugged. 'I know nothing of that, but I do know that they are restless – especially at this time of year. They follow no rules of nature.

We could return tomorrow and find this place gone.' He fixed his black, bottomless eyes on his king and pulled back his lips in a revolting grin, revealing his long yellow incisors. 'Torr-Goholoth is rarely far from its twin, Torr-Marloch. You might remember that stone, even if you do not recall these.'

Orion frowned. His memories were still a jumble of fragments. At the mention of Torr-Marloch he saw a glimpse of an earlier life. He saw himself as he was centuries earlier, drenched in blood, standing on a flame-licked rock, holding a lifeless, broken corpse aloft, egged on by a roaring crowd. He nodded as the scene grew clearer in his head, but almost immediately, a fresher memory replaced it. He saw the beasts from the pool, sneering at him as he staggered back into the water, pleading for their faith.

Orion forgot the stones and turned to his equerry with a look of sudden recognition. 'You could take me back to them!'

The smile vanished from Atolmis's face. 'Who?'

'You know who. You let them judge me.' Orion's voice was hoarse with bitterness. 'You led me to them. You could do it again.'

Comprehension dawned in Atolmis's black eyes. 'Ah, I see.' He hesitated and glanced at Finavar, unwilling to speak in front of a lowborn. 'You saw that which no mortal could comprehend. You saw the Brúidd.' There was a note of awe in Atolmis's voice. 'The Great Gathering. The portal is open once a year – at the time of the trial. If we were to return to the pool now, you would find nothing but weeds and mud.'

Orion continued staring at Atolmis.

Atolmis shrugged. 'My knowledge is limited. The Queen could tell you more. My leaf-liege, you saw the remains of what came before us. You saw the last remnants of the Council of Beasts.'

Orion bridled at his servant's humble tone. 'What came before is unimportant.' He clenched his fists. 'I am here now.' He grabbed the ivy that snaked from beneath Atolmis's skin and hauled him closer, until their faces were almost touching. 'Who rules this forest?' His voice was a furious whisper. 'This Brúidd, or your king?'

Atolmis hesitated. There was fear in his eyes, but it was mixed with something else. 'There are different ways to rule,' he answered finally. 'They say that Ariel consorts with one of them: a prehistoric spirit called Sativus. He is chief amongst the Brúidd. He–'

Orion shoved him back against the old stones, filling the air with dust. The name Sativus filled him with nausea, throwing him back to the awful scene by the pool. 'How can animals question my right to power?'

Atolmis shook his head fiercely. 'No, my lord, you do not understand. They are not animals. They are not at all what they appear. Their physical–'

'You!' snapped Orion, whirling around and looking back at Finavar. 'How do I use these rocks? How do I find this Wrach?'

Finavar blanched and raised his hands. 'I do not know for sure.' He looked anxiously up at the ridge, where his brother was hiding. The truth was that the boy was the only one who had known what to do, but Finavar did not have the heart to summon such a gentle youth into the presence of Orion. He tried to meet the King's gaze again, desperate to know his mind. Finally he managed to bear the briefest glimpse. Orion's eyes were two furious slits of emerald, glittering with sylvan fire. Finavar gasped as they bored into his mind. 'We waited,' he replied, turning away, 'until sunset. Then we hummed an old melody. And then we slept. The Wrach was willing, so when we awoke, at midnight, the branches had sprung to life.'

'Branches?'

Finavar nodded and waved at the faded circular symbol on the stone. 'The Wrach's key unlocks whatever sorcery links these stones.' He grinned apologetically. 'I do not understand how.'

Orion turned back to Atolmis with a raised eyebrow.

Atolmis studied Finavar, cowering in his spiny black robes on the floor of the dolmen, gazing lovingly at his king. 'The bard speaks the truth, my lord. I have heard many such tales. They say the Wrach can manipulate the forest's hidden spaces. You yourself once told me that the Wrach has a talisman – a fragment of a magic stone, with which he commands these old ruins. He is powerful.' He paused, sounding unnerved. 'But such things have never concerned you before.'

Orion did not seem to register this last comment, distracted by the mention of the Wrach's stone. He recalled how the spirit's odd, elongated fingers cascaded over the head of his staff. 'I cannot wait until nightfall.'

Atolmis shrugged. 'If the Wrach allows you onto the Dark Paths, you will have all the time you need. You could return to Ariel's court before you even left.'

Orion nodded vaguely, but his thoughts had drifted into the past again. He felt a chill of shame as he remembered pleading with the Brúidd. 'I will do anything,' he had said, like a cringing infant. The shame of it was almost too much for him to bear and as he turned back to Atolmis it took all his strength to resist tearing him apart. 'Then I will wait.' He crouched on the rock and turned to Finavar. 'And you will sing.'

After Orion left the clearing the celebrants waltzed on, and after watching the King disappear into the trees, Ariel herself joined the dance.

The musicians drummed with renewed enthusiasm as the Queen turned from the trees and, with a single beat of her delicate wings, dropped right into the heart of the dance. She spun and twirled across a carpet of flower petals as her handmaidens formed a circle around her, holding hands and spinning in the opposite direction. As they danced, the Queen and her handmaidens flickered with silver fire, lighting up the awed faces of the highborn who pressed closer. To those who had remained awake it seemed that they were in the presence of stars and comets; the heavens themselves seemed to be rotating before them on the grass.

As she danced, Ariel closed her eyes and allowed her attention to wander. While others sang and talked, she remained quiet, revelling in the eternal sameness of her court. At first she could only hear the fawning tributes of those subjects who were nearest to her, but her senses quickly moved on to the more interesting conversations being held beneath the trees. She smiled to herself. Gossip, she decided, was as unchanging as the cycle of the seasons. She heard one noble boasting of some adorable new slaves: human children, snatched from the outskirts of the forest. Their infancy would now be eternal, blessed, and spent in the service of asrai lords. 'They have such intelligence in their eyes,' exclaimed the noble. 'I swear, you could almost believe they were born in the forest.'

Then another perennial topic caught Ariel's ear: the folly of youth. The shocking appearance of the wardancer, Finavar, was the subject of much debate. They were outraged by his flaunting of protocol and his arrogant demeanour; most of all, though, they were galled by his assumed title. 'The Darkling Prince!' they scoffed. 'Have you ever heard of such a thing? From a rough-hewn lowborn, with no trace of nobility in his blood!' Ariel's smile grew as she heard the force of their contempt. She heard mention of all the usual scandals: whispered secrets, forbidden trysts and shameful, hidden vices. Lord Beldeas's name was on everyone's lips. He had spent the winter amusing himself in a manner that delighted the other nobles. They feigned disapproval, of course, but it was all too clear that they revelled in his exploits. Ariel resisted the urge to laugh as she heard Beldeas's velvety tones, not far from where he was being discussed. He was boasting to one of her servants, telling her how he had recently produced a wonderful piece of artwork, using nothing but moths.

Ariel spun faster through the dance and threw her thoughts even wider. As she listened harder, she heard one refrain that did not seem quite so amusing. Buried amongst the idle notes of flattery and gossip, there was another, darker theme. At first she disregarded it, but the same phrases were repeated so many times, eventually she started to pay heed.

'Outsiders, right on our borders. I've never seen such a thing.'

'Creatures of Chaos, marching straight through the heart of the Iuliss Vale.'

'Bull-headed things. Easy enough to kill, of course, but we found the last of them near Drúne Fell. How could they have reached such a place?'

Ariel's smile faded. The highborn only mentioned these events briefly before moving on to other, more exciting matters, but Ariel felt unnerved by them. It sounded as though some of the kindreds had suffered heavy losses. Outsiders had been seen across the length of the forest, and some of the sites mentioned were right in its heart. The Iuliss Vale was a few short leagues away. The peaks of Drúne Fell were even closer. Such places had not seen violence since the Winter of Woe. The thought that they might be changed in some way appalled her.

As the dance spiralled around her, Ariel allowed all the strength and passion of the nobles to flood her mind, cleansing it of worry. Their thoughts bled through her like sunshine piercing a leaf. She closed her eyes as she danced and let them lift her mind up, over the treetops and down into the surrounding valleys. Spring was already taking hold. Shoots were slicing through the loamy soil; tiny spears of green were sprouting through dead, coppery bracken. The dance whirled faster and Ariel's thoughts flew further. The crowns and domes of her kingdom spread out before her and the Queen felt all the potency and permanence of the forest. The thought calmed her. The outside world had long been pitted against the asrai, but her rule was as endless as the stars. Besides, Orion was born again and nothing else mattered. With the King by her side, she could endure anything.

Ariel was about to begin another dance, when she saw a tall, antlered figure, striding back through the trees. 'Orion,' she gasped, grinning with relief. 'You decided to stay!'

CHAPTER TWELVE

The rock had not been easy to find. The indifferent centuries had left it as hunched as a crone, and clad in thick, velvet robes of lichen and moss. Only the most determined gaze could have picked it out, hidden as it was amongst a grove of solemn, moonlit boughs.

The Blood-kin were nothing if not determined.

Most of them remained hidden beneath the surrounding trees, glaring suspiciously at the old rock, but three stepped close enough to touch the circle carved into its surface. The first was a swaggering brute with a broad, hunched back and a meat cleaver in each hand. It was dressed in filthy rags and scraps of tattered skin and, at first glance, looked no different from those beneath the trees, with a broad, humanoid torso and a snorting bovine head. It was only as the monster emerged from the shadows that its particular mutation was revealed. Its waist rose from the scarred, muscled body of an enormous bull.

'Another firestone,' it said. Its voice was a low grunt and as it spoke it scratched furiously at its flanks. Weevils and mites glittered in its hair and scurried across its long, wide back. 'The sticks told us right, again.'

The second of the three figures nodded in agreement. It was short, slight and leaning heavily on a crooked staff. This creature was much harder to discern. Its tattered robes were midnight black and as its hooves pounded across the clearing the light rippled away. It was as though even the moons were reluctant to examine it too closely.

'*I* told you right, Ghorgus,' it rasped. Its voice sounded like a badly oiled hinge.

The four-legged monster gave no reply and turned to the third figure. This one was taller than the other two. Its origins were clearly just as vile, but its bestial hindquarters were clad in thick plates of armour and its chest was almost as wide as the stone looming over them.

'What does Morgharon say?' asked the creature with the body of a bull.

The third figure drew itself to its full height, clearly revelling in the way it dwarfed the other two. It lifted a roughly hewn club, bristling with shards of iron, and waved it back the way they had come. 'Morgharon has brought the Blood-kin here.' Then it pounded the club against its metal-clad chest, indicating the foul glyphs daubed across the iron plates. A dull clanging sound filled the clearing. 'Morgharon is in the eye of the gods. Morgharon sent the fae back to their flowers. Even the hooded dancer could not stand against me. *Morgharon* deserves to share the prize this time.'

The creatures waiting beneath the trees heard Morgharon's claims and began to snort and low with excitement. As they pressed closer, raising their cruel weapons, it became clear that there were as many beastmen around the stone as trees. They stared hungrily at the three figures, sensing that it might be time for a new chieftain.

The four-legged creature called Ghorgus nodded. Its reply was full of grudging respect. 'Perhaps Morgharon *has* earned the right to touch the firestone this time.' Ghorgus turned to the shadowy figure with the staff. 'What does Belakhor the Unseen think?'

Belakhor waved its staff at the trees. Vague, enormous shadows were arrayed around the clearing – taller even than the old oaks that surrounded the stone. 'We can sip at the flames, but the full draught is not for us.'

Ghorgus nodded eagerly but Morgharon sneered, clearly forming other ideas. 'Look at how that boar-headed oaf pissed his chance away. You should put your trust in Morgharon.'

This claim was met by a ripple of grunts and laughs from the figures under the trees.

Ghorgus looked amused rather than threatened, and turned back to the hooded figure with the staff.

Belakhor the Unseen stepped closer to the stone and planted its staff in the ground, clutching the knotted wood with both hands. Even standing in the centre of the clearing, the creature was hard to see. It was as though the shadows had become caught in its robes and dragged along with them. The beastman began to mutter under its breath. A series of repugnant, guttural snorts fell from its hood, and the figures beneath the trees began to shuffle and pant, excited by the power rippling through their fur.

Belakhor barked, belled and snorted, reciting its spell with such force that its staff began to rattle. The wood was draped with an odd collection of trophies and fetishes: snail shells and bird skulls clattered against gore-drenched rags and the remnants of a human ribcage. As the spell continued, the rattling grew louder, Belakhor's words became more urgent and a pale glow began to emerge from beneath its hood. Finally the sha-man let out a bitter curse and lowered its staff. 'This stone is too big. The fae-magic cannot escape. It must be moved back. It has to fall.'

Morgharon strode forwards, barging the other two aside with its enormous bulk. 'Morgharon is in the eye of the gods.' It growled at the crowds beneath the trees. '*Morgharon* will move the stone.'

The snorts and jeers grew louder, egging Morgharon on, but Ghorgus made no comment as the brute dropped its club on the ground and slammed its shoulders against the old rock.

Belakhor lifted its staff and continued the spell, muttering the words with even more urgency as Morgharon strained against the stone. The staff pulsed with light again and this time the waystone responded. The moss beneath Morgharon's fingers lit up in a circular, knotted design.

As the stone flared brighter it illuminated the beastman's snarling features, revealing the determination in its tiny, feral eyes. Morgharon began to groan, applying more and more pres-sure to the rock, leaning its whole, enormous weight against it.

Then, as Morgharon's groans became a furious howl, the chief-tain, Ghorgus, plunged its meat cleavers deep into Morgharon's back.

The giant figure grunted in surprise and slumped heavily against the rock.

The creatures beneath the trees gasped.

Belakhor the Unseen showed no sign of surprise as the Blood-kin's chieftain wrenched its meat cleavers free and struck again, hacking this time into Morgharon's thick neck.

The bray-shaman's magic swelled as the giant figure dropped to its knees, spraying blood but still clutching the rune-covered stone.

Ghorgus's cleavers rose and fell for a third time, hacking Morgharon's head from its shoulders and sending an even thicker fountain of blood gushing over the stone.

The blood glittered in the moonlight as the chieftain grabbed the severed head from the ground and turned to face the crowds beneath the trees, holding the still gasping head aloft.

As the creatures flinched back into the shadows, Ghorgus's four hooves drummed against the soil. 'Ghorgus is the king! Four-legs *is* the Blood-kin!' The chieftain galloped towards the watching crowds and yelled ecstatically. 'Who else wants my crown?'

As Ghorgus thudded and cantered around the clearing, waving Morgharon's severed head, the warherd raised their axes and clubs and roared their approval. 'Four-legs!' they howled, stamping their hooves on the ground and rattling their weapons, filling the forest with a dreadful din. 'Four-legs! Four-legs!'

Ghorgus's victory dance was infectious and soon the beast-men plucked up the courage to approach, emerging from the trees and clambering over the stone. They danced gleefully on Morgharon's corpse and stole pieces of armour, quick to forget the hopes they had recently invested in the brutish giant. Then they grabbed leather flasks from their tattered robes and doused Ghorgus in spirits, before drinking thirstily.

Only one figure remained indifferent to the orgy: the small, hooded shape of Belakhor the Unseen, hunched next to the stone, still muttering furiously and clutching its crooked staff. Morgharon's blood had filled the hieroglyph on the stone's surface with fire. After a while the whole stone began to pulse with pale, glowing mist, lighting up the vile celebrations that surrounded it. As the mist flashed brighter Belakhor looked around for the chieftain.

Ghorgus had a flask in each hand and was glugging furiously

at the pungent spirits. After every few swallows it had to pause to laugh, recalling how easily Morgharon had fallen for the trick devised by Belakhor.

'Ghorgus,' called Belakhor, lifting its voice over the din.

The chieftain lowered the flask and snorted furiously. 'Is it ready?'

Belakhor nodded, tapping the blood-slick stone with its staff. There was a note of excitement in its screeching voice. 'There is more here than any of them.' The creature snickered in its hood. 'Morgharon's blood has served you well, Four-legs.' The monster glanced at the shadows looming over the clearing. 'Take your reward before we feed our pets.'

Ghorgus thudded up to the stone. 'Now?' it asked, readying its meat cleavers.

The hooded figure nodded and uttered one last, foul syllable.

As the mist flared, Ghorgus Four-legs hacked down with both cleavers and the blades clanged against the rock.

There was an explosion of light that sent the chieftain staggering back across the clearing.

Belakhor's frail body was lifted from the ground and slammed into the whirling crowds.

A blinding light filled the clearing, followed almost immediately by pitch darkness. The celebrations ceased and the beastmen fell silent, blinking and cursing as they staggered blindly back towards the trees.

Ghorgus Four-legs lay sprawled on the ground, dazed by the blast and looking vacantly at the branches overhead. Then the creature shook its head and looked down at its bloody cleavers. The pitted metal was now shrouded with the same mist as the old rock. Ghorgus started to laugh. The vapour was even snaking up through the veins in its scarred forearms. 'The fae-magic is in me!'

The hooded bray-shaman hurried over and knelt by the chieftain's side. It threw back its black hood and there was a flash of white as its head was revealed. All that rested on its shoulders was the bleached, bloodstained skull of a ram. 'The firestones are getting more powerful as we get deeper into the forest,' it said, looking at the arched path through the trees ahead of them. 'We are on the right path.' The bray-shaman tapped one of Ghorgus's cleavers with its staff. 'Try it.'

The chieftain leered back at Belakhor and stood up. Then it closed its eyes, raised the weapons to chest height and held them out at arm's length, muttering another vile incantation. The blades pulsed even brighter and spewed thick columns of fog into the trees.

The Blood-kin muttered and hissed, still shocked to see their chieftain using the strange magic of the forest.

Ghorgus's words grew in volume and ferocity and then the chieftain hauled back the meat cleavers towards its chest. The trails of mist lashed back into the clearing, dragging with them clumps of bushes and branches and a whole menagerie of creatures: rats, voles and foxes tumbled across the bloody earth, then scampered back into the shadows as Ghorgus lowered the weapons and allowed the mist to evaporate.

The chieftain turned to the skull-headed shaman with its crimson eyes blazing. 'You were right, Belakhor. This power *is* greater.' Ghorgus bellowed with excitement, jabbing the blazing weapons at the moonlit clouds. 'Four-legs is the king of the forest!'

Belakhor pulled its ram-skull head back beneath its hood and nodded. 'We have reached the greatest of them. The stick-thing was right. We can cease our wandering. The Blood-kin will be homeless no more.'

At this the figures waiting beneath the trees began to howl

again, rattling their weapons against their crude wooden shields and stamping their hooves on the ground.

'Quick,' came a thin, rustling whisper, from somewhere near the stone.

Ghorgus and the others had already lost themselves to another frenzied dance and did not hear the voice for their own hooting din.

Belakhor, however, whirled around and hurried back towards the shattered stones, peering into the shadows.

The shaman was rewarded with a glimpse of a foot-high figure: a tiny cluster of twig-like limbs topped with a tall, skull-shaped head. The spectre glittered as Belakhor crouched next to it.

'What did you say?' hissed Belakhor.

The bundle of sticks giggled as it clattered jerkily up onto the smouldering remains of the stones, slipping briefly in Morgharon's cooling blood. 'The firestones are not a toy, cloven one,' it said in its odd, rasping whisper. It reached the tallest fragment of stone and pointed at the giant shadows waiting in the trees. 'Feed *them*.'

'Of course.' Belakhor stooped closer to the spirit. 'And then do we unleash what we have gathered?'

'Not yet! You must come further! There are bigger firestones.'

Ghorgus noticed the strange light and rushed over. 'What does it want?' The chieftain's voice was full of suspicion and it lifted one of its still-glowing cleavers.

Belakhor stopped the chieftain with a raised hand. 'Wait. It says there are even bigger stones, further in the forest.'

Ghorgus sucked its yellowed fangs and lowered its voice, staring at the trees. 'And then the forest will be ours?'

The flickering shape on the stone nodded at the shadows. 'Soon you will have all the power of the firestones. Just a few more to go. Locrimere is all that stands in your way.' It clenched one of its tiny fists. *'Crush* it.'

Ghorgus frowned. 'What is Locrimere?'

The spirit giggled again and nodded at Ghorgus's meat cleavers. 'A sheath for your blades.'

CHAPTER THIRTEEN

Few sounds could have dragged Caorann from such a deep sleep, but the bright, ringing tone of Eremon's war horn was one of them. The sound cut into his nightmares and dragged him, trembling, from his bed of skins and straw.

'Fin, wait,' he groaned, lurching naked across a gloomy chamber, pursued by dreams of towering, goat-headed monsters and screaming friends. 'There are too many of them!'

'Wait,' cried a voice, full of alarm.

Caorann staggered and dropped to his knees. Only then did he wonder where he was. He looked around and saw that he was high up in one of Locrimere's lofty spiral towers. Through an opening at the far end of the room he could just glimpse the distant crowns of the forest. The treetops were capped by a sliver of dawn light. Caorann frowned, wondering how long he had slept.

Crooked, calloused fingers clasped his shoulders, catching him just before he dropped onto his face. 'You are too weak, Caorann,' said the voice.

Caorann turned to see a familiar face. 'Elaeus,' he gasped, meeting the concerned gaze of Locrimere's oldest healer.

'Your friends have left you in my care,' said Elaeus, with a gentle smile. 'And I will not incur the wrath of the Darkling Prince. You must rest.'

Caorann's frown deepened. As he looked around he saw dozens of other, similar chambers, but they were all empty. 'Fin has left me behind? Where has he gone?'

Elaeus helped Caorann to his feet and ushered him back to his bed. 'Eremon has allowed him to greet Ariel and Orion with tidings of war.' He frowned. 'A strange decision, if you ask me. Who ever heard of a lowborn demanding an audience with our immortal sovereigns?'

Caorann flopped back into the bed and closed his eyes, trying to recall how he had arrived in Elaeus's care. His chest was tightly bandaged in linen and every inch of his frame was bruised, but he could not for the life of him remember why. Panic gripped him as he peered into a featureless void. Then the fog began to clear and he saw a brief glimpse of battle. He gasped. 'The cloven ones. They are in league with the forest.' The horn rang out again and Caorann opened his eyes, grabbing Elaeus by the shoulders. 'What is it? What's happening?'

Elaeus shook his head and smiled. 'There is nothing to be afraid of, Caorann. Eremon is summoning a gathering of the kindreds.' He looked around at the jars of salve, tassels of dried herbs and poultices hanging from the walls. 'If my skills lay in another direction I might be able to see for myself.' He waved in the direction of Locrimere's southernmost borders, and a note of awe softened the time-worn gravel of his voice. 'I imagine it will be just like the harp songs you and Finavar like to sing. There will be a great, glorious battle. Eremon has been preparing for days. The blood-rites have all been observed. I hear that he has the steel of Khaine in his eyes.'

The healer clenched his fist and stared at it for a second, wishing it clutched a longbow. His frail old body grew tense and he spoke through clenched teeth. 'How wonderful to have a *warrior* at our head for a change.'

Caorann understood the allusion and frowned. 'Then where is Lord Beldeas? And Lady Ordaana?'

Elaeus opened his fist and exhaled, relaxing his muscles. 'They left before Finavar and the rest of your friends.' He sneered. 'They had other matters to attend to. Apparently, it was essential that they see in the new year in the presence of the other highborn, whatever danger might be threatening Locrimere.' A distant look came into his eyes. 'Perhaps they could stay in the Council Glade forever, and leave us in more capable hands.'

Caorann shook his head and was about to reply, but then he wrinkled his nose and scowled. The sharp, acrid smell of burning pitch had entered the chamber.

Elaeus focused back on the present and noticed Caorann's grimace. He looked back over at the opening. 'There *is* something odd on the wind.' He rose from the bed and crossed the room. He had taken no more than a few steps when he gasped and clutched his pale robes. 'By the gods,' he groaned, leaning heavily against the wall.

Caorann climbed to his feet and quickly dressed himself in a loincloth. Then he limped to the healer's side. As he looked out he saw a scene far worse than the nightmares he had just escaped. The coils and curlicues of Locrimere's towers were ablaze. Hundreds of flaming arrows were pouring out of the forest, flickering like fireflies in the early morning gloom.

'How can this be?' gasped Elaeus, leaning out and peering at the fires. 'Why are the sentries not doing something? Where is Eremon?'

Caorann peered at the flashes and sparks erupting in the trees. 'Look!' he snapped, pointing at an odd shimmer of light, mingled in with the flames. 'That is what I saw with Fin. It is just the same.'

Elaeus shook his head desperately. 'I don't understand.'

'The creatures of Chaos have turned the forest against us,' said Caorann, scouring the chamber for his weapons. The two blades were lying near the bed, so he snatched them from the floor and slid them into his belt. Then, with a groan, he lowered himself from the chamber and out onto a walkway, heading for the forest floor.

Elaeus continued shaking his head, watching the distant fires with a shocked expression. Then, after a few minutes, he realised his charge had left and was halfway to the ground. 'Wait!' he cried, leaping out of the chamber and vaulting down through the branches. 'Caorann! You must remain here!'

Caorann gave no reply and hurried on down the walkway. His chest was throbbing painfully but his head was much clearer. As he dropped to the ground, he saw that Locrimere was abandoned. Every glade and avenue was empty. Everyone is at the borders, he thought, hobbling off in that direction. So why is Locrimere going undefended?

Elaeus caught up with him and grabbed his shoulder, forcing him to halt. 'You are too weak to be of any use, Caorann. You need rest!'

Caorann rounded on him with a snarl. 'Am I to lie dozing while outsiders destroy Locrimere?' He shrugged free of Elaeus's grip and pointed at the trees up ahead. There was a waist-high blanket of smoke, drifting beneath the boughs. 'Can *you* rest while our home burns?'

Elaeus looked at the forest and reeled away from Caorann, his face full of anguish.

'Forgive me, old friend,' said Caorann, softening his voice and grabbing his friend's arm. 'I know you meant well, but we must find out what is happening. Perhaps what I saw with Fin may be of some help?'

Elaeus nodded slowly, but was too shocked to reply. He allowed Caorann to lead him on into the smoke, muttering dark oaths under his breath as they went.

A squall of embers followed them as they hurried through the trees and an ominous heat washed over their faces. Soon they heard sounds of battle and the crackling of burning wood. Arrows whistled past, wrapped in pitch-soaked rags and spitting flames. Branches exploded as the arrows struck home and asrai voices rang out, calling desperate commands.

Caorann handed one of his blades to Elaeus and held the other before him like a beacon as he limped through the thickening smoke. The fumes filled his lungs and when he coughed his chest was wracked by a dreadful pain. Elaeus was still at his side though, so Caorann gave no sign that he was struggling and hurried on, holding his hand over his mouth.

After a few more minutes, they began to glimpse slender figures dashing through the trees, some sparsely clad like Caorann and covered in tattoos, others wearing green leather armour and olive-coloured cloaks.

At the sight of Caorann's vivid blue hair and tattooed limbs, one of them cried: 'Bard! Is the Darkling Prince with you?'

Caorann shook his head as he reached a group of guards and realised that he knew the one who had called out. 'Ilbrec,' he said. 'Where is Eremon?' Nausea was washing over him and he felt as though a hot brand was being forced against his chest. As he leant weakly against a tree, he noticed that his linen bandages were dark with blood.

Ilbrec noticed his pain and his eyes filled with sympathy. 'Of course, you are Caorann. I did not recognise you.'

Another wave of flaming arrows whistled through the trees, thudding into trunks and branches all around them, and they ducked behind one of the larger trees.

'Eremon was leading the attack,' gasped Ilbrec, his hands shaking with shock, 'but the Chaos creatures are using sorcery.' His eyes flicked anxiously around the group. 'It is like they have one of our own magi in their ranks.'

'How could that be?' asked one of the other guards, a note of hysteria in his voice.

'It could not be,' stated Caorann flatly. The agony in his chest gave his voice a certainty he did not feel. 'There must be some other explanation. Some other kind of sorcery.'

'But what?' asked Elaeus, leaning closer to Caorann.

'The power comes from the creature that leads them,' gasped Ilbrec, peering back into the smoke. He grimaced. 'It is a vile union of man and bull, and it carries a pair of axes that feed on the forest. They hurl mist into the trees.' He grabbed Elaeus and shook him. 'It captured hundreds of our kin and then–'

'Yes,' interrupted Caorann, placing a hand on Ilbrec's shoulder and trying to calm him. 'I have seen such a thing.' He looked down at his bloody bandages and finally remembered how he had been wounded. 'We must stop this bull-thing, then. It is our only chance.' He stared at Ilbrec. 'Where is it?'

Ilbrec blanched and recoiled from Caorann's grip. 'You cannot stop it!' he cried. 'Did you hear me? It dragged hundreds of guards from the trees. They were butchered in seconds.' He waved his longbow at the arrows whirring through the smoke. 'You have never seen such a host! They are in the thousands, Caorann. Even Eremon could not–'

'Which way?' boomed Caorann, rising to his full height.

Ilbrec blushed and lowered his bow, ashamed of his outburst.

'Very well,' he muttered, looking as though he had just volunteered for his own execution. 'I can show you.' He looked at Elaeus, hoping he might be a voice of reason, but the old healer remained silent.

'This way,' said Ilbrec, nodding to the next grove of trees.

With the other guards in tow, they dashed through the banks of smoke, glimpsing groups of archers as they went. The voices they heard were odd and muffled and nobody paused to acknowledge them as they passed.

As they approached the borders of Lord Beldeas's realm, the scene grew far more disturbing. Hulking, goat-headed beastmen were charging through the glades, spreading fire as they went and hacking down anyone they met. Many of them stumbled, dropping to their knees with arrows embedded in their necks or their tiny, crimson eyes, but they were so numerous that most hurried on through the smoke, making for the heart of Locrimere.

Ilbrec and the other guards shot as they ran. Even in such a state of panic, their marksmanship was incredible. They were vaulting over flaming stumps as they fired, but not a single shot went wide.

Caorann cursed as an outsider exploded from the hedges to their right. He lashed wildly with his leaf-shaped blade and opened the monster's throat, sending it reeling back into the smoke. The thing died immediately, but Caorann had wrenched open his chest wound and incredible pain washed over him. He groaned as the world went black.

He awoke seconds later, sprawled in Elaeus's arms and surrounded by asrai. They had abandoned their usual tactics of slipping in and out of the trees, and formed a static circle around the fallen wardancer. They were clearly exposed, huddled on the side of a small hill, and the beastmen were quick to single them out. Dozens of the monsters began loping out of the shifting gloom, leering and snorting and brandishing brutal weapons.

At a nod from Ilbrec, the asrai raised their longbows and loosed a volley of arrows. Every shot found its mark, but there were already dozens more of the beastman approaching. The asrai moved with lightning speed, preparing to shoot again, but the monsters were already on them.

Caorann still had his sword in his hand and lurched to his feet, severing the throat of the first creature to reach them and slamming his forehead into the face of the second.

Elaeus downed a third with a brutal backhanded slash.

Ilbrec and the other guards dropped their longbows and drew blades of their own, hacking furiously at the axe-wielding monsters pouring over the hill.

The asrai slipped between their hulking opponents with ease, but as they fought, dozens more thudded through the trees, bellowing victoriously and waving tattered, bloody scalps over their heads.

A guard fell, with blood spurting from his plates of leather armour. As he dropped to his knees the other asrai rushed to his side, but before they could reach him, a beastman's axe thudded into his face, shearing half his head away.

As the guard died, Ilbrec's foot landed in the beastman's face and sent the monster spinning back through the air.

Elaeus howled as he saw Ilbrec vanish beneath a wave of blades, fur and teeth. He shouldered his way through the fighting but, before he could reach his fallen friend, the haft of an axe crunched into his frail chest and knocked him flat on his back. His sword slipped from his grip and, as he tried to roll clear, the old healer saw to his amazement that it was not just the axe's haft that had struck his chest; the blade was embedded deep between his ribs and his robes were quickly turning crimson. He drew a breath but before he could let out a scream the axe was wrenched free, taking his life in a spray of blood and splintered bone.

More of the asrai fell as the monsters continued to flood over the hill.

Caorann ignored his pain, vaulting up onto the shoulders of a beastman and flipping through the air.

He landed several feet away and gagged as blood rushed up from his chest.

The beastmen hacked down the last remaining asrai and lurched in his direction, grinning wildly.

Caorann ran, weaving drunkenly through the trees, with no idea which way he was heading. Battling figures whirled past him, shrouded in smoke and trailing terrified screams. The fires were spreading quickly now, leaping from tree to tree, and above it all, Eremon's horn was still ringing out.

Despite the agony and grief that threatened to overwhelm him, Caorann picked up his pace and managed to leave his attackers behind. The smoke had transformed Locrimere and after a few minutes he paused, unsure which way to go. Eremon's horn rang out again and he realised it was not as far away as he had thought – it was just the smoke making the sound seem distant. He tightened his blood-drenched bandages and headed off in a new direction.

After crossing a high, slender footbridge, Caorann finally recognised where he was. He had reached Locrimere's spiritual heart: the peaceful wildflower meadow surrounding the waters of the Idolan.

It was peaceful no longer.

The air was clearer here and Caorann was able to see a pitched battle, raging through the long grass. Hundreds of archers were assembled on the southernmost side of the meadow with their backs to the lake, filling the air with arrows and howling commands. The other side of the field was swarming with outsiders. Ranks of goat- and bull-headed monsters were advancing, trailing tattered banners and cowering behind shields that bristled with arrows.

Caorann groaned at the sight. The Idolan was surrounded by burning glades and beastmen were pouring into it from every direction. He heard the sound of hooves clattering across the bridge behind him and raced on, making for the lines of archers. As he ran Eremon's horn rang out again and then he saw the captain himself, at the front of the asrai lines, clutching a torn banner emblazoned with a pair of black yew trees.

The wardancer was drunk on pain and blood loss and as he approached the ranks of archers, his peripheral vision vanished, leaving him only a dark tunnel with light at the end.

'Eremon,' he croaked, raising his bloody sword as he ran.

The captain was wearing a tall leather helmet and his face was mostly hidden, but Caorann caught a glimpse of blazing eyes and a firm, set jaw.

Eremon was drenched in blood and dying soldiers were stacked against his legs. He nodded at Caorann and was about to reply when light flashed in the smoke. It scorched Caorann's face and sent him spinning back onto his knees, then it coiled around the ranks of archers and wrenched dozens of them towards the advancing beastmen.

Caorann climbed to his feet and hurried on, but when he looked again, there was no sign of Eremon, or his banner.

The ranks of asrai collapsed as the outsiders tore into them, bellowing victoriously as they swarmed across the meadow.

Pain exploded in the back of Caorann's head and he dropped to the ground. As darkness threatened to wash over him for a second time, he noticed that the sun had finally lifted above the treetops.

I will not die on the first morning of spring, thought Caorann.

He dragged his aching body back onto its feet and staggered on into the battle.

CHAPTER FOURTEEN

As the sun dipped beneath the trees, Finavar's voice began to falter. He had recited the same incantation so many times that the words had taken on an odd, meaningless quality. The rite was starting to make him feel as though he was losing his mind. He had other reasons to question his sanity. Orion, Consort-King of the asrai, was slumped at his feet – a great snoring mound of immortal, antlered muscle, wrenched from the dreams of his childhood. Watching over the King was a figure no less terrifying: Atolmis the Hunter, whose black, pitiless eyes glared at Finavar every time his voice failed.

The other riders were sleeping next to their king, snoring just as loudly, but Atolmis clearly had no intention of leaving Orion unguarded and had remained awake.

After the first couple of hours of Finavar's song, his kinband had plucked up the courage to approach. At the sight of more tattooed warriors Atolmis had clutched his spear and growled. For a second it looked as though blood might be spilled, but Finavar had explained that they could help with the ritual and somehow managed to calm the situation.

Thuralin, Alhena and Jokleel were now hunkered next to Finavar, adding a little harmony to the repetitive phrase. At first, they had stared at the horned giants in awe, unable to believe what they were seeing, but long hours had passed since then and, as the light faded and the King showed no sign of waking, the others started to quietly ask questions of Finavar, taking it in turns to maintain the song.

'Did you speak to him?' whispered Jokleel, his eyes glistening with wonder.

Finavar nodded, and his chest swelled with pride. He could barely believe it himself.

Thuralin leant closer. His gloomy features were a sharp contrast to the boy's youthful stare. 'Locrimere is doomed if we do not return soon. And we need to return with an army in tow.' He massaged his crippled arm and looked anxiously at the figures sleeping under the dolmen. 'Even the King could not face such a host alone.'

Finavar shuffled back so that Jokleel was between him and Atolmis and he took a break from singing. 'Orion is not coming to Locrimere yet,' he whispered.

The old wardancer narrowed his single eye. 'What?'

Finavar shrugged. 'He wishes to find the spirit who brought us here. He will not listen to talk of anything else. I made one mention of the Wrach and he demanded I lead him to the Dark Paths.' His eyes widened. 'He has some great purpose.'

Thuralin shook his head. 'How will that help Locrimere?'

Finavar spoke without taking his eyes off Orion. 'We have no need of an army. Once the King is ready to join us we will butcher those mongrels by the thousand.' He pictured himself, riding to battle beside Orion. 'He is a god made flesh. He is the Lord of the Wild Hunt. Why would we need anything else?'

Thuralin continued to frown as he picked up the tune and gave Jokleel a chance to speak. 'No, Finavar,' Jokleel insisted, staring at the horizon. 'He does not intend to help us.' He closed his eyes and held his hands up to catch the breeze. 'I can feel it. We still need an army. Perhaps you could return to the Queen's court and beg her for help?'

Finavar was about to reply when Orion sat bolt upright. His eyes were still closed, but he levelled one of his fingers at the side of the dolmen. The faded inscription had grown as dark as a bloodstain. As they watched, the branches began to writhe and undulate, as though they were alive.

'He is here!' cried Orion, with his eyes still closed.

The tune faltered and came to a halt as the four singers backed away in alarm.

Atolmis frowned in confusion as the other riders climbed to their feet. Their eyes were also closed but they were facing in exactly the same direction as Orion, staring at the black inscription.

'My lord?' asked Atolmis, but Orion suddenly stood and barged past him.

Atolmis watched in alarm as Orion and the other sleepers stumbled off towards the trees. 'Wait,' he grunted, hurrying after them, but before they even reached the line of trees, Orion and the others rippled oddly, like stones dropping through water, then they vanished completely.

Atolmis staggered to a halt, shaking his head.

Finavar and his brother looked at each other in recognition. There was an earthy, herby aroma on the air that they all recalled. It was the smell of the Dark Paths, the smell of time being wrenched out of true.

Alhena shook her head in dismay, staring at the spot where Orion had last stood.

'They have gone,' called Finavar to Atolmis, grinning with pride. 'The Wrach was willing.'

Atolmis turned and glared at him in disgust, appalled that such a person would dare address him. He walked back without a reply and stared at the wall of the dolmen. The hieroglyph was faded and motionless once more. He grunted and shook his head, then stepped out of the dolmen and mounted one of the horses, leading the others behind him as he rode back down the gulley.

As Finavar watched him go his smile faded, and, once Atolmis had disappeared back into the trees, he turned to his kinband. 'I thought he would take me with him.' He looked at the three faces staring back at him: Thuralin's gloomy frown, Alhena's vicious scowl and the boy's soft, mournful stare. He laughed and shook his head. 'Look at you! My own personal storm clouds!' He threw his arms out and embraced them in a fierce hug. 'Do not fear! There is hope!' He grinned idiotically. 'I have already made the acquaintance of a king today.' He looked at the trees. 'He will return, I am sure and then he will ride with us, but, in the meantime, I think I should make the acquaintance of his queen.'

CHAPTER FIFTEEN

Although he would never show it, Orion felt afraid. As he strode away from Torr-Goholoth he found himself in a world he could not explain. It was midday and he was surrounded by fields of rippling, windswept corn. There were only two breaks in this ocean of gold. One was the path before him, a broad expanse of dark, glossy cobbles that caused his hooves to clatter and clang as he walked; the other was the hunched stones of Torr-Goholoth.

With a rising sense of panic, Orion realised that there was not a single tree in sight.

'Where have I come?' He stared at the sun-drenched fields and the cloudless sky. 'Is this the Tenderfoot Way?'

The forest might have gone, but three of his priests had followed him into his dream. They stared back at Orion with confusion in their black eyes. He was starting to recall who they were. They had served him faithfully through the centuries. Sélva, the tallest, wore a cloak of shimmering grey wolfskin. Like the others, he had veins of ivy running beneath his pale skin and a pair of slender horns that curled up from the sides of his wooden helmet. Beside him was Olachas. He wore no helmet, and his straw-coloured hair was bound in long plaits, woven with feathers and dried flowers. Rather than a spear, Olachas carried a longsword that shimmered slightly as it caught the light. Orion remembered that it had a name, Baecor, and that it was alleged to contain some kind of ghost, or soul. The third of them was named Ilaruss. His face was completely hidden by his helmet but Orion recognised him easily by the long, jagged scar that stretched from his belly to his neck; a memento from a previous year's Wild Hunt.

Sélva waded into the waist-high corn and shook his head. 'My lord, the Dark Paths do not just lead to other places. They lead to other times.' He turned to Orion. 'Perhaps we have slipped forwards into another era? Or back, to the dawn of the world?' He nodded at the dolmen. 'Perhaps we are in the era when the stones of Torr-Goholoth were first laid?'

'My lord,' said Olachas. 'If this is not what you sought, perhaps we could just return through the stones?'

Orion shook his head. He knew he could not return until he had wiped the doubt from the Wrach's strange, pale face; or silenced him forever. He turned away from the others and looked back up the road. At the horizon, it vanished into a rippling heat haze, but a few miles to the east of it Orion thought he made out a patch of darkness in the fields; a building of some kind.

'Follow me,' he grunted and headed off into the corn. As he strode through the field, he had to resist the urge to stoop. Never in all his many lives had he felt so exposed. Without the cover of trees the sky seemed alarmingly vast. The King had the strange sensation that it might fall on him at any time. He was conscious that the priests were following, though, and kept his antlers proudly raised. 'There is something in the corn,' he cried, lifting his chin. 'This spirit guide must be here somewhere – the wardancer would not dare lie to me.'

Orion walked for what seemed like hours, scattering hares and mice before him as he marched though the corn. He was sure he had travelled for several miles but the dark shape never seemed to be any nearer. He walked for so long that the sun rolled across the sky and began to sink towards the horizon. His pulse started to hammer in his temples and he juggled his spear from hand to hand, itching to vent his rage on something. How could it be that the dark shape always remained the same distance away? Finally, just as he was about to suggest they try heading back to the road, Orion realised that he had reached his destination.

He let out a howl of frustration. Standing before him were the stones of Torr-Goholoth and the beginning of the same long, cobbled road. The only difference was that the dolmen was now silhouetted against a grey, cooling dusk and the fields of corn now looked like a sea of silver, rather than one of gold.

Orion hurled his spear at the old rocks and it bounced off them with a clang.

'Show yourself!' he cried, climbing up on top of the dolmen and scouring the gloomy fields. 'Accuse me, as you did before!'

Sélva and the others looked at each other in confusion.

As Orion's cries faded into the half-light, they seemed to be answered.

The King's horned equerries climbed up beside him on the sunken capstone and saw a white shape, drifting out of the darkness towards them. A pale mist was rippling across the fields, rolling and churning in the hollows and sending thin tendrils up into the pewter-coloured sky.

Orion dropped to the ground and grabbed the battered spear he had taken from Atolmis. The tip was bent out of shape, but the weight of it felt good. As the fog tumbled towards him, he recalled every damning phrase that had been levelled at him by the Brúidd. He hoped that the strange weather was a sign that they were about to appear. He recalled the great stag, Sativus, looking down at him as he cowered in the pool, and prayed for a chance to face the creature under less shameful circumstances.

Orion stepped away from the stones and approached the corn, peering into the fog. 'Show yourself!' he cried, holding his spear aloft. 'Let us see who is weak!'

There was no reply, but before Orion could repeat his demand, agony exploded in the calf of his right leg. He looked down and saw that a slender white snake had slid out of the corn and fastened its jaws upon him. The pain was sharp and deep. Orion reached down with a curse and wrenched the snake free, hurling it back into the corn. It was only as the serpent flew from his grip that Orion noticed how odd the corn looked. He had thought the field looked white because it was drenched in moonlight, but he realised now that the corn had vanished, replaced by thousands of anaemic, writhing snakes.

He cursed as another one clamped onto his leg, igniting his flesh with a fierce heat.

Sélva dropped from the stones and hacked down with his sword, slicing the snake free.

'Face me, you coward!' cried Orion, as they both backed towards the dolmen. He glared at the banks of fog. 'Who is the mewling wretch now?'

'Still you.'

The voice was no more than a whisper and it came from behind them. It came from the shadows beneath the dolmen.

Orion whirled to see that the fog had pooled between the stones and formed into a small, hunched figure, leaning on a staff. At the sight of the hooded old man, Orion felt all the fury and shame of their last encounter. His frame shook as he levelled his battered spear at the Wrach. Then, as he stepped closer, he saw the reason for the creature's odd, shifting flesh.

The shape beneath the robes was constructed entirely of writhing white snakes.

Orion's lip curled in distaste. The Wrach was nothing more than a bundle of serpents held together by tatty robes. 'You will kneel to me,' he snarled. 'For I am the King. I will have your allegiance.'

'You are a false king,' hissed the Wrach. There was a clump of pallid, worm-like snakes where his mouth should be and as he leant on his staff, they rippled into a snarl. 'You will fail us.' Some of the snakes' tongues flickered from his lips. 'I can *smell* it.'

'You are a liar!' Orion strode forwards with his spear raised. 'Kneel to me!'

'I will not,' whispered the Wrach. As he spoke, the fog spiralled around him and obscured him from view.

Orion thundered through the dolmen and found that it was empty. He howled again, jabbing the spear into the remnants of fog. 'I am the King!' he roared, arching his back in fury.

'Prove it,' came the Wrach's whispered reply.

Orion spun around and glared out at the squirming, white landscape. The mist had rolled back to create a drifting avenue over the rippling snakes. At the far end of the avenue, about half a mile from where Orion was standing, was the hooded old man, still leaning heavily on his staff.

'Come to me,' said the Wrach. His voice was still a sibilant whisper, but it echoed around the stones of Torr-Goholoth.

Orion lurched down the slope towards the mass of snakes, but Sélva grabbed his arm and held him back.

'Look at your leg,' said the Wild Rider as Orion turned to glare at him.

Orion looked down and cursed. Where the snakes had attacked his leg, his flesh had shrivelled away, revealing the glistening tendons beneath and a flash of white bone.

'Of course, you cannot,' came the mocking whisper. The Wrach raised his staff and the entire ocean of snakes lifted their heads. 'There would be pain. And you are afraid.'

Orion strained against Sélva's grip, but his servant held firm. 'Even if you manage to reach him, you would die.' Sélva shook his head. 'Is he worth your life? What has he done?'

'He doubts me,' growled Orion, freeing himself from Sélva's grasp.

'Of course,' continued the Wrach, 'you could easily leave.' He waved his undulating staff at the stones behind them. 'The forest is waiting.'

Orion and the others turned to see that Torr-Goholoth now looked onto a peaceful wooded glade, full of dappled sunlight and the sound of birdsong.

'I will not let him mock me,' snarled Orion, furiously massaging his brow.

Olachas stepped to his side. 'My lord, Sélva is right.' He waved his sword at the snakes. 'Their venom would destroy you.'

Orion dropped to his knees, breathless with rage. Then, as he pawed the ground in desperation, an idea struck him. He recalled something Atolmis had said earlier, while they were talking to the lowborn bard. Perhaps there was a chance, he thought; a way to prove himself to this wretched creature.

'Wait here,' he muttered, without looking up.

Olachas and the others looked at each other in confusion but, before they had chance to react, Orion launched himself into the fog.

He landed heavily in the rolling mass and gasped as dozens of fangs punctured his skin.

'Wait!' cried Olachas, rushing to the edge of the snakes, his voice a wild screech. 'They will kill you!'

Orion remained crouched and motionless. Agony flooded his limbs and for a second he thought he would be unable to even take the first step. Then he crushed his doubt. I am equal to *anything*, he told himself and leapt forwards, racing towards the distant figure of the Wrach, with snakes trailing from his limbs like ghostly pennants.

As he raced down the corridor of fog, dozens more fangs sliced through his skin and the pain blossomed at an incredible rate, but there was no trace of doubt in him now. He divorced his thoughts from the agony and locked his gaze on the hunched, robed shape of his enemy.

The Wrach shook his head in disbelief as Orion charged through the snakes, but he made no move to withdraw. As the King staggered towards him, the Wrach sounded shocked, but no less disdainful. 'You are braver than I thought,' he whispered, 'and far more stupid.' As Orion towered over him, the Wrach raised one of his arms. Dozens of slender serpents trailed from his voluminous sleeve, masquerading as fingers. He pointed the longest of them at Orion's chest. 'You have killed yourself,' he said, turning his whisper into a reedy laugh.

Orion looked down and saw the snakes' venom had acted with incredible speed. His skin was melting into a bloody slush and pooling around his hooves. His organs were visible and blackened, pouring with smoke and the stink of decay. He gasped and dropped to his knees, allowing the white snakes to tumble over him, tearing into his face and neck.

The Wrach nodded, seeing that all his doubts had been well founded. 'I have killed you.' He sounded almost sympathetic.

With seconds of life remaining, Orion dragged his thoughts away from the pain and forced himself to recall his plan. 'You cannot kill me,' he gasped, through bloody teeth, 'if I was never here.'

The Wrach shook his head, confused.

With a final, agonised curse, Orion rose up and raised his hand to strike the Wrach across the face.

The blind spirit raised his staff to defend himself.

Orion changed the direction of his blow and, rather than striking his hooded enemy, he grabbed the ball of black stone that topped his staff.

'Wait,' gasped the Wrach, as Orion wrenched the talisman free. 'You don't understand!'

Orion replied with a punch. He hammered the lump of stone into the Wrach's face. His fist tore through the knotted snakes and burst out the other side in a shower of blood and coiled serpents.

The spirit toppled to the ground and rolled away.

Orion staggered after him, thrown forwards by the momentum of his punch. He saw the fog gather around the Wrach and lift him back to his feet, restoring his head to its former shape. Then the spirit's robes fell away, revealing a contorted spiral of writhing snakes, rearing and hissing furiously as they tried to regain humanoid form.

'You have no idea what you have!' howled the spirit.

Orion's ruined body was collapsing in on itself. Blood was spraying from hundreds of open wounds and his head was lolling drunkenly on his broken shoulders.

'Kneel to me!' he gasped, holding the stone aloft.

The Wrach screamed horribly and tried to reassemble himself, reaching for the stone.

Orion smashed the mass of snakes to the ground. 'Kneel!'

The Wrach made a pitiful attempt to do as Orion requested.

The King let out a long sigh of satisfaction then turned away and fixed his gaze on the stone. It was polished to such a sheen that it resembled a pool of oil, glittering in his fist. It even seemed to be rippling, as though currents were drifting through its centre. He saw his mutilated face, glaring back at him. The flesh was falling away and he realised he had seen this moment before, in a dream. He held his nerve and stared deeper into the stone, picturing other shapes moving through the void.

With a stomach-wrenching lurch, Orion's mind plummeted into the blackness and whirled away on the currents of time. He saw a torrent of places and people: a bewildering collection of scenes that left him reeling. For a second he felt an awful doubt; had he set himself an impossible task? What did he know of the Wrach's Dark Paths? How could he navigate such places? Then, with a gasp, he glimpsed a face he knew: a blazing point of light, surrounding a pair of bottomless, mournful eyes.

He threw his thoughts at Ariel like a spear.

And vanished from the world.

Orion smashed through the bracken and lashed out furiously, thinking for a moment that he was still surrounded by snakes. Then, as he came to a halt, he opened his eyes and saw a beautiful grove of oak trees, dappled by midday sun. At its centre was an oddly-shaped hill, and he grunted in recognition. The turf looked as though it had been draped over stone slabs, just like the ones at Torr-Goholoth. 'This is one of his gates,' muttered Orion, stamping a hoof on the turf and feeling the hard rock beneath.

He heard voices and looked through the trees. Beyond the oaks there was a wide clearing, surrounding a raised grassy dais and a pair of tall root thrones. Hundreds of figures were gathered on the lawn, watching a tall figure stride away from them.

Orion gasped as he saw the figure more clearly. He realised that he was watching himself, a day earlier, marching away from the Queen and heading off to find the Wrach.

As his earlier self approached, Orion caught his eye and raised a fist, displaying the Wrach's bloodstained talisman as a warning, dangling a nest of dead snakes from his fingers.

As he looked deep into his own eyes, Orion felt of rush of joy. He had cowed one of his accusers. The Wrach could never again question his divinity. I am the master of time, he thought, clutching the stone tighter and feeling drunk on the possibilities it presented. As he watched his former self continue on his way, he felt a pride so powerful it bordered on awe. They were all wrong, he realised, taking a deep, shuddering breath. I *am* destined to rule this forest; and I will rule it more surely than they ever could. They will kneel to me, all of them, before I am done.

He looked down and saw, without surprise that his body was unmarked. Then he started to climb down towards the clearing, ready to begin his rule in earnest.

As Ariel saw Orion emerging from the trees, her eyes lit up with excitement and surprise. 'Orion! You decided to stay!'

As Ariel embraced the King, Ordaana felt a rush of nausea. The crowds on the dais were still reeling from the King's earlier outburst but as their sovereigns talked and Orion's rage seemed to pass, the highborn resumed their ritual dance. 'What ridiculous games we play,' Ordaana muttered under her breath. She and Lord Beldeas had been swallowed up by the surging crowd and she felt no need to hide her distaste. 'How we grovel and fawn. We debase ourselves like worthless chattel, even though Orion would tear any of us apart as quickly as look at us. And Ariel can barely recall our names.' She ran a trembling hand over her immaculate silver hair. 'They crave nothing but our subservience.'

Beldeas frowned at his wife's bitter tone. Most of his attention was fixed on one of Ariel's handmaidens, but he could not help noticing Ordaana's bile. He turned to face her. 'My love, this is ridiculous. You adore them, more than anyone. You always have.' His eyes narrowed. 'I am not such a fool as you might think. You may wish to play the part of dutiful wife again, but I know you did not marry me through love.' He waved at the surrounding nobles. 'Our nuptials bought you entry into this world. These "ridiculous games" are all you have ever wished for.'

Ordaana stared at her husband with hatred and disbelief. Even now, he was unaware of the hurt she was carrying. He had never asked her why she was no longer required as one of the Queen's handmaidens. He did not even seem to have noticed that she was not up there, next to Ariel's throne. She was on the verge of explaining everything when she noticed something odd. Beldeas's beautiful green robes were behaving strangely. As he edged closer to her, she noticed that the bronze-coloured stitching around his collar had slumped out of shape. She peered at the needlework in confusion for a second, then realised she was seeing the noble face of Aestar Eltanin, gazing back at her from her husband's chest. He was looking at her with stern disapproval.

Ordaana was too shocked to speak for a moment and Beldeas frowned. Then she snapped her mouth shut and gave Aestar a subtle nod.

'Forgive me,' she said, meeting her husband's confused gaze. 'Of course, you are right. I *do* adore them. I have more respect for our king and queen than anyone.' She attempted a brittle smile. 'That dreadful bard has unnerved me, that is all.'

Beldeas grimaced, recalling how the youth had embarrassed them. He looked over at the trees and saw to his relief that, although Orion had returned almost immediately, there was no sign of Finavar. 'I'm sure he will not dare show his face again.' Beldeas felt a brief flush of shame as he recalled giving Finavar control of the kinbands. Perhaps he was responsible in some way for this pretend prince's arrogance? He dismissed the feeling. Of course not. How could he have predicted that the vile youth would show up at court, ranting about invasions and annoying the King?

'I understand completely,' he said, softening his voice and taking Ordaana's arm. 'When we return home I will order Eremon to arrest the wretched outlaw. Such behaviour is unforgivable.' He shook his head. 'The very idea of a lowborn, here in the Council Glade… It is quite awful. I do not…'

Beldeas's words trailed off as he noticed he had lost his wife's attention. She was watching Ariel and her Consort-King as they made their way back to their thrones. As they moved through the whirling crowds, Ariel scattered greetings like gifts, lighting up the awed faces of her subjects with a single well-placed word, but Orion had no interest in pleasing his guests. He barged through the crowds without any sign of recognition, glowering intently at something he was clutching in one of his hands.

'The King looks well,' muttered Ordaana, as she watched them take their seats, surrounded by a fluttering entourage of spirits and handmaidens.

'Of course.' Beldeas did not notice his wife's odd tone. 'Imagine what the summer solstice will bring.' As Beldeas admired the scene, his gaze fell back on the Queen's beautiful handmaidens and his attention wandered. After a few minutes of pleasant daydreaming he turned to find that his wife had vanished into the crowds, swallowed up by the dance. He shrugged and allowed to the music to drag him off towards the thrones.

Ordaana hurried through the crowds towards the edge of the glade, her heart pounding. Had she placed the knife in the wrong place? Or had she recited the incantation incorrectly? Something had clearly failed; Orion showed no signs of illness or frailty. In fact, he looked more virile and powerful than in any previous spring. What would he become at the time of the summer solstice? Panic gripped her. Aestar Eltanin would think her such a fool. How could she have failed in such a simple task? Would he find another disciple to help him?

She reached the towering oaks that bordered the glade and lost herself in the shadowy groves beyond. Even here, the trees were crowded with highborn. Many of them were sprawled idly across the roots and branches, either locked in the arms of their lovers or simply contemplating the beauty of the Queen's realm. Ordaana hurried past them, ignoring their languid greetings and making for a secluded hollow, half a mile from the Council Glade. She reached the gloomy spot and sat down, perching on the mossy bole of an alder tree. After scouring the shadows and assuring herself she was alone, Ordaana began to mutter. 'I anointed the knife, I recited the incantation, I stabbed the shadow of the tree; why is there no effect?'

'Patience, Ordaana,' came a reply from the darkness.

Ordaana recognised the voice immediately and rose to her feet. 'Aestar! Where are you?' As the words left her mouth, she realised she could already see him. There was a tangled clump of branches and leaves on one side of the hollow and, as she watched in delight, it reared up from the ground, adopting a tall, humanoid form and stretching out its arms in greeting.

'You have performed your task admirably, like a true daughter of Asuryan.'

Ordaana edged closer, with even more awe in her eyes than the nobles she had left paying homage to Ariel and Orion. Aestar remained in the shadows, but she could just about make out his long, imperious features, gazing down at her.

'But,' she glanced anxiously into the trees, checking again that they were alone, 'if the curse was successful, why does Orion seem so powerful? He nearly split the ground with his voice.'

Twigs snapped and popped as Aestar nodded in reply. 'Exactly! This is all just as I had hoped.' He reached out with one of his brittle, mossy hands and stroked Ordaana's perfect silver hair.

She closed her eyes as the cold bark moved lower and caressed her cheek.

'Misguided as they are,' he explained, 'Ariel and her Consort-King are the envoys of gods. If we were simply to butt heads with the King, he would crush us. Nothing would change. Your kindreds would remain, withering in this doomed forest.'

Ordaana felt childlike before such ancient, noble intelligence and, try as she might, she could not understand. 'Then what was the use of my curse?'

Aestar Eltanin smiled graciously and squeezed her shoulder. 'We are not trying to smother the fire, child, we are trying to stoke it. Understand this: Orion's strength is Ariel's weakness. Your curse was not intended to drain him of energy, it was intended to add to his vigour.' Aestar paused. 'And fuel his wrath.'

Ordaana shook her head, still confused.

'The Queen's reign is predicated on one thing,' he continued. 'Harmony. As long as she can maintain balance, the forest will permit her to remain. Equilibrium is the key. You are all here under sufferance, Ordaana. Perhaps Ariel has forgotten it, but you should not. If it suited the forest's needs, it would abandon Ariel without a moment's pause.'

The creaking shape stooped closer to Ordaana. 'Your curse has sown doubt in Orion's mind. However Ariel tries to placate him, he will desire now nothing more than to prove his dominion. And the harder he tries, the more he will turn the forest against Ariel.'

Ordaana gripped her master's brittle hands, starting to understand.

CHAPTER SIXTEEN

'My own mother wouldn't know me now!' cried Finavar, turning on the spot with his arms raised. 'Even if I had one!'

The wardancers were standing by the side of a small, glittering brook, on the borders of the Council Glade. They were close enough to hear snatches of song and harping, but they had been denied entry to the Queen's court. Even Finavar's most winning smile had failed to sway the stern-faced sentries. It seemed that his uninvited appearance earlier in the day had earned him enemies.

Alhena was crouched like a cat on a branch above his head. 'Why are we wasting time here?' She tugged angrily on her single plait. 'Locrimere needs us.' She sneered and looked south through the trees. 'Our home is in the hands of Eremon. What hope is there in that?'

Finavar waved proudly at his disguise. He had removed his distinctive black cloak and painted his entire body white. He had also fashioned a mask from bark and painted that white. The outfit was completed by a leering, red, toothy grin, painted across the mask. 'But am I not the perfect Bel-Geddon?'

Thuralin looked as gloomy as ever and gave no reply, but Jokleel's gentle features creased into a smile. 'Indeed you are, brother. No god could wish for a better attendant.'

Finavar grinned behind his mask. 'Quite! And what more suitable character is there for this festival than Bel-Geddon?'

Jokleel nodded, still smiling. 'He *is* Loec's favourite attendant. And everyone knows he's a herald of spring. And he's funny.'

'Exactly,' said Finavar. 'Even those humourless sentries would not dare refuse such a guest!'

Thuralin massaged the heavy lines of his face and gave Finavar a despairing look. 'What exactly do you hope to achieve by telling jokes? The minute you take off that ridiculous mask, you will be removed, or worse. How can you gather support if you can't even admit who you are?'

Finavar shrugged. 'I have yet to solve that particular problem, but I'm sure I will find a way. If I can just get near the Queen again, I can make her realise the seriousness of this attack.' He shook his head. 'You should have seen the courtiers, Thuralin. They are utterly self-absorbed. They can see nothing beyond the boundaries of that glade and their own pretty robes. They were far too busy swooning over each over to heed my warning.'

'Of course they were!' cried Alhena, slapping the branch she was perched on. 'So why don't we leave them to their ridiculous pageants and get back to Locrimere while there is still time?'

Finavar shook his head. 'Until Orion returns, the Queen is our best chance. If I can just get close to her, I'm sure she will listen. She saw how much credence Orion gave my message. Just think: if Ariel requested it, we could have a thousand archers at our disposal. Two thousand! Who knows how many?' He looked up at Alhena. 'Trust me. I'm sure I can make her listen. Then we will head straight for Locrimere.' He looked around the faces of the three wardancers. 'Just give me one hour, then we will go.'

Alhena dropped from the tree and stepped to Finavar's side. 'And what if you don't return?'

Finavar grinned again. 'Think of a way to come and find me.'

Before Alhena could answer, Finavar turned on his heel and dashed through the trees, adjusting his wooden mask as he went.

Hooded sentries were waiting at the edge of the Queen's Council Glade and Finavar came to a halt a few feet away with a flamboyant bow.

A few of the guards raised their eyebrows at the sight of his bright white limbs and his leering, toothy grin.

'I think my foal has a sore throat,' muttered Finavar, stepping up to them.

The sentries kept their gaze fixed straight ahead.

'Well, it's certainly a little horse!' cried Finavar, performing another exaggerated bow.

None of the sentries smiled, but one of them relented and stepped aside, waving for Finavar to enter the glade.

He hurried past, before they took too close a look at him, and entered the broad, grassy clearing. The ritual of Ostaliss was still in full swing. Finavar saw wardancers from other parts of the forest, flipping and twirling through the crowds, scattering rhymes and trailing tiny, glittering spirits. Robed magi were crowded on the royal dais, paying homage to the Queen and summoning visions from the smoke-filled air with their long, pale fingers.

Finavar headed for the heart of the crowd, spouting rhymes and jokes as he went. The lords and ladies were a far more appreciative audience than the sentries; drunk on sorcery and heady wine, they grasped Finavar by his gleaming arms and spun him around, ordering Bel-Geddon to make them laugh. Finavar punned and rhymed, but never stopped for too long in one place, moving all the while in the direction of Ariel's throne.

The sound of harps and flutes swelled as the celebrations became more raucous. Finavar found himself snatched and dragged in different directions by gangs of red-faced, wild-eyed devotees, draped in garlands of spring flowers and howling their praises at the Queen and King in the Wood.

Finally, with petals and ribbons plastered across his white body paint, Finavar reached the centre of the royal dais and staggered out in front of the Queen.

He stumbled to a halt in shock. Sitting beside Ariel, in his tall root throne, was Orion, conversing angrily with Atolmis the Hunter.

Finavar forgot his role as a playful deity and stared in amazement. He knew Atolmis would head back to the celebrations, but Orion should be halfway across the forest by now, wandering the strange paths of the Wrach. His pulse raced. This was even better than he had hoped. He had proved to Orion that he was no fool. Surely now he would be ready to lead his hunt to Locrimere?

There was another row of sentries arrayed before the thrones, selecting who should be able to approach Ariel and Orion, and as Finavar shook his head in confusion he noticed that they were staring at him suspiciously. To his dismay, one of them nodded in his direction and muttered to another one of the guards.

Have they recognised me, wondered Finavar? He immediately reassumed his role and began regaling the nobles nearest to him with the most lurid, bawdy jokes he could recall. The lords and ladies frowned and he realised that, in his panic, he had struck the wrong note and offended them. As they muttered their disapproval, he quickly backed away into the crowd, desperate not to be removed before he had chance to garner help. As he shouldered his way back, away from the thrones, he wondered how Orion could have beaten him to the Council Glade. The Wrach must have led him astray and sent him back to where he started. Finavar peered through the crowd at the huge, antlered figure of Orion, hunched on his throne like a cornered beast, snarling orders at his equerry, Atolmis. That must be why he looks so furious, decided Finavar, emerging from the crush of bodies and finding himself next to one of the blazing ceremonial fires. The Blind Guide has evaded Orion and hurled him back to his queen.

The faces around the fire were flushed with drink and as Finavar looked through the flames he met eyes that were glazed and distant. The celebrants' faces had an ethereal quality that made Finavar doubt they would be as suspicious as the Queen's guards. He was safe, for the moment, but what use was that? He needed to catch Orion's attention somehow. He sat down on the ash-covered soil and pouted, wracking his brains for an idea. The guest next to him was a drunken harpist, swaying and muttering to herself as she plucked a clumsy, staccato melody from the instrument in her lap.

Use the gifts you have been given, thought Finavar, grinning to himself.

He grasped the harpist's shoulder and leant close, giving her a broad grin. 'Play me something I can sing to.'

The harpist ceased playing and struggled to focus on Finavar's white mask. After a few seconds of looking confused she grinned back. 'Bel-Geddon!' She nodded her head and tried to adopt a serious expression. 'Whatever you, I, whatever you request, O servant of the gods, I play shall...' Her words trailed off and she frowned, unsure what she had been trying to say. 'Play-I-I. I will play for you!' she managed finally, proud that she had managed a coherent sentence.

Finavar rose to his feet and nodded. 'The Lamentations of Gavra,' he demanded, clearing his throat.

The harpist frowned. 'Really?' She looked around at the wild scenes that surrounded them. 'On the first day of spring? Have a heart, Bel-Geddon! Is that... Are you sure? Is the... Is that the song the really you want?'

Finavar nodded eagerly. 'Trust me. Do I not know the will of my own masters?'

The harpist raised her eyebrows, trying unsuccessfully to look disdainful, but she did as she was requested and began playing the mournful tune.

The other guests groaned as they recognised the music but Finavar lifted his voice over the crackling flames and within a few seconds they had closed their eyes and were sighing with pleasure. The Darkling Prince had a voice of such poignancy that it transformed even the simplest lullaby; and the Lamentations of Gavra was no simple lullaby. It told the tragic story of a double suicide, alleged to have occurred many centuries earlier, during the bitter war known as the Winter of Woe. As the harpist's shimmering strains grew louder, Finavar sang the maudlin tale. The myths of the asrai recorded how Gavra the Black and his brother, Aefa, were led to ruin by their terrible arrogance. As the Winter of Woe grew more hopeless the forest called on them for aid, but the brothers remained in their own kingdom, claiming that they were too busy to leave. It was only after several days had passed that the self-obsessed nobles discovered that their wives, ashamed of the brothers' cowardice, had left to join the defence of the forest. The two brothers, filled with shame, rushed to the battle but arrived too late. The fighting was over and their wives had already been slain.

As Finavar's song reached its heart-rending climax, the lords and ladies of the asrai fell quiet, touched by the warm, plaintive tones of his voice. Even those kneeling before Ariel and Orion turned around, intrigued to see who would dare to sing such an inappropriate song at the festival of Ostaliss; and sing it so beautifully.

To Finavar's dismay, Orion continued talking urgently to his equerry, tapping one of his talons on something in his fist and seeming quite deaf to the music; but Ariel turned from her handmaidens and frowned, listening intently to Finavar's song.

Everyone who looked for the source of the song was surprised. They expected to see a regal noble, but they saw instead a scruffy, bedraggled performer, daubed with white paint, wearing a crooked mask and plastered with flower petals.

Seeing how her audience had grown, the harpist rose drunkenly to Finavar's side and played the final chorus with a dramatic, slightly clumsy flourish.

Finavar ignored the harpist's mistake. His voice soared through the final phrases, describing how Gavra and Aefa bound themselves with heavy stones and stepped into the bottomless waters of a mountain pool, known as the Eomain Tarn. He stared at Orion as he recounted how the brothers' shame only died as they drowned beneath the cool, still waters.

As the music ceased, the Council Glade fell quiet.

Orion was still oblivious and Ariel had lowered her gaze to her lap. Finavar thought he saw her wipe a tear from one of her pale cheeks.

Hundreds of nobles held their breath and waited, along with Finavar, to see what would happen next.

The Queen dried her eyes and gazed through the crowds in the direction of Finavar. For a few dreadful seconds he felt all the weight of her timeless gaze. Then she turned to one of the iridescent figures hovering by her throne and began whispering. The handmaiden nodded sadly and looked over at Finavar. Then Ariel smiled wearily at her subjects and indicated that the celebrations should continue.

Another musician struck up a jauntier tune and the nobles resumed their wild, ritualised dance, relieved that the awkward moment had passed.

Orion remained engrossed in his conversation with Atolmis and had not even noticed the interruption.

Finavar's shoulders slumped and he dropped back down beside the fire. He had been sure his song would capture Orion's attention. He had hoped it might illustrate a point – that the call to war should be ignored at one's peril, that life was about more than celebration – but his tale had clearly fallen on deaf ears. If anything, the festival was now even wilder. It was as though the nobles wished to expel the memory of Finavar's gloomy song by dancing even more energetically. The sun was now directly over the glade and scented fumes hung low over the dancers, shrouding their delirious excesses in shifting robes of grey and gold.

The figures sitting by the fire glared at Finavar and the harpist.

The drunken musician shook her head in disbelief as she sat down next to Finavar. 'Lamentations?' she groaned. 'What were you, what, what were you thinking?' She leant closer to the wardancer, peering at his mask. 'What kind of Bel-Geddon are you? I thought you were going to turn that dirge into a… I thought it was some kind of joke.'

Finavar was too busy wracking his brains to pay her any attention.

Colour flooded the harpist's cheeks as she saw that she was being ignored. With the wild grace of the drunk, she lashed out and sent Finavar's mask spinning into the flames.

Finavar cursed as sparks and ash exploded all over him. 'What have you done?' he gasped, pressing his hands to his face and looking anxiously at the nearest dancers.

'You shouldn't wear to deserve that costume,' slurred the harpist. 'You're not funny.'

Finavar panicked as he remembered he did not even have a hood to hide beneath. He sat on the grass with his head in his hands, unsure what to do next. His conversation with Orion had been witnessed by dozens of nobles. It would only take one of them to recognise him and the sentries would drag him from the clearing, or maybe even imprison him.

'You should be careful,' said a voice from above. 'A song like that has the power to wound.'

Finavar's heart sank as he realised he already been recognised. He looked up, expecting to see a scowling guard, but saw instead a flutter of damselfly wings and a shimmering, sylph-like figure, hovering a few feet above him. Finavar clambered to his feet, backed away and bowed, realising he was face to face with one of Ariel's handmaidens. Her limbs trailed a web of spectral, glittering ivy and she wore a flashing diadem of fine plaited silver. Her hair was roughly cropped in a boyish mop and her pretty, elfin face was locked in a wry, crooked smile.

'Was your intention to make my lady weep, Darkling Prince?' Her uneven smile grew more pronounced, forming dimples in her pale cheeks.

Something about the dimples made Finavar unable to speak

for a moment, then he shook his head and bowed again. 'Forgive me…'

'Laelia,' said the handmaiden, still smiling.

'Forgive me, Laelia,' muttered Finavar. Only the asrai's most
powerful magi were allowed to attend Ariel, and Finavar was
not fooled by her youthful, playful appearance. He knew she
was far more dangerous than any sentry. 'I will leave immediately,' he said, bowing again. Behind him, the drunken harpist
climbed to her feet and bowed too, glaring at Finavar with
even more disgust.

'No, stay awhile,' said Laelia, placing a firm hand on Finavar's shoulder. 'I would like to talk.' She gave him a look of
mock suspicion. 'As long as you aren't intending to sing again.'

Finavar's heart sank. So it was to be imprisonment of some
kind. He had no idea how the Queen dealt with unwelcome
guests, but he doubted it would be a pleasant fate. He nodded
sadly and met Laelia's eye. Even with the threat of imprisonment hanging over him, Finavar could not remain entirely
downhearted. 'I think a song might actually be less dangerous
than one of my jokes.'

Laelia laughed. It was a genuine, unforced sound and Finavar
relaxed slightly.

'Come,' she said, taking his hand and leading him through
the crowds. A few of the nobles paused at the sight of her.
To see one of the Queen's own sorcerers so close was a rare
privilege; something to boast of when they returned to their
own kingdoms. They were so distracted by the sight of the
winged handmaiden that they did not pay much attention to
the bedraggled entertainer hurrying after her.

Laelia led Finavar down a quiet, leafy arbour for half a mile or
so and said nothing more to him. They eventually emerged in a
grove to the south of the Council Glade. The trees surrounded

a tall mound, topped by a pile of splintered branches and logs. There was something strange about the wood and Finavar peered at it in confusion. He realised that the logs had been transformed into chunks of gnarled rock, but that was not the strangest thing about them: they looked oddly mobile and shimmered with a silvery light. As he looked closer, Finavar thought he could make out images – scenes and faces, captured in the shifting stone.

Laelia's damselfly wings folded behind her back as she sat at the bottom of the mound and indicated that Finavar should do the same.

He dragged his gaze from the mound and sat awkwardly next to her, noticing that she was still looking at him with the same crooked smile. 'Am I so ridiculous?' he asked, pouting slightly.

Laelia looked at his bedraggled frame and raised her eyebrows.

Finavar looked down and saw that his white paint had smeared in several places and the ash from the fire had turned what remained into a speckled grey mess. His pout became a smirk. 'You needn't answer,' he said.

Laelia sat in silence for a while, watching birds fluttering and spiralling through the grove.

Finavar shuffled awkwardly next to her, anxious to know what his punishment would be for sneaking into the Queen's presence a second time. After a few minutes his thoughts wandered. He pictured his doe-eyed little brother, waiting anxiously for his return; then he remembered the deathly pallor he had seen on Caorann's face as they left him in the care of Locrimere's healers. He wondered if there was any way he could pass a message on to his kinband before he was imprisoned. To lose their trust seemed more terrible to him than anything else.

This far from the Council Glade the sounds of celebration

were distant and muffled and Finavar noticed an odd atmosphere in the grove. He looked up at the pile of stones and felt a strange chill. There was something sinister about the sculpture. Such artifice was unnatural. He wondered who might have placed it here.

Finally, sensing Finavar's discomfort, Laelia turned to face him. The crooked smile was gone, but there was still a hint of mischief in her eyes. 'Do you know this place?'

Finavar shook his head.

'Cerura Carn,' she said, looking up at the pile of petrified logs. 'Even amongst the court of the Queen there are few who remember its purpose. Atolmis the Hunter perhaps; Naieth the Prophetess, certainly. She comes here often, especially during the festival rites.' She lowered her voice to a whisper, as though the stones could hear. 'The logs were placed here after the Winter of Woe and preserved by the will of the Queen. The carn is a memorial, but it is also a living prophecy.' She looked at Finavar's fidgeting legs and his twitching fingers. 'And it is a place of quiet contemplation. Here we may remember the price of our forest home and give thanks.' She gave Finavar a meaningful glance. 'Naieth once told me that the wives of Gavra and Aefa are buried beneath this mound, so I thought perhaps you should see it for yourself.'

Finavar blanched and stared at the strange rocks. 'Surely such people never lived? I thought the song was nothing but a story.'

Laelia shook her head. 'All songs contain a truth, one way or another. You, of all people, should know that. Your version was fanciful, certainly, but the deaths occurred. My lady witnessed them first hand. They died defending these very glades.'

Finavar recalled the pain he had seen on Ariel's face and felt a dreadful guilt. 'She knew them?'

Laelia nodded. 'Of course. They were sorcerers; handmaidens to the Queen, just as I am.'

Finavar cursed his stupidity. 'I had no idea the song carried such meaning.'

Laelia looked at him closely. 'All words carry meaning, bard, however sweetly sung.' She shrugged. 'It is fortunate though, in a way, that you sang that particular tune. My lady was unaware that you had returned.' She looked at Finavar and the humour in her eyes sparked again. 'Thanks, no doubt, to your elegant disguise.'

Finavar remained silent, eager for Laelia to reach her point.

'But your song caught her ear in a way that no other would have done and she realised that we were once more in the presence of the child who feels able to question the will of her Consort-King.'

Finavar raised his chin and adopted an uncharacteristically severe expression. 'I am no child. And I never meant to defy Orion. I only wanted to warn him.'

Laelia's humour vanished. 'It is your warning that piqued my interest. My lady has heard other tales, similar to your own: rumours of an enemy that knows more than it should. She gives them little credence.' The handmaiden looked uncomfortable as she questioned the will of her queen. 'She believes her rule is as assured as the cycles of the moon, but something in these rumours scares me.'

Finavar stared excitedly at Laelia, delighted that his warning had found an audience at last. 'I have seen these creatures. They are like nothing I have seen before.' Forgetting himself for a moment, Finavar grabbed the handmaiden's slender arm. 'It's not just the numbers that are so alarming, Laelia: they *know* the forest. They know the routes to our halls and they know how to steal power from the branches of trees.' He waved in the direction of the Council Glade. 'They may even know the way to Ariel's court.'

Laelia withdrew her arm but smiled as she did so, amused by Finavar's ignorance of court protocol. 'I see,' she said. 'And this is why you felt it was acceptable to enter the Council Glade, and disturb the rites of spring.'

Finavar nodded, not even noticing the disapproval in her voice. 'I thought Orion would help.' He looked anguished as he recalled the vast army that was descending on his home. 'I wished to find aid, before it was too late. Locrimere is on the verge of ruin, but Lord Beldeas does not seem to care.' He shook his head in exasperation. 'And Lady Ordaana would rather die than speak to one such as me.'

The crooked smile returned to Laelia's face. 'Surely that at least is a blessing.'

Finavar smirked. Then his eyes flashed with hope. 'Do you think you could persuade the Queen to aid me in some way? Then perhaps Orion would follow? What do you think? Would Ariel loan me even a fraction of her power?'

Laelia's smile grew. 'Well, she didn't send me here just to entertain you, Finavar.'

CHAPTER SEVENTEEN

Spring came to the shores of the Idolan, blackened by fire and hungry for revenge. As Caorann lay bleeding on his fallen kin, he laughed. Figures were bursting from the smoke in all directions: immense, inhuman goliaths and hunched, spindly wraiths, shadowy beings of thorn and bark that raced through the crimson dawn, towering over the ranks of minotaurs. Awful sounds filled the air, loud enough to be heard over the fire that was still raging through Locrimere: the harsh crack of breaking limbs and moist tearing of flesh.

Caorann lifted himself up onto his elbows and watched the reborn forest rise up to defend itself. 'Of course,' he croaked, still laughing despite his pain. 'Ostaliss.' He knew that somewhere, on the far side of the forest, Ariel and her Consort-King were emerging from their winter-long slumber. And as they performed the ancient rites of spring the world around them was returning to life; not just the tangible world of fronds and sap, but the hidden realms of shadow and magic – the ancient heart of the forest, pounding with hate and hunger.

Caorann stared in wonder as a brittle, wooden ocean flooded through the smoke, crushing and devouring everything that moved. Many forest spirits were bound within the rotten bark of dead trees – bark that was now black and glinting as a result of the outsiders' pitch-soaked arrows. They vented their outrage in a frenzy of lurching and stabbing, flinging goat-headed bodies through the air and tearing them apart in jagged wooden jaws. Despite their size, the spirits had a vague, intangible quality that made it almost impossible to see them clearly. It was only as they paused next to one of the beastmen that their shape could be even guessed at, and after a few seconds of wrenching and crunching they were gone again.

Another sound rang out through the carnage: a defiant horn blast that dragged Caorann to his feet. 'Eremon,' he gasped, wiping a string of blood from his mouth. He and the grizzled old captain had never seen eye-to-eye, but now, just knowing he was still alive made Caorann deliriously happy. 'He still stands,' he muttered, staggering off through the glittering, ember-filled smoke. Even in daylight it was impossible to see more than a few feet ahead, but the asrai had long ago learned to navigate by instinct. Caorann paused only to grab a sword from one of his fallen kin, before hurrying in the direction of the lake.

After a few terrifying minutes spent dodging between grinding, ghost-like shapes, he glimpsed a stretch of water, flashing through the pall. As he emerged from the smoke, clutching his wounds and swaying like a drunk, Caorann heard dozens of voices cry out in greeting.

Spread out along the shores of the Idolan, fighting furiously for the soul of Locrimere, were the remnants of Eremon's army. Less than three hundred were left to raise a cheer for Caorann, but at their head, still clutching his ragged banner, was Eremon himself. His helmet was gone and his armour was in tatters, but he was as straight-backed and determined as ever, and as he hacked and lunged with a battered sword, he even managed to nod at Caorann.

At first the wardancer could see little reason for hope – the asrai were surrounded by vast numbers of the braying, goat-headed monsters and it was impossible to see how Eremon could keep them alive much longer – but as Caorann neared the rows of archers he frowned. What he had at first taken for strands of mist, rising up behind them from the lake, were actually serpentine figures: coiled, writhing monsters of weed and silt that slid past the ranks of asrai and unfurled themselves into the smoke, joining the tree spirits in their orgy of destruction.

Caorann hacked wildly as he approached the asrai lines. His blows were weak and clumsy with pain, but as he made his way through the crowds of beastmen, it did not matter. All their attention was fixed on the creaking, whirling spirits smashing through their ranks. Caorann saw brutish, bull-horned creatures torn apart by strands of pondweed and animated, sharpened roots piercing the chests of goat-legged monstrosities. He shouldered his way through the carnage, sure at any moment that he might be snatched up by one of the tall, groaning shapes looming through the smoke. After what seemed like an age, he finally reached the shore of the lake. The lines of archers parted as he approached, allowing him to stumble past and collapse behind them, still clutching his bloody chest.

Most of the archers could only spare him the briefest words of welcome as he tumbled to the ground, but one lowered his longbow and stooped by his side. It was a pale, bloody-faced youth, with copper plaits of hair and wide green eyes.

'Your chest,' he gasped, placing a hand on Caorann's sodden bandages.

Caorann shook his head. Then he waved at the battle raging around them. 'Why is Eremon making his stand here? There is nowhere to pull back. There is no cover.'

The young archer nodded at the expanse of water. 'He spent the night communing with seers and prophets. They laid a stern command on his shoulders. They reminded him that the Idolan must never be polluted by beastman flesh.' He glanced at the mounds of fallen archers that surrounded them. 'Eremon said we must hold this spot until the dawn, at whatever cost. The forest demands it.'

Caorann nodded, seeing the sense in Eremon's decision. Tactical decisions should never be a matter of cold logic. Wisdom would not be revealed by drawing lines on the ground, but by listening to the will of trees.

The youth waved his bow at the figures rushing through the crimson smoke. It was a nightmarish scene; jagged, ethereal shapes were rending and hacking their way across the hazy, burning meadow, while the numbers of beastmen grew ever more incredible. But there was a glimmer of hope in the youth's eyes. 'And now spring has come, and Locrimere is rewarding Eremon for his loyalty.'

Caorann nodded again, then flinched, as a cold clammy figure slipped from the water and rippled past him. It was moving with unearthly speed, but he managed to glimpse barb-like talons and rolling, watery eyes, before the shape vanished into the smoke, eliciting a chorus of bestial howls as it looped and lassoed its way through the battle.

The youth helped Caorann to his feet, picked up a bow from the ground and handed it to him. 'Lend us your skill. There is hope now. The spirits are abroad once more.'

Caorann dropped his sword to the ground and grasped the bow. It was scorched and blood-slick, but he could see it was still true. 'Of course,' he gasped, wrenching a quiver from a nearby corpse.

The young archer lent him his arm and they hobbled back towards the fighting.

Caorann aimed into the whirling mass of bodies and smoke, firing as he walked. He smiled grimly as his arrow found its mark. For a while he abandoned himself to the cool thrill of revenge, picturing the kind, crumpled face of Elaeus. For a while, the asrai were free to fire on the enemy without need to defend themselves; the beastmen were far too busy fending off the forest spirits to deal with the thin waves of arrows that were whistling through the smoke.

After a few minutes, Caorann had exhausted his arrows so he looked around for another quiver. As he did so, he noticed that Eremon had lowered his own bow and was scowling at the far side of the clearing.

Caorann followed the direction of his gaze and felt a thrill of joy. An even taller shape was lumbering through the smoke: a colossal silhouette that had appeared behind the beastman army. There was something unique about this spirit, though, and Caorann could understand why Eremon looked so puzzled. Unlike the other giant shapes, this goliath was draped in shifting light.

'Locrimere will defend its own,' gasped the young archer at his side, grinning as he caught sight of the newcomer.

Caorann shook his head and looked over at Eremon again, noticing that the captain was now scowling thunderously. 'That thing is not of the forest...' muttered Caorann as the immense shape strode through the rolling smoke and loomed into view, '...whatever it is.'

The lines of asrai cursed and faltered as they saw the shape clearly. The giant figure resembled the beastmen at its feet, ox-headed, cloven-hoofed and draped in human bones and skin, but it had been magnified to insane proportions. It reared over the tree spirits, more than thirty feet tall and crowned with enormous, horizontal horns. As it entered the smoke-wreathed battle it glared down at the mayhem with an enormous, cyclopean eye.

'Isha preserve us,' Caorann heard one of the archers say. 'What is it?'

Eremon howled another furious order, demanding that the kinbands maintain their fire, but some of the archers were too shocked to obey. As they watched the giant approaching through the smoke, they lowered their bows and backed towards the water, muttering prayers under their breath.

Caorann frowned as he watched the monster's advance. It moved with odd, lurching bounds, shaking embers from the surrounding trees as it pounded across the sacred meadow. Its movements were random; there seemed no logic to its erratic lunges and it appeared confused by the crowds surging around its legs. Then Caorann gasped as he saw the giant fix its lantern-like gaze on a forest spirit: a ghostly blackthorn, tearing and hacking its way through the battle. The giant beastman abandoned its erratic wandering and leapt with shocking speed, reaching down with unnerving accuracy and wrenching the spirit from the ground. There was a groan of splintering roots as the monster lifted the thrashing shape up into the air and bit into it like a choice cut of meat.

Caorann watched in horror as the cyclopean creature gorged itself on the spirit. As it did so, the light in its enormous eye blazed even brighter. Then it fixed its malevolent gaze on another forest spirit, wrenched it from the ground and destroyed it with a snort of pleasure. It was as though it could see the ghostly spectres with more ease than its own army.

'Its eye,' muttered Caorann. 'It is not fixed on this world. It sees the realm of the spirits.'

'Blind it!' he cried, raising his bow and loosing an arrow into the smoke. But his words were lost in the clamour of the battle.

As the giant lumbered across the meadow, the tide of the battle started to turn. As soon as the cyclopean monster captured a forest spirit, the beastmen were able to attack too. In a matter of minutes, dozens of the writhing shapes were torn apart and cast into the growing flames.

Caorann shouldered his way through the ranks of archers and after a few minutes he reached Eremon's side. The captain's brutal, heavy-browed face was covered with fresh scars, and he was knee-deep in corpses, but there was no trace of fear in his eyes as he turned to face the wardancer. As he took in Caorann's blood-drenched bandages and countless other wounds, he softened his glare a little.

'You should not have left your bed,' he growled, loosing another arrow.

Caorann could not help but smile. Barked and furious though they were, the captain's words were the closest he had ever come to speaking kindly to him. Caorann realised that he must have made a good impression on the tough old veteran.

'If we wait here, we'll die,' he said, matching the captain's gruff tones. 'We have to advance.' He pointed his bow at a hill to the north of them, still free of fire. 'If we could make that vantage point we would be in range of the giant.' He nodded to the writhing, splintering shapes in its hands. 'And we would have a chance of saving them.'

Eremon grimaced as he looked at the ranks of beastmen between his archers and the hill, but he nodded all the same.

He turned and stared at Caorann for a moment. 'But will we save ourselves?'

Caorann shook his head, unsure what to say. Breaking through the beastman army would result in horrific casualties, but he could not bear to watch the forest's soul being torn out by such a vile creature.

Eremon looked around at the flaming towers of Locrimere. Left unfought, the fires were tearing through the glades and groves of their home. He clenched his jaw and nodded, then clapped a hand on Caorann's shoulder. 'You have a heart of oak. And you are right.' He took a deep shuddering breath. 'Whether we live or die will be decided by the gods, not me, but we cannot stay here and watch the forest die.'

He drew his horn from his belt. As the flames raged higher he let out a long, true note and ordered the asrai to advance.

CHAPTER EIGHTEEN

'It *should* work,' said Orion, turning the blood-slick stone in his hand. 'Such power is fit for a king, not a beast.'

The festival rites were over. The only strains of music were quiet, wistful airs and most of the lords and ladies of the forest were sprawled across the royal dais in an exhausted stupor. Behind them the sun was sinking, framed by the silhouettes of branches and a vivid, turquoise dusk. There was still a devoted group of supplicants fawning at Ariel's feet and Orion had to keep his voice low to avoid being overheard.

'Am I not the King?' he growled, staring at Atolmis.

Orion's equerry was standing next to the throne, peering at the Wrach's talisman. His black eyes were full of doubt. 'The Brúidd are the guardians of these things. Only they understand them. No one else knows the mind of the forest. Even our most skilled magi would struggle to–'

'Do I not have dominion? Am I not the lord of every leaf, branch and beast?' Orion's shoulders were trembling as he placed a hand over the hard lump buried in his chest. 'Did you

235

not select me, Atolmis, out of everyone, for this duty?'

'Of course,' said Atolmis. 'You are my leaf-liege.' He hesitated. 'But without the strength of the Brúidd the forest would fall apart.'

Orion only heard the first part of Atolmis's reply. 'And yet, I had to prostrate myself before those *creatures*.' He glared at the lifeless stone. 'I had to endure all their ridicule and doubt.'

He looked over at Ariel, graciously listening to the nonsense spewing from her awestruck subjects. Her head was tilted to one side and she maintained a benign smile, even as they smothered her with tales of their tedious, melodramatic little lives. She looked up for a moment and caught his eye. For a moment, everything fell away and they were alone, standing beneath the boughs of the Oak of Ages at the dawn of their reign; victorious and blazing with passion, filled with hope. Even then, Orion realised, all those long centuries ago, there had been something otherworldly in Ariel's eyes. Her gaze had always been fixed on the unknowable.

I will never fail you, he thought, feeling again the weight of his burden.

The Queen's smile was unfaltering and she held out a hand to him.

It was immediately grabbed by the dreamy-eyed poet, Khoron Belidae, who covered it with kisses and began regaling her with some ridiculous tale.

Ariel held Orion's gaze for a second longer and then she began to laugh, softly, as the crowds moved between them.

Orion turned back to Atolmis with his heart pounding. His voice was low and urgent. 'There was a child. He had golden eyes. He treated me as though I were some kind of pathetic fraud.' Orion shivered at the memory. 'They called him Zephyr.'

Atolmis stepped back and shook his head. 'I know nothing

of such things.' He nodded to Ariel. 'Your queen would be able to tell you more than me. She has communed with the Brúidd for centuries. She knows the forest's spirits more than anyone else. Ask her about Sativus.'

Orion grimaced. The thought filled him with nausea. How could Ariel have anything to do with such a being? The idea of discussing it with her made his head spin. 'Who else knows of them?'

Atolmis looked out across the Council Glade. The lawn was a network of long shadows and it was hard to make out the crowds with any clarity. 'Perhaps Naieth, the prophetess, but she rarely mingles with her own kind. You will see her on Midsummer's Eve. She will come to pay her respects, and witness the start of your Wild Hunt.'

Orion peered at the polished stone. 'I cannot wait until summer.' He met the eyes of his equerry. 'I am no fool, Atolmis. I understand what you have done to me.' He looked around at the sprawled remnants of the festival. 'You have bound me to the seasons. I have no time. I must win the allegiance of these wretched spirits now.'

Atolmis narrowed his eyes, unnerved by Orion's words. 'But have you won the allegiance of the Wrach, my lord?' he asked. 'Or just his hatred?'

Orion leant back in his root throne, stretching his broad, ivy-clad chest. 'I made him kneel, Atolmis, I made him *kneel*. That is enough. He will not question my strength again.'

Atolmis looked again at the bloody stone. 'But at what cost?' Pain flashed in his eyes. 'Sélva and the others have been left to wander the Dark Paths. They may *never* find their way back without the Wrach to guide them. Without that key you hold, who knows what strange shores they will wash up on?' He pointed one of his talons at the stone. 'That is no toy.'

Orion was about to reply when he noticed that someone was edging hesitantly towards the throne.

Atolmis backed away and Orion looked up to see who would dare approach him. As the noble rose from a deep bow, Orion realised it was one of the guests he had noticed earlier: the bare-chested warrior with golden, wing-shaped torques coiled around his biceps and a network of scars gouged into his face.

'Prince Haldus,' said Orion. 'A rider of hawks.'

The guests who were still crowded around the thrones ceased their babbling to watch the exchange.

Ariel nodded at the warrior and as he bowed in her direction she smiled in recognition.

'Orion, Lord of the Deepwood Host,' replied Prince Haldus. His voice was gruff and his cheeks were flushed with embarrassment. As he spoke, he kept glancing around at the assembled nobility, clearly uncomfortable in their presence. He dropped awkwardly to one knee, in a clumsy attempt to observe the etiquette of the Queen's court. He spoke slowly and carefully. 'You remember me. I am honoured.'

Orion felt an immediate kinship with the warrior. His rough manners set him apart from the crowds. He clearly had no interest in their gossip or poetry and Orion wondered what had brought him to the Council Glade, when he would obviously prefer to be anywhere else.

Orion scoured his memory. After a few seconds he pictured the two of them riding together, many years ago, way above the eaves of the forest. Orion could almost feel the wind howling around his face as they plunged through the rain towards an unseen prey, laughing wildly as they hurtled towards the trees. As he returned his gaze to the kneeling prince, Orion realised that, despite his awkwardness and his scowl, this warrior was a friend; more so than any of the other nobles present.

He softened his voice slightly. 'We hunted together.'

The prince's scarred, weather-beaten features flushed even darker and he continued staring at the ground. 'Yes, my lord. Many times. Since I was but a boy.' He dared to meet Orion's eye for a second and his thin, cracked lips gave the slightest hint of a smile. 'Perhaps, come the summer, we will hunt again.'

Orion leant back in his throne, still clutching the Wrach's carved, black eye. He realised that the whole gathering was watching the exchange and filled his voice with the same ferocious tones he usually used. 'What do you want, Prince Haldus?'

'My lord, I...' His words trailed off and his scowl deepened as he struggled to speak clearly. He coughed nervously and began again. 'Please forgive me, but I have come to offer you my aid.'

'Your aid?' Orion tightened his fingers on the stone and lowered his voice to a rumble. 'What need do *I* have for aid?'

The threat in his voice was tangible and several nobles backed away. Finavar's disappearance had not gone unnoticed. There were already rumours that Orion and his equerries had devoured him.

Prince Haldus remained on one knee but kept his voice slow and deliberate. 'The King has no need of aid but he does, on occasion, indulge his most loyal subjects by allowing them to serve him.'

Ariel pursed her lips in a smile, clearly amused by the warrior's diplomacy.

Orion leant forwards in his throne, keeping his voice low. 'What do you want?'

'My lord, as my subjects wintered in their lofty eyries, I have travelled.' His blushes deepened. 'I wished to escape my duties for a while.' He coughed again. 'At first, all I wished was a chance to be alone, but as I crossed the forest I began to witness sights that troubled me deeply.' He looked from Orion to Ariel and back again. 'While you and the Queen slept, the winter snows have been red with blood.'

Orion narrowed his eyes and his breathing quickened. 'Are you afraid of blood, Haldus?'

'Of course not, my lord.' He paused and spoke even slower, desperate not to be misunderstood. 'This is not the natural cycle of life and death.' He waved at the sky. 'From the clouds I see things others might miss.'

Ariel's smile vanished and she leant forwards, listening intently. Courtiers and nobles pressed closer, eager to hear the exchange.

Orion remained silent.

'My lord,' said Prince Haldus. 'This winter I have travelled the length of the forest, from the Grey Mountains to the Wildwood, and everywhere I look, I see signs of destruction. The creatures of Chaos are taking your kingdom for their own.'

He paused, choosing his next words with particular care. 'And they could not do such a thing without help. Someone has betrayed us.' He looked around at the shocked faces of the nobles. 'The halls of your subjects are in danger. If you do not unite the kindreds under your banner, the whole forest is at risk.'

Scorn and ridicule poured from Ariel's courtiers.

'Unite?' cried one of the nobles. 'Is he saying we cannot defend our own?'

'Ridiculous!' cried another one of the highborn, flinging back his robes in outrage. 'Are you giving us orders, barbarian? Would you tell us how to defend our own glades?'

After a while the nobles fell silent, waiting to hear how Orion would respond to such strange ideas. There was no sign of emotion in his eyes, but his mind was racing. This was the first time they would see how well he carried his mantle of kingship and he filled his voice with scorn. 'Our borders are a snare, Prince Haldus. Any mongrel that stumbles through them is sport, nothing more. If it pleases me I will hunt such things down. If it does not please me, I will not. Either way, there is no threat.'

Orion's words were met with applause and laughter and the nobles continued to glare at Haldus, appalled by his suggestion that they should bind their armies together in some way.

Orion returned his gaze to the stone in his fist and seemed to forget all about Prince Haldus.

He heard Ariel pick up the conversation. There was an incredulous tone in her voice.

'You said we had been betrayed?'

'Yes, my queen,' replied Haldus. 'All through the winter I have been watching. Outsiders are travelling through the forest as confidently as if they were born beneath its boughs. They follow secret routes only an asrai could know of. This is why we must join arms together.'

At the mention of secret routes, Orion thought of the Wrach, and his old stones, but he remained silent.

'Who would betray their own queen?' asked Ariel, genuinely confused.

The prince shook his head, looking distinctly uncomfortable. 'I cannot be sure, your majesty.' He hesitated. 'But I believe it must be a member of this court.'

There was another chorus of gasps from the nobles and some of them placed hands on their weapons.

Ariel held up a hand and the crowd fell silent. 'So,' she said, utterly bemused, 'you came here to offer us your aid.'

The prince's discomfort grew. He glanced hesitantly at Orion, but the King was muttering to Atolmis and seemed uninterested in the exchange.

'I came to pay my respects and offer to help the King unite our armies. I intended to lead him to the outsiders, so that he might see for himself. Every mile they cross sees them grow more powerful.'

He glanced around and singled out two slender figures, standing at the edge of the dais. 'That young bard, Finavar was right – the halls of Lord Beldeas and Lady Ordaana are already in grave danger. There is an army gathering outside Locrimere unlike anything I have ever seen. Alone, the kingdoms will be unable to–'

'Did you see the beasts?' snarled Orion.

Haldus shook his head, confused. 'Beasts, my lord?'

'Beasts.' Orion turned to Atolmis, his voice full of bile. 'What did you call it? This council of spectres that claim to rule my forest?'

Haldus struggled not to flinch as Atolmis stepped from behind the throne. He was almost as terrifying as Orion, with his featureless black eyes and his bloody, ivy-clad skin.

'The Brúidd,' he replied, his voice a low growl.

Ariel's eyes widened and she rose from her throne. 'What has he told you, my love?' She frowned. 'Why do you speak of them with such hate?'

Orion could not meet his queen's eye, remembering again all the shame of his encounter by the lake. He leant forwards instead and stared at Haldus. 'They are like the ghosts of animals: freakish serpents and bloated toads that speak in mockery of our own language, wolves made of moonlight and eagles that speak gibberish.'

Haldus shook his head, looking over at the Queen for an explanation, but she was too shocked by Orion's bile to speak. Then Haldus raised his eyebrows. 'Did you say a great eagle?' He narrowed his eyes. 'An eagle that speaks?'

Orion nodded and leant forwards in his throne.

'I *have* heard of such a thing,' said Haldus, 'but not while I was abroad.' He pointed to the far side of the clearing. 'Less than half a mile from here is my own mount, Nuin. She is truly a great eagle. There is no more noble creature in...'

The prince's words trailed off as he saw that Orion was shaking his head.

The nobles began to jeer and laugh as they realised Haldus was losing Orion's interest. Several of them barged past the prince, causing him to stagger away from the throne.

As the King turned away and began to speaking to Atolmis again, Haldus looked desperately at Ariel for support, but she was whispering furiously to one of her handmaidens.

'You *must* act, my king,' he said. 'The forest is in grave danger.'

Orion barely seemed to hear him and Haldus was jostled further back by the nobles.

'An eagle that speaks?' he called, raising his voice above the tumult.

Orion looked back at him.

'Perhaps you are talking about Amphion.'

Orion leant forwards again. 'Amphion?'

Haldus barged his way back through the crowd and knelt before Orion's throne again. 'There is a kingdom in the Pine Crags, a lonely vale by the name of Fincara. The kindreds who dwell there are a strange people. They pay homage to a spirit named Amphion. I have always dismissed the tales that come from that place, but my daughter Clorana delights in them.' He smiled at the memory. 'She recites them incessantly. In the stories, Amphion appears in the form of an enormous eagle, and speaks to the people of Fincara in their own tongue.'

Orion stood up, towering over the prince. 'What else does she sing? Does your daughter sing of its wings, or its plumage?'

Haldus wracked his brains for the details of his child's stories. 'Yes. There was something else: Amphion has two pairs of wings.' He shook his head and scowled. 'And there is something about its feathers. I believe Clorana said they are sculpted from fire.'

CHAPTER NINETEEN

For the first time in his short life, Orion felt free. The forest was gone. It had sunk beneath him in a haze of grey cloud and all that remained was the endless, blinding azure of the evening sky. Skólann's enormous bulk was beneath him and she was no longer trembling. The giant eagle had grudgingly accepted her new rider and she was at ease once more, and revelling in the power of her enormous wings.

As she soared up into the blue, Orion leant forwards, as Prince Haldus had instructed, gripping her between his thighs and muttering the gentle phrases he had learned. He looked to his left and saw the prince was only a few feet away; close enough for Orion to see the wind rippling through the feathers of his mount. The trailing spines of Haldus's headgear and the swirling scars on his face made him resemble a spirit of the air and his eyes were blazing with excitement. The awkwardness that had marked him out in the Council Glade had vanished. He rode Nuin so lightly that he and the bird seemed to be joined; a single glorious being, gilded by the sun's fading light.

As he caught Orion's gaze, Haldus hopped up into a crouching position and looked back at him without a trace of servility.
For a brief moment they were equals beneath the spring sky
and Orion felt as though he had slipped back into a previous
life. He revelled in the sensation, happy to enjoy the simple,
physical pleasures of the wind on his face and Skólann's warm
feathers beneath his legs.

They flew in silence for several long, blissful hours, heading
east towards the Grey Mountains, a jagged row of snow-capped
peaks that marked the furthest reaches of the forest. Then, as
the sun sank lower and the skies shifted slowly towards a deep
cobalt, Prince Haldus called out, pointing his longbow to the
foothills below and a patch of open land beside the silver
ribbon of a small brook.

Orion nodded in reply, attempting to maintain his magiste-
rial demeanour, but wondering how he could steer Skólann
back down through the clouds. Then, as Prince Haldus guided
his mount down towards the ground, Orion sighed with
relief. Skólann needed no encouragement to follow her sister's
descent.

Orion gripped her feathers a little tighter and leant back as
she dived through the clouds, letting out a long, gleeful screech.

'This is all that matters,' said Prince Haldus, leaning closer.
They had built a small fire beside the brook and the light was
rippling over his face, picking it out from the evening gloom.
The lines on his thunderous brow had softened and, with the
flames glittering in his eyes, Prince Haldus looked as happy
as the supplicants of the Council Glade. But his was a different kind of happiness, Orion realised. Haldus was not dazed
by intoxicating herbs or drunk on fruit wine. His cheeks were
red, but only as the result of the wind and warmth of the fire,

and his voice was calm, unlike the wild songs that filled Ariel's court. He spoke with the same ponderous care as before, but there was a new edge of emotion in his voice. 'To be in the heart of the forest, alone.' He stretched his limbs and groaned with pleasure. 'To feel the exhaustion of a long day's riding.' He looked up the stars that were unveiling themselves overhead. 'Far from one's duties and obligations.'

Orion recalled that he and Prince Haldus shared a bond: they both had kingdoms and subjects that hung shackle-like from their limbs. He nodded and lay back across the damp grass, hypnotised by the flames. 'Do you crave nothing but escape? There are many tales of Arum Tor. All of them mention its beauty.'

Haldus continued gazing into the fire, considering his reply carefully before he spoke. 'Arum Tor is as much a part of me as my family and my kindred. And yes, my king, it is beautiful beyond anything you could imagine.' He closed his eyes for a second, picturing the lofty eyries of his home. 'Perhaps one day I will show you my halls at the roof of the world: Cáder Donann, the jewel of Arum Tor. Its reach is so high that you might believe you were in the realm of the gods.'

He opened his eyes and peered into the inky darkness pressing in around the fire. Two huge shapes were just visible at the edge of the trees. 'It is the nesting place of the noblest eagles; birds of true dignity. They would rather die than bring shame on their race. If you called the kindreds to war, the great eagles would lead your armies. I promise you.'

Orion realised that he could remember Cáder Donann. With every hour that passed, he saw his previous lives a little better and he smiled as he saw Haldus's home, perhaps even more clearly than the prince himself. Then he recalled all the countless generations of princes that came before Haldus, riding to war on raptors that could trace their proud ancestry even further back than the asrai.

The combination of the fire and his kaleidoscopic memories weighed heavily on Orion's eyelids. He spread his massive frame further across the grass, relaxing each of his tired muscles one by one and relishing the sleep that loomed over him. Then, as he turned onto his side, Orion felt the eye of the Wrach, secreted in a deerskin pouch attached to his belt, digging into his thigh. At the memory of the Blind Guide his tiredness vanished. He sat up and shook his head, ridding himself of drowsiness.

'Tell me again of Amphion,' he said.

Prince Haldus looked disappointed by the question. 'I know nothing of the spirit itself, or if it even exists for sure. All I know are songs and legends.'

Orion felt his muscles tensing as Haldus entered another one of his long, deliberate pauses.

'These are the facts I *do* know,' said the prince after a few moments, sitting upright. 'Since long before I was born the Vale of Fincara has trod a lonely path; it is sundered from the other asrai of the Pine Crags. Many centuries ago they ceased paying fealty to my ancestors and severed ties with all the other kindreds of the forest.'

He looked away, then stared down at his rough, calloused hands. 'The lord of Fincara no longer attends the festivals of the Council Glade – whether it is the rites of spring, or the summer solstice. You will see no envoys from his realm; not a single kinband.' He shook his head. 'Beyond that, my knowledge is little more than rumour and conjecture. My waywatchers tell me that Cyanos, the current lord of Fincara, has styled himself King of Turas-Alva.'

'Turas-Alva?'

'It is an ancient name for the Pine Crags.'

Orion was unable to hide the impatience in his voice. 'And the spirit, Amphion?'

Prince Haldus met Orion's eye again, and chose his next words with care. 'These are the rumours I have heard. Lord, or "King" Cyanos does not attend festivals like Ostaliss because he considers himself quite above such things. He believes that he is a regent in his own right and therefore does not need to pay homage to the King and Queen in the Woods. The kindreds of Fincara do not even consider themselves asrai any more. As I mentioned, they refer to their home as Turas-Alva, which means the Land of the Sky. They imagine themselves an entirely separate race. They call themselves alvaír, or the Children of the Sky, and Lord Cyanos has become, by all accounts, very strange. Even more than the other kindreds that surround his realm, he is obsessed by birds and flight, and the nature of the wind. And like his father before him, he is a hoarder of strange antiques – obscure texts left in the forest by our forefathers. Apparently his years of research have enabled him to transform his flesh in some way, some vile tribute to his master – a forest spirit that he worships under the name of Amphion. The same spirit my daughter sings of. I'm told that Cyanos is so enamoured of this being that he pays no heed to true gods such as Asuryan.' He paused and glanced at Orion. 'Or even Kurnous.'

Orion leant even closer to the fire, clutching the stone in his pouch.

Haldus continued. 'I cannot be sure if the avian spirit he worships is the same as your Bru...' Haldus frowned, unsure of the name.

'Brúidd,' growled Orion, tasting the word like a poison. 'Atolmis called them the Council of Beasts.'

Haldus nodded. 'The Council of Beasts. I cannot be sure if we are describing the same being, but the details are oddly similar.'

'Four wings.'

'Four wings and the odd markings that resemble flames.'

'It was a kind of brindle,' said Orion, 'but the feathers were red and gold and they shimmered.' He was now leaning so close to the fire that his mantle of ivy was beginning to smoke. 'It *must* be the same creature.'

Haldus frowned. 'It is the same description, certainly, but I cannot be sure that Cyanos really sees such a thing. Who knows what effect all his strange collections have had on him. I have never spoken to him myself. I have heard rumours and songs, nothing more.' He grimaced. 'Scrolls and books have no place in the forest.'

He shrugged, looking a little embarrassed by his own vehemence. 'My advisors say I should wage war on Fincara, or open up some kind of negotiations.' As he described such onerous duties, Haldus looked quite nauseous. 'But I would rather spend my time on the wing, where I can forget such complicated matters.' He looked up at the stars, and gripped the knife at his belt. 'I would rather be hunting by your side, my lord, than playing political games. Should I be ashamed of that?'

Even through the filter of his rage, Orion noticed again the bond he shared with Haldus. They both felt the weight of an inheritance they could not escape. He shook his head and softened his voice again. 'How long until I can see this "King" Cyanos for myself?'

Haldus shrugged. 'We are already in the foothills. By midday tomorrow we shall reach the Vale of Fincara.'

Orion gave no reply and for a few minutes they were both lost in their own thoughts.

Haldus prodded at the fire with a stick, sending a cloud of sparks spiralling up into the darkness and flooding the riverbank with a brief flash of light. The flare picked out a row of tiny shapes that had gathered at the foot of the trees, not far from the sleeping eagles. Haldus frowned for a second, unsure what he was seeing. Then he noticed that the shapes had faint, glimmering wings and spiny, twig-like bodies. He realised the forest's tiny spirits were intrigued by his companion. The sight of them reminded him why he had originally approached the King.

'My lord,' he said, stirring Orion from his thoughts. 'My reasons for travelling the forest this winter were selfish, I admit, but what I told you in the Council Glade was true. I have seen armies of beastmen larger than anything I have ever heard described.'

Orion looked up. The prince's words were almost identical to Finavar's and the memory of the wardancer immediately conjured another image: a row of bestial faces, jeering at his weak, ruined flesh.

Haldus took another long pause before he continued, and the frown returned to his low, heavy brow. 'Will you do nothing?' His question was so quiet it was almost a whisper.

At first it seemed that Orion had not heard. He continued looking blankly through Haldus, as though he had slipped into some kind of trance. Finally, after a few minutes, he refocused his gaze and nodded. 'I will do something,' he said. 'I will prove to this forest that it is mine.' His voice rumbled from his chest. 'I will teach the Brúidd that the Queen and I are the twin beating hearts of this realm. They must pay fealty or die.'

Haldus looked pained. 'And the outsiders? Will you hunt them?'

Orion revealed his long teeth in perfect mimicry of Atolmis's vile grin. 'I will hunt *everything*.' He reached into the fire and gripped a flaming log. His skin rippled in the heat, starting to blister, but then something odd happened. The fire burned a deep red where it touched his hand, then it became a bright white, pulsing across his knuckles. After a few minutes, Orion withdrew his hand and held it up in the moonlight. It was completely unharmed.

'I am becoming *strong*.' He turned his hand back and forth and stared at it in awe. 'All the strength of Kurnous is in me.' He turned his gaze back on the prince, remembering something Ariel had said.

'By summer there will be nothing that can stand against me.'

They awoke with the dawn, stiff from the cold and covered in a filmy layer of dew. The fire had died and the spirits had vanished with the stars. Orion climbed to his hooves and stretched his powerful arms, looking down at the rippling stream. He saw his reflection and for a moment he was confused. In his dreams he had been Sephian, the wanderer from the Silvam Dale; weak, powerless and mortal. The vision that glared back at him from the water's undulating mirror was a god in the making. It seemed incredible, but Orion was sure he had grown during the night; surely his antlers were taller and more knotted than before? And weren't his talons thicker and more ridged? They looked like they could tear through rock.

'My lord?' said Haldus, indicating the cold remains of last night's meal – a brace of hares they had caught in the neighbouring meadow.

Orion wolfed down the food in one grunting mouthful and followed Haldus back to the eagles.

As he approached Skólann she eyed him calmly for a few seconds and then lowered her head. Orion felt a rush of pride. The noble creature was going to let him fly without any encouragement from Prince Haldus. He muttered a few words of thanks as he climbed onto her back, attempting to temper his brutal growl.

Smaller birds exploded from the trees as the two great eagles pounded their wings and launched themselves into the morning light.

Haldus led the way, steering his mount low over the treetops, following the backs of the foothills as they tumbled towards the looming mass of the Grey Mountains.

After several hours of wordless flight across the canopy of the trees, Prince Haldus called out a warning and headed up through the clouds.

For a while Orion was enveloped in greyness. Then, after a few minutes, they cleared the clouds and Orion saw a scene of such beauty that for a few seconds he forgot to breathe. The Pine Crags sheared up from the foothills; jagged, unforgiving, blazing in the morning light and draped in a cloak of gloomy fir trees.

Prince Haldus looked back over his shoulder, and as he saw the look on Orion's face he beamed with as much pride as if he had wrenched the rock from the ground with his own hands. As they banked to the north, across the sheer face of the peaks, he pointed his longbow at a crevasse – a deep, brutal gash in the mountainside, surrounded by dozens of circling hawks.

'Fincara,' he called, straining to be heard against the buffeting wind.

Orion nodded eagerly in reply and leant forwards for a better look. The crevasse was deep in shadow but, as they looped down towards it, he began to make out caves in its walls and more birds, drifting lazily in the thermals.

Haldus steered his mount straight down towards the narrowest part of the gulley, plunging like a stone, with no sign of slowing as he neared the rocks.

Skólann followed suit, dropping into a steep dive, and Orion had to clutch wildly at her feathers to avoid tumbling from her back.

Hawks and ravens scattered as the great eagles plunged into the chasm and were enveloped by the cool shade within.

Haldus landed his eagle on a narrow bridge of rock, jutting out like a jetty from the side of the ravine thousands of feet above the valley floor. The bridge was a geological wonder: a needle-like sliver of granite that arched across the chasm, linking the great hulks of mountain on either side. A few seconds later Skólann landed a few feet away, scraping her talons across the rock and letting out an indignant screech as she came to a halt, facing a tall, gate-like opening in the wall of the mountain.

As soon as the eagle had settled, Orion dropped from her side and paced across the bridge, filling the ravine with the sound of hooves against stone.

Prince Haldus dismounted and hurried after him.

'Wait, my lord,' he called. 'The caves will be guarded.'

Orion gave no answer and strode onto a broad lip of rock at the far end of the bridge, making for the cave opening.

'A weapon!' he cried, without turning.

Haldus hurriedly drew a sword from his belt and held it out to his king.

Orion snatched it from his grip and swung it back and forth through the crisp mountain air, creating a thin whistling sound as he disappeared into the gloom of the cave.

It seemed to Orion that he had entered a forest glade. Then, as his vision grew accustomed to the dark, he saw that the tree-like columns surrounding him were actually towering fingers of rock and the dappled light came from hundreds of tiny holes in the cave's ceiling, spilling sunlight down through the shifting, dusty air.

Tall, long-limbed guards hurried towards him: asrai, certainly, but clad in strange, tawny-coloured robes of feather and moss. Even stranger than their cloaks were the masks they all wore: hoods of animal hide with long snouts of carved bone, designed to resemble the beaks of eagles.

The guards carried slender wooden javelins, but as they neared Orion they lowered them in confusion and fear. Even after centuries of isolation, the asrai of Fincara could recognise such a ferocious, snarling likeness of Kurnous, God of the Hunt. The image of the horned god was carved deeply into their ancestral memory and it filled them with dread.

A few of the guards turned on their heels and ran back into the darkness, taking word that a spirit had fallen from the heavens, but most edged closer, staring at Orion in awe through the sagging eyeholes of their masks.

Prince Haldus hurried to Orion's side. The lights flickered over his face as he drew an arrow and the guards muttered nervously at the sight of his mutilated skin.

'Which of you is Cyanos?' cried Orion, filling the cave with his feral roar.

The guards turned to one another in wonder, clearly amazed that this green-hued monster could speak a language they understood.

After a brief, whispered debate, one of them broke ranks and approached Orion with his spear raised.

'Are you a god?' he asked. His dialect was odd, and the words were interspersed with strange clicking sounds, but the meaning was clear.

'I am Orion: Consort-King of the Queen, Master of the Wild Hunt and Lord of the Deepwood Host. The blood of Kurnous is in my veins.'

The guard seemed unsure whether to attack or bow. He looked back at his companions for guidance, but they looked as confused as he did. 'I am Síngas of the alvaír,' he replied eventually. A noticeable tremor entered his voice and he lowered his gaze. 'The King of Turas-Alva does not receive guests.'

Orion replied with such violence that the guard took a few steps back. 'I am not his guest. I am his king.'

Síngas cowered but kept his javelin raised. 'Word of your arrival has been sent, but King Cyanos will not–'

'Step aside,' growled Orion, striding forwards and raising the sword he had taken from Prince Haldus.

The guards cowered but held their line, raising their javelins with trembling hands and pressing closer together as Orion approached.

Orion paused, shaking his head in amazement. 'Would you deny your king?' he asked, looking up and down the line of hooded figures.

'Cyanos is our king,' replied Síngas, raising his chin, despite his fear. 'And he does not receive guests.'

Orion let out an odd, snorting bark and drew back his sword.

'Wait, my lord,' said Prince Haldus, placing his hand on Orion's arm.

Orion hesitated and Haldus moved past him, holding up his hands as he approached the line of guards.

'I am Prince Haldus of Arum Tor,' he said to the one called Síngas. 'My father fought alongside Cyanos's father at the Battle of Amathíon Head, when your king was still a boy. Even here, I'm sure that must still mean something. If you mention my ancestry to your master, I am sure he will admit us.'

Síngas replied in a sneering tone. 'We remember the princes of Arum Tor.' He threw back his feathered cloak and raised his voice, so that the rest of the guards could hear. 'We remember how you took our bravest sons and sacrificed them, so that Ariel's children could continue nestling in their pretty little bowers, whether they're wanted there or not.'

The disdain in the guard's voice emboldened the others and they began to advance, training their javelins on Haldus and Orion.

'We remember how the Prince of Arum Tor grovels to those who have planted themselves in ground that has no love for them.' The guard's bile grew as he stepped closer, jabbing his javelin as he approached. 'You and your kind are not fit to—'

Síngas's words became a wet gargle as his head flipped back. He dropped to his knees as his head fell away, still contained in its strange hood as it bounced across the rock.

For a few seconds the other guards were unsure what had happened; Orion's sword had moved so fast that they only realised what he had done when he drew back the blade for a second strike.

One of the guards drew back his javelin to fling it at Orion.

Prince Haldus moved faster. He stepped back and calmly fired an arrow.

Before the guard could loose his javelin he reeled backwards with the arrow sunk deep in his throat.

There was a brief pause, then the shadowy cave exploded into violence. The guards threw themselves at Orion and Haldus, lunging and jabbing with their slender spears and drawing long, curved knives from their belts.

Orion lashed out with the sword a few times and then seemed to find it an encumbrance. He sent it clattering to the ground and tore into his opponents with talons, fists and antlers. As he wrenched necks and gored faces, the King roared. It was a cry of pleasure.

Prince Haldus continued to edge slowly backwards, loosing arrow after arrow as he walked, dropping every figure that emerged from behind the pillars of rock.

The cave was filled with the sound of grunting and tearing and the clatter of Orion's hooves.

Guards continued to pour from the shadows, but none could land a blow on the King. His movements were as wild and frenetic as a cornered animal.

After several minutes of fruitless carnage, one of the more clear-thinking guards ordered a retreat, forming a second row several feet away from the fighting.

As Orion continued to snarl and punch, Prince Haldus lowered his longbow for a second, realising that the alvaír were about to launch dozens of javelins at Orion, regardless of who else might be injured.

He whirled around and squinted out through the entrance of the cave, to the slender bridge of rock outside. The two eagles were still waiting patiently on the ledge and he raised his fingers to his lips, summoning them with a shrill, sustained whistle.

The enormous birds responded immediately. They launched themselves into the air with a single beat of their vast wings and hurtled towards the cave.

The alvaír stumbled and lowered their javelins, crying out in fear as the eagles swooped through the cave mouth and crashed into them.

There was a flurry of talons and feathers as the eagles attacked. Their wings were edged with sharpened bone and they tore open the guards' chests, sending their weapons clattering across the stone floor. Their beaks hammered back and forth like pickaxes and their steel-tipped talons grasped and tore.

The line of guards collapsed. Several of them fell, clutching at mortal wounds and wailing in fear, and the rest dropped to their knees, begging for mercy. Not one of them fought back.

Prince Haldus frowned. Terrifying as the eagles were, the response of the guards seemed odd. Rather than defending themselves, they wailed pitifully at the sight of the enraged eagles, drawing invisible symbols in the air and begging the birds for forgiveness. Haldus considered their strange, bird-like masks and long, feathered robes and guessed the reason: they saw the eagles as gods. His own kindreds revered their noble winged mounts but, in their isolation, the kindreds of Fincara had taken such beliefs to an extreme conclusion.

The eagles turned to face Haldus. Their feathers were slick with blood but none of it was their own.

Orion downed his final opponent with a fierce backhanded blow. Then he raised his bloody fists and howled, surrounded by a mound of bodies. He was too lost in the moment to notice the strange sight of the kneeling guards, fawning and pleading with the eagles.

Haldus sprinted across the body-strewn cave towards the eagles. As he reached their sides he scowled at the cowering guards. 'Take us to your king!' he cried, pointing at the eagles. 'Or face the wrath of your gods!'

The alvaír looked at each other. Several of their bird masks had been torn away and their pale, bloody faces were filled with terror, but none of them seemed willing to accede to Haldus's demand.

Orion lowered his head. Blood flew from his antlers as he turned to look at Prince Haldus, finally noticing that the remaining guards were all kneeling in a half circle around the eagles.

Seeing their hesitation, Haldus turned to the eagles and made a subtle clicking sound with his mouth.

The birds stepped towards the guards, unfolding their enormous wings.

The alvaír wailed again and one of them raised his hands to Prince Haldus. 'We will do as the spirits command!' The other guards nodded their heads in desperate agreement. 'Tell your masters.'

Orion trotted across the mounds of corpses and stood next to Prince Haldus, shaking his head at the oddness of the scene.

Haldus raised his eyebrows at Orion, then he turned back to the guards. 'One of you must lead us to your king. The rest will remain here and attend to the spirits.' He waved to the eagles with his longbow. 'If we do not return safely, their fury will be like nothing you have seen so far.'

The guard who had spoken climbed hesitantly to his feet. 'I am Elpenor,' he said 'I will lead you.' His eyes were straining with terror and his words tumbled from his mouth. 'King Cyanos would not deny such a command. I did not realise you were envoys of gods. Forgive me, I…' His words trailed off as he looked at the pile of bodies Orion had left. He shook his head. 'We did not realise.'

Orion was still trembling from the frenzy of his attacks and as he turned his gore-splattered face to Haldus, he revealed his long teeth in a snarl. 'What game are you playing? I do not need *tricks* to gain entry.' He nodded to the dead and dying, sprawled between the columns of the cave.

Prince Haldus bowed to the King. 'My lord. Forgive my impertinence. I merely thought that we could spare any more bloodshed and save a little time.'

Orion continued to scowl at the prince for a while. His chest was still heaving from the exertion of the fight and he was flexing his claws, clearly itching for more violence. He gave a grudging nod, but the snarl remained on his face.

Prince Haldus bowed again and turned back to the cowering guard. 'Take us to Cyanos.'

A spiralling coil of stairs ran up through the heart of the mountain. After a steep climb, Orion, Prince Haldus and the guard emerged on a ledge of rock, way up in the clouds and high enough to be dusted with a layer of snow. As Orion looked up at the surrounding peaks, his breath snaked around his face and trailed after him like a scarf.

Elpenor hurried ahead, snapping orders to figures that loomed out of the mountain mist. The other alvaír watched in amazement as Orion clattered past them, his blood-splattered antlers held high and his emerald eyes blazing.

'This way,' called Elpenor, directing them to another long stair. They climbed again, for longer this time, until they were high enough to look down over the clouds, which were so motionless Orion felt that he could step from the mountain and walk towards the horizon. It was late afternoon, and as they climbed higher, the sun was sinking lower, painting the white peaks with amber light.

The air grew thin and, after nearly an hour of climbing, even their guide grew short of breath. He paused for a while on a jagged precipice, panting slightly as he leant against the rock and looked warily at the ivy-skinned giant climbing towards him.

Orion and the prince were both growing lightheaded and they slumped against the icy granite, glad for a chance to rest.

After a few minutes, Prince Haldus peered up to the summit and saw another series of cave mouths. 'Is it true,' he gasped, keeping his gaze fixed on the caves, 'that Cyanos has changed?'

Elpenor frowned at him with a mixture of confusion and fear. 'Changed?'

Prince Haldus looked at the guard's feathered cloak and his strange, blood-splattered mask. 'Physically, I mean. In Arum Tor there are rumours. They say that his long years of worship have changed his flesh in some way.'

Elpenor drew back his shoulders and nodded proudly. 'It is true; after years of religious study King Cyanos has begun the ascent to divinity. Amphion has adopted him as a son and begun remaking him in his own image. He also made him a gift of the Silverwood – a spear carved from the tusk of the great drake, Tamarix.' The guard's eyes glazed over at the thought of his king. 'At first, not all of the kindreds understood the importance of King Cyanos's Great Work, the Ìobrass, but with the Silverwood in his hands, none could deny him. It is a weapon from the dawn of the world. There is a vein of Tamarix's fire running right through it. Nothing is impervious to its bite.' The guard lowered his head for a moment, awed by his own words. Then he sighed with pleasure. 'Every life given will be worth a hundred taken. We will burn in the flames of Amphion's wrath.'

Prince Haldus frowned. He had heard legends of the Silverwood, but he could make no sense of the guard's other words. 'The Ìobrass? What is that? I have–'

Orion had been staring out at the clouds, but at the mention of Amphion he rounded on the guard. 'Tell me of your god,' he said, interrupting Prince Haldus's question. 'What does this Amphion look like?'

The guard cringed under Orion's intense gaze and muttered his reply into his mask. 'He is the father of all the great eagles. His feathers were forged in the fires of the summer sun.'

Orion nodded eagerly. 'And how many wings? How many wings does he have?'

'Four,' replied the guard, as though the question were ridiculous. 'One for each of the seasons.'

Orion grasped Prince Haldus's shoulder. 'We have found him.'

Elpenor stared at Orion, as though he were only now recognising the strangeness of his appearance. He muttered a prayer under his breath, then turned and nodded to the remaining stairs. 'This is the final ascent. We have almost reached the High Hall of King Cyanos.' His voice was filled with awe. 'Perhaps you will be permitted a glimpse of Amphion yourself.'

They emerged on a broad spur of rock, dusted with snow and ending in a tower-like peak, networked with caves and tunnels so that it resembled a piece of bleached, worm-ridden wood. Word of their arrival must have somehow reached Cyanos, because hundreds of archers were waiting for them. They wore the same masks as Elpenor and they had formed into two long lines, leading all the way to the tower. Every one of them had a bow trained on Orion and the effect was of a bristling, arrow-lined corridor.

Prince Haldus cursed under his breath. If the archers decided to loose their arrows there would be nothing he or Orion could do. He wondered whether they should return to the steps and summon the eagles but, before he could suggest the idea to Orion, he realised that the King was already halfway down the avenue of archers, striding between the two lines as though he were in no danger at all.

Haldus spat another curse and hurried after him, dragging Elpenor with him as he went.

'Where is your king?' Orion snapped, turning briefly to face the guard.

Elpenor nodded to the base of the tower. There was a wide

tear in his mask that revealed an inane grin. 'He has come to meet you.'

Orion squinted at the distant figure, but the light was fading fast and he could not be sure what he was seeing. He picked up his pace and after a few minutes he began to make out the figure more clearly. For a second, his heart raced. In the half-light he thought it was Amphion. He saw a pair of broad, glittering wings that unfurled briefly and shimmered in the gloom. Then he recalled that the spirit he met in the grove of linden trees had two sets of wings, not one. Also, as he approached the tower of rock, he realised that the figure waiting for him was no eagle, but a king.

As Orion approached King Cyanos, he barely noticed the rows of archers and spearmen that flanked him. The king's appearance was so striking that for a brief moment, Orion forgot everything else. The king was much taller than his guards, as tall as Orion in fact, and he was unusually beautiful, even by the standards of the asrai. His hair was long, black and parted in the centre, in sharp contrast to his bone-white face, and his eyes were an odd, piercing green. His chest was clad in a breastplate of black, burnished iron, hammered to resemble the feathered breast of a bird, and he carried a long, sharpened piece of bone that was as tall as he was. Dozens of objects were clasped to his belt and chest: scrolls, pouches and odd, glass-fronted cases, all covered in intricate, indecipherable glyphs. Oddest of all was the enormous pair of wings folded behind his back, glimmering with an oily blue sheen.

Despite his severe appearance, King Cyanos greeted Orion with a smile of such gentleness that they might have been the oldest of friends.

'The Lord of the Deepwood Host,' he said, nodding his head in place of a bow. 'This is an honour I never expected.'

Orion narrowed his eyes as he studied the king of the alvaír. He had expected violence or resentment, but not this disarming, softly spoken welcome. He kept his gaze locked on Cyanos's, expecting him to look away, but to his annoyance Cyanos continued smiling calmly back at him.

'I have come in search of a forest spirit,' said Orion. 'A great eagle, by the name of Amphion.'

King Cyanos's smile faltered. For a moment he was too surprised to speak. He shook his head. 'Can I have been mistaken about you? Perhaps...' He waved at the surrounding mountains. 'You have come to the right place, Orion. Turas-Alva is the one kingdom in all the forest where my father has been made truly welcome.' He waved his bone spear at the tower behind him. There was a wide cave mouth at its base. 'Let me show you what we have wrought in his honour.'

With that, King Cyanos turned and strode into the tower.

Orion moved to follow but Prince Haldus grabbed his arm. 'My lord.' He waved at the hundreds of archers and spearmen that surrounded them. 'Is this wise?' He looked suspiciously at the tower. 'We have just butchered dozens of his guards. If he knew we were coming, he must also know that we are enemies.'

Orion wrenched his arm free and scowled at the prince. 'Cyanos would not dare lay a finger on me.'

Before Haldus could protest further, Orion vanished into the cave mouth, hurrying after their mysterious, winged host.

He looked around to face a row of expressionless masks. Then he let go of Elpenor and followed Orion, still muttering under his breath as he went.

The tower was ablaze with light. Countless sconces lined the walls, filled with crackling fires. The first cave was a small antechamber but, as the king led them further, they entered a cave so vast that the light of the braziers was unable to reach the ceiling. The centuries had wrought a kind of natural clerestory and more archers looked down at Orion and Prince Haldus, following them with their arrowheads as the king led them through the flickering shadows.

At one point they passed an opening in the wall of the cave, revealing another chamber filled with rows of leather-bound books and strange, enormous paintings showing oceans and continents. Orion and Haldus both frowned at the sight. Such things were the hallmarks of outsiders, with their stone-built colleges and their ink-smeared scribes. Why would an asrai noble indulge in such strange pursuits?

Finally, as they the exited the far side of the chamber, Orion and Haldus saw the hollow centre of the tower. The peak was a dormant volcano lined with hundreds of caves. At its centre was a sight more incredible than anything they had seen so far.

'My Great Work,' announced Cyanos, holding out his arms to encompass the vast shape that loomed over them. 'The final penance of the alvaír: the Ìobrass.'

Hunched in the heart of the mountain was a colossal statue. It had been sculpted to resemble a great eagle, gazing up at a distant patch of sky. Orion's head swam as he considered the work that must have gone into creating such a vast, absurd structure. The whole thing was hollow and its surface was a network of stone bars. It was a huge, beautiful cage and at its base there was a single door.

Orion frowned as he looked closer and saw movement. Eagles and hawks were gliding back and forth inside the enormous sculpture and there were other shapes sprawled across the floor of the thing. As the torchlight waxed and waned, Orion struggled to see them clearly at first, then he grunted in surprise. The shapes were corpses. They were in various stages of decomposition and some of them were little more than skeletons, picked clean by the birds circling overhead.

'What is this?' asked Orion, noticing that the cage-like statue had four wings folded behind its back. 'Is this where Amphion lives?'

Cyanos was still smiling, but there was now a slight hesitance in his voice. 'This is our last hope for repentance.' The white bone of his spear flashed in the torchlight as he pointed it at the crumpled remains in the statue. 'With every life we offer, Amphion grows a little stronger, but these offerings are only a precursor to what will follow.' He closed his eyes and clutched the spear to his chest, clearly moved. 'By the summer solstice the Iobrass will be complete. Then we will offer our final sacrifice and atone for your wrongs.'

'Iobrass!' hissed Prince Haldus, finally recognising the statue's obscure name. 'Sacrifice.'

'Exactly,' replied Cyanos. 'At the time of the solstice we will fill the Iobrass and offer our bodies as kindling. We will not only atone for your crimes, but we will fill Amphion with such power that he will cleanse the forest of all its foes.' He glanced meaningfully at Orion. 'Whatever form they take. And then, the forest will live.'

Dozens of voices echoed from the shadows overhead, repeating the king's final words: 'The forest will live.'

Orion shook his head in disgust. 'You mean to sacrifice yourselves?'

The king nodded, but his smile had vanished. 'We will join our souls to Amphion's and ascend into the unknown. It will be as it was written: the lifeblood of the alvaír will create a being of such incredible power that nothing will stand against it. The forest will be free. As it was in the beginning. Your crimes will be forgotten.'

The sound of Orion's hooves rang out as he stepped closer to the king. 'My crimes?' His voice was low and full of menace.

'Of course.' Cyanos frowned. 'Why have you come here, if not to atone for your crimes? Surely you wish forgiveness for what you have done?'

Orion shook his head. 'What have I done?'

Cyanos's voice remained soft, but his odd, green eyes flashed dangerously. 'What have you done? Is that a joke? You have violated the forest, Orion. You and your queen have imposed yourselves on a world that was never meant for you, and in doing so you have wounded it so horribly it can barely hope to survive. But surely you know this?'

Orion was about to reply when Cyanos gasped in surprise.

'Drop your bows!' cried Prince Haldus, pulling back Cyanos's head and pressing a knife to his throat.

Cyanos's voice grew taut. 'Be careful.' He tried to pull back from the knife. 'Think of what you're doing. I *must* remain alive until the solstice.' The colour drained from his face. 'By the gods! You could ruin everything.'

The archers that surrounded them gasped and looked at each other in horror. Some did as Prince Haldus demanded, lowering their weapons, but others stepped closer, on the verge of firing.

'Tread carefully,' said Cyanos, holding up a hand to his guards. The smile returned to his face, despite the knife at his throat, and he extended a hand to Orion. 'You were brought here. Don't you see? Amphion has offered you a chance to atone. The forest is dying because of you. Your illegitimate reign has left it unable to defend itself. You have disturbed an equilibrium that existed for thousands of years before you came. The beasts of Chaos are roaming, this very minute, through the trees. We must give the forest back.'

Orion shook his head and was about to reply, but King Cyanos was growing more impassioned with every word.

'Imagine what would happen if you joined us!' He waved at the statue, almost slitting his own throat as he turned to face it. 'Imagine if your soul met ours in the flames. This must be why you have come! Think what a wonderful symmetry it would make. The King – the very being responsible for the ruination of the forest – offering his strength to the Great Eagle. The Brúidd's power would be restored. They would be invincible once more.'

There was disarming, simple honesty to Cyanos's words and Orion noticed that Prince Haldus was looking confused.

'I am not here to prostrate myself before those animals,' he snarled. 'I am here to subdue them.' He turned to the anxious-faced guards huddled in the doorway. 'Your king is a either a lunatic or a liar, and he is leading you all to a pointless death.'

Some of the guards looked outraged and raised their bows again, but others were clearly unnerved by Orion's words, looking anxiously at each other for reassurance.

'Lies,' said Prince Haldus, shrugging off his doubt and pressing his knife back against the King's throat.

Just as it seemed blood would be spilled, a warm breeze flooded the caves, causing the torches to gutter and spit.

Cyanos trembled with fear and excitement. 'He's here.'

Orion whirled around but saw nothing.

The breeze blew harder and many of the torches were extinguished: hundreds of them, all around the inner walls of the mountain, fluttered and died, plunging the caves into darkness.

'What are you doing?' demanded Orion. He could just about make out Haldus and the king, but everything else was a confusing shroud of shifting shadows.

'It is not *my* doing,' replied the king, his eyes straining in the dark.

Orion was about to demand an explanation when he noticed a new source of light. It was coming from the base of the cage-like sculpture: a faint, amber glow, that shifted and writhed in the breeze. It flickered across the pools of blood and grew in brightness, like a miniature sunrise. Then it settled and stretched out, growing larger and assuming the form of a great eagle with four wings that glimmered and rippled, like the embers of a fire.

'Amphion,' cried Orion, forgetting all about the impasse between Haldus and the alvaír. He grabbed King Cyanos's arm. 'How do I enter the cage?'

The king's face was rigid with fear and he was unable to tear his gaze away from the dazzling creature. 'Stairs,' he gasped, pointing vaguely into the darkness.

'Wait here,' ordered Orion, catching Haldus's eye briefly, before striding off along the circular balcony that surrounded the statue. As he went he reached out to the wall and snatched one of the few torches that were still blazing, using it to light his way through the gloom.

No arrows were fired as he clattered down the stairs. Several of the guards had backed away at the sight of the spirit, muttering prayers under their breath, and the rest were unable to target Orion in the flickering light.

It was a short climb and within a few minutes Orion reached the entrance to the statue. This close he saw how cleverly designed the thing was. It was an enormous mesh of slender stone columns and thick oak beams, built over a mound of kindling that must have taken years to collect. Once locked inside, it would be impossible for a sacrificial offering to change his mind and flee. Cyanos and his alvaír would have no opportunity for second thoughts once the flames took hold. For now,

however, the gate was left open and Orion strode inside, hypnotised by the creature taking shape before him. Despite the
feelings of anger and shame it evoked, Orion could not deny
that Amphion was beautiful. In the linden grove he had only
half-glimpsed its form, but now it revealed itself quite clearly:
spreading its four shimmering wings and throwing back its
head to let out a deafening screech.

Orion staggered to a halt a few feet away from his prey and
held up his torch. There was no doubt – this *was* the spirit he
had seen by the pool. It was also, however, much larger than he
remembered.

Amphion reared up over his head, spreading all four of its
wings to their full, impressive span and fixing its coal-black eyes
on him. 'Are you lost, little king?' Its voice was a thin shriek,
and as it spoke its wings erupted into flames, creating such a
blast of scorching air that Orion had to lean forwards to stay
upright.

'You are my subject, Amphion!' cried Orion, levelling one of
his talons at the eagle. 'I demand your fealty!'

'You mewling runt,' laughed the eagle, hopping towards him.
'Why would I worship you?' It lowered its head until its eyes
were level with Orion's. 'You are the weakest in a long line of
weaklings.'

Orion's mind flooded with hatred. He lunged at the towering creature, trying to land a punch, but Amphion continued
laughing as the blow passed straight through the shimmering
blaze of its feathers.

Orion cursed and staggered across the floor, realising that the
spirit was as intangible as smoke. He dropped to his knees and
found himself staring at the mounds of dry kindling beneath
the statue. Then he let out a short bark of laughter as an idea
occurred to him.

'How long has Amphion been ruling you?' he asked, waving his torch at the rows of anxious faces staring down at him. 'How long have you been working towards this sacrifice?' He curled back his teeth in what could either have been a grin or a snarl. 'Just a few months now, and it will be the summer solstice. Then Cyanos's Great Work will be complete. Is that right?'

Amphion turned its head on one side, fixing Orion with one of its eyes.

'But what if there's nothing left by then?' Orion dropped his flaming torch through the grilled floor.

A chorus of wails erupted from the figures watching overhead.

The torch looped and fluttered, then landed in the kindling with an explosion of sparks.

Orion turned to Amphion and pointed up at the masked figures. 'Their souls are not yours to take.'

'By the gods!' wailed Cyanos, still trapped by Prince Haldus's knife. 'The Ìobrass! Get down there! Stop the flames.'

A few of the alvaír shuffled towards the stairs, but most did nothing, clearly terrified. Orion's torch had already caused a small fire and the mound of kindling was the size of a hill. Even if they crawled beneath the statue, it would be impossible to climb through the sticks and branches to reach the torch.

Orion watched proudly as flames spread beneath him. 'I will teach you to kneel,' he growled, glaring up at Amphion.

To his amazement, the enormous eagle began to laugh again. It threw back its beak and let out a series of hysterical shrieks. 'Do you think I care about this? Do you think I care about these idiots and their pointless rituals?'

The alvaír on the stairs paused in confusion and even Cyanos ceased his yells.

Amphion spread its wings, indicating the cage-like statue.

'This hideous thing would never have channelled their souls. It is just another example of your people's idiocy.' A note of disgust entered the spirit's voice. 'Do you really think I would mingle my essence with such pathetic, unnatural creatures?'

Up on the balcony, King Cyanos slumped back into Haldus's grip, shaking his head.

Haldus lowered his knife and managed to catch Cyanos before he collapsed.

Cyanos recovered and rushed to the edge of the lip of rock. 'My lord! Why are you saying such things?' His face was ashen as he jabbed his spear at the statue. 'We have built the Ìobrass, just as the old texts described. Every detail has been attended to. Our sacrifice will atone for Orion's hubris. The books of our forefathers say–'

'Your forefathers were fools,' screeched Amphion, whirling around to face the king. 'Every one of your miserable lives could never atone for what has been done to the forest.' The eagle looked around at the rows of guards and archers, wailing and clutching their masks. 'But it would have given me some satisfaction to watch you all burn.'

Orion shook his head in frustration. The flames were spreading quickly beneath him, sending columns of smoke up into the statue, but he realised it was pointless. Cyanos had been deceived. Whether the cage burned now or at the summer solstice made no difference to Amphion. It was all a lie.

As the flames began to reach up through the grilled floor of the Ìobrass, Prince Haldus called out in alarm. 'My lord! Leave the cage!'

Orion looked around and saw that fire was racing across the mound of kindling. Anger erupted in his head, with even more violence than the flames. He could not leave without bending Amphion to his will, but the towering eagle was already spreading its wings – embracing the flames and pulsing with golden light as it looked down at him, still shaking with mirth.

A terrible, agonised scream sliced through the tumult.

Orion looked up to see Cyanos, transformed by grief and shock. His gentle smile had been replaced by a horrified leer and he was stumbling like a drunk. 'A lie?' he kept repeating, shaking his head. 'A lie?'

Prince Haldus had backed away from him, forgotten in all the excitement and unsure what to do.

'Of course it was a lie!' screamed Amphion. 'How could you hope to atone for thousands of years with one absurd sacrifice?' The eagle fixed one of its eyes on Orion again. 'Although I was quite looking forward to watching them try.'

King Cyanos let out another horrible screech. Then he spread his jet black wings, launched himself from the balcony and hurled his spear.

There was a flash of white as the shaft of bone sliced through the whirling smoke and sank into Amphion's shoulder.

To Orion's surprise, the weapon did not pass through Amphion's rippling feathers, as his punch had done; the enchanted weapon lodged deep in its flesh and sent it fluttering back across the floor of the cage.

Amphion's laughter twisted into a croak as it crumpled to the floor.

Orion had to leap clear as the eagle collapsed towards him, causing the columns of smoke to billow and roll.

'What have you done?' cried Amphion, writhing in pain and shock and straining to reach the spear. However much it struggled, it could not reach the weapon.

'Take back your gift!' cried Cyanos, hovering outside the cage with tears glittering in his strange green eyes. His voice was filled with even more pain than Amphion's. There was such horror and desolation in his words that even Orion paused to stare at him. 'The Silverwood can pierce anything! It seems you were honest about that, at least.'

Amphion screeched again, thrashing its wings and trying to dislodge the spear.

The flames had now spread right across the mound of kindling. The few alvaír who had obeyed King Cyanos's orders were now starting to climb back towards the balcony, seeing there was no hope of extinguishing the fire. Orion, however, had other ideas. Rather than make for the door of the cage, he raced back through the smoke and leapt into the air.

Amphion was too lost in pain to notice his approach and only realised what was happening when it was too late.

Orion latched both of his hands around the shard of dragon tooth and rammed it down with all his strength.

There was an awful grinding sound as the weapon sank even further through the eagle's shoulder and into the stone beneath, pinning Amphion to the floor.

Orion rolled clear, tumbling through the flames, and came to a halt a few feet away.

Amphion screamed, straining its back and thrashing its wings, but the spear was now buried deep in the stone and would not move.

Orion staggered back to Amphion's side and jammed the spear even deeper, filling the cave with another grinding screech. The heat was incredible but he paused long enough to lean over his horrified foe.

Amphion glared back at him.

'I am your king,' said Orion in a calm, flat voice.

Amphion arched its back and thrashed its wings furiously, trying again to free itself from the floor, but when it slumped back the spear had not moved an inch.

Orion nodded. 'I will leave you to think.'

He raced across the floor of the cage and left Amphion to the flames, slamming the door behind him as he went. He paused briefly to say: 'Perhaps by the summer you will see things more clearly.'

As Orion climbed back up the stairs, the whole mountain was filling with smoke and heat. The Ìobrass was built to burn. The flames were already washing over the walls.

Prince Haldus was waiting for him at the top of the steps, his countenance more severe than ever. The alvaír that had not fled were utterly dazed by what they had seen and made no move to attack him. 'My lord,' he said, grasping Orion's hand and hauling him back onto the lip of rock. 'What have you done?'

'I have shown the Brúidd who rules this forest,' he replied, wiping ash from his face and looking past the prince.

King Cyanos had landed on the balcony and slumped to his knees. He was sobbing violently, utterly destroyed by Amphion's treachery.

Orion stepped to his side, grabbed him by the shoulder and hauled him to his feet.

Cyanos stared at Orion with red-rimmed eyes. 'Let me die,' he whispered.

'I will not.' Orion's voice had all the weight and authority of an ancient oak. 'You will live. And you will serve your king.'

Cyanos shook his head, his eyes full of bitterness and confusion. 'How can I serve a king that has wrought such harm on his own realm?' His words lacked conviction and as he spoke them his eyes were filled with confusion. He began to choke on the fumes billowing around them. He continued speaking, but in a monotone – as though he were reciting a text. 'While you and Ariel exist, the forest has no hope of survival.'

'The Queen and I are the forest's *only* hope. It has always been so and it always will be.' Orion pointed through the smoke and flames, to the struggling shape of Amphion. The great eagle had vanished, replaced by a bewildering succession of thrashing, screeching creatures – bears, hounds, unicorns and wildcats – all straining to free themselves from the Silver-wood, but Orion's unnatural strength had jammed the spear so deep into the stone that it would not move. 'These beings despise me,' Orion's revelation came to him only as he spoke it aloud, 'because they cannot survive without me.' He pulled Cyanos close, fixing the king with his emerald eyes. 'They are *perfidious*. They are unknowable. They are like foxes, cowering in a den. But I will bend them to my will. I will bring every creature in the forest to heel. That is my burden.' He placed Cyanos back down on the floor and considered him. 'Can you carry it with me?'

'My lord, we must leave,' cried Prince Haldus.

Smoke and embers billowed around Orion and Cyanos, but they kept their gazes locked on one another: Orion's full of pride and certainty, Cyanos's full of doubt, and the beginnings of awe.

'My lord!' repeated Haldus, as the remaining guards barged past him and fled from the cave.

Orion gave no reply as the flames rushed closer, keeping his eyes locked on the king of the alvaír, letting his question hang over them.

Cyanos looked down at the writhing shapes in the cage. The creatures were snarling and spitting, but could not free them-selves. Despite all his rage at Amphion's betrayal, Cyanos could not help but feel pity. Pity quickly led him to disdain, and he shook his head. 'I have been deceived. After all these years I have–'

His words were interrupted by a violent fit of coughing as the smoke filled his lungs.

Prince Haldus called out for a third time, but still Orion would not move. Flames were now licking across the stones, but he kept his gaze locked on Cyanos, waiting for him to continue.

The fit passed and Cyanos turned back to Orion, his eyes full of terror and shame. 'I am a fool. I have failed you.'

Orion replied with a slightly softer voice. 'The year is still new, Cyanos.'

A faint glimmer of hope appeared in Cyanos's eyes. Then another fit of coughing rocked his body. This time it was so violent that he dropped to his knees.

Orion lifted Cyanos as easily as a child and threw him over his shoulder. Then he strode from the cave.

As Orion emerged onto the snow-covered mountainside, the alvaír swarmed around him. They watched in stunned silence as he placed their king on the ground and looked back at the spire of rock. Smoke was belching from its peak and embers were drifting through the air.

Orion looked around at the crowds of dazed figures pressing around him. 'The eagle will remain, even after the fire has died. You must stand guard. All of you. Watch over Amphion until I return for him. If you do this, you will earn my forgiveness.'

'You are not our king,' cried one of the alvaír.

Orion's eyes flashed. He drew back his shoulders and was about to reply, but another voice called out before him.

'We will not fail you,' gasped Cyanos, clambering to his feet and placing a hand across the black metal of his breastplate. 'We will earn your forgiveness.'

CHAPTER TWENTY

For a long time she wept; hot, bitter tears that rolled down her face as she staggered through the ruins. Then she laid herself down in the ashes and robed herself in blood, assuming the form of a wounded archer: one of Ariel's simpering whores, frail, beautiful and rotten with lies.

She picked a spot where she knew she would be seen; a wide, smouldering patch of grass on the side of a hill, drenched in pale, morning light. She glanced at Liris and Melusine and they withdrew, fading back into the smoke, obscuring themselves amongst the butchered trees. Then she clicked her limbs into grotesque, unnatural angles and waited to be found.

The wait was not long. They came from the south, grunting and jeering and trampling through the wasteland they had created. Hate pulsed through her veins, but she quashed it, remaining on the ground and acting the part of a febrile, muttering victim, waiting to be put out of her misery.

There was an explosion of growls as the outsiders reached the hillside. There were two of them: hunched, axe-wielding mongrels, with spiralling ram's horns and gore-splattered hooves.

Centuries of hunting had taught her many things, some more pleasant than others. Vile as they were, the words of the outsiders made sense.

'And here's one for you, Arghob,' cried the first of them, its voice a guttural snarl of laughter.

'Finally!' roared the second creature, lurching towards the hillside and staring hungrily at her broken body. The monster was clearly drunk. Its first attempt to approach her sent it veering off to the far side of the clearing, where it stumbled over a burnt stump and fell onto its face.

The first outsider rocked with laughter, snorting snot and alcohol. 'Useless worm!' It grinned and licked some blood from its axe. 'Let me deal with this.'

The drunkard lurched to its feet and rushed back towards the hill, shoving the other creature aside as it raced towards its prey.

She loosed a little power and the outsider stumbled to a halt, its eyes rolling in their sockets. Only once she was sure she had it under control did she loose her grip and allow it to approach.

It fingered the haft of its axe as it studied her, sensing that something was amiss. Then bloodlust washed away its doubt.

'You've had all the fun,' it growled to the other creature. 'This one's mine.'

As the beastman stepped over her, she spoke to it in her most pitiful, whining voice. 'Why here?' she asked.

The monster's grin faded. It had not expected to be addressed in its own tongue. 'What?' it barked, grabbing her by the throat.

She flopped pathetically in its grip. 'Why have you struck here?'

The other monster trotted closer and clutched its head, trying to clear its throughts. 'Kill her.' It looked nervously around at the trees. 'Remember what Four-legs said. The plan is secret.'

'Idiot,' snapped Arghob. 'She's going to die anyway. Let's tell her.

She can die knowing there's no hope.'

The monster pulled her face closer, so that she could smell a previous victim on its breath. 'The forest is for us now.'

'How?' she groaned, trying to sound afraid. 'How can you overcome the magic of the Queen?'

'Four-legs has a friend.' The monster pressed the edge of its axe against her blood-slick neck. 'Four-legs has magic of his own.'

'The magic of your dark gods has no power here.'

The monster shook its head and grinned. 'This is other magic. Old magic. Magic from the time before gods. Magic of the firestones.'

For a moment she forgot her glamour and the creature flinched, catching a glimpse of the truth. Then she whined again, filling her voice with sorcery. 'Firestones?'

'Stop talking, moron,' hissed the other monster. 'Kill her.'

Arghob frowned, sensing something was wrong.

The monster drew back its axe to strike but it was already too late.

The pain was incredible, but even more powerful was the sense of confusion that flooded Arghob's tiny brain.

The last thing Arghob saw was its own headless torso, lying far below on the hillside, jerking and pumping blood across the grass.

She watched Liris and Melusine with delight as they tore the two monsters apart in a frenzy of thorns and sharpened roots. She shared their joy as they unleashed their pent-up rage. Then, as the bloody remains slopped onto the hillside around her, she considered what she had learned.

'Firestones?' she whispered, abandoning her disguise and cladding her limbs in cold, knotted bark. Her voice was trembling as she turned to face her sisters. 'Could they have discovered the Sínann-Torr?'

Finavar strode from the trees with his head held high and a grin on his face. He felt as though he were a line from a song. The figure by his side shone with a cool, lunar glow and glided so lightly through the grass that her feet rarely touched the earth. Laelia had the light of Ariel in her gaze and the strength of Isha in her wings. She had led them home in less than a day, taking bewildering, impossible routes that Finavar had tried desperately and unsuccessfully to remember. Even the Wrach's Dark Paths seemed slow and wearisome in comparison.

Thuralin, Alhena and Jokleel emerged from the trees behind them, shaking their heads in mute surprise as they recognised the borders of Locrimere. They had barely spoken to Finavar during the journey, stunned, yet again, by his daring. As Laelia dropped lightly to the ground and began to speak, they huddled a few feet away, not daring to approach.

'Now, at least, you should know where you are.' The handmaiden graced Finavar with one of her crooked smiles and waved at the tree-lined valley spread out below them.

Finavar blushed and nodded. 'We will see the towers of Locrimere from the top of the next rise. It is a few more miles at most.' He smiled. 'Then, perhaps, I can introduce *you* to a wonder of the forest: the sacred heart of Locrimere – the Idolan.' He looked through the thick mesh of branches and recalled how his thoughts of Locrimere had changed. Until a year ago, he was snubbed and reviled – a figure of ridicule at best. But he was Finavar the fatherless no more. He looked back at his kinband and basked in their gaze. He had a family now. He was their Darkling Prince and he could see the respect in their eyes. He had braved the court of the Queen and returned with a sorceress in tow. He laughed to himself, remembering that Eremon had told him to return in better company. What would the old captain think when he saw Laelia?

He was about to hurry down into the valley when Laelia placed a hand on his arm. The smile faded from her face as she pointed at the sky. 'It is mid-morning, and we are facing east.'

She lowered her voice. 'Why is the sky so dark?'

Finavar shook his head and peered up into the gloom. 'Storm clouds?' he muttered, but there was doubt in his voice.

'We are too late,' said another voice.

Finavar and Laelia turned to see that Jokleel had approached. He turned to face them with his odd, lizard-like slowness and spoke with the same leisurely drawl he usually employed, but his eyes were wide with fear and his hands were shaking. 'We are too late, Finavar. The battle is already lost. They are all dead.'

Laelia looked closely at Jokleel, intrigued by his strange, ethereal manner. 'How do you know?'

Finavar grabbed Jokleel by the arms. 'Calm yourself, brother. How can you be sure?'

Jokleel pulled away and dropped to his knees, sinking his fingers into the earth. A strange keening sound came from the back of his throat. 'The darkness is smoke,' he said, staring at the soil. 'They burned everything. *Everything.*'

Finavar looked back across the valley and his pulse began to race. 'Smoke? It can't be. The whole sky is black. How could there be so much?'

He looked at the others, but nobody needed to answer his question. The reason was obvious, and dreadful. Only the destruction of an entire kingdom could account for such a blaze.

They raced down into the valley and clambered up the opposite slope, with Jokleel staggering after them.

Locrimere was gone, replaced by a vast, smouldering expanse of black.

Finavar groaned in pain and dropped to his knees.

Laelia turned away.

'No,' gasped Alhena, clutching frantically at her shaven head. 'It cannot be.'

Thuralin's countenance grew even more dour than usual.

He peered through the shifting haze and glimpsed a stretch of water. 'The Idolan,' he muttered.

Finavar followed the direction of his gaze. The ancient meadows that surrounded the sacred lake were as blackened as everything else. He stared harder and realised that amongst the trails of smoke there were banners: broken, tattered and bearing the heraldry of Locrimere.

Laelia forced her eyes to take in the horrendous sight. Then she looked down at Finavar, hunched by her feet, crippled by grief.

'Caorann,' he whispered. 'I left him to die.'

Thuralin placed a hand on the youth's shoulder and spoke with an uncharacteristic note of kindness. 'Perhaps not. They may have fled, before the cloven ones arrived.'

'Eremon would never flee,' Finavar replied. 'Not while there was hope.'

'What if there *was* no hope?' insisted Thuralin.

Alhena let out an anguished gasp and staggered down the hillside, horrified by the destruction of a home she had never known. 'It cannot be!' she howled, drawing her blades and hacking wildly at the air.

No one made any effort to call her back and, after a few seconds, they followed suit, dashing towards the ruined trees with tears in their eyes.

Quickly, they began to find bodies. Many of them were so charred it was impossible to recognise asrai from outsider, but some were clearly the remains of their kin: long, elegant limbs, twisted into unnatural shapes by the heat of the blaze.

They walked in silence, stunned by the desolation, and eventually they stepped out into the meadow that surrounded the Idolan. The blaze here had been less fierce, with no trees to burn, and the bodies were horribly recognisable.

Most affected of all was the boy, Jokleel. He stared wide-eyed at the corpses, muttering and singing to himself as he staggered through the burnt grass. 'How could we ever redress such an act?' he whispered. 'It is too much. Too much.'

Finavar trudged wearily towards the lake, muttering to the pair of polecats following him through the carnage. 'We should have stayed. We should have died with them.' He turned to the creatures, as though expecting an answer, and noticed that one of them had paused and was staring through the smoke, as though it were hunting something. Finavar narrowed his eyes and peered in the same direction.

'Your weapons!' he hissed, drawing his swords.

The others rushed to his side.

'What do you see?' asked Alhena, curling her lip and raising her blades.

'We're not alone,' whispered Finavar, nodding at a hunched silhouette moving awkwardly through the smoke towards them.

Laelia nodded and raised her staff. Light shimmered along its length, pulsing through tendrils of ivy and snaking along the copper filigree. As the light grew, Laelia closed her eyes and mouthed the words of a spell.

Finavar and the others watched in awe as the smoke rolled away to form a shifting corridor between them and the approaching figure.

Caorann nodded sadly at them through the haze. He seemed on the verge of cracking a joke, but the words failed him and he simply trudged towards them.

Finavar howled in relief and sprinted towards his friend.

Caorann was covered in fresh wounds and he winced as Finavar hugged him. 'Have a heart, Fin,' he groaned, managing a faint smile.

The others rushed to his side, shaking their heads in wonder.

'What happened?' asked Alhena, looking around with her blades still raised.

Caorann was about to reply, when he caught sight of Laelia. 'My queen,' he gasped, trying to bow but only managing to lower his head.

Laelia glided to his side and placed a hand on his back, dimming the light of her staff as she did so. 'I am no queen,' she said with a wry smile, 'and even if I were, you have been through too much to hang your head. Please, sit. Tell us your story.'

Caorann looked up at Laelia's words, but his eyes were still full of doubt.

Finavar helped him to a seat, winking as he did so. 'Even lowborn wastrels like us can have powerful friends. Let me introduce my travelling companion: Laelia, handmaiden to the Queen.'

Caorann shook his head in disbelief, but as he saw the smile on his friend's face, he let out one of his deep, booming laughs. 'By Loec, you have some nerve, Fin.'

Finavar replied with a smirk.

Thuralin hobbled to Caorann's side and waved at the blackened ruins that surrounded them. 'Please, tell us what happened.'

Caorann flinched at the sight of the old warrior. In the time since he had last seen Thuralin, he had become even more twisted and stooped and the portion of his face that was visible behind his mask looked even more lined with exhaustion. The distance of time allowed Caorann to realise something for the first time. He's dying, he thought, staring at Thuralin's ruined, scarred face. His eyes flicked to Alhena, wondering if she realised.

'Please,' said Jokleel, stumbling over with a dazed expression on his face. 'What happened here?'

Caorann shook his head and told them his sorry tale. Eremon had led the defence with bravery and determination, but eventually it was the enemy's decision to move on. On the second day of fighting they had suddenly withdrawn. It was as though they had no interest in Locrimere itself, and had attacked with the sole purpose of slaughtering Eremon's army. With that achieved, they charged north through the glades, leaving a pitiful group of survivors left to trail after them, seeking vengeance.

'But you remained,' said Finavar, still clutching his friend's shoulder. 'Why?'

'It was Eremon's decision,' replied Caorann. 'We were wrong about him, Fin.' He shook his head and looked out across the mounds of corpses. 'He may be highborn, but he is nothing like Lord Beldeas. He has a good heart.'

Finavar shook his head. 'But why did he leave you behind?'

'I told him you would return.' Caorann looked up at Finavar with a meaningful glance. 'And that you would bring help. I persuaded him that you are not as foolish as you might appear. You have done a good job of convincing him otherwise, but he now knows you are a true master of the shadow-dance, and he wants you by his side.'

'By his side?'

Caorann nodded and met Jokleel's tearful stare. 'Eremon is undefeated. Locrimere may have fallen, but its heroes have not. He is stalking the enemy through the forest, striking at their flanks whenever they pause. Eremon will never let them forget the crime they have committed here.'

Caorann waved at the bloody rags that covered his chest. 'I am not at my best, so we agreed I might serve him best as a messenger.' He grinned. 'Eremon humbly requests your company, Fin. The enemy are making for Drúne Fell. Loec knows why, but with your help, Eremon plans to make their journey a painful one.'

'Eremon lives,' said Alhena, trembling with excitement and clutching the hilts of her twin swords. 'And he is not alone. The fight is not over.'

Caorann nodded.

'Who is this Eremon?' asked Laelia, turning to face Alhena.

As the handmaiden's gaze fell on her, Alhena's cheeks flushed with colour. She refused to lower her gaze, though, and stared defiantly back. 'He is the witless captain of Locrimere's kinbands.'

'I see.' Laelia started to give Alhena one of her crooked smiles, but it was met with such a ferocious glare that she quickly abandoned it. 'Then I may still be of some help.' She looked down at Caorann, who was still clutching the bloody bandages that covered his chest. 'Give me your hand.'

Alhena and Thuralin glanced at each other. They had both heard stories of the magic wielded at Ariel's court, and they were relieved they did not have to proffer their own hands.

Pale fire rippled from Laelia's fingers and spread across Caorann's chest. He gasped and threw back his head, and when the light faded the pain was gone from his eyes. The lines of his face softened and he climbed to his feet, taking a deep breath and stretching out his limbs. 'My lady,' he said, bowing low, with as much grace as he ever had.

Alhena clenched her jaw and when she spoke it was clear she struggled to keep her voice soft. 'Are we just going to stand here?' She turned to Finavar. 'Are we going to trust vengeance to a fool like Eremon?'

Finavar looked up from his miraculously healed friend with doubt in his eyes.

Laelia gave him a sympathetic smile. 'I will follow you, whatever you decide.'

Finavar looked around at the ashes that surrounded them and rage flickered in his eyes.

Alhena watched his fury grow with elation. Her whole body was trembling with emotion and she wrapped her fingers around the hilts of her swords.

Laelia looked carefully at Finavar. 'We cannot balance one act of violence with another. The scale of this is beyond anything–'

'We must avenge them,' interrupted Alhena, keeping her stare fixed on Finavar. She waved her swords at the mounds of corpses. 'We *must*.'

Thuralin tried to speak, but his words became a hacking cough. Once the fit had passed he wiped his mouth and looked at Finavar. 'If Eremon lives, we cannot just leave him to his fate. Caorann is right.' He glanced at his daughter. 'The captain has a noble soul. We must find him. We must help him.'

Laelia was about to disagree again, but she hesitated. 'I owe you an apology,' she said to Finavar. 'You were right to interrupt the rites of spring. This is the murder of an entire people. If Locrimere can fall, nowhere is safe.' She looked at the mounds of bodies and shook her head. 'The Queen did not foresee anything of this magnitude, but she sent me to aid you. What would you do, Finavar? This is your kinband. You must lead them.'

Finavar did not respond for a moment. Then he nodded and looked to the north.

SUMMER

Sólis-Leith
Burning
The Season of the Hunt

CHAPTER TWENTY-ONE

'It had to be done,' said Ordaana, hauling herself over a boulder and leaving behind a smear of blood. Her voice was hoarse and her face was ashen. Above her were the sun-drenched slopes of a mountain and below her was the forest, basking in the heat of a summer's afternoon. As she crept along a narrow precipice she kept one hand pressed against her robes, trying to stifle the flow of blood from a wound in her side. She looked exhausted. Her angular cheekbones strained against her taut, pale skin and her hair was a tumble of knotted silver.

There was a clattering as Death's-head appeared. 'The four-legged one has arrived.' The little bundle of sticks gave a screeching, grinding laugh. 'Even with Ariel, they will not be able to stop him. There is nothing they can do without Orion.'

Ordaana gave no reply and looked up the slope. Drúne Fell: the Lost Mountain. A slender, crooked peak looming over the trees, several miles from the foothills of the Grey Mountains. It was as though it had been ostracised on account of its ugliness. From her vantage point on the mountain's western face,

Ordaana could see for several miles. Looking in this direction it seemed as though nothing was wrong. The forest was an explosion of growth and movement. The glossy crowns of Ariel's oak groves were clearly visible and swallows were drifting overhead, chasing each other lazily through the sky. There was something timeless and torpid about the scene, but Ordaana knew what she would see from the south side of the mountain and the thought of it made her heart pound.

'Perhaps not,' she said, with fear in her voice, 'but I must be sure.'

She peered up to the summit. Only the most arrogant of Ariel's subjects would have dared such an outrage: to drag the Queen from her sacred glades and lead her to this raw, wind-blasted peak. If Orion had been present, they would never have dared, but his constant absence was part of their complaint. No one but Ordaana could understand it. All spring he had ignored the call of his disciples and roamed the forest. Now summer had come and still he was absent. Hints and rumours followed in his wake, ominous tales of a belligerent king, at war with his own domain. The forest rang with dreadful sounds: the cracking of bones and the hollow screech of spirits dragged from their dens. A few kindreds dared to hunt the hunter, but they found themselves facing a beast, blood-slick and feral, his eyes full of hunger. As the summer solstice grew nearer, there were rumours that he might even abandon the Wild Hunt.

Ordaana shook her head and continued her weary ascent. 'I must be sure,' she repeated. As she climbed, she waved at her clattering familiar, ushering it back into the shadows.

After half an hour of scraped knuckles and stubbed toes, Ordaana finally reached the broad shoulder of granite on which the lords of the asrai had gathered. The wind here was even fiercer and she had to lean into it as she walked, struggling to keep her slight frame upright. There were eight of them. Her spineless husband, Lord Beldeas, was the nearest. He looked ridiculous amongst such company, with his feeble, ungainly limbs and his pallid, academic air. He was clutching a sword in his hands but Ordaana noticed, without surprise, that there was no trace of blood on the blade.

The figure by his side could not have been more different. Prince Haldus was bare-chested and bronzed from his years on the wing and, with his spiralling mask of scars, he looked every bit the warrior. He was scowling as fiercely as ever, and still looked uncomfortable in such august company, but Ordaana knew he had forced this gathering. With the forest burning and Orion gone, the nobles had finally listened to his warning.

Standing behind Prince Haldus was another hawk rider. He was a stranger to Ordaana, and a mysterious one at that. He had arrived with Haldus and no one could remember seeing him at Ariel's court before. He was tall, with the features of an aristocrat, but he kept his gaze fixed on the ground and when, occasionally, he lifted his eyes, they were full of shame. His chest was encased in a cuirass of black metal, hammered into the shape of feathers, and he had announced himself simply as a servant of Orion. During the skirmishes of the spring he had fought with astonishing ferocity, but he had given no other name and refused to explain the bloody, bandaged stumps that arched up from his back.

To Ordaana's eyes they looked like the remnants of wings.

Beside the stranger there was a pair of young brothers from the north of the forest: Lords Salicis and Alioth. Ordaana had known them since they were children and could not help but pity them. From the gleam in their eyes it was clear they considered this gathering the beginning of a brave adventure, rather than the extinction of their race.

Kneeling beneath the glittering presence of the Queen was her rakish poet, Khoron Belidae, speaking in mellifluous tones to another kneeling figure: the elderly warden of the Silvam Dale, Prince Elatior.

They were all too engrossed in their conversation to notice Ordaana as she clambered over a lip of rock and began staggering towards them. Before addressing them she paused and looked to the south, studying the subject of their discussion.

The forest below her was horribly wounded. Black, smouldering lines networked its face, all pointing towards the mountain. Acres of trees had been put to the torch and a host of figures was moving through the smoke. Ordaana gasped as she saw the full extent of her treachery.

'What have I done?' she hissed, growing rigid with panic. Then she calmed herself, repeating the stern words of Aestar Eltanin. 'She is a monster and we must unseat her.' She had come straight from talking to him and as she thought of his regal face her nerve steadied. This was her chance.

From this side of the mountain she could hear the battle. Horn blasts and screams drifted on the wind, seeming closer than they actually were. She peered down the ragged slopes and saw where the enemy had been halted. Waves of arrows were pouring from the glades on either side of them and shadowy figures were dancing through the boughs, waltzing through the ranks of ram-horned brutes and lumbering minotaurs.

Ordaana sneered at the thought that one of her own wretched subjects was leading the defence. 'Darkling Prince,' she muttered, her voice full of disdain. All through the spring she had heard tales of his supposed bravery. Since the fall of Locrimere, he had fought alongside Eremon, hounding the cloven ones as they tried to advance through the forest, delaying her plans at every turn.

She flinched as a voice called out her name. She had been so lost in her thoughts of Finavar that she had forgotten the nobles gathered behind her.

Her husband dashed to her side, his face full of concern. 'Are you wounded?' He frowned at the stain on her robes. 'What happened? I told you to remain in the Council Glade.'

She waved at the gathering. 'And leave *you* to lead our defence?' she sneered. 'When did you last kill anything, Beldeas?'

He immediately forgot her injury and his face flushed with pride. 'Our great kingdoms are about to join as one.' He waved his bloody sword down the slope. 'Prince Elatior's kinbands have almost reached Eremon's lines. When our forces meet, we will halt the advance completely.'

'Eremon?' Ordaana's voice remained cool, but her disbelief was clear. 'Do you really believe *he* is leading our soldiers? Haven't you heard? That wretched orphan leads our subjects now.'

'What does it matter?' Beldeas raised his voice so that the others could hear, adopting a lordly tone. 'Whoever leads the assault, we have a duty to preserve the forest, Ordaana. This revolting horde must go no further. Prince Haldus was right all along, I knew it. We must stand as one. The Queen herself intends to aid us in the final attack.'

Ordaana could not believe what she was seeing. Her husband was as deluded as the youths from the north. He had never shown the slightest interest in warfare, but now his eyes were gleaming with excitement. He clearly had no idea of what was waiting for them down there. She met the gazes of the other nobles and realised that they all wore the same ridiculous expressions. Only Prince Haldus and his companion looked troubled; the rest wore their bloodstains with pride and were clearly itching to rejoin the battle.

'Then what are you doing up here?' she asked, resisting the urge to laugh at them all.

Beldeas raised his chin and gave Ariel a deferential wave. 'Before the Queen would spare any more of her handmaidens, she wished to see the threat with her own eyes. Prince Haldus suggested–'

'*More* handmaidens?' interrupted Ordaana, raising one of her eyebrows. For a moment she forgot that she had been released from the Queen's service and wondered if Beldeas was referring to her. Then she recalled that she was a handmaiden no longer and felt a rush of shame.

Beldeas nodded eagerly and grinned. 'Do you think that Finavar would have been so successful on his own? In her wisdom, the Queen foresaw this whole situation.' Beldeas did not notice how horrified his wife looked at this idea. 'So, when she sent him away from the Council Glades, she made sure he did not go alone – he returned to Locrimere in the company of her most powerful mage.'

Ordaana shook her head and was about to ask who this mage was, when she noticed that the Queen was drifting across the mountaintop towards her, followed by a cluster of her adoring subjects.

'You are wounded, Ordaana,' said Ariel, dropping lightly to her side. 'You must return with me.' She waved at the battle below. 'We have seen enough of this bloodshed. We must leave Prince Haldus and the others to their games.'

Ordaana bowed and kissed her queen's hand. Only then did she see the fear in Ariel's eyes. At first she thought it was fear of the monsters that were crushing against the mountain, but she quickly realised that Ariel was not even looking at the battle.

Her thoughts were elsewhere. Had she uncovered her betrayal? Was she about to take her revenge? 'Yes, my lady,' Ordaana replied, filled with dread.

Ariel took Ordaana's arm and led her away from the assembled warriors, taking her across the small plateau without a word of farewell to the others.

'Let me,' said the Queen, pausing at the edge of the lip of rock. She placed her hand over Ordaana's wound and muttered a soft prayer.

Ordaana felt a flash of heat in her side as the wound closed. When she looked again, even the tear in her robes had vanished. Ordaana blushed as she saw the Queen's expression. There was no accusation in her eyes, only concern. 'I met some of the creatures,' Ordaana muttered, feeling utterly ashamed, 'as I made my way up the mountain.'

Ariel frowned, as though confused by something, then she nodded and indicated a natural stair that led down the far side of the mountain.

As they climbed, Ordaana noticed how distracted Ariel seemed. She did not ask her any more questions, but just stepped lightly at her side, gazing out across the treetops with a pained expression on her face.

After a few moments, Ordaana plucked up the courage to address her. 'Is it the battle, my lady? Is that what troubles you?

Ariel did not respond for a while, keeping her gaze fixed on the horizon. Then after a few minutes she seemed to realise she had been addressed. 'I'm sorry, Ordaana.' She turned to face her. 'What did you say?'

'Is it the battle that troubles you, my lady?'

'Ah.' Ariel shook her head. 'No, not that.' She smiled sadly. 'I have no doubt that Prince Haldus will hold them together. At least until they have all claimed ownership of the victory.'

Ordaana tried to smile back, but she was so nervous she might laugh that it was more of a grimace. She had always known that Ariel had little grasp on reality, but she was still shocked by this casual tone. How could she fail to see the danger that was hanging over her?

'Then, what?'

Ariel's smile faded. She dropped to Ordaana's side and looked down at her. It was clear from her expression that she wished to unburden herself. 'You must not speak of this,' she said, placing a hand on Ordaana's shoulder.

Ordaana shook her head, fighting another terrible urge to laugh as she realised the Queen was about to confide in her.

Ariel lowered her voice. 'Orion has grown strange to me, Ordaana. I no longer recognise him.'

She paused, shocked by her own words. 'I am *afraid* of him.'

CHAPTER TWENTY-TWO

Finavar laughed as he sprinted from the trees. His prey saw very little: a barbed cloak, a flutter of black, and then he was on them. His blades flashed in the dappled light as he flipped and rolled, slicing throats and severing limbs. Others figures followed in his wake, performing the same lethal dance; a whirling storm of limbs and steel. The creatures grunted and tried to parry, but the fight was lost before they realised it had begun. Within seconds the clearing was still once more, and carpeted with a mound of steaming bodies.

Finavar's cloak settled over him as he dropped into a crouch, surveying his work. 'Another twelve,' he said, counting the corpses. His face was barely recognisable. Usually it was open and animated; now it was locked in a determined scowl.

There was movement all around them. Ram's horns and spears flashed through the gaps between the trees; there was a whole army passing by, but Finavar's kinband killed in ghost-like silence, and before they were spotted, they would be gone. The same scene was being repeated many times throughout the foothills of Drúne Fell. The survivors of Locrimere were avenging their home.

'Next?' snapped Finavar, turning to his companions.

There were five figures gathered around him. Thuralin, Alhena, Caorann and Jokleel were covered in fresh scars and their faces were drawn with exhaustion, but they looked at the fifth of their number as eagerly as Finavar.

Laelia was the only one present whose demeanour had not changed over the last few months. Her delicate frame still shimmered with otherworldly light and, as she dropped lightly to the ground, she wore the same crooked smile that had first greeted Finavar. 'Do you wish to rejoin Eremon?'

Finavar shook his head, watching the shapes rushing past the clearing. They had little time before they were discovered. 'Not yet. We keep moving until we hear his call, as we agreed.'

Laelia nodded. Eremon's plan was to avoid a head-to-head battle for as long as possible. 'Haunt them like wraiths,' he had roared, as they began their shadow war against the outsiders. 'Hide your faces. Show them your blades.'

Laelia closed her eyes and her skin shimmered with light, throwing shadows across the broken remains of the outsiders. 'Half a mile to the west,' she said, waving through the trees. 'There is another of the giants.' She grimaced as she pictured it: a grotesque, cyclopean monster, lurching hungrily after the forest spirits, devouring their energy with disgusting relish.

Finavar's only reply was to launch himself off in the direction she indicated, vaulting over a wall of twisted bracken and vanishing into the shadows.

The others were ready and sprinted after him.

Seconds later, dozens of outsiders crashed into the clearing.

The monsters howled in frustration as they saw a still-twitching pile of corpses and no sign of those responsible.

Finavar slowed to a jog, then came to a halt beside a brisk, glittering stream. The water rippled and gurgled over dozens of corpses, hunched brutes with the symbol of the enemy branded into their hides – interlocking ram's horns, formed into an eight-pointed star.

'What is it, Fin?' asked Caorann, eyeing the surrounding trees. 'We cannot wait here.'

Finavar looked up through the branches, studying the bright face of Drúne Fell. 'Do you see that?' He scaled a nearby tree for a better view. 'Eremon has found us some friends.'

The others followed his gaze and saw that he was right. There was a haze in the air. Banks of arrows were raining down from the crevasses and peaks of the mountain.

Laelia raised her arms and drifted up through the branches. She smiled as she glimpsed groups of archers, rushing down the slopes. 'There are hundreds of them.'

There was a crack of breaking wood and Finavar turned to see a pair of crimson, goat-legged runts, with stunted black horns and axes in their hands. They staggered to a halt as they saw the figures looking down on them from the trees.

The first of them snarled and raised its axe, preparing to cry out a warning, but before it could speak, it stumbled back into the trees, a long, leaf-shaped blade buried in its throat.

As the second tried to run, Alhena dropped into view and loosed her second blade. It flashed through the air and slammed, hilt-deep, into the face of the monster. The thing reeled around the clearing for a few minutes, gargling blood and clutching at its face; then it dropped to the ground and lay still.

Finavar gave Alhena a brief nod as she wrenched her blades free and began gouging at the mouths of the monsters. Since the fall of Locrimere, her trophy-taking had become even more demented. Her wiry frame trembled with excitement as she added to her morbid assortment of teeth, fingers and dripping scalps.

'They're gathering on the mountain,' said Laelia, turning away from Alhena with distaste and looking at the distant figures.

Thuralin was standing a few feet away. His face looked more lined and weary than ever and he was leaning heavily against a tree. He seemed on the verge of collapse, but then he drew some seeds from his pouch, and as he crunched them between his teeth, a little colour returned to his sunken cheeks. 'We should join them. We could fight like this forever, stalking them in shadows, but to face such a horde in open battle would require all the kindreds of the forest.'

Finavar nodded eagerly. 'Perhaps that's what we're seeing.' He stared at each of them in turn, his eyes bright with mania. 'I knew the King would not forsake us. He must have been gathering the kindreds.' He waved one of his blades at the figures on the mountain. 'Don't you see? The Wild Hunt has begun. Orion is here.'

Jokleel turned hopefully to Laelia. 'Could it be?'

The smile faded from Laelia's face and she gave no reply.

Thuralin saw her hesitance and sneered. 'The King is chasing ghosts. He has no time for the living.' He nodded at the foot of the mountain. 'But if Eremon has chosen to make his last stand here, we should fight by his side.' Then he turned and limped off through the trees, making for the slopes of Drúne Fell.

The Lost Mountain had long ago grown accustomed to war. Its foothills formed the shape of a horseshoe and were peppered with a network of caves and tunnels. For centuries Drúne Fell had been the asrai's final bulwark against the few invaders who made it this far into the forest. As Finavar emerged from the trees, trailing his kinband behind him, he wondered if Alhena might be right. The bloody rag that had once been Eremon's banner was flying from a lip of rock, overlooking a meadow of tall grass, swarming with archers and spearmen. Finavar saw kindreds from every kingdom of the forest. He had never seen so many assembled in one place. As he climbed to the top of a small hill he saw hundreds more, flooding from the trees and racing towards Eremon's banner. He ran his fingers across the tips of the chest-high grass and shivered with hope.

Who could summon such a gathering, but the King?

He turned and looked back into the forest. The sun was dipping towards the treetops and throwing long shadows out over the valley. Dusk was upon them but as yet, the enemy had not emerged from the trees. Their handiwork was unmistakable, however – plumes of smoke that filled the sky for miles around and the explosive crack of falling trees, ringing out every few minutes and cutting deep into the hearts of every asrai present. There was no mistaking the enemy's route – they were making directly for the mountain.

Finavar frowned. 'Why here?' He looked across the valley at the twisted face of the mountain. 'Why Drúne Fell?' Then, as Caorann and the others reached his side, he nodded. 'The standing stones.'

'What?' Alhena was looking at the gathering army with undisguised awe, but Finavar's words made her pause. 'Standing stones?'

Finavar nodded. 'It has been the same every time. They always make their way to one of the dolmens – like the one we showed Orion. Do you remember?'

'Yes, I've seen them, but what does it matter?'

Finavar shrugged and peered up at the mountainside. 'There must be a collection of the stones on Drúne Fell, or on the far side.' He nodded at the ragged banner. 'We should take our place beside Eremon. They will be here soon.'

As they climbed to the outcrop, Finavar spied the weathered, craggy face of Eremon. He looked surprisingly well. In the months since the fall of Locrimere, the veteran had mended his leather armour and regained his proud, straight-backed posture. The anguished look that had haunted him for years had evaporated in the face of honest, desperate warfare.

It was not Eremon's health that gave Finavar pause, though, it was the figures by his side. There were dozens of nobles standing on the rock, all of them grilling Eremon for news of his campaign, but only one of them was familiar to Finavar and his stomach turned at the sight of him: Lord Beldeas, the dispossessed warden of a realm that no longer existed.

'Ah, here is our prince,' said Beldeas, with an insincere grin on his skeletal face.

'Finavar!' Eremon had been engrossed in his conversation with the nobles and had not noticed the hooded youth until he was a few feet away. He rushed towards him and grasped his hand. 'Loec be praised.'

Finavar's face remained stern, as he recalled how Beldeas had forsaken him at the festival of Ostaliss, but there was clear affection in his eyes as he shook Eremon's hand. The enmity that had once existed between them had long since vanished. Over the last few months they had saved each other's lives on several occasions. As Caorann approached, Eremon grasped his shoulder in a tight grip. The bond between the three of them was unmistakable.

Lord Beldeas's smile faltered for a moment, but he forced it back into place as he turned to face the other nobles. 'My shadow-dancers are the pride of the forest. They are the finest warriors you could hope to meet. See how wisely I choose my servants.'

Finavar turned from Eremon and, ignoring Lord Beldeas, he bowed to the other nobles. He studied each of them in turn, undaunted by their regal stares. He saw the two young brothers and immediately dismissed them as unimportant. The excited gleam in their eyes told him everything he needed to know – they were pampered children, even younger than he was, with no idea of war, or loss. They were both dressed in the most incredible finery – long ermine cloaks, amber necklaces and tall, elaborate headdresses crowned with carved, looping antlers. They were the cream of asrai nobility and Finavar doubted either of them would see the dawn.

He looked past them to someone less easy to place. He had straight black hair, parted in the middle, he was almost as tall as Caorann and he wore a haunted-looking expression on his face. His wiry limbs had clearly been hardened by years of combat, but he only met Finavar's gaze for a brief moment, before looking back at the ground. Strangest of all were the two stumps jutting out from the back of his black cuirass. Finavar recognised pain in his eyes, mingled with determination. He felt a rush of empathy. If they were not on the edge of a battle, he thought, it might have been interesting to learn the stranger's story.

Then he turned to the final noble. He recognised Prince Haldus from the festival of Ostaliss – his scarred, furrowed brow was unmistakable, as were the winged torcs that snaked around his biceps – but Finavar sensed a change in him. At the rites of spring he had been awkward and reticent, but now, on the edge of battle, he looked proud, and quite at ease. All eyes were on him and, however much Lord Beldeas waved his arms and boasted, it was clear where the power lay.

Prince Haldus waited for Beldeas to finish speaking then stepped over to Finavar. 'You are the pebble that started a land-slide, Finavar.' His mouth remained almost closed as he spoke and it was clear he did not enjoy giving praise. 'You have shown great bravery. Your interruption of the spring rites shocked us all, but without your example I might never have dared to address the King.'

Finavar clenched his jaw. 'Perhaps if I had shown a little more foresight this army could have mustered in time to save my home.'

'The past is gone, Finavar, but you are here now. You can fight *now*.' Haldus raised his spear and waved it at the figures crowding round them. 'What happened on the shores of the Idolan will not be repeated. These curs wish to defile one of our most holy sites – a place called the Vaults of Winter. It lies just beyond these peaks.' His eyes glittered. 'But they will not be expecting to meet us.' He raised his chin. 'The highborn have been summoned.'

'Summoned by Orion?' asked Finavar, unwilling to abandon such a long-cherished hope.

A shadow crossed Prince Haldus's face and his voice faltered. 'Our king is pursuing other matters.' He waved at another group, gathered further down the ledge of rock. They were clad in an assortment of flowing robes and lustrous furs and had huddled around Laelia, whispering excitedly and waving at the forest. 'But Ariel has blessed us with some of her handmaidens. The forest has been generous. I never dreamt of such a gathering.'

Finavar's shoulders dropped and he gave Caorann and Ere-mon a questioning glance.

They did not reply, but Prince Haldus noticed the exchange. 'What is it? Eremon?'

Eremon shook his head. 'Orion or not, we will gladly fight by your side.'

Prince Haldus's expression darkened. 'But you think we will fail?'

Eremon hesitated, noticing how many faces had turned in their direction. Dozens of nobles had gathered on the rock to see the infamous lowborn who styled himself the Darkling Prince.

Eremon drew back his shoulders and shook his head. 'We will not fail, but you must understand what we face. These creatures have grown strong. The forest is feeding them somehow – lending them its magic. And there is something with them. Something we faced in Locrimere.'

There was a flicker of doubt in Prince Haldus's eyes, then he remembered his audience and raised his voice. He waved at the magi gathered around Laelia. 'What magic is more powerful than the servants of the Queen? Ariel's handmaidens will hurl the very soul of the forest against these runts. We will stop them here. They *will not* reach the Vaults.'

Eremon looked at the magi and nodded. 'You're right.' He turned back to Prince Haldus. 'Nothing is more powerful than the magic of the Queen.' He turned to Finavar and Caorann with a grim smile.

'The running is over. We face them here.'

CHAPTER TWENTY-THREE

Ghorgus cursed. Smoke was leaking from its hide and blisters were bubbling across its muzzle. There were flames racing through the forest, but they were not to blame. No, the smoke was coming from *inside*. Ghorgus felt an odd mixture of emotions as it considered the changes overtaking its flesh. The most noticeable was the pale glow – it had begun leaking from its hide after the fall of the fifth stone. Now, weeks later, it had become incandescent, and uncomfortably hot. This was the cause of Ghorgus's shroud of smoke, not the fire in the trees. The monster was slowly being cooked from the inside out.

The hunched, hooded figure at Ghorgus's side spoke up. 'What?' Belakhor's dry screech cut through the din of the army below.

Ghorgus sneered back. 'Nothing.' The pain was not worth mentioning; not when the other symptoms were so wonderful. With every stone they toppled, Ghorgus moved closer to godhood. Godhood. That was the only suitable word. As the old magic bled from the rocks, it flooded Ghorgus's mind, throwing light onto hitherto unknown corners and sparking ideas at once strange and wonderful. Each thought blossomed, flower-like, as the monster focused on it, and then rippled through its flesh, adding thick layers of muscle and other, stranger powers. Ghorgus began to laugh as it considered what lay ahead. The bundle of sticks said there was another collection of fire-stones in a frozen cave, somewhere beyond the mountain to the north of them. Ghorgus shivered with delight, considering what another draught of magic would do to their pets.

Ghorgus's mind filled with visions of a forest devoid of the fae. With Belakhor's help, Ghorgus would become the new King in the Woods: a tyrant with the strength to rule the whole kingdom. Ghorgus glanced furtively at the hunched shaman. Perhaps even Belakhor would be unnecessary. After all, why should a god share its power?

Belakhor turned and light flashed on the bleached bones of its skull. Ghorgus had the unpleasant sense that the shaman had guessed its thoughts.

The ram's skull stared at him with its empty sockets. 'We are close now. So close.'

CHAPTER TWENTY-FOUR

Orion waded through the knee-deep waters of the Líath-Mael. The river looked as ancient and venerable as ever, but, like much of his kingdom, he knew it was a beautiful lie. He crashed through its dark, white-topped currents, recalling how many times he had encountered it unexpectedly, snaking through far-flung corners of his realm. Always, it appeared to be a permanent fixture of the landscape, and always it vanished, to reappear miles away, with a hint of laughter in its inky depths and a new horizon glittering across its surface.

Orion's hunt had lasted months and his skin was covered with mementos of his conquests: scars, weals and bruises, all worn with pride. While feuding lords and squabbling princelings fretted about warfare, Orion had been busy, carving his name across the knotted heart of the forest. Four of the Brúidd had already knelt before him, grovelling for mercy as he ground them beneath his hooves. Now his hunt had led him far to the south-east, near the halls of Coeth-Mara, and the kingdom of Lord Aldaeld.

Orion had never encountered the Líath-Mael so close to the Wildwood and he paused for a moment, sensing that something was not right. What business did the Líath-Mael have here, in this most dangerous corner of the forest? The river might be perfidious, but it was no fool. The Wildwood was a realm of ruin and loss. The Líath-Mael knew better than to wind through such a place.

He paused and placed his hands in the fast-moving water, trying to understand its reasoning. Despite the afternoon sun, it was deathly cool and as he peered closer, he noticed pale shapes drifting by. He reached out and grabbed one, lifting it up into the morning light. It was a fish: a silvery, foot-long trout that flopped pathetically in his grip. It was not dead, but it had made no move to evade him. Orion frowned as he turned the fish over in his hands. Its belly was twitching with dozens of tiny, black, arachnid limbs. They scuttled and recoiled as Orion ran a finger over them. He cursed and dropped the fish back into the water. It drifted away, trying to swim but enfeebled by its hideous mutation.

Orion growled under his breath. His sense of unease grew as he studied the other shapes drifting past. The forest was a place of magic and wonder, but the grotesque shapes moving through the river spoke more of disease than of sorcery. His lip curled as a clump of pale, tubular limbs floated past. They were coiled around a bloated, sack-like head, and as it rolled and tumbled, Orion glimpsed an anguished, humanoid face. He waded after it, but the Líath-Mael was not willing to indulge him, and its currents snatched the creature away.

There was a crash of breaking wood as Atolmis emerged from the trees further downstream. 'My lord,' he called, levelling a spear at the trees on the far side of the river.

Orion's doubts were fogotten as he glimpsed a flash of gold, slipping through the forest gloom. This latest prey had eluded him for weeks, but the chase was almost up. The summer solstice was only days away and Orion was delirious with power. He leapt easily from the river and bounded into the trees. As he ran the forest carried him – an extension of his own flesh, lifting him with glossy green tresses and dropping him onto a deer path that wound between the trunks.

The sound of his hooves rang out, thudding down onto the path, and Orion's prey looked back at him.

Orion's heart pounded as he saw its face. It was crouched in a patch of sunlight, watching his approach with disbelief and terror. Doubtless the thing had never dreamt Orion would be so tenacious. In all the long miles of pursuit, this was the closest he had managed to come to the spirit and now that it was almost in his grasp he saw that it was not as he remembered. It still resembled a lithe youth with golden, shimmering skin, but its crown of autumn leaves was gone, replaced with a circlet of summer flowers. Its eyes were as gold as its flesh.

Orion paused and frowned. Something was flickering in the corner of his vision; it looked like blue flames rippling through the trees, but when he turned to examine it, it was gone. He shook his head and returned his attention to his prey.

'Zephyr,' he said, edging slowly closer and attempting to steady his breathing.

The spirit recoiled at the sound of its own name.

Orion smiled. 'You did not expect me to remember you.'

The spirit was rigid with horror. 'What do you want with me?' It stared at Orion's ivy-clad antlers and long, filthy talons.

Orion knew that Atolmis would be circling around behind the spirit, along with the other equerries. Just a few more minutes and they would have the thing surrounded. All he needed to do was keep it from bolting. Again, he thought he saw blue lights, somewhere in his peripheral vision, but this time he ignored them, putting them down to the strange power that was transforming his body.

'Would you say I have assumed the correct mantle?' Orion drew himself erect and threw back his chin.

'What?' The spirit shook its head, not recognising its own words. 'What mantle?'

From the corner of his eye, Orion saw Atolmis and the others moving silently into place, but the spirit was staring intently at the King and failed to realise the danger.

'You doubted me,' whispered Orion, 'but now you will kneel, like all the others.'

The spirit edged closer, looking horrified. 'All the others? What do you mean? What have you done?'

As the spirit stepped closer, Orion prepared to pounce. 'I have spent the spring hunting you all down, one by one,' he said, lifting his spear.

Understanding flashed in Zephyr's eyes and it whirled around, finally realising it was surrounded.

'Let me show you how to treat your–' Orion's words became a strangled cough and he staggered backwards, with thick roots wrapped around his throat. The blue lights flashed again but this time they blazed inside his skull.

He howled as he was dragged back along the deer path, as powerless as a newborn.

'Who dares to…?' he began, clutching at the roots, but his words trailed off as the lights faded and he saw what was happening to him. The path was erupting, vomiting roots and vines and lashing them around his body. He whirled around as the tendrils tightened web-like over his face.

Orion's stomach lurched horribly as he tumbled into the hole that appeared beneath him. Then his thoughts grew dark as consciousness slipped away.

The last thing he saw was Atolmis, staring down at him in horror as he plummeted beneath the earth, feeling his flesh disintegrate.

'Help her out!' cried a voice, from somewhere nearby. 'She's in pain.'

Orion opened his eyes, expecting to see the earth and roots, but seeing something else instead – something equally strange. He was in a small clearing, filled with hundreds of pulsing lights, all of them emanating from a tall mound of branch-like stones. There was a female figure trapped inside the mound, wreathed in blue flames and howling in pain. As she screamed, a bird thrashed back and forth above her head. Orion realised it was an owl, and the thought filled him with a dreadful sense of déjà-vu. As his vision cleared, he saw other figures crowded around the prisoner in the stones, attempting to grasp her flailing hands.

Orion felt a rush of relief as he saw that Ariel was standing near the screaming woman. She had her back to him but her mantle of glittering tendrils and her tall, shimmering wings were unmistakable. His head was spinning from his flight across the treetops, but he realised that the other figures were handmaidens and advisors. There was another noblewoman he could not immediately place. Her gaunt, angular face was a sneer of disdain, and her hair was a jumbled mess of silver tresses, which had once been plaited in some complicated style. She looked as though she had recently been involved in a fight. Her robes were in tatters and there was a dark stain just below her ribs. She looked briefly at Orion and her eyes flashed with emotion. They were filled with either hatred or lust, but Orion was too dazed to be sure which.

'I have her!' gasped a young nobleman, reaching into the stones.

Orion recognised Khoron Belidae – the effete youth who had almost ruined the festival of Ostaliss with his endless poetry. He had grasped the screaming figure in the mound and Ariel and her handmaidens rushed to help him.

Orion remained slumped on the grass, watching with a bemused expression as the stones rippled and undulated, before spitting their prisoner out into the clearing.

One of the handmaidens caught her and as she lowered the woman gently onto the ground, her cries finally ceased and Orion saw her more clearly as she turned to face him. She had an intense, piercing gaze and wore delicately woven robes of spun gold, decorated with hundreds of intricate runes. As she clambered to her feet, she leant heavily on a staff of knotted twigs.

Naieth, thought Orion, realising whose hands had wrenched him all the way from the south of the forest to the Cerura Carn: the Queen's most powerful sorceress. Who else would dare to drag him beneath the earth, just as he was about to seize his prize?

He cursed and tried to stand, but his legs collapsed beneath him and he felt a dreadful wave of nausea. He thought for a moment that he might make himself look even more ridiculous by vomiting, but managed to steady himself by crouching on the ground and taking deep slow breaths.

'Take a moment to rest,' said Naieth, stepping towards him. She was still leaning on her staff and it was clear from her pained expression that she felt as terrible as Orion.

'What have you done, witch?' He glared at her. 'How dare you summon your king in such a way? I am not an errant child.' He tried again to stand but was still too weak and fell back. 'Who gave you the right to–?'

'My king,' interrupted Ariel, stepping between the two of them and dropping to her knees at Orion's side. 'You must forgive me. I asked Naieth to do this.' Her eyes were wide with concern as she grasped his hand. 'I have heard such strange stories, my love. I had to see you. I need you, my king.'

Orion's rage faded a little as he saw the fear in Ariel's eyes. 'It is almost Sólis-Leith,' he said, managing to keep his voice low. 'I would have returned then. Could it not wait?'

Ariel waved at the others, watching anxiously from the foot of the mound. 'They have told me such tales, my love. Prince Haldus told me that our reign is danger; that outsiders are threatening the sanctity of the Council Glade. He has gathered an army without you.'

Orion climbed slowly to his feet and grasped her by the shoulders. 'Our reign is eternal.' He struggled to dampen the fury in his words, enraged by the thought that the hawk rider had spread such rumours. 'If I am left to finish what I have begun, nothing can harm us.' He ran a bloody talon across the pale perfection of her cheek. 'We are one, my queen. Nothing can come between us.'

Ariel nodded and attempted a hesitant smile.

'Are you already dealing with this threat, then, my king?' asked Naieth. She tapped her staff against the mound of stones. The lights were quickly fading, but images were still drifting inside and Orion caught a glimpse of a laughing, gold-skinned child, sprinting along a deer path.

Naieth's eyes were narrow. It was clear that her question was loaded with accusation.

Orion's veins were throbbing with strange vitality. The nearer he got to midsummer, the more powerful he felt. It was intoxicating and wonderful, but such unnatural vigour did not lend itself to quiet debate. Naieth's tone was like a spark set amongst kindling. He reeled away from Ariel, threw back his head and howled until his whole body shook.

Khoron Belidae and the handmaidens cowered away from him, backing off beneath the trees, but Naieth stood her ground, closing her eyes and grasping her staff with silent determination until Orion fell quiet.

Before Ariel could stop him, Orion thudded across the clearing and levelled one of his talons at the sorceress. 'I am dealing with the *real* threat!'

His face flushed and he waved at the runes on her golden dress. 'These shades and phantoms you worship would tear us apart if they could.' He pointed at the surrounding glades. 'They have no love for me, or my queen. *They* are the ones who must be brought to heel.' He waved dismissively. 'Not bull-headed runts, snuffling in the undergrowth. I know the stories and they do not interest me. Come the Wild Hunt they will flee like rats, but until then I have more important matters to attend to.'

Naieth dared to open her eyes and meet Orion's furious, blazing stare. She nodded at a carved stone, tied to his belt. 'And is this why you destroy things you could never hope to understand? I see you have stolen the eye of the Wrach and thrown his paths into chaos. Is that how you intend to prove yourself? Destroying the things you profess to rule?' She pointed at the stone. 'Such tools are beyond us, Orion; they were not made by mortal hands. You will never control it.'

Orion's frame stiffened with rage. Naieth was infuriatingly accurate. Try as he might, he had never been able to replicate his initial success with the stone. Every time he tried he found himself peering into a black void. He glared at Naieth, but could think of no reply.

'Orion, my love,' said Ariel, her eyes clouded by doubt. 'Is this true? What have you done?'

Orion turned to face her and his rage was briefly replaced by shock as he realised how unearthly his queen had become. She seemed half phantom. A terrible thought crossed his mind: *Are* we still one? Unlike him, her life was a continuous stream. There was no cycle of death and rebirth for the Queen – she simply lived and lived and lived. For thousands of years, she had been becoming less Ariel and more Isha. Since they emerged from the Oak of Ages, Orion had not taken the time to really study her face. He did so now and balked at what he saw. Her gaze was as vague and distant as the stars. She had no idea of how precarious their rule really was. He stepped closer and peered into her eyes, desperate for a sign of recognition.

She saw his concern and her face broke into a gentle smile.

For a second Orion saw a bright speck of Ariel: a precious stone of mortality, glittering in the inferno of her divinity.

His pulse steadied and he nodded at her.

They *were* one; unbroken.

'I have done nothing.' His voice was calm. 'Other than remind our subjects that they owe us fealty.'

As they realised Orion's wrath was under control, the others stepped back into the clearing. Orion noticed that the silver-haired noblewoman was still studying him closely and he finally recalled her name. 'Ordaana,' he said.

She bowed low to the ground, looking deeply uncomfortable. Her pale face flushed with colour and she hurried to Ariel's side.

'The forest is not our enemy, my love,' said Ariel, still smiling.

'The Queen is right,' said Khoron Belidae, stepping to the

Ariel's side and throwing up his arms in a dramatic, encompassing gesture. 'You *are* the forest: every oak, every alder, every blessed, bleating fawn.'

Orion shook his head, irritated by the poet's dreamy tone. This was exactly the kind of thinking that made Ariel feel so remote. He grew even more irritated as he saw the delight with which Ariel greeted the poet's words.

Orion felt his bile returning. 'Why have you dragged me here?' He turned to Naieth so that he did not have to look at the poet any more.

Naieth studied him in silence for a moment then stepped back towards the stones. 'Let me show you.'

Orion's anger grew as he studied her, but he held it at bay. He was intrigued, despite himself, to know why she had put herself through such pain. Summoning him had clearly been agony for her.

Naieth leant the head of her staff against the mound and closed her eyes. Light rippled through the knotted twigs and passed into the stones, causing them to stretch and unfurl like new leaves. As the mound rippled away from the staff, Naieth held out her hand and said: 'Othu'. There was a flutter of wings and Orion recalled the owl he had noticed earlier. The bird flew from its cage and settled on Naieth's forearm, swivelling its head to study him as its mistress worked her spell.

The sorceress kept her eyes closed and more of the light leaked from her staff into the ancient memorial. After a few moments, a circular window formed at the heart of the cairn and Naieth raised her staff, so that the eye-shaped carving at its head was hovering in the centre of the space. Spokes of light arced out from the wood, turning the window into a corona of blue fire. The light grew so fierce that some of the handmaidens had to avert their gaze.

Orion stepped closer, fascinated by the display. As he peered into the blaze he began to make out shapes, smashing through an inferno of burning trees: a vast host, swarming around the foothills of a mountain. 'Drúne Fell,' he breathed, recognising the jagged peaks and realising how close this scene was to where he now stood.

Naieth nodded and twisted her hand, causing the lights to flicker and change, revealing a new image. Orion saw Haldus and the other nobles of Ariel's court, preparing for battle. When he last saw them they had been clad in pale robes and circlets of flowers, chanting hymns to the new year, but now they were dressed in blood and scarred leather, howling desperate commands as they raced into position.

Orion saw that many of them would go into battle already wounded. As he wandered the forest, hunting down the Brúidd, his people had been fighting for their lives. He felt a vague doubt. Many of his courtiers were fools, but Haldus was a noble soul. He did not deserve to be abandoned.

Then, as quickly as it came, Orion's doubt was gone. He could do nothing while the Brúidd still doubted his power. Everything else could wait.

Naieth gasped and the lights dimmed. She reeled back from the stones and Orion barely managed to catch her before she dropped to the ground. She slumped in his arms and groaned.

Ariel rushed to her side and took her hand. 'Naieth, you must rest!'

The sorceress freed herself gently from Orion's grip and managed to support herself with her staff. She looked more exhausted than ever and her copper-coloured hair was plastered across her pale, sweaty face. 'What did you see?' she said, turning to Orion.

The King sneered, conscious that all eyes were on him and

determined to hide his moment of doubt. 'Yes, yes – outsiders, in the heart of the forest, as you said. I understand.' He shook his head. 'They would not last an hour against me.'

'Then lead us.' Naieth's voice was an urgent whisper. 'Lead your subjects to war. Haldus is not a king. He can't do this alone.' She waved at Orion's ivy-clad limbs. His green-tinted flesh was glimmering with arboreal power and his muscles were like slabs of oak, carved and worked with the most intricate spiralling designs. 'Now is the time to strike.'

She placed a hand on his arm. 'Soon you will be at your most powerful. Sólis-Leith is only days away. But once autumn comes…' She left the thought unfinished.

Orion recoiled from her touch and pounded across the clearing to stare out at the trees. He knew exactly what Naieth was referring to. The mention of the summer solstice caused his heart to race, but also reminded him how short his time was. Half the year had almost passed. The thought terrified him. He had no fear of death, but what if he were to die with his work unfinished? He turned to look at Ariel. What if he failed to subdue the forest spirits before he laid himself out to die? The distant look was back in Ariel's eyes. She had no idea how precarious her rule was. Her mind was in the heavens and the trees; she could not defend herself.

'I must finish what I have begun,' he said, taking a deep breath. 'Then, when Sólis-Leith comes, I will truly become the King.' He glanced at Naieth. 'I will run no errands, witch, but when the Wild Hunt begins, nothing will stand against me.'

A low, bestial rumble came from his chest. '*Nothing.*'

The handmaidens flinched at the sound of Orion's rage, but Naieth nodded calmly. She had expected this response and had her argument prepared. She opened her mouth to reply, but Ordaana chose that moment to speak up.

'My queen,' she said, bowing low again. 'What is this Sínann-Torr you mentioned? Perhaps the prophetess would know something more on the subject?'

Naieth frowned, annoyed by the interruption. 'Yes,' she snapped, 'the Sínann-Torr. Echoes of a previous world. A link to the other realms.' She shrugged. 'Somehow these outsiders are using them to create a bond with the forest. That is how they have come so far.'

She turned back to Orion, but saw that the mention of old stones had distracted him. The King was now examining the carved rock attached to his belt and muttering under his breath. Naieth stepped towards him, eager to draw his attention back to Haldus and the battle at Drúne Fell, but before she could speak, Ariel replied to Ordaana.

'Ah yes,' she said, smiling gratefully at Ordaana. 'The forest rings with that name: Sínann-Torr.' She placed a hand on Naieth's arm. 'Perhaps the Chaos creatures are making for another one of these stones? Perhaps that is their goal, rather than my sacred glades?'

Naieth nodded impatiently. 'Yes, my queen, that is quite possible. They have found several of the ancient sites: Torr-Dobár and Torr-Cirrus have been defiled in just the last week.'

The thought of such ancient power distracted her for a moment and she lowered her gaze, recalling what she knew of the stones. 'There is a legend of a keystone, located to the north of Drúne Fell. It was hidden deep in the Vaults of Winter, long before we came to the forest. The ancient runes referred to it by various names, but I have always known it as the Torr-Ildána. It is said to be hidden in a place called Dhioll Hollow.' She shook her head in frustration and scowled at Ordaana for changing the subject.

Ordaana raised her voice and glanced at Orion. 'The Vaults

of Winter.' She spoke slowly and clearly. 'The place forbidden to us.'

Orion had been moving slowly back towards the trees, bored by the talk of old stones, but Ordaana's choice of words caught his attention. 'Forbidden?'

Ordaana nodded. 'One of the places in the forest we would never dare enter.'

Orion laughed. 'There are no such places for me.'

Ordaana turned to Naieth with a raised eyebrow.

The sorceress blanched as she saw where Orion's thoughts were leading. 'My king, your forebears swore long ago never to enter the Vaults of Winter. It is the dark heart of the forest: a repository for its most closely guarded secrets. All of the old accords between the asrai and the–'

Orion held up one of his hands to silence her. 'What would happen if the outsiders reached this final collection of stones – this Torr-Ildána?'

Naieth glared at Ordaana, then reluctantly answered Orion's question. 'The Sínann-Torr are scattered across the forest. Some of our most potent magi have devoted their lives to the mystery of them but, even now, we have little idea of how many there are, or who made them.'

Despite her frustration at this distraction, Naieth began to warm to her theme. 'In my youth I spent decades trying to decipher the runes carved into the few stones we know of, but it is a thankless task. They are born of an intelligence that bears no relation to our own. The most I could discern was a repeated mention of something called the Gyre, or the Dark Paths – a circular web of magic linking the ancient sites, centring on the one known as Torr-Ildána.'

Orion stepped closer to her and stooped until their faces were level. 'And what does this have to do with the outsiders?'

Naieth shrugged. 'They are able to find these sites with ease. It is almost as though the forest wants them to discover its secrets.'

'Of course,' growled Orion. 'The forest is loaning them the power to overthrow my rule.'

Ariel shook her head, horrified by the suggestion. 'That cannot be.'

'What will happen if they reach the final stone, this Torr-Ildána?' repeated Orion, keeping his gaze fixed on the sorceress.

She sighed. 'Well, if the legends are true, and the Torr-Ildána is some kind of keystone, they would tap into the heart of the Gyre. Whatever power links these old stones would be theirs.'

Orion threw up his hands. 'So why all this talk of Drúne Fell?' He shook his head. 'If you are truly afraid of these runts then it is clear what I must do.'

Naieth's eyes lit up. 'Yes! If you join Prince Haldus and the others at Drúne Fell, you can prevent them reaching the final stone. You can halt this–'

'I must enter the Vaults of Winter.' Orion drew back his antlers and stared at the sky. 'I must find these old stones and take the power for myself; or at the very least prevent the outsiders taking it.'

Naieth moaned in horror and grasped his arm. 'No. No you must *not*. That is not what I meant. Understand me, Orion, your forebears swore an oath. The Vaults are forbidden, and for good reason. The balance of life is precarious. If you enter the forbidden–'

'Forbidden?' Orion snatched back his arm. 'What king is *forbidden* from his own realm?' He began pacing around the clearing, churning the earth with his hooves. 'Again, the spirits seek mastery over me.' His voice rose in volume. 'Again, they would bind me to their will.'

'Orion,' said Ariel, stepping to his side with fear in her eyes. 'Something has changed in you. You are different.'

As the Queen placed a hand on Orion's arm his lips curled back in a snarl and he drew back his fist.

There was a hiss of alarm from the handmaidens and they raised their staffs defensively.

Orion froze, seconds away from striking Ariel's face. His mouth fell open as he realised what he had nearly done. Then he backed away to the edge of the clearing, staring at his fist as though it were not his own.

As the handmaidens rushed to Ariel's side, Naieth hastened past her, following the dazed-looking Orion. She lowered her voice, sounding almost sympathetic. 'You're not thinking straight, my king. Make for Drúne Fell. Otherwise your subjects will die. They cannot hold back this threat without your aid. Would you leave them all to their fate?'

Despite his shocked expression, Orion replied with certainty. 'And what if some of the outsiders are already inside the Vaults of Winter? Have you considered that? Do you think they will honour your old accords? They will take whatever they find there and hurl it against us; whatever happens at Drúne Fell.'

He looked at Ariel with an apology in his eyes, but she did not meet his gaze, so he turned away and glared at Naieth. 'I will find this Dhioll Hollow,' he tapped the rock tied to his belt, 'somehow. And I will harness the stones for myself.'

He filled his lungs and drew back his shoulders. 'I *will* be king.'

The sorceress blanched and shook her head, but her fear betrayed her. 'You would never find it. I'm the only living soul who could show you the way and I will not take you. The path to Dhioll Hollow must stay hidden, even from you.'

The King laughed and looked at the Wrach's stone again.

'Then I will use a different kind of guide.' He strode towards the mound of stones and looked through the rippling window in its side. The remnants of Naieth's spell were still coursing round its frame and a torrent of images was rolling through the air.

'Wait!' cried Naieth, guessing his intent. 'You have done enough damage already.' She pointed her staff at the rolling coils of light.

Orion ignored her plea and unclasped the black stone from his belt. He saw that flashes of light were flickering inside the talisman. They were coiling and spinning around the stone in a way he had never seen before. He looked back at Ariel. 'Our rule will not fail.' His voice was husky with emotion. '*I* will not fail.'

Ariel shook her head, unnerved by the fear in Naieth's eyes. 'My love,' she said, but before she could continue, Orion stepped inside the stone sculpture and gasped as blue fire enveloped him. He lifted the stone and raised his voice over the sound of the flames. 'Come for what is yours!' he cried.

The light flared brighter and Orion heard a hideous grunting sound. At first he thought a huge beast had appeared next to him inside the cairn, but then he realised it was his own breath. As his eyes grew accustomed to the glare, he saw that the world outside had stopped. Ariel, Naieth and the others were still watching him in horror, but they were as motionless as the rocks above his head. Naieth was frozen in the act of pointing her staff at him, a look of abject terror on her face. Ariel was caught mid-stride, dashing across the clearing, and the others were preserved in the same instant: either cowering or reaching out to him. Only Ordaana looked unafraid. If anything, the expression fixed on her face was one of triumph.

Orion realised that his breath seemed so loud because there

was no other sound. The world was silent. His ragged gasps were ringing out in a void. He climbed from the stone in confusion and looked at the sky. A pair of swallows were painted across the clouds, as static as everything else. 'What do I do?' he said, turning to Naieth.

She could no more reply than the grass. The prophetess had been petrified, as surely as the stones behind him. Orion leant closer and saw that even the tiny strands of her copper hair were motionless, trailing behind her head like delicate metalwork.

Fascinated, he reached out and touched her face. Her skin was warm and yielding. She was a living statue. Orion moved around the clearing, feeling a growing sense of anger. The old witch been able to harness the stones, why could he not?

As he strode around the clearing something caught his eye, back down the avenue of trees leading to the Council Glade. His breathing quickened as he realised something was moving in the stillness: a shape, drifting between the rigid shadows.

He crossed the clearing and walked beneath the canopy of trees, keeping his gaze fixed on the undulating shape. As he passed Khoron Belidae, he lifted a spear from the poet's lifeless fingers and tested its weight. It was a good weapon, tipped with a large metal blade. He grunted in satisfaction and continued on his way.

As he approached the shape, a low growl rumbled in his chest. The movement he had seen was a hooded robe, fluttering despite the absence of a breeze. The robe was draped over a small, familiar figure with long, numerous fingers that rippled and coiled as they reached out towards him.

'Have you have learned,' asked the Wrach in a thin, rasping voice, 'what a weakling you are?'

Orion felt an overwhelming urge to hurl the spear, but he kept it at his side, remembering his purpose. 'Have you already forgotten,' he replied, 'that you are my subject?' He raised the weapon. 'Need I prove myself a second time?'

The Wrach wheezed with laughter. 'Your proofs are meaningless. What do you want?'

Orion held up the stone. 'To enter the Vaults of Winter. Take me there and I will return this useless rock.'

The spirit looked up, revealing the pale, writhing mess of its face. 'The Vaults of Winter?' There was hesitation in its voice.

'Do not play ignorant, serpent,' snapped Orion. 'You see everything. You know the way.'

The hooded spirit waved at its blind eyes and shrugged. 'I see nothing, weakling, remember.'

Orion nodded. He had expected this. He tightened his grip on the stone. Strands of ivy rippled beneath his skin as his muscles swelled.

'What are you doing?' The Wrach stepped closer and reached out with a nest of snapping, sibilant fingers.

Orion gave no reply but pressed harder on the stone, closing his eyes and hunching his shoulders as he applied all his newfound strength.

There was a cracking sound and a trickle of black dust fell from his fist.

'Stop!' screamed the Wrach, breaking into a run. 'I know the way! I will take you!'

Orion was unable to stop at first, delighted by the power throbbing in his arm. He felt the stone beginning to break. Shards of it splintered off, slicing into his skin, but even the pain gave him pleasure. Then, as the Wrach stumbled to a halt in front of him, he nodded and relaxed his grip, holding the stone out before the Wrach's face. It was bloody and cracked, but otherwise intact.

'What have you done?' The Wrach sounded utterly horrified.

Orion closed his meaty palm around the stone again and raised his eyebrows.

'I will take you!' The spirit wrapped dozens of serpentine fingers around Orion's forearm. 'If you swear to return the stone!'

'Take me and the stone will be yours.'

Still, the spirit hesitated. It let out a strange hissing sound and caressed Orion's arm. 'But the Vaults? Really? Why there? You will find nothing but pain in those cold pits. I could show you glens of such beauty–'

Orion grabbed the Wrach's hood, pulled it close and hissed, 'The Vaults.'

The spirit slumped pitifully in Orion's grip and replied in a flat, defeated voice. 'Of course. Press the stone to my flesh.'

Orion grimaced as the Wrach's robes sprouted dozens of white snakes. They quickly enveloped his forearm and wrapped around the stone. He was about to speak, but then he noticed another horrible sensation, prickling against his shoulders and chest. *Snow*. He looked up in wonder. The sky overhead was midnight black, but filled with colossal, drifting banks of whiteness.

'What are you doing?' he asked, glaring at the spirit. 'I did not ask...' His words trailed off as he realised that the forest was gone, replaced by a dazzling, snow-covered mountainside. He stepped back, remembering to keep a firm grip on the stone. He could see nothing but snow, rocks and heavy, low-hanging clouds. A bitter north wind lashed against him and he felt it more keenly than a sword blow. It sliced through his skin and clamped around his organs. 'Is this it? Is this the Vaults?' He wrapped his arms around his chest, still clutching the spear in one hand and the stone in the other.

The Wrach shook its head and pointed at a steep crevasse, a few feet away.

Orion frowned and lurched across the mountainside, still clutching his chest. 'This cold,' he muttered, 'it burns.'

The Wrach nodded but gave no reply as it followed Orion towards the crevasse.

As he reached the edge, Orion knelt and leant out over the drop, peering down into the shadows. The thick banks of snow made it hard to see clearly, but it was plain that there was no easy way down. The chasm was sheer-sided and glittering with frost and ice. There were a few footholes and ledges but no visible bottom.

'The stone,' said the Wrach, extending a writhing limb of serpents.

'What is this?' Orion waved at the crevasse. 'I'm no eagle. How do you expect me to find my way down there?'

'There is no other way.' The Wrach kept its hand outstretched. 'You swore you would return what you took from me.'

Orion hurled the stone back across the ice with a sneer. 'Take the useless thing.'

The Wrach unfurled one of its limbs and caught the stone before it vanished in the snow. The spirit sighed ecstatically as it fixed the black orb onto the head of its staff.

'How do I reach the Vaults?' demanded Orion, jabbing his spear at the sheer drop.

The Wrach backed away into the dark and the snow, shaking its head.

Orion leapt to his feet and followed, keeping his spear raised. 'You said you would lead me to the Vaults of Winter!'

There was one last reply as the hooded figure vanished into the blinding whiteness. 'Take back your slaves,' said the spirit. 'Ask them to carry your corpse.'

Orion cursed and turned back to the crevasse. 'There is no way down,' he said, studying the treacherous climb. Then the wind lashed across the slopes even more ferociously and Orion felt the dreadful pain again. The cold was leaching the life out of him. He looked around for shelter, but it was obvious there was only one place to go. He strapped the spear to his back, dropped to his knees in the snow and prepared to climb. The nearest ledge was thirty feet away and the descent was gleaming with ice.

'Impossible!' he cried, looking around for a sign of the Wrach. 'No one could survive such a drop!' It was only then that he noticed three figures, emerging from the snowstorm. 'Sélva,' he said, recognising the wolfskin cloak and tall birchwood helmet of his equerry. Behind him was Olachas, with his flaxen plaits and his glittering longsword. And finally came Ilaruss, his face completely hidden behind his wooden helmet.

Orion climbed to his feet and waded through the snow to greet them.

The equerries knelt at the sight of their king and Sélva held out his hand. 'My lord,' he said. 'I just watched you vanish into a field of snakes. Now you are here.' He looked around in confusion. 'In the snow.' He peered at Orion's green-tinged flesh. 'And unharmed.'

Orion indicated that his servants should rise. 'The Brúidd are playing games with us. I left you months ago, at Torr-Goholoth. Spring has passed since then. Midsummer is almost upon us.'

Sélva narrowed his eyes. They were as black and pitiless as Atolmis's. The surprise left his face and he nodded. 'The Dark Paths follow their own seasons. Only the Brúidd fully understand such things.' He pressed his palm to his chest. 'How can we serve you, leaf-liege?'

Sélva's words needled Orion even more than the cold. *Only the Brúidd can understand such things.* Bile rose in his throat. Even his own equerries considered the Council of Beasts more powerful than their own king. 'We climb,' he growled looking back at the crevasse. 'Then we destroy.'

CHAPTER TWENTY-FIVE

Figures hurried across the slopes of Drúne Fell, picking vantage points and checking weapons. Despite the horrors of the last few months, Finavar could not help but smile. He had never imagined he would see such a thing. The ridge where he crouched was lined with hundreds of survivors of the battle for Locrimere, shadow-dancers like himself; lithe, tattooed figures, clutching their leaf-shaped blades as they waited in the dark for Eremon's order to attack. Their captain had a banner raised above his head: a slender pennant fluttering in the warm summer's breeze, emblazoned with the mark of their fallen kingdom – two black yews, on a field of pale green. The hiding was over. The children of Locrimere now waited in full view of their enemy, their eyes glittering as dangerously as their blades.

Finavar relished the chance to finally look his enemy in the eye, but he understood that they were little more than bait. Prince Haldus had placed his full strength out of sight. Before the outsiders could climb to Eremon's banner, they would discover the true size of the army waiting for them in the gloom. At the foot of the mountain was the entrance to a passage, the fastest route through the foothills to the Vaults of Winter, and Haldus had positioned the bulk of his force there: hundreds of spearmen, proud, stern-faced guardians of the Queen's glades, wearing thick leather body armour and helmets as they waited silently in the trees. They were led by the pampered young nobles, Lords Salicis and Alioth, and Finavar noted with surprise how well the brothers had scattered their force – the spearmen were gathered in great numbers, but the minotaurs would have no inkling of their presence, right until the moment the spears started to fly.

And that would not be the only surprise. Laelia and the magi were also waiting in the trees, and in the caves above Finavar's kin were hundreds of archers – marksmen from right across the forest, united under the command of the scowling Prince Haldus. Death would come from the air in other ways, too. There was no sign of the pale stranger in the black cuirass, Lord Cyanos, but Finavar knew Prince Haldus had sent him off to the eastern slopes to prepare his own forces for the attack.

Caorann noticed Finavar's pouting expression and smiled. 'The Darkling Prince,' he said, waving at the noble figures that surrounded them. 'Finally you are moving in the correct circles.'

Finavar laughed. 'Did you see how much it pained that prince to address me?' He adopted a haughty expression and mimicked Haldus's stiff tones. 'You have shown great bravery.'

Caorann grinned and shook his head in mock despair but, before he could reply, the enemy broke from the trees.

A wave of hunched, lumbering runts led the attack: goat-legged fiends with crimson flesh and crooked, wiry limbs. They sprinted across the valley in ominous, frenetic silence, their eyes fixed on Eremon's banner as they approached the trees at the foot of the mountain. They carried spears and crude iron swords and the ram's horns curled around their heads were dark with asrai blood.

Finavar and the other asrai on the ridge looked to Eremon. Their dour-faced captain held up his hand and shook his head, indicating that they should wait. They all understood his reasoning: grotesque as they were, these puling wretches were not the true army.

Finavar tensed as the monsters reached the line of trees. For a few seconds they continued their advance, dodging quickly through the shadowy boughs. Then Lords Alioth and Salicis made their move. Lithe figures dropped from the shadows and launched themselves at the enemy. Some threw their spears, others rammed them through throats and chests, flinging their victims aside before racing on to another target.

Finally, the creatures broke their silence. Howls of pain filled the trees as the asrai tore into them.

Finavar knew the plan, but gave Eremon another hopeful glance.

The captain's expression remained implacable and his hand was still raised in silent command.

Finavar itched to join the fun, but he held his position and continued watching from afar.

After a just a few minutes, the fighting was already nearing a conclusion. Finavar glimpsed a flash of garish colour in the dark and realised he was seeing the two young popinjays leading the final defence.

No more than a dozen of the monsters survived to stagger from the trees and scramble back towards the forest, trailing broken weapons behind them and limping pathetically.

Finavar looked up to see if Prince Haldus would stop them

reaching safety, but his archers remained hidden. Not an arrow was loosed.

The ominous silence returned and it felt to Finavar as though even a loud breath would echo around the curve of the foothills. Then he flinched as a deafening noise filled the forest: a harsh braying of tuneless horns that came from dozens of different directions.

Caorann looked at Finavar and raised his eyebrows as the forest spawned an army of unbelievable size. These were no stooping runts; these were hulking, armour-clad brutes with wide, bull-like horns and the thick, muscled legs of cattle. They stomped through the gloom in their hundreds, if not thousands, pounding drums, bellowing along with the tuneless din of the horns and clutching spitting torches and massive, spike-laden axes.

Finavar shivered as he imagined such a wave of muscle and hate smashing into the spearmen below. He looked at Eremon again. The captain's face still showed no sign of emotion and his hand was still raised.

The minotaurs marched slowly across the valley, and as they reached the survivors of the first attack they clubbed them mercilessly to the ground, mocking them with snorts of derision and trampling them under leaden hooves.

As they approached the trees, Finavar saw them more clearly and realised that the monster at the head of the army was almost twice the size of the others, and clad head-to-toe in plates of hammered iron. The creature was almost as wide as it was tall and the combination of its bulk and thick metal armour caused the ground to shake as it moved. Like the others, it carried a massive, two-handed axe, but this weapon glowed with a light that caused Finavar to shiver.

The outsiders reached the trees at the foot of Drúne Fell

and Finavar heard a rippling note of birdsong. Finally, Prince Haldus was summoning his first surprise.

The minotaurs smashed into the trees and found them bristling with spears. The huge, armoured captain bellowed and raised its axe, ordering a charge, filled with bloodlust at the sight of the spearmen. As the monsters' hooves thudded across the baked earth, they did not notice that a new sound was filling the valley.

Finavar and Caorann gasped as they saw something they had only ever sung about: riders, from every corner of the forest, mounted on beautiful, palomino steeds. The horses were so pale they gleamed in the dark, flooding the valley like a moonlit river. The riders barely seemed to touch them as they rode – few were even holding their reins, clutching spears, pennants and bows instead as they hurtled towards the beastmen.

The monster in the plate armour was so enraged by the spearmen dancing through the trees, that it did not notice the riders until they had sliced through the flanks of its army.

Horns wavered and drums ceased as the minotaurs were attacked from all sides. As the riders harried their flanks, Alioth and Salicis led the spearmen out to greet them, attacking the vanguard with a bristling wall of spears and glaives. At that moment, up on the slopes of Drúne Fell, Prince Haldus whistled for a second time and his archers loosed a black cloud of arrows at the stranded minotaurs. Simultaneously, the forest erupted as Laelia and her coterie of sorcerers teased it into life. Their incantations took physical form, dragging hungry spirits from the ashes and elms.

Finavar felt his pulse hammering in his ears, as though his own flesh was responding to the summons. He looked hopefully at Eremon and, to his delight, the old soldier finally sliced his hand through the air, freeing the kindreds of Locrimere to begin their dance.

Finavar howled and flipped over the rocks, lifting his voice in song as he plummeted towards the battle.

CHAPTER TWENTY-SIX

She waited, savouring the quietness of the snow, nursing centuries of bitter hurt. Behind her lay a network of caverns; glittering and dark, filled with lies, a perfect tomb for a false king. She had ordered her sisters to stand down and Orion would blunder in, unaware that they were sneering at him from the shadows. She stretched the long, knotted bark of her limbs and sighed with pleasure. She had always known that he would come. Such arrogance was bound to undo him eventually, and finally, after all these centuries, her patience would be rewarded. She turned to leave, muttering a prayer to all those she was about to avenge.

'My lord,' came a voice, 'is this wise?'

She paused and let out a hissing sound. He was not alone. She turned and stepped out towards the foot of the ravine, staring through the snow. There were four silhouettes approaching, not one. All of them were broad, and heavily muscled, but one was taller than the others, with a crown of knotted antlers. He has his lackeys with him, she thought. This might ruin everything. She tensed her wooden flesh and crept back towards the caves.

'*Do you question your king?*' replied Orion, emerging from the snow.

He had a metal-tipped spear in his hand and pointed it at the wall of cave mouths. '*This is my realm as much as the King's Glade. Why should I avoid it?*'

One of the other figures shook his head. '*But, my lord – the Vaults of Winter. Nothing has ever emerged from here but madness. Why would you deliberately court such danger?*'

Orion raised his chin. '*It is not your place to question me, Sélva.*'

She crept closer, keeping to the shadows. To her horror, she saw that, despite his fierce tone, there was doubt in Orion's eyes. Out here in the snow, away from his blessed trees, he was finally unsure of himself.

Another underling stepped to his side. '*Naieth the Prophetess knows the history of these caverns. They are forbidden for a reason, my lord.*'

Orion clenched his jaw, enraged by the mention of the copper-haired witch, but the doubt still lingered in his eyes.

Sensing that her moment of revenge might pass, she decided to intervene. How could she ensure he did not leave? What could blind him to madness ahead? She smiled. Of course. His rage. What could be more sure? She dressed herself in the gleaming, flawless hide of a white stag and trotted out to greet him.

They were still at the far end of the ravine, thirty feet or more away, but echoes carried oddly across the snow, and they immediately looked up at the sound of her hooves. She raised the proud, cervine head she had adopted and came to a halt in the centre of the gulley, watching Orion with regal disdain.

The King recoiled, clutching his spear in both hands. '*It's you,*' he gasped. '*Sativus.*' He looked at his guards. '*Can you see this?*'

They nodded and raised their weapons, stepping closer to their king, looking at her in amazement.

She struggled to hide her delight. Even after all these centuries, he had not learned to recognise her.

'Turn back,' she said.

Orion's face flushed a darker green. 'Do you still doubt me? After everything I have already achieved?' He pointed his spear at her and raised his voice to a howl. 'I have crushed your snivelling curs in my fist. Whatever hold you might have over Ariel, I am still your king, Sativus!'

She wanted to laugh with delight at the rage in his voice, but she shook her head instead. 'You are unworthy, Sephian. You are weak. You must turn back.'

At the sound of his former name, Orion's doubt visibly evaporated. He arched his back and howled into the snowstorm, tortured by the thought of his past. Then he raced down the gulley towards her.

She turned and galloped back into the caverns, filling the ravine with the sound of clattering hooves as she disappeared into the gloom.

CHAPTER TWENTY-SEVEN

Orion plunged through the darkness, pursuing the stag as it bounded into a network of frozen caves. He was blind to everything but the white flanks of his prey. As he thundered through the caves, strange, rippling shapes arched over him, but he paid them no heed, moving with such speed that his equerries were unable to keep up.

The caves were not entirely dark. As Orion ran he passed through columns of light, leaking through cracks overhead and refracted by minerals in the rock. The lights threw glittering shapes across Orion's face, twisting his expression into a leering grimace. The white stag always remained a few feet ahead of him and, after a while, Orion began to tire. The cold air was thin and insubstantial and his chest began to ache with every ragged breath. Finally, with a last, bitter curse, he tumbled to his knees and watched Sativus vanish around a bend.

For a few moments, Orion could do nothing but kneel on the ground and gasp for air. The cold seeped into his flesh like poison, draining him of vigour. After a few minutes, still struggling to catch his breath, he finally looked around. Passageways trailed off in every direction: some tall and magnificent, punctuated by glittering stalactites and stalagmites, others so narrow that Orion could never have shouldered his way inside. Every surface glittered, either with ice or crystals, and, as Orion looked around, his breath pooled in thick clouds of vapour, adding to the mysterious appearance of the caves.

'Orion,' he spat, using his own name like a curse. He suddenly felt a fool. What had driven him to race after the stag like that? Without even waiting for the others? He had no idea what kind of place he had entered. Why did he not pause to consider his actions properly, in a manner more suited to a king? He glimpsed Naieth and the others, warning him to avoid this place, and a dreadful doubt filled him. Why was he so determined to ignore them? Now that he looked back over the first half of his new life, he realised that all of his decisions had been made in a blind rage. Is this normal? he wondered, looking down at his hands, as though they belonged to someone else. Fragments of the Wrach's stone were still embedded in his broad, leathery palm, and he regarded them like the spoils of a crime. 'Orion,' he muttered again.

He hauled himself to his feet and called out. 'Olachas! Ilaruss! Sélva!'

He thought he heard a distant reply, but the sound quickly faded and he could not be sure if it was real or just an echo. His sense of foolishness grew. He had abandoned them for a second time, to who knew what fate. Seeing there was nothing else for it, he turned and headed off in the direction he had last seen the stag, muttering under his breath as his hooves clattered across the frozen rock and he entered another gloomy corridor.

Orion quickly lost track of time. The caverns were bewildering and endless, looping and climbing through the mountains and often bringing him back to places he had already seen. He despaired of ever finding Sativus, or the Dhioll Hollow and the Torr-Ildána. As the hours rolled by, it seemed the best he could hope for was to find a way back to the cave entrance. Every now and then he paused, sensing movement nearby, but each time he looked there was nothing – beyond perhaps a slight shifting in the cave walls, like water rippling over the rock.

Finally, Orion spotted a route that he was sure he had not explored: a tunnel that shone brighter than any of the previous ones. He hurried down it, wondering if he had found his way back to the mountainside. As he entered the tunnel, Orion was dazzled by the ferocity of the light, and stumbled to a halt. Once his vision had cleared, he realised that the far end of the cave did indeed open onto the outside world. He grunted in relief. Perhaps he could still find the others and return to the Council Glade. There was no reason for him to lose face. He would simply explain that the Vaults of Winter were empty, dreary caves, containing nothing of value beyond a few glittering rocks. And if that pallid youth, Belidae, decided to make comment, he would witness the wrath of a king. As the oppressive atmosphere of the caves bore down on Orion, the idea of returning to the forest filled him with renewed energy and he hurried towards the light.

As he staggered from the cave mouth, Orion's excitement grew. Somehow, he was back in the forest. A mangled grove of oak trees surrounded him, nestled beneath the slopes of the mountains, and for a few seconds Orion thought he had returned home. Then he realised that this could not be his home. The trees were bare and draped in thick drifts of snow. Horror gripped him. This was a place he was never intended to see: the forest in the depths of winter. Like all of his kind, he understood the reign of the King implicitly: he was Kurnous incarnate. He was a living avatar of a god, but he was bound to the seasons, born with the spring and gone by the first frosts of winter. This was no place for him. The sight of naked, frosted branches turned his stomach and caused his head to pound. As the snow settled on his antlers and his furious brow, he felt it draining even more life out of him. He suddenly felt as though he could barely hold his spear.

He stumbled back the way he had come. Even the caves seemed preferable to the forest in winter. There must be another way, he decided, but as he trudged back through the snow, something caught his eye: on the other side of the clearing were two figures, locked in an embrace. He seemed to be witnessing some kind of tryst beneath the snow-clad boughs.

He paused and called out in greeting. The figures gave no reply and Orion looked warily at the frozen trees again. Then, with a shake of his head, he trudged away from the cave mouth and headed in the direction of the lovers.

As he approached, Orion's distaste mingled with shock. 'It cannot be,' he growled, gripping his spear tighter and picking up his pace, but as he reached the two figures his suspicions were confirmed.

It was Ariel, and coiled around her, snake-like, was her advisor, Khoron Belidae: pale and effete as ever and whispering gently in her ear.

'What are you doing?' roared Orion, but still they did not hear. As he reached the tree, he realised that they were discussing him.

'It is meaningless,' whispered Khoron. 'Let him rage. Let him stomp. You, my queen, my Ariel, are the true, immortal heart of this forest. When the sun grows weary and falls from the sky, you will remain: preserved, unchanging, by the love of your people.'

Ariel blushed and lowered her gaze, clearly flattered by her advisor's words. 'But he is not himself, Khoron. Each year he comes to me, filled with the wrath of summer, clearing away our foes and leading the Wild Hunt, but I have never seen him so erratic before. All through the spring he has been persecuting the forest spirits. Why would he do such a thing?' She looked up, and for a moment Orion thought she must have seen him, but she showed no sign of recognition. 'In my dreams I have seen my oldest friend, Sativus. He has become a beautiful white stag.'

Khoron nodded encouragingly, and gently turned Ariel's face back towards his, until their lips were almost touching.

'Sativus warned me,' Ariel continued, oblivious to Khoron's lascivious expression. 'He said that Orion has been transformed in some way. That he is more dangerous than ever before.'

Khoron stroked Ariel's cheek. 'I have seen it myself. The King has become a stranger to all of us. He no longer understands his role.' He shook his head. 'Or his queen.'

Orion howled in frustration. He had always suspected this fawning dandy, but to see such treachery with his own eyes was more than he could bear. He hurled his spear at the poet.

The weapon passed through his chest and slammed into the tree.

Khoron winced and clutched his robes.

Orion stepped closer, preparing to finish the job with his talons.

'I believe that wine has taken a dislike to me,' said Khoron, backing away from Ariel and frowning.

Ariel laughed. 'You drink like a true poet.'

Orion cried out as he saw that the spear was still embedded in the tree and had left no mark on Khoron.

'I think I may need to lie down for a moment,' said Khoron, nodding towards the heart of the forest.

Ariel smiled and took his arm. 'Let me help you.'

As they stepped lightly through the trees, Orion howled and hurried to his spear. To his horror, the cold had left him with so little strength he was unable to wrench the weapon free. 'I will kill him,' he said and heaved again. Still the spear refused to move. He looked around and saw a rock, about the size of his fist, jutting out of the snow. Incensed by rage and jealousy he hammered the stone down against the shaft of the spear. It finally came free, but as he snatched it up from the snow he realised that Ariel and her advisor had vanished from view. He raced deeper into the forest, trying to catch sight of them, but it was no use. The further he ran, the darker and colder it grew and the more tightly packed the trees became. The forest was his home, but seen like this it was a stranger to him. He felt a palpable enmity creeping through the ice. As he staggered through the frosted bracken he glimpsed movement in his peripheral vision, but when he looked it was gone. He remembered that he had had the same sensation in the caves. 'Who is that?' he cried, whirling around. 'Sélva? Is that you? Olachas?'

There was no reply, so he hurried on, hoping to find a familiar landmark, but the snow was now falling so heavily, and the trees pressed so closely around him, that he could no longer even see the mountains. His anger grew as he pictured Ariel nursing Khoron Belidae. Why had he come to such a cursed place? He wondered again at all the choices he had made and shook his head furiously, trying to jostle his thoughts into some semblance of order. This only added dizziness to his list of problems and he closed his eyes for a moment, trying to steady himself as he ran.

Orion's stomach lurched as the ground gave way. He opened his eyes and realised that what he had taken for solid ground was an outcrop of snow, hanging over a sheer drop.

He fell in glittering silence, wrapping his arms around his head as he spun through an explosion of snow.

The painful landing he expected never came and, after a few moments, Orion realised he did not feel cold any more. He saw a smoke-filled hall, crowded with jostling, indistinct figures. A familiar face was looming over him, smiling in disbelief.

'Isére?' he gasped, recognising his first love. He locked his gaze on her lidded, blue-grey eyes and tried to ignore the rolling sensation in his stomach.

'Sephian,' she said, stifling a laugh as she held out her hand, 'are you drunk?'

Orion looked around and saw that he was in the bowels of the Wilding Tree – back in the Tourmaline Hall, surrounded by the devious, gossiping sorcerers of the Silvam Dale. 'Sephian?' he gasped.

Isére frowned as she helped him to his feet. 'You *are* drunk! Have you forgotten your own name?'

Orion looked down at his body and saw that he had been transformed. The slabs of green, ivy-threaded muscle were gone, replaced by a slender frame, clad in mud-splattered robes and wearing worn leather slippers. 'My spear,' he gasped, looking at his empty hands.

'You never carry a spear,' said Isére, peering at him in confusion. 'What did she say? Has she bewitched you?'

Orion shook his head in confusion. 'Who?'

Isére nodded to a wall of flickering lights on the far side of the hall. The place was too crowded and smoky to see clearly, but Orion could just about make out a frail figure, wreathed in light and drifting above the crowd.

'Princess Asphalia,' said Isére. 'I thought she was all show, but she has clearly dazzled you.' The smile dropped from her face. 'Did you pass on your news? Did you tell her about the outsiders, and Tethea?'

Orion was about to reply yes, but then groaned in dismay. This was more than he could bear: to be mortal again, a simple wanderer, serving the witches of the Silvam Dale. As Isére shook her head in confusion, he broke from her grip and barged through the crowd, shouldering his way through crowds of sneering faces, dazzled by the light of the fireflies drifting overhead.

'Sephian?' cried Isére, but he did not pause, breaking into a run as he spotted the stairs at the back of the hall. The forest. He needed to be back in the forest. He needed to escape the cloying, scented smoke and clear his head.

He raced up the winding staircase of knotted branches and emerged into the cool, crisp air of a dying winter. The twin moons were gliding overhead and he followed their light through the trees, making for the deeps of the forest. No one challenged him as he left the agonised hulk of the Wilding Tree, but he noticed the sentry, Arthron, watching him from the shadows, his face still hidden beneath his hood.

Orion ran on, unsure who or when he was. The name Sephian echoed in his mind, and he grasped desperately at memories of all that had happened to him during the spring and summer. Could he have dreamt everything, as he lay swooning in the roots of the Wilding Tree? Had Princess Asphalia beguiled him?

As his thoughts raced down various avenues, he lost track of his route and barely noticed that the air was becoming colder again and that the trees were coated in snow once more.

The sound of voices dragged Orion back into the present. He stumbled to a halt and listened, realising the sound was familiar. It was a low, rumbling chorus: dozens of powerful voices joined in a melody so lachrymose and beautiful that it snatched his breath away. 'Orion,' he muttered, changing direction and racing down a winding tunnel of yews towards the sound.

They remained as he had left them: the Lords of the Deep-wood Host, assembled in the King's Glade to pass judgement on him, godlike and blazing with stellar fire.

Orion knelt before them, peering through the blaze in an attempt to discern their expressions. He saw that they were each subtly different: some more feral, some more haughty and some more stern than their twins.

'Guide me,' he said, holding out his hands.

They did not seem to notice his presence, but as their voices rumbled on, Orion recognised words in their droning round song. They were singing of Prince Haldus and the Darkling Prince, left to die on the slopes of Drúne Fell, as their king chased the ghosts of his past.

He groaned and clutched his head in his hands. Their judgement was plain: they had found him wanting. He had failed them miserably. Nothing he had done had proven his worth. He plucked a knife from his belt, filled with despair. As the chorus circled around his thoughts, he lifted the knife and studied the keenness of the blade. Perhaps if he ended his life here, in the King's Glade, a new Orion would emerge; one more worthy of Ariel?

As Orion studied the blade, an image flashed into his mind. Cyanos had hacked off his own wings with this knife, before handing it to Orion as a sign of his fealty. Other images arrived in quick succession. He saw Cyanos's shame as he handed over the bloodstained weapon. He had been appalled and awed by Orion's victory over the spirit, Amphion. Then Orion saw the eagle spirit itself, pinned like an insect to the floor of Cyanos's stone prison. His shame began to fade as he stared at the knife. He saw the Wrach, cowering before him, begging for mercy as he took the black polished stone from his staff. Then he saw the other spirits he had hunted down, binding them to the will of Kurnous, as surely as if he were the god himself.

The song faltered and the lights faded.

Orion stood and raised the knife over his head. 'This is a lie,' he said, realising the truth as soon as he uttered it. 'Sephian is cold in his grave. I am the Lord of the Deepwood Host. I am the King. I am Orion.'

As Orion's voice grew in strength, the trees of the King's Glade began to broaden and lose their colour.

'I am the King!' he roared, and the trees became the frozen walls of a cave. The crowned figures shimmered and merged into a single shape, hunched in the darkness.

Orion realised that he had never left the Vaults of Winter. He was still surrounded by columns of ice-clad rock and bathed in the rainbow colours of the crystals that lined the walls. His spear was still in his hand and his body was still his own: sinewy, green-hued and threaded with vines. Sephian's robes and slippers were gone, replaced by a loincloth and a pair of thick, ridged hooves. He had been beguiled, but it was Sativus who had planted the illusions in his mind, he was sure of it.

'Face me!' he bellowed, levelling the spear at the figure in the shadows.

'You must leave,' answered the shadows, without approaching. The voice was odd and inhuman, like two slabs of rock scraping against each other.

'You are my subject, Sativus,' said Orion in a quieter voice, calmed by the accuracy of his guess – the images that had tormented him were a glamour, nothing more, and he had seen through them. Sativus had been proved wrong. There was nothing in the forest he could not face.

The figure stepped into the shifting light and revealed itself.

It was not a stag; in fact, for a moment, Orion strained to understand exactly *what* it was. It was as though the wall itself were moving towards him. Then the stranger abandoned its stooped posture and straightened its back, drawing itself to its full height. Orion realised that the figure was not hunched in the cave, it *was* the cave. He reeled back in shock as the walls and ceiling collapsed, assuming the form of a colossal humanoid figure. The snow-filled sky was revealed as the cave unravelled, collapsed and stood up, with all the grinding din of a landslide.

Dust and pebbles rained down on Orion and he was forced to shield his face with his arms. Then as the rocks settled he peered up through the whirling banks of snow and dust, trying to understand the thing that was towering over him. He saw a stone goliath of absurd proportions. As it stretched its limbs and pulled back its enormous shoulders it resembled a mountain chiselled into the shape of a man, with a broad outcrop for its chest and a crumbling, snow-capped peak for a head. Beneath its craggy brow was a pair of dazzling lights that passed for its eyes and, rather than hands, its arms ended in two hammerheads of rock.

'By the gods,' muttered Orion as he realised the impossible scale of giant. As he peered at its jagged torso, he noticed something carved into its chest; some kind of circular design, he thought, but with all the dust billowing around it, he could not be sure.

The stone giant looked down at Orion with a sombre expression and spoke with a voice so booming that more rocks tumbled from the remaining walls of the cave.

'The asur are forbidden.' It formed the words slowly and with obvious difficulty. It turned its head, shedding clumps of snow and soil, and spoke even slower. 'There. Was. A. Vow.'

The words were so loud that Orion had to clutch his hands over his ears, but as he did so, he glimpsed something on the far side of the giant's feet. There was a small valley beneath him, on the other side of the giant, and at its centre there was a circle of beech trees. Despite the unnatural winter the trees were dressed in glossy red leaves. It was hard to see clearly through the dust and snow tumbling from the giant, but he thought he could make out a structure of some kind.

He peered through the haze and gasped. There was no mistaking it. There was a dolmen in the centre of the trees, on top of what looked like a burial mound. The stones were polished and black, just like the orb on the Wrach's staff. 'Torr-Ildána,' he said, stepping towards the valley.

He had reached his goal.

'A *vow*,' boomed the stone giant, stepping sideways and crashing one of its feet down in front of Orion.

'Who are you to block my way?' cried Orion, reeling back into the remains of the cave. Once he was steady, he pointed his spear at the mournful face looming overhead. 'You have no power over me.'

'I am…' the giant hesitated, struggling to find the right word, 'the protector.'

Then its other foot slammed down and barred the entrance to the valley.

CHAPTER TWENTY-EIGHT

Finavar whirled through the air, his blades held at shoulder height, gleaming in the moonlight as they sliced through iron, flesh and bone. All around him arrows found their mark, thudding into the tiny black eyes of the minotaurs. The skill of the archers was incredible. Even in the dark, not a single shot went wide. Finavar and his kindred fought with wild, animal grace, secure in the knowledge that they would never be mistakenly hit.

Finavar's black cloak fluttered around him as he waltzed through the fighting, its barbs shredding the skin of his foes and hazing his movements. His lumbering, armour-clad opponents lurched after him, snarling curses and swinging their axes, but by the time they struck he was gone, flickering above their helmets like fire.

Dozens of similar figures vaulted after him, hacking and slashing as they careered through the enemy lines: the wild children of Loec, unleashed at last. Their dance might end in victory or death, but either way it would be a thing of heartbreaking beauty. There was a flash of blue as Caorann rolled across a row of shoulders and plunged his twin blades into the neck of a roaring brute.

Behind him came Thuralin, gasping and wheezing as he fought, but still too fast for the enemy to catch. His daughter was at his side, pausing every now and then to rip bloody trophies from her gasping victims.

As Finavar and his kin performed their vicious dance, the riders continued to harass the enemy flank, charging in fluid, seemingly random waves that left the minotaurs reeling and confused.

Finavar paid no heed to the cavalry or even the dancers behind him. His gaze was locked on a towering shape at the rear of the enemy lines. It was a grotesque mixture of bull and man, like all the other outsiders, but it towered over the rest of the army, as tall as an oak and staring back at him with a single enormous eye that blazed like another moon, hovering over the battle. There was no mistaking the repugnant light. Finavar knew from his conversations with Eremon and Caorann that this was the villain who had torched their home. As he vaulted through the battle, even Alhena and the others fell behind. His face was locked in a stern pout as he considered each footfall and sword strike with hair's-breadth precision, but with every particle of his being he was singing. His fluid, tumbling movements were a hymn to the glory of war. If he were struck down at this moment, he would achieve the most perfect, most beautiful death he could imagine. This was all that he had ever dreamt of: a moment to serve the forest with all the skill and grace he could muster.

As he neared the cyclops, Finavar saw that it was lumbering wildly through the dark, smashing and rending anything it encountered and screaming gibberish to itself. Every now and then it would pause to swing wildly at the air, as though battling foes only it could see.

It's insane, thought Finavar, landing briefly on the ground and dashing across the bloodstained earth. He ducked and weaved around the bellowing minotaurs, moving so fast that most of them barely registered his passing.

Finavar was nearing his goal when the towering cyclops suddenly strode off through the battle – not in flight, but making for something that Finavar was unable to see. The enormous monster crossed the battlefield with great, loping strides, its grotesque eye locked on the trees below Drúne Fell.

Finavar struggled to keep up, but as he ran he saw what had drawn its attention. Near the foot of the mountain, where the enemy lines were smashing through rows of asrai spears, the earth had sprung to life, heaving like an ocean and sprouting dark, coiled limbs.

'Laelia,' said Finavar with a grin. Such powerful sorcery could only be the work of the Queen's handmaidens. As he watched in amazement, Finavar saw great, crumbling behemoths of root and soil, lashing out of the ground and dragging dozens of minotaurs to their deaths.

His smile faltered as the cyclops waded frantically through the battle, heedless of the damage it caused its own troops as it made for the patch of writhing earth.

Finavar forced his aching limbs into one last sprint, trying to intercept the giant before it reached Laelia.

As he neared the disturbance, Finavar saw that he was right: it was Laelia, drifting several feet above the trees with her arms raised and her head thrown back. Her wings were fluttering behind her and light was coruscating between her extended fingers. The other magi were drifting at her side and beneath their dangling feet the earth had become a heaving vortex, groaning as it rotated, dragging outsiders underground with thrashing roots. Dozens of the minotaurs had already tumbled into the pit, clawing desperately at the soil as the knotted tendrils grasped and crushed.

Laelia's voice was raised in song and her eyes were closed. Her boyish mop of hair was fluttering around her face and her wiry limbs were jerking with erratic, spastic movements.

Finavar realised that she was consumed by the ferocity of her own spell, and unaware of the giant shape striding towards her. His fear grew as he realised he might not reach the cyclops in time to stop it.

He bounded across the back of one of the howling minotaurs and hurled himself though the air, diving for a patch of open space at the heart of the battle.

The air exploded from his lungs as a fist connected with his stomach.

He crashed into the toiling ranks of monsters and rolled across the earth.

For a second he was too disorientated to rise and was still crumpled on the ground, gasping unsuccessfully for breath, as his attacker lurched into view.

It was a mountain of scarred muscle, with a thick crest of hair from the small of its back to the top of its bull-like head. Two long, iron-capped horns swooped down from its forehead and its massive fists were clad in plates of thick, studded iron.

Despite the pain of his screaming lungs, Finavar managed to roll aside before the monster's fist destroyed his face. As he flipped back up onto his feet, Finavar brought both his blades down on the minotaur's wrist.

Rather than severing the monster's hand the blades clattered against the iron bracers and sent a shock of pain jangling up his arms.

He cursed and staggered back, raising the blades in front of his face as the monster punched again. He parried the blow, but knew his luck would not hold. Spinning lightly across the heads of an army was one thing, but fighting for his life on the ground was another.

He leant to one side in a feint, suggesting that he was about to flee.

The minotaur lurched after him, and Finavar dodged in the opposite direction, placing his feet onto the monster's back and launching himself off through the battle.

Axes and fists flew after him, but he flipped clear and vaulted up into the air, trying to glimpse Laelia.

To his horror, he saw that he had moved even further from the Queen's handmaiden, whilst the cyclops was only moments away from her. Its stream of gibberish had grown so violent that its head was jolting with the force of its words, spraying arcs of drool through the air.

'Laelia!' he cried, but it was no use. She was still consumed by the power of her spell. Her head was still thrown back and the ground beneath her was a volcano of tendrils and broken bodies.

Finavar looked back at the cyclops and saw that its eye was pulsing with light and rolling wildly in its socket. Its mouth was hanging open in anticipation as it neared its prize.

After landing in another open space, Finavar placed two fingers in his mouth and whistled, hoping desperately that he was not too late.

Nothing happened.

The cyclops was now just a couple of strides away from Laelia but Finavar was forced to back away as the surrounding mino-taurs spotted him and lunged in his direction.

Desperate, Finavar whistled again. 'Loec bless you!' he cried, as he saw a pair of tiny shapes race up one of the giant's legs.

The polecats were like mites compared to the enormous bulk of the cyclops, but to Finavar their undulating movements were unmistakable.

The cyclops was oblivious as Mormo and Mauro scuttled higher, circling its enormous gut and making for its jowly face.

Finavar laughed as the polecats reached their goal. They raced across the monster's massive eye and sank their claws into its flickering pupil.

The cyclops threw back its head and roared. The sound was ear-splitting and the surrounding figures stumbled to a halt, looking up to watch as the cyclops clawed desperately at its eye. It clamped its hands over the bleeding orb and staggered backwards, spraying a mixture of flames and blood from between its fingers.

At the sound of the cyclops's roar, Laelia and the other sorcerers opened their eyes and finally saw the monstrosity that was looming over them.

Laelia gasped in alarm and let out a cry of command, levelling her finger at the monster. As one, the magi redirected the currents of magic rippling through their flesh. The earth detonated and a forest of tendrils slammed against the cyclops, enveloping its limbs and lashing around its face.

Finavar stumbled to a halt, looking anxiously for two tiny shapes on the staggering giant.

The cyclops roared again, arched its back and wrenched the net of roots from the ground, showering the sorcerers with earth and turning its bloody eye back on them.

Laelia cried out another command, but before the words had left her lips, the cyclops reached down and clutched one of the handmaidens. Her body exploded in a cloud of blood and, as Laelia wailed in horror, the cyclops stuffed the mangled corpse into its mouth.

As the cyclops ate, light blazed through its skin and it moaned in ecstasy, pawing at its face and shivering with pleasure as it swallowed its still-twitching victim.

Laelia repeated her command with still greater vehemence, and now the sorcerers had time to respond. The ground erupted with even more violence and this time, as the net of roots hurtled towards the cyclops, they took the form of humanoid creatures, crying out in rage as they latched onto the monster's face.

The cyclops tried to wrench itself free for a second time but the roots held firm.

The brief pause that had gripped the battle evaporated and the armies threw themselves at each other, crashing around the feet of the struggling cyclops.

Finavar was still unable to see any sign of Mormo and Mauro and he felt an awful dread. Had he sent them to their deaths? Such an action would have terrible consequences, he was sure of it. Then, as he scoured the cyclops for a sign of the polecats, he saw something unexpected.

'Eagles,' he gasped, watching sleek, dark shapes drop from the stars. Finavar dodged another axe blow and raced towards Laelia and the magi. As he ran he snatched glimpses at the sky. Raptors were diving from the heavens, with archers crouched between their pounding, steel-tipped wings.

Finavar laughed as he saw the noble in the black cuirass riding the first of them. As the one-eyed goliath struggled to free itself, Lord Cyanos's mount locked onto its face and tore away a section of its cheek. As it did so, Cyanos loosed an arrow, at point-blank range, into the centre of its pupil.

Fluid and light sprayed from the wound and the cyclops roared in pain.

It snapped free one of its arms and reached out to grasp its attacker, but Cyanos's mount had already swooped clear, taking its rider with it.

The cyclops wrenched the arrow from its eye, spraying another column of blood and fire.

Finavar ran on, still making for Laelia, but, as he neared the sorcerers, he realised there was no way he could reach Laelia through the heaving vortex. He also realised that there was no longer any need. She and the five remaining sorcerers were lashing root after root around the struggling cyclops.

Finavar ducked beneath an axe blow, plunged his blades into the chest of his attacker and ran on, past the sorcerers and into the trees. He vaulted up into the branches and looked out across the heaving crowds, watching in amazement as the hawk-riders continued diving and looping, tearing chunks from the cyclops's face and allowing the riders to fire dozens of arrows into its enormous, rolling eye.

Pain shuddered through the colossal creature and, with a last desperate lurch, it wrenched one of its legs free and stamped down on the circle of magi.

There was a screech and a flash of light and another handmaiden died, pulverised beneath an iron-shod boot.

Laelia howled with grief. Only four of her sisters now remained.

To Finavar's horror, she launched herself through the air on a tide of branches, landing on the cyclops's chest.

As the monster ground its boot into the handmaiden's corpse, its eye blazed brighter and it let out another roar of pleasure. As the light grew, so did its strength and it wrenched free its other leg, forcing the remaining handmaidens to break their circle and scatter.

Laelia rode across the cyclops's chest on a wave of verdure and thrashing roots, screaming curses as she went.

Alarm flashed in the monster's eye but its arms were still held fast and, before it could react, Laelia drew back her arms and made a throwing gesture. Vines tumbled from her palms, smashing into the cyclops's face and flooding its bloodstained mouth.

At the same moment, Lord Cyanos swooped back into view and loosed another arrow into the monster's pupil.

The combined assault was too much.

The cyclops's body went slack and it let out a low, guttural moan.

The combatants behind saw the danger, but most were too crushed to move aside as the gargantuan creature rocked back on its heels and smashed to the ground.

A cheer erupted from the asrai as they watched an eagle swoop back up into the clouds, carrying both Cyanos and Laelia to safety.

Finavar began to cheer with them, but almost immediately fell silent. From his vantage point in the tree he was able to see what they could not: a wall of enormous figures striding out of the distant forest. He slumped against the trunk of the tree and groaned. Just one cyclops had almost turned the battle against them but, as he peered across the enemy lines, he counted dozens, all blazing with hunger as they strode towards the slopes of Drúne Fell.

Finavar cursed his stupidity. As the absolute hopelessness of their situation overwhelmed him, he could not shake the feeling that he was to blame. He pictured a pair of polecats, lying somewhere, broken in the mud.

'We cannot win,' he gasped, watching the giants advance.

'There are too many.'

CHAPTER TWENTY-NINE

Orion cursed and rolled across the frozen rocks, his arms singing with pain. He had tried to jam his spear into the shin of the stone giant, but had succeeded only in jarring his nerves and buckling the blade. He looked up, expecting the goliath to strike back, but it continued studying him with the same mournful expression.

'The asur are forbidden,' it repeated, keeping its feet firmly planted at the entrance to the valley.

'You do not understand,' cried Orion. 'Those stones must be destroyed. Outsiders are coming. They mean to steal this power.' He waved at the circle of trees and the dolmen at its centre. 'You must let me through!'

The giant gave no reply.

Orion groaned in frustration and sprinted across the rocks, attempting to circle around the guardian's legs.

As he neared the side of the gulley, the giant punched one of its hammer-like fists into the ground.

The blow landed a few feet away from Orion and enveloped

him in a cloud of dust and spinning rocks. He rolled across the ground, scraping skin from his legs and arms and howling in rage.

As soon as the dust settled he bolted in the opposite direction, but the giant simply pummelled the ground with its other fist, sending Orion rolling back down into the caves.

As he thudded against the shattered walls he cracked his head against the rocks and sprayed blood across his chest.

He remained there, slumped in the snow, breathing heavily. Then he leapt up and hurled his spear at the stone giant's face.

The giant shuddered as the weapon clattered across its eye and Orion bolted in the opposite direction, trying again to circle around its enormous legs.

The giant punched and Orion tried to block the blow, raising his own fist.

There was a flash of pain as he flew back across the ground and rolled to a halt, groaning in pain. Then, as he staggered clear, Orion stared at his throbbing fist.

'By the gods,' he muttered.

It was shrouded in pale, shimmering mist.

He stood and wiped the blood from his face, ignoring the fragments of antler lying next to his hooves, and looked up at the snowstorm. Something flickered at the edge of his thoughts – a faintest ghost of an idea. When his fist connected with the giant he had felt something more than just pain.

Was it power?

Far on the horizon, beneath the leaden mass of clouds, there was a thin sliver of gold. For a moment, Orion could not understand what it was, then he realised that dawn was rising from the forest. Even the Vaults of Winter could not entirely blind him to the power of the summer sun. Something stirred in his chest at the thought of summer. Any day now it would be Sólis-Leith. As he staggered through the bloody snow, he pictured the rites of summer. He would be anointed. He would be armed. He would become Kurnous incarnate: Lord of the Wild Hunt.

Suddenly, the howling of the storm reminded him of hounds.

He stood, fixing his eyes on the distant shred of summer, and as he did so, he felt his strength returning. He threw back his head and wallowed in the memory of every summer he had known; every glorious hunt. Fire kindled in his wooden heart, sending a shiver through his battered limbs. 'I will not fail you,' he whispered, as the oak apple thudded in his chest. He gasped as the power surpassed anything he had previously felt. Midsummer was hours away.

Orion took a deep, shuddering breath and closed his eyes. As he plumbed the depths of his growing power, he realised it was more than just physical. His thoughts were as crisp and bright as the snow. He found he could see everything with incredible clarity. Previously disconnected thoughts began to coalesce, sending shoots of ideas spiralling through his mind. He saw, in quick succession, the stones of Torr-Goholoth, carved with a circle of branches; he saw the chest of the stone giant, engraved with the same symbol; he saw Atolmis's bottomless black eyes as he explained how the Wrach used his stone to weave through time; and, finally, he pictured the palm of his own lacerated hand, filled with shards of the Wrach's glittering talisman and trailing pale mist.

He nodded as everything came together as one: the black of the carving, the black of Atolmis's eyes, the shards of stone in his hand and the gauntlet of mist around his fingers. They expanded to fill his mind until he saw a single, polished stone, engraved with a spinning circle.

He smiled and opened his eyes.

Kurnous had looked down on his child and revealed the truth. He had anointed him with the light of the summer sun. Orion's doubt melted away as he saw everything that had previously eluded him.

'I will not fail,' he whispered, stepping towards the giant.

The giant's expression remained unchanged as Orion broke into a sprint and raised his bloody fist.

'I will not fail!' howled Orion as he raced across the rocks, throwing up clouds of snow with his hooves.

'I will not fail!' he roared, reaching the giant's legs and punching with all his strength.

His fist exploded with pain.

Blood showered his face and chest.

Orion howled, but stayed upright and wrenched his hand free.

The giant stumbled backwards, letting out a booming curse.

As the giant swayed to one side, Orion bounded up a steep incline and leapt through the air.

The giant raised an arm in front of its face, but Orion aimed lower, hammering his bloody fist into the circular symbol on its chest.

There was a flash of light and a plume of glimmering mist.

Emerald blood pumped from Orion's fist as he landed heavily on the ground, but strands of magic were also bleeding through his skin.

Orion shivered with a mixture of agony and ecstasy as he saw the answer Kurnous had sent to him with the dawn. As his blood rushed over the stone, it was flickering with cold, unnatural fire. He was delirious with pain, but he knew what this was. He knew that he was not hallucinating.

'The eye,' he groaned, his voice hoarse with pain, picturing the shards of black stone embedded in his flesh – shards of the black stone used by the Wrach to manipulate the Sínann-Torr. The fist he had smashed against the giant still contained the magic of the Blind Guide; the key to the ancient stones.

Orion raised his ruined fist and let out an incoherent howl as he saw the symbol on the giant's chest twitch into life.

'I will not fail!' he cried again, feeling his body swell with power.

Orion staggered away from the giant, raising his fist higher. As he did so, another glut of blood poured from between his fingers, but he barely noticed the pain. All his attention was now fixed on the cords of pale mist trailing from his hand to the giant's chest.

As the fog grew, the giant's eyes blazed sapphire and the branches carved into its chest shivered even more violently.

As Orion raised his bloody fist the giant did the same, mimicking his movements like a colossal marionette. Orion turned to face the valley, and the dolmen at the centre of the trees, and the giant followed suit, letting out a cry of alarm as it did so.

Orion paid no heed to the giant's rumbling protests and strode towards the valley.

Strands of mist flashed between Orion's fist and the symbol on the giant's chest, and despite its obvious horror, the guardian of the caves was unable to resist, crashing through the snow and descending into the valley with all the noise of an avalanche.

Orion's power grew as the distant band of sunlight flashed in his eyes. He raised his fist again, and hammered it down.

With a despairing cry, the giant did the same, smashing its fist straight through the ancient stones of Torr-Ildána.

The valley shuddered.

There was silence, then blinding light, then a roar as loud as the ocean.

The explosion slammed into Orion, lifting him off his feet and hurling him through the air. He hit the ground hard and, as he passed into unconsciousness, he saw the face of his queen, smiling at him through the flames.

'I will not fail,' was his final thought.

'I know,' she said.

Lights pulsed from the shattered rock, washing over the snow-covered slopes and flickering through the clouds. As the light grew, the valley began to collapse. The burial mound, already crooked from the giant's blow, slumped in on itself, spewing clouds of ancient dust. Fragments of dolmen rolled into the surrounding drifts, followed by rocks and stones from the gulley walls. Within seconds, the stream of pebbles became a torrent of larger boulders, bouncing and clattering from the slopes.

As the landscape dissolved, the stone giant swayed back on its heels, shaken by a series of enormous, grinding tremors. It staggered away from Torr-Ildána, looking at its fist in horror.

The earth groaned and screeched and the giant stumbled again. The reverberations of its blow were growing, rather than fading, and as it staggered away from the caves the giant began shedding great slabs of limestone. Its fist splintered, dropping enormous digits to the ground, then its shoulder slumped and tumbled down the length of its arm, smashing against its feet like broken crockery.

The giant tried to pick up its pace but its legs cracked and folded beneath it, sending its whole colossal mass smashing to the ground. It struggled for a while, reaching up to the tumultuous sky, then the leaves carved into its chest unfurled and its arm fell apart.

There was a final, brittle *crack* as the giant's head tumbled from its neck, then it lay still.

The avalanche did not end with the death of the giant. A while later, as a masked figure staggered from the caves, he was forced to cower beneath a lip of overhanging rock, peering out at the destruction.

He wore a tall birch-wood mask that hid his face, revealing only a pair of thin, spiral horns that jutted out of his forehead. He had a spear in his hands and, after a few minutes, he used it to haul his way up the trembling rocks, and looked down into the valley.

A voice called out to him from the caves, but it was drowned out by the noise of the falling stones.

The masked figure looked back. 'What?'

'What do you see, Ilaruss?' cried the voice from the caves, as another priest of Kurnous staggered into view.

'Stay back!' replied Ilaruss, using his spear to block a boulder that was about to slam into his face. 'The mountains are falling!'

He turned back towards the caves, but as he did so, he heard another voice: a pained burst of guttural words that emerged from the entrance to the valley.

Ilaruss hesitated, peering into the banks of dust and snow.

There was still a glimmer of light amongst the piles of rubble, like fire trapped beneath the rocks.

Ilaruss staggered through the shifting snow, batting away more stones with his spear and glancing anxiously at the surrounding slopes. He was still several feet away from the light when Orion climbed from the wreckage of Torr-Ildána.

The King was a vision of bloody defiance: his skin was smeared with gore, his hand was pulverised, his antlers were broken and his spear was lost, but Ilaruss saw none of this. He saw the immortal Lord of the Wild Hunt, rising to greet the dawn. He gasped in shock. His master had become his god.

Where there had once been doubt and rage, now there was only the white heat of eternity, blazing through Orion's eyes.

Ilaruss lowered his gaze in awe.

'My lord,' he gasped, falling to his knees.

Orion glared down at him and his voice rang out over the avalanche, trembling with pride. '*Now* I am king.' He looked at the distant line of sunlight. 'Take me home, Ilaruss. Take me to the Oak of Ages. Summon the hounds.' He tilted back his head and closed his eyes, breathing heavily.

'I am ready to hunt.'

CHAPTER THIRTY

Silver light poured down through the branches, filled with the power of the infinite. It shone first on a circle of priests, flashing across their wooden masks and in the bottomless pits of their eyes. Then, as the moons aligned overhead, the light fell on the figure kneeling at their feet: a trembling, scarred ruin with shattered antlers and a broken, bleeding fist. The tree had endured the ritual countless times and as the soul of a god descended through its branches it shivered, recognising the dreadful hunger of Kurnous, come again to taste blood.

There were nine disciples and their droning chant was led by the High Priest, Atolmis, whose spear was resting on Orion's shoulder. At the crescendo of their song, he drew a knife and dragged it across his naked chest. The other priests followed suit and, as the blood fell, they caught it and hurled it over Orion's back. The blood slapped against his skin, the moonlight flickered and Orion shuddered in pain.

The priests closed their eyes, sensing that Kurnous was amongst them, and knowing it was not their place to look upon divinity.

As the blood ran down his back, Orion's bones cracked and elongated. He gasped but did not cry out, despite the agony.

Atolmis began the song again, raising his voice to drown out the sound of Orion's splintering bones. It was a droning round tune that was joined after a few moments by another voice.

Ariel stepped slowly into the Oak of Ages with her head lowered. She was dressed in a long white mantle, girdled by wreaths of larkspur, and in her hair she wore a chaplet of delicate blue vervain. She carried a cloak that shimmered in the moonlight: an intricate weave of leaves and spun gold that rippled between her fingers like water.

The song reached another solemn crescendo as Ariel entered the circle and stood over her immortal, blood-drenched lover.

Sensing her presence, Orion tried to stand. At first he was unable to rise. His body was still wracked by a series of jolting changes and he stumbled, dropping heavily back to his knees.

Ariel looked pained, but remained motionless.

Orion tried again to rise and this time he succeeded. He towered over his disciples and his queen, swaying slightly as he looked up at the shafts of moonlight. Then he turned his gaze on Ariel. His was face contorted by pride and pain but he managed a nod of recognition.

She nodded in reply, still singing as she floated gently into the air and placed the cloak of leaves over his shoulders.

Orion's spine gave one last crack as he shrugged the cloak into place. He was now nearly ten feet tall and as he looked down at his disciples power rippled from his flesh, filling the chamber like a heat haze.

At a nod from Atolmis the priests stepped back into the recesses of the chamber, fading into shadow as Orion walked past them. The final transformation of his flesh was complete and as he approached the centre of the tree he stretched his enormous limbs and smiled. There was no trace of his injuries and he could feel his oak-apple heart pounding in his chest, fierce and virile. The weariness that had overcome him in the Vaults was a memory.

At the centre of the tree there was a natural alcove and a broad, uneven shelf of root. Lying on the wood was a gilded horn on a strap of vines and, next to it, there was a spear, its blade inscribed with an intricate network of knotted runes. Orion took the horn and slung it around his neck. Then he lifted the spear, tested its weight and turned to face Ariel and the priests.

'The Wild Hunt has begun,' he said, striding from the tree.

Hundreds of nobles were assembled on the moonlit dais outside, clutching torches and wearing masks of birch wood, painted to resemble the snarling faces of animals. As Orion emerged, they threw petals before his hooves and garlanded him with flowers, but he was deaf to their prayers, peering through the ranks of masked figures, looking for something.

After a few minutes of staring into the darkness, he raised the gilded horn to his lips and let out a long, lowing note.

The nobles gradually fell silent until the only sound was the crackling of their torches and the echoes of the horn blast.

Then, from deep in the trees, there came a reply: a chorus of baying howls, ringing out from every direction.

Orion blew his horn for the second time and, around the edges of the clearing, the shadows rippled into life. Grey, rangy hounds emerged from the trees, sniffing and growling as they caught the scent of his divine blood. They padded around the masked figures for a while, with moonlight flashing in their eyes. Then they began circling Orion, regarding him with cool, wary intelligence.

Behind Orion, Atolmis stepped from the Oak of Ages and

saw the hounds. He revealed his yellow incisors in a grin and thrust his spear into the air. 'Kurnous has risen! Let the Wild Hunt begin!'

The nobles raised their torches into the air and joined their voices to the cry of the hounds. 'Orion!' they screamed, delirious with bloodlust. They drew knives and spears and crowded around their king, howling his name like a warning. 'Orion!'

CHAPTER THIRTY-ONE

Finavar clasped his head in his hands, still picturing the dead polecats. How could he have been so callous? He climbed higher in the tree, staring at the approaching goliaths, sure that he was responsible. There were too many to even count. How could they face such a foe? The handmaidens were scattered and grieving and, below him, the kindreds were locked in desperate battle. The darkness was alive with screams and the clanging of swords as the Battle of Drúne Fell raged on, oblivious to his pain.

Something caught Finavar's eye and he forgot his shame for a second. The night was punctuated by countless lights – the flicker of enemy torches, pale, moonlit steeds and, in the distance, the vile, cyclopean eyes, swaying towards the fighting like a row of lanterns – but it was something else that caused him to pout in confusion. On the far side of the battle, beneath the eyes, there was a small cloud of mist. It was not impressive in itself, but what caused Finavar to stare so was the fact that each time the mist flickered with light, the lantern-like eyes pulsed in time with it.

He climbed out along a branch and peered into the dark. The outsiders had scorched everything in their path and the distant trees were shrouded in smoke but, after a moment, he saw it again: a faint pulse from between the trunks that seemed to drive the towering monsters forward.

'Something is controlling them.' Finavar's smile returned as an idea began to form in his mind. Loec had not abandoned him, he decided, he had simply set him a challenge. If he could reach that distant light, and extinguish it, he would atone, in some way, for the death of his two scouts. To Finavar's mind, the logic was clear.

He climbed to the crown of the tree and held his swords aloft, calling out to the eagles swooping across the battlefield. His voice was lost in the clamour of the battle but his weapons flashed in the moonlight, and, after a few minutes, a pair of the raptors swooped away from the fighting and flew in his direction.

'I knew it,' he said, waving his blades even more wildly, sensing the hand of Loec guiding the eagles to him.

The eagles dropped to the ground at the foot of the tree and a mocking voice called up to him. 'Has the Darkling Prince abandoned his subjects?'

Finavar recognised the brooding, scarred face and the coiled, wing-shaped torcs on the rider's arms.

'Prince Haldus!' he gasped, leaping down from the tree. Beside him on the second eagle was the stranger in the black armour.

'We must act quickly!' cried Finavar, hurrying towards them.

Haldus's face was grey with pain, but his eyes remained defiant. 'I have the enemy exactly where I want them. Many brave souls have passed to the Unknowable Realms, but, by dawn, we shall have cleansed these abominations from our home.' He closed his eyes, overcome with emotion. 'Did you see it, Finavar? Did you see the power of Ariel's handmaidens?' He shook his head. 'Their bravery has saved us all.'

Finavar's only reply was to point one of his swords across the battle, to the distant lights emerging from the trees.

Haldus shook his head, seeing nothing, but the other rider spoke up.

'What *is* that?' asked Lord Cyanos, peering through the darkness.

'More of the one-eyed creatures,' whispered Finavar. 'Dozens more.'

The colour drained from Prince Haldus's face as he saw the truth of Finavar's words. 'So many,' he said, his voice a hollow croak. He stared at Cyanos in shock and for a second it looked as though he might fall.

'There is still hope,' said Finavar, throwing back the hood of his cloak and stepping closer to them. 'This is the will of Loec, I know it. I created disharmony in the forest. I sent innocent creatures to die on my behalf.' He grimaced at the memory of it. 'But Loec has shown me a way to redeem myself. With your help I can lead us to victory.'

Haldus shook his head and looked again at the blazing eyes swaying from the trees. They were already nearing the battle and their grotesque silhouettes were starting to take shape. 'What are you talking about? What creatures?' His voice was hoarse. 'How could you stop such things, when even Laelia, with all her power, struggled to halt even one of them?'

Finavar lowered his blade and pointed to the foot of the trees. 'That's how.'

Haldus saw the mist, flickering in the darkness, but continued shaking his head. 'I don't understand.'

'Watch,' said Finavar. 'See how it flashes in time with their eyes.'

Haldus stared at Finavar as though he had lost his mind, but Cyanos nodded slowly in recognition.

'I have read of such things,' he said quietly, clearly ashamed by his admission. 'By themselves they are blind; they see only what we do not, the hidden realms beyond our own. Something must be guiding them to us. Something is driving them on.'

Finavar nodded eagerly. 'Exactly.' He nodded to the eagles, watching them intently from a few feet away. 'Take me to that cloud of fog, Prince Haldus. Help me kill whatever it hides. I'm sure that's the answer.' He placed a hand over his tattooed chest. 'Loec has spoken to me.'

Prince Haldus saw the wild passion burning in Finavar's eyes and nodded. 'When you first blundered into the rites of Ostaliss I thought you were an arrogant fool, Finavar – an arrogant fool who was about to ruin my one chance of speaking to Orion.' He grabbed Finavar's arm. 'But I was wrong. You have stayed true when many would have faltered.'

He looked down at the archers and spearmen, slowly pushing back the enemy. As yet, they were still unaware of what was wading towards them out of the darkness, but the pounding of the giants' feet was already starting to shake the ground. It would only be a few more minutes before the asrai glimpsed the horrors bearing down on them.

'We must be fast,' said the prince, turning and summoning Finavar up onto his eagle. 'There will be a rout. They will not pit themselves against such things.'

Finavar laughed as he climbed onto the bird's back. 'Then they have more sense than us.'

Haldus shook his head as he climbed up beside Finavar and

allowed himself the briefest smile. Then, with the lightest of touches, he launched the eagle into the air.

Finavar continued laughing as the summer breeze whistled around them. He tried to explain that he had never ridden an eagle before, but his breath was snatched away as Haldus and Cyanos sent their mounts hurtling across the battlefield.

The speed of the eagles was dizzying and Finavar found himself clutching onto Haldus as they rode. Beneath him he saw the entire battle spread out like a map, and he saw that to the warriors on the ground it must look as though victory was at hand. Emboldened by Laelia's magic, the spearmen were forcing the enemy slowly back across the valley towards the forest. Eremon's banner was everywhere at once as he raced through the heaving ranks of beastmen, leading the kinbands onwards with a booming, defiant cry. The riders at the enemy flanks were also gaining ground, with their pennants held high as they galloped through the carnage. At the foot of Drúne Fell, Laelia and the surviving handmaidens had unleashed all their grief and outrage in a torrent of roots and vines – devouring whole swathes of the enemy with their wild sorcery. It seemed as though the forest itself had risen to answer their call. Shattered, lifeless trunks were moving through the gloom, snapping bones and rending flesh as the magi waved them on. It should have been a glorious sight, but Finavar shook his head in pity. None of them had seen the doom that was lumbering towards them.

The one-eyed monsters were blind to the eagles' approach and Haldus steered a path so close to them that Finavar saw their enormous faces in far more detail than he would have liked.

'That way!' he tried to call out, but his words were lost beneath the buffeting of the wind.

Before he could try again, he saw there was no need – Haldus had already ordered his mount to dive, heading straight for the light flickering beneath the trees, with Cyanos plunging after them.

As they approached the ground, Finavar began to make out a pair of figures in the mist, hiding in the trees and watching the distant battle. The pulsing light was leaking from their flesh but Finavar only caught the briefest glimpse of them.

There was a flash of light as one of the figures raised a staff, then the world turned on its head.

Haldus's mount screeched in pain and tumbled over in an awkward loop.

It shed its two riders and narrowly avoided crashing into the trees, then continued screaming as it soared back up into the night sky.

The second eagle went spinning off into the darkness, with Cyanos clinging desperately to its back.

Hot agony exploded in Finavar's face as he slammed into the ground. Instinct drove him up onto his feet, dazed by the impact, but relieved to find he could stand. Blood poured from his nose and he could tell from the pain that it must be broken. He whirled around like a drunk, unable to get his bearings.

The figures he had seen beneath the trees were still there. He had landed fifty or sixty feet away, at the edge of the drifting fog. He looked the other way and saw that he was just as far from the battle. Here, behind the enemy lines, there was an odd quiet, punctuated only by the groans of the dying, sprawled around him on the scorched turf.

Finavar spun around, looking for Prince Haldus, but there was no sign of him in the dark and all he managed to do was send another glut of blood flying from his nose. He reached up to touch his face. As he thought, the bone was broken.

With a quick, brutal movement, he snapped it back into place.

The pain was intense, but seemed to steady him somehow and Finavar turned back to face the two figures, deciding to look for Haldus once he had completed what he set out to do. He looked down and found, to his surprise, that he was still clutching one of his swords. He raised it and ran silently across the grass.

The smaller of the two figures raised its staff again and Finavar ducked, expecting another blast, but none came and he stumbled to a halt, looking around in confusion.

There was no sign of the strange light, but he sensed that something had happened. There was a charge in the cold, clammy mist. It tingled across his skin. Whatever they were, the two figures beneath the trees had clearly spotted him.

'Think, Fin,' he whispered, looking around at the mounds of corpses for some kind of inspiration. The blank stares of the dead only unnerved him more and he decided there was nothing for it but to continue running with all the speed he could muster and hope he was equal to whatever he found beneath the trees.

Before he had taken a step, Finavar slammed to the ground for a second time.

He rolled, feeling a sharp pain in his back where something had smashed into him. Then he climbed awkwardly to his feet and saw a large mass approaching through the gloom – a deepening of the shadows. It looked as though a hill was lurching towards him.

Whatever it was, the creature with the staff had clearly summoned it, so Finavar backed away, keeping his sword raised.

The shape approached at an alarming speed and, as it loomed out of the darkness, Finavar lowered his sword, dumbfounded.

A mass of slug-like flesh was scuttling towards him, carried by dozens of spindly insectoid limbs. It was almost as large as the one-eyed giants and a pair of enormous fly's wings was mounted on its glistening back. Its drooping, misshapen face was such a mess of horns and tusks that Finavar could not even be sure if the thing had eyes.

Finavar backed away, clamping his eyes shut and trying to block out the hideous sight. The thought that such a thing could exist was more than he could bear and he dropped to his knees, groaning in horror.

'Fight, lowborn!' cried Haldus, grinning fiercely as he sprinted from the darkness and jammed his spear into the monster's heaving flank.

The thing reared up in pain and scuttled backwards like a spider, spewing black blood from the wound Haldus had left in its side.

The sight of Prince Haldus snatched Finavar from the brink of madness. The eagle-rider looked quite calm as he paced after the undulating monster, raising his spear to strike again.

Finavar realised that the grotesque thing was between them and the figures beneath the trees. They were clearly afraid to face him themselves. The thought gave him hope and he rose to his feet, snatching his sword from the ground as he raced to Prince Haldus's side.

CHAPTER THIRTY-TWO

The hunt rode on, smashing through the trees like a river, wrenching up roots and tearing down trees, killing everything in its path. Animals were ahead and behind, some fleeing, some hunting and all drunk on the blood of Kurnous. The baying of the hounds was indistinguishable from the baying of the lords. Violence rippled through them like laughter, making it impossible to distinguish animal from noble; they were all one, hunter and hunted, bound together by a chorus of hitching screams.

At the heart of it was Orion himself, surrounded by his horned riders and drenched in the blood of his subjects. Shreds of fur, leaf and skin trailed from his teeth and his eyes had rolled back into his skull so that only the whites were visible. He thundered on, racing through the Council Glade, past Cerura Carn, through lakes, hollows and dykes, running so fast that even the horses could barely match his pace.

They headed south, growing more ferocious. The nobles began to murder their own kin, tearing throats and smashing skulls, consumed by glorious hunger. Others were dragged to the ground by the hounds, still howling with excitement as the dogs ripped open their flesh.

The delirium was overwhelming, and Orion let go of everything bar a single name: Drúne Fell. He punched, snarled, clawed and spat, but kept those words fixed in his head. He could not recall the significance of the place, but he knew it was his goal. He knew it was the culmination of his hunt. There he would find prey worthy of this consuming hunger; prey worthy of a god. He looked back and glimpsed a moment of bloodshed: nobles and hounds, frozen in mid-air, wild-eyed and maniacal, ripping at each other's faces. He saw nature unfurled in all her wild rage and it was magnificent.

Overhead there was a rolling mass of birds, screaming, thrashing and tearing at each other as they tumbled in his wake. Orion looked up to revel in their fury and realised that the sky was growing lighter. He lowered his horn and howled as the longest day began.

Midsummer had come.

He would greet it with slaughter.

CHAPTER THIRTY-THREE

The monster lashed out with a jumble of segmented legs.

Finavar dodged to one side, focusing on the thing's limbs, trying to spare himself a glimpse of its hideous face. As a leg jabbed towards him, he stepped easily aside and hacked down with his sword, slicing through its thick, glossy skin and drenching himself in black gore.

The monster reared back in pain and Prince Haldus raced beneath it, jamming his spear at its sagging guts. The thing moved with surprising speed and flicked out another of its limbs, sending Haldus tumbling across the ground.

The prince's spear flew off into the gloom and he cursed as he climbed to his feet, realising he was now unarmed.

The monster lunged after him, but Finavar jammed his sword into the side of its face, eliciting another gout of inky blood. Then he dashed clear before the creature could catch him in its gaping jaws. His breathing came in ragged gasps and, as he circled around towards Haldus, he noticed that his sword was buckled and useless. He hurled it to the ground and groaned in frustration. They had been fighting the grotesque hulk for what seemed like an age, with no success.

As he staggered to the prince's side Finavar shook his head and pointed at the battle. 'Look,' he gasped.

Haldus snatched a glimpse back towards Drúne Fell and grimaced. The sun was finally starting to rise and they could see the fighting with horrible clarity. The one-eyed giants had now reached the asrai lines and were stamping through them with glee, wrenching tiny figures from the crowds and stuffing them into their mouths. What had looked like a victory, just half an hour earlier, now looked like a riotous retreat. There was no sign of Eremon's banner and the kindreds were being forced back into the foothills.

Finavar shook his head and was about to speak when the monster lurched into action again. It let out a moist, belching roar as it threw its whole shivering mass forwards.

Prince Haldus sprinted in one direction and Finavar took the other, grabbing the prince's spear from the ground as he went.

The monster opened its mouth wider and vomited a long, fleshy neck that ended in a second, smaller mouth, crammed with rows of needle teeth.

Finavar jammed his spear into the mouth.

The teeth sank into the wood and, as the neck flew back towards the larger mouth, Finavar was lifted from his feet and hauled along with it.

He let go of the spear, but not before he was sent tumbling towards the nest of thrashing limbs.

The monster batted him to the ground, raised its bloated bulk and prepared to drop onto its prey.

Prince Haldus launched himself onto its back and punched a knife through its thick hide.

The monster screamed and reared up in pain.

Finavar rolled to safety, then cursed as he saw the vile thing hurl Prince Haldus to the ground and spear him with one of its legs. He sprinted back towards it, still trying to keep his gaze from its face.

As he approached, he saw that the monster had torn a hole through Haldus's arm. The prince was thrashing wildly on the ground, clutching the wound. Blood sprayed from his arm as the monster drew back its leg and prepared to stab again.

Finavar dived through the air and hauled the prince to safety, seconds before the leg pierced him a second time.

Blood rushed over Finavar as he dragged the prince across the ground.

The monster turned and followed with a horrifying slowness as Finavar looked around desperately for a weapon.

There was nothing. Even the prince's knife was still embedded in the creature's back. Finavar's heart pounded in his chest. Haldus was barely conscious, struggling weakly in his arms and muttering gibberish as blood continued rushing from his awful wound.

Finavar's jaw tightened as the monster reared over them. He rose to his feet, preparing to fight with his bare hands.

He looked up to face his enemy but, as he did so, he saw the thing's face in all its grotesque glory: folds of glistening, mutant flesh, filled with countless mouths and rows of jagged teeth. Finavar cried out as he saw, in the middle of its head, a pair of terrified, human eyes, looking down at him. Finavar found this more dreadful than anything – the thought that the creature must once have been a mortal man was too hideous to bear. As the creature raised its legs to kill him, he found himself watching the scene with numb dispassion. An overwhelming sense of unreality came over him as he waited to die.

A shape flashed along the side of the monster's bulky torso, then vanished from view.

Finavar burst into a fit of high-pitched laughter as the monster's side flopped open, ejecting great mounds of white blubber.

The monster lurched backwards with a roar, but as it did so, a second shape hurtled past, spinning along its back. But, again, it vanished before Finavar could make it out.

The monster's cry became a piercing shriek as its back exploded in a shower of gore.

The sound echoed strangely through the fog and Finavar moaned in dismay. With the creature distracted, he began dragging Prince Haldus across the ground, hauling them both along with one hand and clutching Haldus's awful wound with the other.

A third figure raced into view and bounded onto the monster's head. This time he remained in place long enough for Finavar to see his face.

'Caorann!' said Finavar in a dazed voice.

Caorann glanced anxiously at him, then hammered a spear down between his feet.

There was clanging sound and the weapon buckled uselessly against the monster's hide.

Caorann grimaced and leapt clear, with the still-screaming monster lurching after him.

Finavar saw three other figures line up alongside Caorann, raising their swords to face the monster down. Thuralin looked more cadaverous than ever, Jokleel was drenched in blood from a gash across his forehead and Alhena was limping, but they all wore identical looks of fierce determination. Finavar felt an overwhelming sense of relief as he saw his brother still standing. He staggered towards him, wondering how badly he was hurt. Then he paused and frowned in confusion.

'How did you find me?'

Jokleel managed a brief grin and waved at two slender shapes circling his feet.

Finavar laughed at the sight of the polecats but, before he could say anything, the monster attacked again.

The kinband had done little more than enrage it and, as Finavar staggered towards them, they were forced to scatter, spinning and flipping out of reach as the thing's legs lashed out at them.

As the monster lunged and slashed, Finavar rolled clear. As he rose to his feet a few feet away he noticed the two distant figures beneath the trees. The one with the staff was still waving it back and forth, snatching strands of light from the air and hurling them into the growing dawn. As it gesticulated, Finavar saw the distant giants responding, stomping through the battle and butchering Haldus's fleeing army.

Finavar's joy at seeing his friends faded as he saw that the battle was almost over. The asrai were now openly fleeing into the mountains, or being hacked apart by the jeering minotaurs. Countless hundreds of them were already dead. It was a loss that would take generations to heal.

Something else caught his eye. To the west of the mountain a group of figures had emerged from the trees. Despite their small numbers, they were charging in the opposite direction to everyone else, heading straight for the heart of the battle.

The monster was still busy fighting Caorann and the others, so Finavar watched, fascinated, as the distant figures smashed into the enemy's flank and began ploughing through them. He shook his head, thinking that such a small group of reinforcements would be dead within minutes. The longer he watched, however, the more confused he became. The newcomers grew in number as they advanced, rather than diminishing. As the morning sun began to creep over the corpses and tattered banners, it picked out the figure at the head of the group and Finavar cried out, raising his fist to the heavens.

'Orion!' he howled.

Finavar's despair evaporated. This was all of his childhood dreams come true: the King of the Woods, at the head of the Wild Hunt, tearing through the bloody dawn towards him.

'Orion!' he yelled again, punching the air repeatedly, his voice cracking with emotion.

At the sound of Finavar's cries, his kinband backed away from the grunting monster and looked across the valley.

'Is it really him?' gasped Jokleel, rushing to Finavar's side, his eyes wide with awe.

Finavar enveloped his brother in a hug. This was a moment they had both imagined as children, but never expected to see.

'I *knew* he would come,' said Finavar, grinning at Jokleel with tears in his eyes.

Prince Haldus managed to climb to his feet, clutching his tattered arm and swaying drunkenly as he watched the figures heading towards them. The circular scars around his mouth splintered into a grin as he saw who was approaching.

Finavar turned to look at the prince and noticed as he did so that the hooded figure beneath the trees had lowered its staff and lurched out into the morning light to watch, followed by a large, four-legged beast of some kind. The monster, meanwhile, finally ceased its thrashing and belching. Its tiny, terrified eyes rolled in its head as it stared out across the battlefield.

Hunting horns rang out over the battle as Orion approached. After a few minutes, Finavar's smile faltered. The image thundering towards him was not quite as it had been in his dreams. A cloud of birds were spiralling and swooping around Orion's antlered head, thrashing wildly and screaming as he led them on, tearing each other apart as they tumbled after him. Behind the King were dozens of riders: horned priests with blazing eyes, smeared in blood and sweat as they howled along with Orion's horn.

All around them were the nobles of the Council Glade, but they were barely recognisable as the celebrants Finavar had seen at the rites of spring. Their faces were hidden behind ferocious wooden masks and their robes were in tatters or just abandoned.

They had become animals.

Their bodies were gored and bruised, but so full of unnatural vigour that they did not register the pain. Their mouths were crammed with hunks of raw flesh and their heads were shaking violently as they charged across the valley.

Finavar took a step backwards as he realised why the group was growing larger. As Orion ploughed through the enemy ranks, animals were stampeding from every direction to join his charge: an army of wolves, boars and foxes was pouring from the forest and tearing into everything they encountered.

Orion blew his horn and the animals attacked, falling on beastmen, asrai and each other, consumed by a desperate hunger.

The outsiders tried to put up some kind of defence, regrouping and raising crude, iron-rimmed shields, but it was hopeless – the hunt smashed through them, tearing, snarling and howling in a shower of dismembered limbs.

The sound of the riders' hooves rolled through the valley like thunder but above it all was the keening of Orion's horn, summoning more of his subjects to the slaughter.

Finavar felt dazed as the stampede pounded towards him. Then, with the host almost on top of him, he felt his heart begin to pound. A terrible hunger for violence washed over him and he howled, joining his voice to the wild-eyed nobles and the storm of screaming birds. He lost all thoughts of survival, or even self, and became an animal; abandoning himself to wild, bloody rage.

As the Wild Hunt enveloped them, Finavar and the others joined the charge, lashing out furiously, clawing at sweating flanks and gouging the faces of the nobles nearest to them. The violence was intoxicating, and wonderful.

'Orion is here!' howled Finavar, seeing that victory was theirs. 'The Wild Hunt has come!'

In a brief moment of clarity, Finavar realised they were rolling over the hulking monster he had just been fighting. The hunters flayed it in seconds, tearing the great mass apart like a cut of meat and leaving its legs twitching on the ground, torn clean from its quivering bulk.

The hunt did not pause but made straight for the two figures beneath the trees. The four-legged one – Finavar now saw that it was a mutant bull, with the arms and torso of a man – tried to flee, but countless animals crashed into it, pounding it into the ground. Then, a few seconds later, Orion reached it and wrenched its pulverised body from the blood-drenched earth, tearing it apart with his teeth, grunting and slavering as he fed on its glistening organs.

The charge faltered and milled around the King as he ate.

Finavar dived hungrily onto a passing shape without knowing what it was, and sank his teeth into soft flesh. Blood washed over his face and he moved on, desperate for another kill. As he did so, a light flashed somewhere nearby and he glimpsed the hooded figure with the staff, blasting columns of fire at the wailing, gore-splattered hunters. He saw that it was struggling. With each move it made, flames burst from its robes. It seemed as though the creature was being torn apart by its own power.

Orion allowed the remains of his meal to slip from his jaws as he lurched towards the flashing mist.

He passed close by and Finavar knew that he was in the presence of Kurnous. The King was enormous – towering over the frenzy he had created and pulsing with his own sylvan light. His teeth were bared in a snarl and his body was naked apart from the shredded remains of his victims. As he thudded towards his hooded prey, the outsider levelled a blast of light at him, more powerful than any it had summoned previously.

Orion finally staggered to a halt as the magic slammed into him.

The light rippled over the King like water, causing him to snarl and reel; but as the hooded creature worked its spell, far more light was tearing through its own flesh. Smoke and flames rippled from its hood, and after a few seconds it was unable to bear it any longer.

With a howl of pain and frustration, the beastman hurled its staff to the ground and reached into its hood.

Orion reacted immediately, hurling himself at the smouldering figure and grabbing it by the throat. With a triumphant roar he lifted it into the air, so that its hood fell back, revealing a bleached ram's skull.

Orion raised his prize even higher and turned to face the writhing mass of animals and nobles crashing around him. Their screams rose higher and Finavar joined his voice to the throng, howling until his throat was raw and his eyes were streaming with tears.

Once he was sure he had the attention of the mob, Orion grasped the ram's head with his other hand and crushed it. The bones exploded in a cloud of dust and fire. Then Orion threw back his shoulders and howled at the dawn.

The mist beneath the trees vanished, slipping back under the boughs in seconds.

Finavar joined the others in a desperate struggle to reach Orion's side, kicking and biting in a bestial scrum of pounding fists and strangled barks.

Orion fed on their passion, trembling with ecstasy as he shook the still-twitching corpse. Then he hurled it to the mob and charged on, leaving them to pull it apart with their torn fingers.

Finavar hurried after his king, still screaming wildly as he watched Orion attack everything within reach. The King paid no heed to what he killed. If it was before him, he smashed it to the ground and wrenched open its flesh.

As he ran, Finavar glimpsed something that shocked him out of his bloodlust: an image that wrenched him back to his own mind like a plunge into an ice-cold tarn.

He staggered to a halt as the rest of the hunt thundered on into the forest, still wailing along with Orion's horn.

Before leading the charge off into the distance, Orion had flung one of his victims onto the side of a small hillock and, as Finavar stepped towards it, the corpse's pale face stared back at him in silent accusation.

It was Jokleel.

Finavar dropped to his knees, just a few feet away from his brother's corpse, unable to go any closer.

As din of the Orion's hunt faded, heading deep into the forest, it was replaced by another sound: the gasps of the dying he had left behind. With the King gone, their bloodlust vanished, leaving the mutilated nobles nothing but their agony. As horror and panic consumed them, they began to scream, pawing uselessly at their terrible wounds and begging Finavar for help.

Finavar heard nothing. He stared at his little brother, lying broken on a mound of earth. Orion had torn Jokleel's throat out, leaving his head to flop back at a hideously unnatural angle, lolling behind a fountain of dark blood.

Finavar tried to say his brother's name, but his own throat was ruined from howling and all that emerged was a groan.

He slumped down into the gore-drenched mud, curled into a ball and closed his eyes.

CHAPTER THIRTY-FOUR

Ordaana staggered across the battlefield, clutching her head in hands, numb with shock. She'd been so close, but after Orion had carved his way across the valley, everything had collapsed around her ears. The lights had vanished from the giants' eyes and they had lost all sense of direction, howling in frustration as they staggered blindly through the battle. With the giants careering back and forth, the Queen's handmaidens were free to unleash all their fury, wrenching coils of ancient root from the earth and summoning animated husks of deadwood from the trees. The outsiders might still have succeeded, had Orion's charge not dragged every fleeing kinband back from the slopes of Drúne Fell. At the sight of the King, their thoughts of retreat were replaced by a terrifying hunger for violence and victory. They slammed back into the mutants with all the ferocity of Orion's Wild Hunt.

'Are you hurt?' asked an archer, rushing to her side.

She shook her head, staring at him in mute shock.

He took her arm. 'My lady, the fight is over.' He waved his

longbow at the fleeing mutants. 'The King has routed them. Nothing can stand against the Wild Hunt.'

'Leave me,' she muttered.

'Are you sure you aren't hurt?' He looked at her torn robes. 'I can fetch you some help. Wait here while–'

'Leave!' hissed Ordaana, and white flames shimmered across her skin.

The archer recoiled, gave her an awkward bow and backed away into the cheering crowds.

Figures jostled by Ordaana, howling victory songs as they barged past. 'I failed him,' she whispered, staggering back towards the foothills.

She was just a few feet from the trees when the full horror of it hit her. If she had failed Aestar Eltanin then there was no hope for any of them. The asrai were doomed. The reign of the Queen would remain unchallenged and they would continue on their slow, inexorable path to extinction. All she had done was lead them to a terrible slaughter. She looked around at the mounds of bodies. Hundreds of kinbands had been butchered and it was all her fault. She had led the outsiders to Drúne Fell. She had done nothing more than diminish her dwindling race even more. She moaned in horror as another thought hit her. If she had failed Aestar, she would never atone for what she did, all those years ago.

Tears filled her eyes and she fell to her knees in the mud. Her mind slipped back through the centuries as she remembered the scene she had struggled so long to suppress – the terrible crime that filled her dreams. She saw flames spreading through her home at the heart of Locrimere; flames ignited by her own bitter curses. She recalled the panic she had felt as she realised her daughter was trapped, somewhere inside the furnace she had created.

'Alhena!' she cried, pulling anxiously at her tattered robes and looking up at the sky. 'Alhena, my child. Forgive me. I never meant for you to die.'

Ordaana began to cry, deep, shuddering sobs that shook her slender frame. Then, after a few minutes, she thought she heard someone crying with her. No she realised, not crying but laughing. She opened her eyes and looked around.

A few feet away lay the severed head of one of the mutants. It was a grotesque, bovine thing, with thick, shattered horns and three glassy eyes. It was laughing hysterically, spilling blood from its neck as it rolled across the ground towards her.

Ordaana gasped and rose to her feet, drawing her knife and staggering towards the head.

As she did so, she heard more laughter coming from behind her and turned to see the body of an asrai spearman. He had been torn in half and his torso ended in a ragged mess of skin and intestines, but he was laughing wildly, slapping the ground around him and shaking with mirth. His eyes had rolled back into his head, but he still seemed to be staring at Ordaana.

She reeled away from him, but found that wherever she looked, there was another bloodless face laughing wildly at her misfortune. Worst of all, she realised, was the fact that the soldiers hurrying past her, eager to join the victory celebrations, were oblivious to her plight. None of them seemed hear the braying chorus of laughter.

'Ordaana,' cried a voice from the distance.

Her panic grew as she saw her husband, Lord Beldeas, striding through the carnage towards her. He had a look of insufferable pride on his face and Ordaana realised that she could not face him. She could not face any of her kind again. She knew that she would be unable to hide what she had done. The magnitude of this crime was too great. She turned and fled into the hills, still sobbing as she dashed towards the rising sun.

She ran wildly with no sense of direction, and soon lost track of time. Her feet were torn and bleeding and her breath came in ragged gasps, but nothing was as painful as her shame. Finally, somewhere in the depths of the forest, she caught her foot on a root and tumbled into a ditch. Brambles tore at her skin and caught in her hair, but she relished the pain, knowing it was a fraction of what she deserved. She came to a halt in a pool of stagnant water, pressed her face into the mud and prayed for death.

Hours passed and death never came. Insects crawled over her skin and the water soaked her robes, but she remained horribly alive. Finally, her aching limbs forced her to roll onto her back and look up through the brambles at the cloudless sky.

'Who drove you to this?'

The voice came from the mud beneath Ordaana's head and she screamed in shock.

She tried to sit, but the hook-like thorns prevented her from rising, scraping the skin from her face as she turned to face the mud.

Writhing in the filth was a black, bloated slug.

'Aestar,' she gasped, picking the slug up carefully between her finger and thumb and holding it close to her face.

'Who drove you to this despair?'

Ordaana felt a glimmer of hope. There was no anger in the voice. If Aestar had forgiven her failure, perhaps they could begin again? Perhaps, even now, she could make amends.

'Is there still hope?' she asked, her voice trembling and weak.

'The outsiders are defeated. Orion is more powerful than in any previous age.' The slug writhed between her fingers. 'There is no hope, Ordaana.'

'But Aestar,' she wailed, finally managing to sit up. 'You said–'

'I said many things,' replied the slug. 'All of them were lies.' The slug writhed again. 'Even my own name.'

Ordaana was gripped by a sudden nausea as she began to guess the truth.

'My name is Alkhor,' said the slug, its voice quivering with barely controlled mirth. 'Aestar's soul sustained me for a while, but I eventually had to let it go, back to whatever rock he has bound it to. For a long time I despaired. I knew what I needed to do. I knew only Orion would have the strength to free me, but I needed a friend, someone to lead him to me. And you and your kind are so slavishly devoted to your precious forest I despaired of ever finding an ally. Then, finally, when I felt the pain of your loss, Ordaana, I tasted freedom. What keener pain could there be than a mother who murdered her own child? Your hurt was like a beacon. I followed you into the pits of your despair, waiting until you reached the very lowest ebb. Only then did I approach.'

Ordaana screamed and crushed the slug in her fist. She felt its flesh burst against her palm, then she wrenched herself upright, ignoring the pain of the thorns as they lacerated her skin.

She managed to free herself from the ditch and stumble off though the trees, trying to wipe the remains of the slug on her robes and sobbing hysterically when the tacky liquid refused to come away.

It was now mid-morning and the forest floor was dappled with sunlight. In her tear-filled vision, the patches of sunlight became flames, rippling across the walls of her home. The lights were so dizzying and her grief so overwhelming that, after another hour of directionless running, Ordaana stumbled again, landing this time on the bank of a glittering stream.

She lay there for a moment, taking hitching, shallow breaths. Her peripheral vision grew dark and she curled into a foetal position as unconsciousness threatened to take her.

'Who drove you to this?'

At the sound of the voice, Ordaana's breaths grew even faster. She saw that the surface of the stream had risen up over her head: a tower of foetid water with ragged wings, a battered sword and a leering grin.

'Answer me,' said the daemon, with a voice borrowed from the rushing sound of the water.

Terrified and confused, Ordaana plumbed the depths of her despair, trying to recall the beginning of her fall.

'Ariel,' she said after a few moments, recalling how perfect her life had been until the Queen spurned her. The rage and grief that had drawn this daemon all stemmed from one act of betrayal. All her woes could be traced back to that one point – even the death of Alhena. She had caused the death of her own child, but Ariel had driven her to it. Her breathing grew more regular, steadied by a growing sense of injustice. 'Everything began with Ariel,' she said, keeping her voice to a whisper, afraid that the forest spirits would hear her blasphemy.

'Then there *is* hope.'

Ordaana looked up at Alkhor, trembling with fear and exhaustion. The immaculate, refined noblewoman was gone, replaced by a filthy, bloodstained wreck. Her eyes were raw from crying, her skin was covered in weals and her hair looked like an abandoned nest. 'Orion lives. I can never face my own people again. What hope can there be?'

'Just one,' said the daemon, raising its sword so that the blade of water flashed in the sunlight. 'Revenge.'

Ordaana felt her body stiffen with hate as she pictured Ariel's face. For a long time she was too enraged to speak. Then, finally, she managed two words. 'Yes,' she sobbed, glancing nervously at the daemon. 'Revenge.'

Alkhor closed its eyes and smiled. Then it climbed up onto the riverbank and stepped back into the physical realm. As it approached Ordaana, the daemon's cloak of water rippled away, slipping from its limbs and leaving behind a thing of flesh and blood.

Ordaana recoiled in horror.

Alkhor had almost taken the form of an asrai nobleman, but not quite. Its limbs were crooked and unnaturally long and its body was devoid of skin, so that its glistening cords of muscle were clearly visible. The daemon smiled a lipless smile, and spoke in a moist, buzzing voice. 'Come to me.'

Ordaana crawled through the mud, still sobbing, then she gasped as the daemon reached out with one of its long arms.

Alkhor pressed three fingers against her exposed shoulder.

Ordaana gasped in pain and tried to pull back, but found that she could not.

Her skin began to bubble and darken beneath the daemon's fingers.

After a few seconds, Alkhor stepped back to admire his hand-iwork. Where he had touched Ordaana there was now a perfect triangle, made of three bruise-dark fingerprints.

'What does it mean?' wailed Ordaana, trying to look at the sigil. She watched in horror as a fly emerged from one of spots, breaking through the soft, rotten patch of skin and launching itself into the air.

The daemon's smile grew wider.

EPILOGUE

She picked her way through the snow and the rubble, bristling with rage as she climbed down into the valley. The circle of beech trees had been torn apart by the blast and there were still flakes of ash drifting on the breeze. She pressed her bark against each of the ruined trunks in turn, absorbing their agony; allowing their souls to pass through hers. How could she have been so wrong?

She looked over at the scattered remnants of the stone guardian. How could Orion have achieved such a thing?

Liris and Melusine were waiting a few feet away, respecting her grief, and she turned to face them, wizened and crooked with hate. She wanted to cry out, to accuse, to rail, but words failed her. She turned back to the ruins of Torr-Ildána and climbed up onto the shattered stones; stones that had contained Alkhor for so many centuries. There was a gaping hole in the snow beneath them, marking the place where the daemon had crawled free.

'We can bring it back.' Melusine's voice was hollow with fear. 'We can bind it again – as we did before.'

Drycha shook her head as she considered what Orion had

unwittingly unleashed. 'There are too few of us now. We lack the power. Alkhor will destroy us all.' She spat the words. 'Orion has doomed us.'

Her branch-like fingers traced over the rock. There was something carved into it: a broken fragment of a circle, designed to resemble a wreath of knotted branches. 'But I will make the false king pay before I am done. We will not die alone.'

ABOUT THE AUTHOR

Darius Hinks's first novel, *Warrior Priest*, won the David Gemmell Morningstar award for best newcomer. Since then he has carved a bloody swathe through the Warhammer World in works such as *Island of Blood*, *Sigvald* and *Razumov's Tomb*. Recently, he has ventured into the Warhammer 40,000 universe with the Space Marine Battles novella *Sanctus*. He plans to return to the grim darkness of the far future after he has finished telling the tale of the forest god Orion.

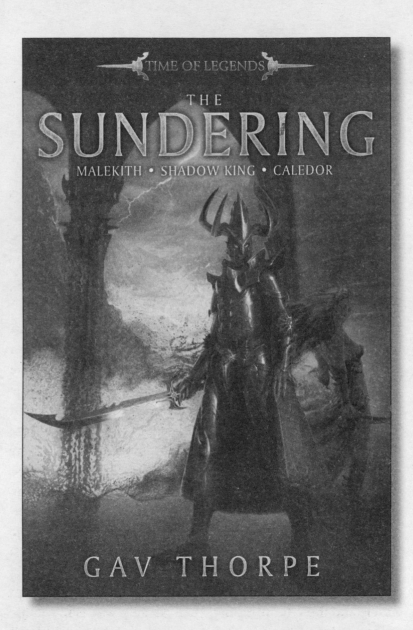

An extract from The Sundering
by Gav Thorpe

On sale October 2012

Yeasir struggled to his knees, still weak from the magical blast that had cast him down. The alarmed shouts of his comrades grew more urgent as the skeletons began to advance up the steps towards the Naggarothi. Crawling to the edge of the uppermost level, he looked down to see the unliving legion marching implacably onwards, each stepping in synchronicity with all the others, guided by common purpose or will. The arrows of the elves had little effect, most bouncing harmless from the glowing bones of their enemies, others simply passing through them as if they were nothing more than ghosts.

As the first line of skeletons reached the uppermost step, the Naggarothi struck out with their spears, driving silvered points into skulls and ribcages. This had more effect than the arrows and no few skeletons crumbled into bones, their golden light ebbing and then disappearing. Their advance was as inevitable as the coming of the tide though, and even as the first rank fell the second stepped forwards, and the third, and the fourth.

The skeletons' blades were as keen as the day that they had been forged, despite the passage of ages, and they bit into shield and flesh as the skeletons attacked back. Cries of pain and fear began to reverberate around Yeasir as he struggled to pull free his own sword, but the scabbard was pinned beneath him and he had not the strength to lift himself from it.

The elf to Yeasir's left gave a cry and toppled down the steps as an unearthly blade slashed through his throat. The skeleton took another pace forwards into the space the elf had occupied and turned its grinning face towards Yeasir. It raised its arm above its head, the wicked black blade in its hand sparkling with golden light. Yeasir gave a cry and tried to push himself away, but the skeleton stepped forwards again, ready to strike. The captain pulled his shield in front of him just as the sword swung down, and the undead thing's blade rang against it with a dull crash.

Again and again the sword smashed upon the shield, with relentless, metronomic ferocity. After the tenth blow, all the strength was gone from Yeasir's arms and the eleventh strike smashed the top of the shield into his face, stunning him. Dazed, he could do nothing as the skeleton's sword arm rose high again. He stared into the guardian's eyes, seeing nothing but pits of darkness.